WICKFORD Hollow

DUET

M VIOLET

WICKFORD HOLLOW DUET
M VIOLET

Cover Design by Sarah Paige. All stock photos licensed appropriately.

Edited by Kat Wyeth (Kat's Literary Services)

Formatted by Champagne Book Design

For information on subsidiary rights, please contact the publisher at authormviolet@gmail.com

GOOD *Girl*

M VIOLET

A NOTE FROM THE AUTHOR

Good Girl is a dark romance meant for 18+ readers only. This is a short smutty novella very loosely inspired by Charles Dickens' A Christmas Carol. But this is not a retelling. And it's not about Christmas. This is something else. Extreme discretion advised. Please see the TWs below.

Trigger Warnings

*Graphic sexual scenes
*Graphic language
*Physical assault
*Sexual assault
*Coercion
*Dubious consent
*Sex with multiple partners
*Group sex
*Sword crossing
*Bondage
*Submission
*Kinks: choking, spanking, restraints, collar/leash, food play, praise, and degradation.

Playlist

"Haunted House "– Neoni

"Just Another Nightmare" – Fae

"Victim" – Halflives

"Motionless but Not Alone (Reaper)" – Andrea Viktoria

"You Made a Monster "– Nick Kingsley and Hannah Hart

"Run Baby Run" – The Rigs

"Faraway Far" – Mavenne

"The Foundations of Decay" – My Chemical Romance

"Smells Like Teen Spirit" – Malia J

"All the Dark Places" – Kat Leon and Jo Blankenburg

To spicy booktok. This one's for you.

All Hallows' Eve

"You're not afraid of the dark, are you, Bailey?" My very sloppy drunk friend Maureen asked.

I laughed and threw back another lime green jello shot, tilting my head back so it could jiggle down my throat. "Hell no I'm not. That's where all the fun stuff happens."

Maureen hopped up on the center island next to me, her tits nearly falling out of her halter top in the process. "So you'll go then? Into the old Wickford place, by yourself with no flashlight?"

I rolled my eyes. "Are you still mad that I didn't want to dress up as a slutty witch with you? Is that why you are trying to ruin my Halloween Eve?"

Maureen laughed. "Oh, come on, Bailey. You know you want

to. Besides, if the rumors are true, then you'll be getting fucked sideways just like you've always wanted. And your burlesque costume is just as slutty by the way."

I glanced down at my bustier right as Maureen made a grab for one of my breasts. I squealed and swatted her hand away playfully. "No more jello shots for you, missy," I teased.

"Seriously, though, Bailey. The party isn't until midnight, and I'm bored as fuck."

"Remind me again why Billy decided to throw a party so fucking late?"

"*Because* it's officially Halloween at midnight," Maureen whined as if that was the most ridiculous question I'd ever asked. "Now, let's go check out that creepy mansion and see what all the fuss is about."

I did love a good dare.

The old Wickford mansion had been the subject of superstition our whole lives. Last summer, after graduation, a bunch of kids got busted for throwing a party there and almost burning it down. The cops have since taped it off and it's scheduled to be demolished later this year.

Legend has it that every year on Halloween Eve, when the veil between the dead and the living fell down, three angry spirits demanded to be set free. They were locked away in one of the rooms there. Whoever let them out would be stuck with them until they gave them what they wanted. It was probably started by a bunch of horny frat boys who were just trying to lure unsuspecting drunk girls into the dark.

It sounded like a bunch of bullshit to me.

"Fine. Why not? It's not like any of that stuff is real. But you have to promise that you won't tell anyone about this later." Partying there with other people was one thing, roaming around by yourself like a weirdo was grounds to get labeled as such.

Maureen dipped one of her long pointy fingernails into

another jello shot, scooping it out and sucking it off. "Shit, like *I'm* going to tell anyone. It will be our little secret, slut."

I shoved her a little too hard, and she toppled over. I reached out to catch her, and we both went tumbling to the floor, laughing. "Oh, fuck. Are we that drunk already?" I spurt out between hysterical bouts of laughter.

She pulled me on top of her and pretended to dry hump me. "Fuck yeah, bitch. You gonna set some spirits free tonight."

I pulled her up and steadied myself against the counter. "Alright, fuck. Let's go before I change my mind. Grab the rest of those shots for the walk over. I'm not doing this sober."

"Yay!" Maureen stumbled in front of me, trying not to drop the tray of shots as we left her house.

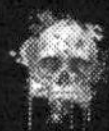

I fluffed my blonde hair as we walked, annoyed that the mist was starting to deflate my curls. I wanted to look hot tonight. To find some beautiful man at the party to make out with. Lord knows it had been way too long. But now I was traipsing through the streets in stiletto heels and fishnets, freezing my ass off. Hopefully we could go back to Maureen's house after and freshen up before the party.

The old Wickford house was a crumbling heap of decay. Just a hollow frame with barely anything left holding it together. I glanced up at the roof just in time to dodge a squirt of bird shit. It splattered on the cobblestones inches away from me.

Maureen howled with laughter. "Fuck, that almost landed on you."

There must have been a half a dozen birds' nests up there. "So gross," I groaned.

The rickety shutters banged against the house, creaking in

the unforgiving wind. A shudder trickled up my spine. This place was creepy as fuck. "So what do I get for doing this stupid dare of yours?"

Maureen tapped a finger on her chin. "Hmm.. Let me think. Okay, if you go in there by yourself and manage to get that door unlocked, I'll let you call dibs on anyone you want at Billy's party tonight."

I rolled my eyes. "As if I need your permission on who I choose to make out with later."

She hissed. "Well, good luck trying with me pussy-blocking you all night."

Fuck. She would do it too. "Seriously, Maureen?"

She shrugged. "Fine. I'll let you borrow my red Balenciaga bag for a week."

A smirk pulled at my lips. That bag cost more than most people's rent. Her parents gave it to her for graduation. "All right. Deal. I go in alone and get the door open. Then I get dibs at the party *and* the Balenciaga bag."

"Both?" Maureen pouted.

I nodded. "And if I'm not out in fifteen minutes, you better come and get me, bitch. Psychos could be squatting in there."

A gust of wind rushed past us, blowing one of the shutters hard against the house. We both lurched back. Goosebumps prickled my arms. We should have brought coats, but no, we just had to be more concerned about how hot we looked.

An eerie sensation pulled at me. "I'm going to get you back good for this one, Maur," I called back to her as I moved toward the decaying porch. The wind picked up again, drowning out her response. All I could hear was the faint sound of giggling.

The floorboards creaked under my pointy high-heels. I was half-expecting to drive a hole straight through one of them. "I swear to god if I get my shoe caught in one of these things..." I cursed under my breath.

The house was empty, devoid of any furnishings or decorations. A little burst of adrenaline tingled through my veins. Ever since I was a kid, I'd been obsessed with horror movies and the occult. Walking around this spooky old house was so fucking dangerous, it almost turned me on.

I tested the railing as I started up the staircase, jiggling it to make sure it would hold. Using caution, I crept up the stairs, my heart pounding the closer I got to the top. Thanks to the busted-out windows, it was freezing inside. The wind howled through the house without anything to hinder it. It roamed wild and free. As if it lived here.

There were all sorts of sounds that would make a sane person jump. Make them run out as fast as they could. Aside from the shutters banging against the house, there was the unsettling sound of rodents scratching the wood as they scurried up and down the walls. They never bothered me much, but Maureen, on the other hand, would have shrieked and leaped onto my back.

She never had the stomach for creepy things. Not like me. While I pretended to be annoyed or bored with her dares, I secretly relished them. The thrill of getting caught doing something dangerous was worth every second. I dreamed of things that would make grown men keel over. Dark and depraved things. Regular stuff bored me. I could only fuck missionary so many times before I'd die of boredom. Only so many of the same monotonous blow jobs I could give without wanting to scratch my own eyes out. I didn't want a normal guy. I wanted a monster. A deviant. Someone who could make me feel fucking alive for once.

But my type only existed in books and in my dreams. Hence why I was traipsing through a creepy condemned house without even a can of mace. For the thrill. The rush. It was the closest I could get to whatever it was I was looking for. That thing that I just couldn't grasp or name. *Fuck, I wish I could bottle this feeling.*

I paused at the top of the stairs and looked back over my

shoulder. These abandoned houses tended to harbor less than savory characters. Despite my adrenaline addiction, having a run in with a crack-head or a serial killer was not what I had in mind.

Confident that no one was stalking me, I continued down the hall. The first two rooms I passed were empty just like the rest of the house. The doors torn off their hinges. Empty paper cups rolled around the floor, most likely remnants from that party a few weeks back. The doorframes were charred yet still looked sturdy enough to withstand a hurricane. That was the thing about these old houses—good bones.

The hall dead-ended with one last room. The only room that had a door still attached to it. I stood in front of it, and a chill snaked down my back. It was as if the temperature dropped another ten degrees in this spot. I've heard some people say that ghosts can make a room colder. The adrenaline junkie in me got off on that, but my inner skeptic was convinced it was just a wind tunnel, pulling the chill farther down.

I gasped as I wrapped my hand around the doorknob. It was ice cold. I tried to turn it, but it wouldn't budge.

"Come on," I groaned.

I jiggled it some more and leaned against the door but still nothing. I pulled out one of my hair pins and stuck it in the keyhole like they do in the movies, but I had no fucking clue what I was doing. *How the fuck is there still a locked door in an abandoned house?*

This is why that stupid superstition got started to begin with.

Fuck it.

I backed up a few steps and charged forward, slamming my body into the door. "Fuck," I cried out as I bounced off it. That was going to leave a fucking bruise. I really needed to stop thinking I was some kind of cat burglar.

I rubbed my shoulder, already feeling a lump forming. This was pissing me off. It wasn't about the Balenciaga bag or first dibs on some vapid frat guy. No. I wanted that rush. *Needed it.* And I was just a tad bit curious to know if the legend was true. What if there really was three spirits in that room, ready to pounce on whoever let them out?

Waiting to do dark and dirty things. A tingling began between my thighs. *Only someone as fucked up as me would get aroused by that.*

I grabbed the doorknob again and jiggled it with all my might. "What the fuck?" I hissed. "Fucking open already." I slammed my hands on the door and sighed in defeat.

As I pulled out my phone to text Maureen that it wasn't happening, I started to turn when I felt a warm breath blow against the back of my neck. I whipped around, my heart racing, only to find no one there.

Fuck.

It felt like a man's breath. Footsteps thudded behind me. I spun around again just as a force rammed into me, knocking me backward. I crashed into the door like a wrecking ball. The wood splintered and gave way as I barreled through it.

"Oh, shit," I yelled.

I tumbled face forward and smacked my palms against the floorboards as I broke my own fall.

Okay, this was a bit more than adrenaline. Someone was fucking with me. I scrambled to my feet and glanced around only to find myself completely alone. There was no fucking way.

"Maureen?" I called out. "You better not be fucking with me, bitch."

My heart thudded in my chest. I ran to the open window and looked down. Maureen sat on a tree stump filing her nails. There was no way she could have run up here, pushed me, and then run back down in that amount of time.

I whirled around, the hairs on my neck standing straight up. It was dark. The wind had calmed to a whispering murmur, but the air was still freezing. Crisp and chill like a meat locker.

I snapped a quick picture of the broken door and darted back down the hall. The floor creaked behind me as if someone was following. I didn't bother to turn around this time. I flew down the steps, taking them two at a time. I ran as fast as one could in four-inch-high heels. But it was my adrenaline that carried me.

While I raced through the doorless entryway and down the front porch, I could barely catch my breath, my teeth chattering. Maureen leaped up from her stump to meet me, but I walked past her.

"Hey," she called out. "Did you do it?"

I didn't stop until we were a block away from the house, Maureen whining over the wind the whole time.

"Bailey, what the fuck happened?"

My hands trembled as I held up my phone. "It's done. I got in."

She nodded, arching an eyebrow at me. "Why do you look like you just saw a ghost?"

I didn't know what I saw or felt. But I wasn't alone up there. That was for fucking sure. "I don't want to talk about it. I just want to get really fucking drunk."

Maureen grinned and handed me a jello shot from the tray that I'd completely forgotten we'd brought. "Bottoms up."

I slammed three shots in a row on the walk back to Maureen's house. It wasn't enough to shake the eerie feeling of being watched. "Can we just stay here at your house tonight? I'm not in the mood to party with those assholes anymore."

Maureen stuck out her lower lip in a fake pout. "Don't be a downer, Bales. There will be plenty of drugs, alcohol, and chiseled abs to get you in the mood."

I shook my head. "Nah. I'm good. I think I'm coming down with something actually. I don't feel like being around a bunch of people."

She sighed and tipped back another jello shot. "Well, *I'm* going. I've been looking forward to this party all year."

I knew that if I told her what really happened she would stay

If I told her how freaked out I was, she wouldn't go. But I did have a bunch of shots before I stepped into that house, and my mind was probably just playing tricks on me. I didn't want to ruin her night just because I was coming down off a rush.

I nodded. "Okay, have fun, be safe, and use condoms. Call me tomorrow and tell me all the sordid details?"

Maureen planted a kiss on my cheek. "You know I will. Text me if you change your mind, bitch."

Lingering at her front gate, I watched her strut down the block toward Billy's house. A part of me was tempted to follow. But I just couldn't shake this feeling that had crept into my skin. I wanted a hot shower, a stiff drink, and to forget this night ever happened.

CHAPTER One

It was midnight.

Happy fucking Halloween to me.

I wiped away the steam from the mirror and knocked back another shot of whiskey. I had brought the bottle with me. But despite the hot shower and copious amounts of booze, I could not escape this chill in my bones. It gripped me.

I slipped on a pair of black lace panties and my favorite T-shirt. It was big enough to cover my ass but not enough to keep me very warm. But all my sweatpants were still in the washer. I'd been so excited to go out with Maureen tonight that I had forgotten to change them over to the dryer.

Fuck me.

I scurried into my bed and pulled the thick blankets up around my chin. It wouldn't be long before I'd be hot and throwing them off anyway. I was disappointed that I didn't have a hard cock against my ass right now, though. Ugh, I should have gone to the party.

It was just a few minutes after midnight. Maybe I could still muster up the energy to go? I know I'd have a good time. And maybe it was what I needed to shake off this creepy sensation that had followed me all the way home from that fucking cursed mansion.

As I lay there contemplating getting dressed again and going out, movement flashed in my periphery. What the fuck?

My breath hitched as I laid as still as possible. Was I imagining things in the dark now? A soft wind brushed past me. And then I saw it.

The shadow moved across my bedroom.

It growled, breathing heavy. It stretched as it got closer. My stomach flipped. This was no shadow, but a man with broad shoulders.

I gasped as he came closer and towered over my bed. I shivered, terrified yet aroused.

What was wrong with me?

His green eyes peered down at me, filled with lust and malice. Like he fucking hated me. Like he wanted to own me.

I was afraid to breathe. Afraid to move.

He leaned over me and pressed his fists into the mattress, boxing me in. His lips hovered over mine. "Do you understand what's about to happen? I'm going to do bad things to you, Bailey. Dirty, filthy, depraved things. And you're going to like it. And you're not going to beg me to stop. You'll demand me to finish. You know why? Because the brutality makes you feel alive. You've been dying in your own skin for so long. That ends tonight. I've come to awaken every vile piece of you."

Oh, fuck.

He wrapped his strong hands around my wrists and yanked

me from my bed, tossing me onto the floor. I gasped as he kept coming, stalking toward me. I scrambled back, my heart pounding.

But where would I go? I couldn't run. No. Not from him. He would never let me get far.

He hissed, his lips pursed, as he dug his fingers into my hair. "This way, little fox."

I yelped as he dragged me across the floor by my strands. "You don't get to cum in your own bed. Not yet. You cum when and where I say you can. When *we* say you can."

We? Oh, fuck. *There is more of them?*

My skin burned against the carpet as he pulled me across it. He kicked open doors as he dragged me. We passed through rooms that used to belong to me. This was his house now. There was no escape. I had done this to myself.

We stopped in the living room. Two other shadows lurked in the dark. Their breaths were heavy. I could sense their arousal. Their lust. *Fuck, fuck, fuck.* Did I want this? Did I have a choice?

The man's fingers twisted in my hair, pulling me up to a half crouch. "This is your life for now, little fox. You live at our mercy. Time to see how well you behave."

A second man growled. "Take off her clothes. Show us what we've won."

I hugged my arms to my chest as the man with the black hair and green eyes hovered over me. A sinister chuckle erupted from deep in his gut. He trailed a finger across my jaw, so soft as if he were the gentlest man in existence. He was not.

"Do you deny us our release, little fox?"

I trembled as he crouched down, putting himself at eye level with my clenched pussy. The only thing covering it was my thin lace panties. Why was this making me so wet?

"We can't force you, but we aren't leaving until we get what we want. The sooner you give in to your own desires, the sooner you admit your carnal appetite to yourself, then the fun can begin. And when we've had our fill, we'll leave you alone forever."

I can't believe that fucking curse is real. What a stupid fucking girl I was. But in my defense, who would actually believe that unlocking a door in a supposedly haunted house would send three scary—though hot as hell—spirits to my house in the middle of Halloween night? Three angry spirits with tattoos and chiseled abs who have been sex starved for centuries.

But he just revealed a secret. They can't make me do anything. Sure, they can torment me and occupy my house for the rest of my life, but they can't *make* me do anything. But would they really have to?

As I looked each one up and down, my nipples pebbling at the sight of their wild eyes already undressing me, their heaving chests practically panting for me, I wondered, would they really have to make me do anything? What if he was right?

Maybe I wanted this just as much as they did. Maybe more. They weren't the only ones who had been starving for sexual touch. I craved it. And I would be lying to myself if I didn't admit that my fantasies lately have started just like this. Only this time, it was real.

CHAPTER Two

My heart pounded. "I'm not taking my clothes off for you." I wasn't ready. "I don't even know your names."

The dark haired one smiled, looking back and winking at the other two who sat perched on my living room windowsill. "She makes an excellent point."

He sat down next to me, and I flinched as he wrapped an arm around my shoulders. His grip was hard and firm, the muscles flexing to show me just how strong he was. "You can call me Poe." He pointed to the blond, blue eyed one, the one with the deep scar going through his eyebrow. "That's Grim."

Poe nodded toward the third disturbingly sexy man-spirit who had yet to utter a single word. He just glared at me hungrily with his sharp brown eyes. He barely moved a muscle except for when he was running his tattooed hand through his dirty blond locks. "And that silent beauty over there, he's called Saint… I assure you he's anything but."

Grim growled as he fingered the buckle of his belt. "Now she can choose which name to scream out when we're defiling that tight little cunt of hers."

Saint licked his lips, his throat bobbing as he swallowed. But he remained quiet. And this is why he scared me the most. The silent assassin, watching me like I was a bird in a cage. A cage that only they held the key to.

What the fuck did I let out last night?

My breath hitched. "So you want me to have sex with all three of you? Are you insane? You break into my house and tell me I have to fuck you. This is absurd. I will *scream*."

Poe grabbed my throat and whispered in my ear, "Yes. You will."

Grim chuckled. "But no one will hear you, little fox. Not out here."

Poe tightened his hold on me. "Starting to regret moving out to the woods?" he drawled.

I should run. Call for help. But where? There's no way I'd outrun them. Even if I could, no one would care. They'd say I deserved it. It was no secret that I'd had my share of men in this town. It was okay for them, but I was the one who was judged for it. *Bastards*.

Poe pulled me into his chest. His other hand rested on my bare thigh. Heat radiated off of him. His breath tickled my ear as he whispered, "It will be so much more than sex, little fox." He nodded at Grim, who stalked over and sat on the other side of me.

Grim nestled in close. His hard body was like a brick wall against mine. He placed his hand on my other thigh, higher up than Poe's, and squeezed. "This is the fucking nightmare you've dreamed about," Grim rasped in my ear.

His fingers inched further up, lingering at the edge of my panties. "A part of you wanted it to be true. That's why you opened the door. I can fucking smell your sweet, little, wet cunt from here. I can feel the pulse in your leg, hammering, aching for us to give you what you've never had."

"No," I rasped, shaking my head. No, no, no. This couldn't be real. There was no such thing as ghosts. These were just three run of the mill, albeit sexy as fuck, psychos.

Grim slid his free hand to the nape of my neck, tangling his fingers in my damp strands. He jerked my head back and hovered over my mouth, licking his lips as he watched me tremble. "You *will* let us play with you. *You'll beg us to.*"

I was completely pinned yet neither would make a move until I gave permission. It was terrifying and arousing at the same time. I clenched my pussy tight. *Damn my body for betraying me like this.*

Saint finally stirred. He slowly rose from my windowsill and ambled forward. His lips curled up into a smirk that was so heavily laced with lust and malice that I almost had a fucking heart attack. Saint planted himself across from me, using my coffee table as a chair. He pushed my legs apart and scooted closer, forcing himself into my space.

Grim shoved my head toward Saint until our lips were almost touching. Adrenaline spiked through me as his breath danced across my face. Saint let out a low growl, so soft I almost thought my ears were playing tricks on me.

His fingers dug into the sides of my knees as he kept me from retreating. "*Say yes,*" he breathed.

Poe nodded. "We have all the time in the world, little fox. If you won't let us begin, there are other ways we can torture you..."

Fuck.

As soon as he said it, I knew that they would make good on that promise. They were so beautiful it hurt to look them in the eyes. Brutal fucking savages with unsatiable appetites. But it made me feel something dark and twisted and fucking alive. I could take from them as much as I wanted. *What I've always wanted.* But what would they do to me? How deep down the dark rabbit hole was I willing to go?

But I couldn't make that mistake again. To trust. Not like that night in the back of my ex-boyfriend's truck. The one time I tried to explore my desires, tried to show him what I wanted, and he called me a slut.

When he accused me of fucking everyone he knew. Because how could a chaste girl like me possibly know what I wanted sexually? Surely if I knew how to touch myself, how to ask for what I wanted, then I must be a slut, right? *Fucking simple-minded asshole.* He had been my first of many after that night. A string of boring one-night stands where my excitement was as fleeting as my orgasms.

I squirmed out of their grip, twisting out of Grim's hold on my hair and swatting Poe and Saint's hands away. "You don't know anything about what I want," I snapped.

They let me stand.

I moved away from them, toward the window seat, shivering with nothing to keep me warm without their body heat except a thin white T-shirt that barely covered my ass.

Poe smiled at Grim. With a quick nod, he was on his feet, crossing the distance between us. I shrunk back against the throw pillows.

Grim stopped just inches in front of me. "Let the torture begin."

CHAPTER *Three*

I held my breath as he unbuckled his belt and slowly slid it out of its loops. I jumped as he snapped it in front of him. "Let's see how much wetter I can get you, little fox."

My heart hammered in my throat. What the fuck was he going to do?

Grim unbuttoned his jeans, pushed them down, and stepped out of the rumpled fabric, kicking them across the room. I gasped at the sight of his smooth, hard cock standing at attention.

He chuckled as he peeled off his black T-shirt, revealing his beautifully carved body. There wasn't a single flaw. With a six pack of abs and two steel rods piercing through his nipples, he looked like a runway model. Only his dark sinister gaze reminded me what he really was.

A predator.

Grim stood completely naked in front of me while Poe and Saint looked on, leaning back and seemingly enjoying the show. Grim moved closer, forcing my legs apart with his knees as he towered over me.

Fuck. He was gorgeous.

I gasped as he wrapped his left hand around my throat, firm but not hard enough to restrict my breath. The feel of his grip on my neck had me clenching again. *Why did this turn me on so much?*

My heart skittered as I anticipated his next move. Was he going to force me to suck his cock? Would I even put up much of a fight? I was practically salivating over it.

His eyes hardened and his lips pulled tight. "Watch," he commanded.

"Watch what?" I murmured.

He fisted his cock with his right hand and began stroking his shaft up and down. I tilted my chin up to look away from his throbbing cock, and he gave my throat a quick squeeze. "*I said, fucking watch.*"

"Oh, shit," I whimpered, struggling for breath. I nodded and he relaxed his grip on me slightly.

"*Good girl.*"

He began stroking his cock again, back, and forth. He circled the tip with his thumb, pinching it between his fingers as a little spurt of pre-cum pooled out.

"You want a taste, don't you, little fox? You want to slide those pouty lips up and down my cock until they're bruised and swollen. If you say otherwise, than you're a fucking liar," he breathed.

Was he right?

I couldn't move or look away. Heat flooded my body as he took his time, languishing in each stroke of his veiny shaft. My nipples ached as they pebbled against the cotton of my shirt, imagining what his hands could do to them. My panties were soaked.

"Say yes, little fox. Just one word and I'll give you what you want. I can see your swollen nipples through that sweat-soaked shirt. I know they're aching to be sucked."

Grim squeezed my throat a little tighter. "*Aching* to feel the scrape of my teeth against them."

Oh, fuck.

Sweat beaded down my back. I was falling apart. Unraveling. Every breath shorter than the last. I kept my eyes glued to his glistening cock, for fear that if I looked into his eyes he'd know. That everything he said was true. That I wanted him. I wanted all three of them.

I fisted my hands at my sides as his breaths grew more rapid. He let out a soft moan and rubbed himself harder, faster. Tingles erupted inside my aching pussy. Watching him, as he held me in place with one hand and fondled himself with the other was vicious. It was fucking brutal. But only because I would not let myself give in.

"Uhh," he moaned. "Fuck. Get ready for it, little fox."

What the... oh, fuck. He grunted and moved his hand to the back of my neck. I whimpered as he tugged my head back and released his cum on my throat. It came out thick and hot. Dripped down my shirt. I quivered as it oozed in between my breasts. I stared at the ceiling as he surrendered to his orgasm, feeling his warm sticky cum drip all over me.

He yanked my head hard and rubbed his fingers over my neck, smearing his cum across my jaw and over my tightly closed lips. I would not give in, dammit. *But fuck how I wanted to.*

Grim pulled me upright, smiled and stepped back. "I look good on you, little fox."

Poe rose and stalked over to us. My heartbeat fast. He took a seat next to me. "We can keep playing these games, or you can give us what we want. *What you want.*"

I looked around the room, soaking in their hungry stares. They didn't look like ghosts. No. They were solid and formed like men.

Beautiful men. Poe with his black hair and green eyes, the way they slinked over every inch of me like I was about to be devoured.

Then Grim, the tallest of the three. His black and grey tattoos swirled and climbed over almost every inch of his skin, highlighting every inch of his hard muscled body. The sexy V-shape that dipped down below his abs, aching to be licked. His blonde hair was slicked back off his forehead revealing the undersides shaved and imprinted with more tattoos. His blue eyes pierced me like razors.

And finally, Saint, he was the biggest of the three. Not in height but in stature. He looked like a bouncer or like he belonged in some fight club. His dirty blond hair was tied up in a top knot. Shadows flickered behind his brown eyes.

A tremor shot through me as Poe stroked my cheek with the tip of his finger. "Give in to your desire, little fox. Let us give you what you've been too scared to get for yourself."

My heart hammered. I could barely control my breath. "I-I'm not scared."

Grim stepped back into his black jeans, pulling them up slowly. He tucked his cock back inside but left the zipper and button undone. He stood over me and cupped my chin in his hand. "You're terrified, Bailey. And it makes you so fucking wet, you couldn't clench your legs together any tighter if you tried."

I tried to swallow, but my throat was so dry. "I need a drink."

Saint made his way into the kitchen and returned with a bottle of wine and a glass. He poured it and as he handed it to me, he kept his fingers curled around the stem. I inhaled a sharp breath as his skin grazed mine. "This will help you relax, little fox."

Or it would just make me make stupider decisions.

I gulped down half of it in one sip. "This is great. Just fucking great. I'm being haunted by three sex starved ghosts. How is that even possible? This can't be real."

Poe inched himself closer to me. "Stop talking. There are better uses for that sexy mouth of yours."

Grim nodded, heat rising in his stare. "Open up for us. We've waited a long time for you, Bailey. Our sly little fox…"

Why were they calling me that? "No. Please, just leave. I can't give you what you want."

Poe sighed. "Wrong answer."

I gasped as he yanked me to my feet. He whipped me around and pulled me to him. His stiff cock ground against my back. Without warning he walked me forward into the wall and pressed harder into me. He fisted my hair tight in his palm. He pressed my face to the wall and breathed heavy into my ear. "You're the only one who can give us what we want."

He smelled so fucking good. I whimpered as he reached around and began slowly pulling up the edges of my shirt. "Spread your legs, little fox."

I wriggled against him, trying to squirm out of his hold but all that did was make him grip me tighter. He shoved his foot between my ankles and knocked them apart, forcing me to widen my stance. My clit ached as he pressed me further into the wall. "Tell me you're not wet right now, and I'll let you go."

I grunted in frustration. "I'm not wet."

He ran his teeth over my earlobe as he whispered, "Liar."

"Prove it, little fox," Grim taunted. "Let him touch you."

Oh, fuck. I wanted to be touched so bad.

I squirmed again. Poe pressed into me. I could feel the hem of my shirt getting higher. My panties were exposed now. My legs spread open. He stroked my belly in soft small circles with his fingers. I quivered. "*Fuck*," I whispered underneath my breath.

"Relax, little fox. Let me touch you," Poe rasped.

I was practically panting. I'd never been exposed like this. This vulnerable. I bit down on my lower lip and shook my head. "I-I don't want you to."

He snickered and released me. "Liar," he repeated.

I turned around and leaned back against the wall. "You don't know me."

Poe twirled a lock of my blonde hair. "We know you better than you know yourself. The sooner you give into what you want, the more alive we'll all be."

He stalked away and sat down on the couch while keeping his feral gaze on me.

Saint smirked. I didn't even realize he was capable of any expression. "Aren't you tired of always being in control, Bailey? Hmm?" He grabbed a black duffel bag from behind the couch that I hadn't noticed until now.

He unzipped it slowly. "We can do things to you that even your wildest fantasies couldn't muster."

I clenched my pussy again, praying my slick juices didn't pool any farther down my thighs. "What do you want to do to me?" I asked, terrified and more aroused than I'd ever been in my whole life.

Saint reached inside the bag and pulled out a black leather riding crop. He caressed the tip of it and then smacked it against his palm. I flinched.

"You think you're wet now, little fox... Submit to us. Say yes, and you will feel pleasure unlike any you've ever known," Saint breathed.

My legs began to shake. I had never been spanked before. But I'd be lying to myself if I said I hadn't always wanted to be. Fuck. How did they seem to know all the dirty things I wanted done to me?

CHAPTER Four

I'd heard about fight or flight moments, but this wasn't that. In this moment, it was either fuck or flight. And what was really starting to scare me was how I didn't want to flee at all. But I should. I needed to. What kind of girl would I be if I let three strangers do dark and dirty things to me? It was shameful. I needed to take care of this myself before I exploded.

"I-I need a second." I shot past them and darted for the bathroom. I was almost to the door when Saint caught my wrist.

"*Shit.*"

He pushed me back against the wall and pinned my wrists above my head. He sniffed my hair like a wolf about to attack its prey. "Don't close that door."

"Excuse me? I have to pee. I'm not doing that with the door open." I could feel my cheeks heating.

Saint twisted his fingers around my wrists. "Liar. You and I both know what you are going in there to do. But if you want to make yourself cum, you'll have to do it in front of us."

Fuck. Of course, they knew. No matter how much my mouth protested, my body gave them every ounce of proof they needed to know I was aching for release.

"Or do one better, and let *us* make you cum," Poe chimed in as he approached, admiring Saint's grip on me.

Grim joined us now too. I was surrounded, pinned against my own hallway wall. By all three of them. Trapped, with Grim's cum still all over me. And I was disgustingly, ridiculously, viciously aroused.

"Please, just let me go," I murmured. *Please don't.*

Grim stroked my cheek. "You belong to us, little fox. Time to accept it."

Poe nodded. "There's no shame in wanting this. Let us show you."

"Say yes." Saint pleaded.

My head spun. My heart hammered. Every inch of my body was on fire with lust. Every nerve ending erect and aware of their effect on me. I was wetter than rain, my nipples ached, my clit throbbed in anticipation. This is what I'd fantasized about. It was finally happening.

So why was I so afraid to give in?

Grim lifted my shirt, exposing my belly while Poe traced the edges of my panties, taunting me. "Let us inside, little fox. I want to feel that tight little cunt clench around my fingers."

Grim placed his hand on the small of my back, tracing small circles over the base of my spine. "Spread your legs, little fox. Open up," he rasped.

Saint lowered his lips to mine, stopping just short of kissing me. "Submit... *Say. Yes.*"

A blast of sensations hit me at once. Heat spread between

my legs. Sweat dripped from every crevice. I panted at the stimulation of all three of them surrounding me, teasing me, begging me to give in.

"Fuck…I-I just…" The scent of their sweat mixed with night and musk and desire was overwhelming. It was seductive and every inch of my skin was raw. Tingling. Every nerve twitched at the thought of giving up control to them.

Poe pulled at the edges of my panties a little firmer but still holding back. "You're so close to the edge, little fox… time to jump."

My chest heaved. I couldn't take it anymore. I took deep breaths, locking eyes with each of them as I did. The tension in the room grew thick as they waited. As they watched my chest rise and fall. As they watched my lips tremble.

I swallowed and willed moisture back into my mouth, but all I could muster was a throaty whisper, "*Yes…*"

A collective swoosh of air peeled back as all three of them pressed in closer to me. Poe slipped a finger inside my panties, stilling it right above my swollen clit. "*Good girl.*"

Grim cupped my ass and gave it a hard pinch. "You belong to us now, little fox. Every single piece of your flesh belongs to us."

Saint wrapped his hand around my throat, and I flinched slightly. Was I really ready for this?

He held firm. "You're no longer in control, Bailey. We're going to do whatever we want with you."

I couldn't catch my breath. "What-what are you going to do?"

"Shh… Let's get you more comfortable," Poe hushed in my ear.

Saint reached into his back pocket and pulled out a switchblade. He grabbed the hem of my shirt and cut into it, dragging the blade up in short little jerks as it tore through the fabric. I leaned back against the wall as Grim and Poe each held one of my wrists over my head.

Saint split my shirt wide open, the air hit my nipples and I gasped.

"So fucking beautiful…" He traced the tip of the blade delicately across my collarbone.

He tipped my chin up with the blade. "Say it."

I looked back and forth between the three of them, confused.

Grim growled in my ear. "Say you belong to us."

This was it. I had made my decision. I couldn't escape it. And I didn't want to. I licked my lips. "I'm yours. God help me, but I belong to you now."

Saint nodded at Poe. He flashed me a grin as he dipped a finger below my panty line, sliding it down my slick slit. I moaned as he pressed against my nub. "So fucking wet for us. I knew you were a fucking liar. But now you're going to be a good girl, aren't you?"

I bit down on my lip as he slid his finger in and out my pussy, slowly. It was agonizing. I nodded. "Yes, I'll be a good girl."

Poe drew in a sharp breath. "Go sit on the couch."

I staggered over to my brown leather cushions and started to sit down when Grim called for me to stop. "Panties off. I want to see that sweet cunt bare against the leather."

Saint was behind me in seconds. I felt the press of the blade against my thigh, then the pull from it ripping the fabric of my panties wide open and away from me.

"*That's better*," Grim growled.

My legs were shaking. I was completely naked, vulnerable, and exposed for all three of them to see.

And they eyed me like prey, hungrily.

I sat on the couch, perched on the edge, my knees locked together.

Saint came from behind and grabbed my shoulders. "Relax, little fox. Lean all the way back."

Oh god, I really was giving up control now. I didn't resist as he pulled my shoulders into the cushions.

Grim and Poe retook their positions on either side of me.

"Open up, little fox. I want to see everything," Poe murmured.

I spread my legs apart just as Saint's hands slid down my chest and cupped my breasts. I gasped as he pinched both my nipples between his fingers, rubbing them back and forth. I could feel the heat flooding me, the intensity of his grip driving my body to near convulsions.

"That's our good girl. So naughty. You're our dirty girl, too, aren't you?" Grim asked.

I licked my lips, my throat dry. "Um… I-I don't know," I squeaked out.

Grim dragged his tongue across my jaw. "Yes, you do. You're so fucking filthy. So beautifully dirty. Say it."

My nipples swelled as Saint pinched and rolled them tight between his fingers. It was getting harder to concentrate on what stimulation was coming from where.

Grim jerked my chin and kissed me hard. "I asked you a question, little fox."

"Yes… I'm a dirty girl," I panted.

Grim snickered. "You know what happens to dirty girls, Bailey? *Hmm?…* Dirty. Fucking. Things."

Poe locked eyes with Grim, a sinister smirk flashed on both their faces. "Open her up for me."

CHAPTER Five

I had never been with more than one man at the same time.

He was right. It *was* dirty. But I didn't want it to stop.

I drew in a sharp breath as Grim pulled back the lips of my pussy. "Uhh," I whimpered.

Poe teased my entrance with his long fingers and without warning, shoved one inside.

"Fuck yeah, little fox. You're so wet for us. So ready."

I gasped as Saint pinched my nipples harder. Grim stroked the outside of my pussy, pressing his thumb on my swollen nub as Poe pushed his finger deeper inside me. I couldn't breathe.

Ripples of ecstasy hit me, wave after wave as I struggled to remain in control of my body. I was going to cum faster than I'd even thought possible. Grim stretched me wider apart as Poe inserted a second finger. I clenched my walls around him and screamed from the pleasure.

"It's too much," I panted.

"Shh, relax. You're doing so fucking good." He pumped his fingers in and out.

I arched my hips, rolling against his hand. "*Fuck*, that feels… amazing."

Grim rubbed the outside of my pussy, gliding his fingers through my slick folds. "This is just the beginning, little fox."

Without warning, Saint released my breasts. Grim spun me sideways so I was laying across the couch in his lap, my back against his chest. His cock stiffened and pulsed against my ass.

Poe hovered over me; the length of his torso wedged between my thighs. This was fucking insane and exhilarating. He kissed my belly, dragging the tip of his tongue down my wet slit. His tongue was soft and hot and firm.

Saint came around the side, a rope dangling in his hands. He grabbed my wrists. I panted as he held them over my head and fastened the rope tight around them. He tied the other end of the rope to a leg of the couch.

I couldn't move. And it fucking drove me wild. This was truly giving up control. I was at their mercy.

Grim drew light circles around my nipples with his fingertips. "Such a good fucking girl. About to burst so we can all taste that sweet cum of yours."

"Oh shit," I rasped.

Poe worked my pussy with his tongue, licking and sucking and scraping his teeth gently across my folds. I bucked wildly, flailing as the overstimulation pushed me to the edge.

Saint kneeled down beside me. "Arch her up."

With his tongue buried deep inside me, Poe lifted my hips, making a space for Saint to wedge his hand between me and Grim.

Grim squeezed my breasts while Saint yanked Grim's pants down and fisted his cock.

"*Fuck*, Saint, that's right," Grim moaned. Saint guided Grim's shaft up and down the line of my ass, sandwiching it between my needy flesh. Poe sucked my clit harder. I clenched around him, feeling every single pulse and flick.

I cried out as my orgasm began to climb inside me. Grim squeezed my nipples tight as he sucked on my earlobe. Saint pushed down on my abdomen with one hand while he rubbed my ass raw with Grim's huge stiff cock in his other hand.

"Little fox…" Saint breathed. He pressed down on my belly. "You have no idea how dirty I'm going to get you."

I moaned as the pressure built. They were right. I could never have dreamt this up. This was unfathomable. I was over stimulated.

With Grim's smooth shaft wedged between my ass, sliding up and down, seeking entrance. Poe's tongue devouring me like I was a bowl of his favorite ice cream. And Saint. The one who barely speaks, orchestrating it all. He was barely touching me, but I was most aroused by him.

"Oh fuck, I'm…com…coming." I screamed and arched my back, ignoring the burns around my wrists as I pulled on my restraints.

The three of them nestled in close, not letting up as all the blood in my body rushed to my head. Stars studded my vision as I moaned out the longest and most satisfying orgasm I'd ever had.

"Fuucckk…"

They stroked me as I came down.

"Breathe, little fox. Don't want to wear you out just yet," Poe cooed.

Grim adjusted himself underneath me, while Saint untied me and pushed me back up to a sitting position.

"We have so much more planned for you," Saint rasped.

I was so dizzy I almost blacked out. It was better than my

fantasy. And I knew that the night was just beginning. This sent a tingling sensation back to my middle, as I still rode out the wave of my orgasm. I wanted more.

Poe cupped my face and pulled my face to his. "I want you to taste yourself on my tongue." He kissed me without warning, and I melted into him. Tasting myself was so naughty. So fucking dirty. I nearly came again.

Grim rubbed my back as Poe explored my mouth, his kisses deepening with every whimper I let out. When he finally broke away, he stole my breath with him. I felt like I was on fire.

"Tell us, little fox," Grim urged, "Why are you afraid of your own pleasure? Hmm?" His hands were tangled in my hair. He stroked the back of my neck. It was soothing and stimulating at the same time.

I was ashamed to answer. "Not everyone likes what I like."

Poe wrapped his hand around my throat and planted a kiss on my jaw. "*We* are what you fucking like, baby girl. And we are right fucking here to worship you. Don't be afraid."

Saint nodded. "You're beautiful."

There was a strange connection between me and Saint. At first I didn't even think he liked me. Now I was starting to wonder. He took such care with me. As if I would break in his hands. I'd let him fucking break me if he wanted to. I craved him most of all.

But something else was bothering me. Despite my lack of belief in ghosts and spirits, I know what I felt back at Wickford mansion. I *know* something unseen pushed me into that door. I hadn't had that many jello shots to where I would hallucinate that.

I curled my legs to my chest, blanketing myself with my own body. "What happened to the three of you? Why are you… dead?"

Grim's breath hitched. He moved my arms and replaced them with his. "Don't cover yourself. If you're cold, we'll keep you warm."

His strong arms wrapped around me, protectively. He hugged me to his chest, placing one arm across my breasts while cupping my pussy with the other. A new wave of tingles shot through me at the instant heat from his palm.

Grim chuckled. "Relax, little fox. They'll be plenty more of that later. This is just to keep the heat flowing in all the right places."

The warmth spread to my belly. My nipples pebbled underneath his forearm. Fuck. "You're trying to distract me," I breathed.

Poe smirked as he fixated on the way Grim was holding me. "And it's working, isn't it?"

Saint grunted as he stood up. "She needs nourishment. I'll get her something to eat and drink."

I couldn't help but squirm a bit against Grim's palm. It radiated like fire through my pussy. I wanted to grind against it. To feel my orgasm climb again. It felt so fucking good.

Grim tsked in my ear. "Such a dirty girl. Don't think I can't feel you trying to rub against me."

My breath grew heavy. "I'm just cold."

"Lie all you want, little fox, but your cunt tells the truth." Poe lounged back against the other end of the couch and pulled off his shirt.

I gasped. His chest was perfect. Carved like stone. "I'm not lying." I was.

Saint returned with a glass of water and a bowl of fruit. He sat down on the coffee table again and set the bowl beside him. "Drink." He handed me the water and I obeyed.

Grim slid his arm back and forth across my breasts. "Good girl."

Saint then picked out a peach and began carving it with his knife. I reached out to take a slice when Poe snatched it from him instead. He dangled the juicy fruit over my lips. "You are not in control anymore. Remember?"

I nodded, my heart racing.

He rubbed the fruit against my lips. "Open your mouth."

As soon as I parted my lips, he shoved the peach slice in. It tasted like heaven. Like fucking ecstasy. Not because it was a good piece of fruit but because Poe had fed it to me. I was practically purring.

Saint started to feed me another slice when Poe stopped him. "You know what, Saint? I feel like something is missing... Grim, what would make our good girl enjoy her meal more?"

His grip on my pussy tightened, reinvigorating the need between my thighs. "Her cunt is as wet as that peach. Would you like to see?"

Poe nodded. "Mmm, very much."

"Make her cum for us," Saint growled.

Oh fuck. My senses were back into overdrive.

Grim shifted his hand and slowly started to caress my outer folds. I parted my legs wider as he stroked, needing to feel every inch of him inside me.

"Grim, please," I panted.

Saint brought a slice of peach to my lips but didn't relinquish it. "Suck."

I moaned as the sweet peach filled my mouth. I sucked on Saint's fingers as he held it, the fruit between my lips.

"Fucking hell, little fox," Poe cried out. "I want a taste."

I gasped as Poe grabbed another slice of the bright tangy fruit and dragged it down my pussy, slathering the juices across my skin. I trembled as the sticky juice coated me and the soft flesh tickled my clit.

"Do you like that, little fox? How does it feel to be so fucking dirty?"

I arched back, panting. "Don't fucking stop," I pleaded.

Poe chuckled as he shoved the fruit that was now coated in my cum into his mouth. He moaned as he savored it. "Fuck, you taste so good."

Grim slipped a finger inside my pussy. "I don't think you're dirty enough, little fox." He pumped another finger in, hooking up toward my G-spot.

I moaned. Oh, fuck. My head was buzzing. Still sucking on Saint's juice covered fingers, I spread my legs as far as they could go. Grim pulled the lips of my pussy back. He slid his fingers up and down my slit, then in and out, while Poe licked every trace of peach juice off me. I bucked my hips, arching up as he pressed down hard on my clit with his thumb.

Poe's eyes fixated on all of it. "Fuck, yeah. Just like that, Grim."

He moaned into my ear. "You're so fucking tight."

Poe gripped my thighs, digging his fingers into the side of my knees, and spreading me wider apart. "You want it harder, don't you, little fox? Faster?"

Saint grunted, fisting his own cock, rubbing himself as he watched us.

"Tell him, little fox," Poe repeated.

I was going to black out. The pressure was building to the point where I couldn't even see straight. "Fuck, yes. Harder. Please, Grim."

"Oh, fuck." Grim pushed his fingers deeper inside, pumping so fast I could barely breathe.

Poe stroked the inside of my thighs. "That's our good girl. So fucking good."

White lights sparked in my vision as my orgasm rumbled from the center of me and burst out. I clenched around his fingers and screamed.

"Fuck," I whispered as I came down, trying to reclaim my breath. "Fuck..."

I rolled my head to the side to look at Saint. His dick was still hard as a rock, but he was no longer holding it as it tented his pants. He let out a deep quivering breath and closed his eyes for a moment. "I'm not ready to cum yet."

He handed me the glass of water and I drank it down in one

sip. That was already two orgasms in the span of one hour. That had never happened to me before. No one had ever even bothered trying before.

My head was spinning. "I'm going to need more sustenance than just a couple of peach slices. And I'd like to at least wear my robe."

Poe started to protest, but I cut him off. "I think I've been a *very good girl*. I've earned a respite for a little bit."

Saint nodded. "Yes, she's right."

Grim smiled devilishly down at me. "Already making demands and owning what you want. I knew you were fucking perfect."

Poe got to his feet. "I'll be right back with a robe for our sly little fox."

As the night carried on, I was beginning to realize that as much as I belonged to them, *they belonged to me*. I was their good girl, but they were my beautiful savage devils. We would break each other. And then we'd put each other back together.

CHAPTER Six

I sat on the edge of the windowsill with a steaming cup of coffee, my fluffy gray robe tied tight around me. I gazed out the window, getting lost in that space between dusk and dawn. When the sky was a dark blue. It was the quietest time of day. Not even the birds were awake yet.

The guys watched me intently from across the room. Their breathing growing heavy again as they looked on. I felt the tingling begin to stir again. Knowing how bad they wanted me. Was I just as insatiable as them?

I locked eyes with Poe. "Tell me what happened to you. How did you die?"

"We were poisoned," Poe snarled.

"All three of you?" I asked. "When? Who poisoned you?"

"So many questions," Grim drawled. "Let's just enjoy our time together. The past doesn't matter."

"I want to know." I raised my chin in defiance.

"It was a long time ago, Bailey," Saint grumbled.

Poe licked his lips. "Keep being a good girl and maybe I'll tell you what happened." The way his gaze traveled over the length of my body was enough to make me shiver.

"I need to use the bathroom."

Poe nodded. "Don't linger in there too long though, or I'll have to drag you out."

I shuddered and reminded myself that they were predators. No matter how gorgeous or sexy, or how skilled they were with their tongues, they were apex predators. And I had bargained with them. Traded my body for their souls. The night was far from over.

I shut the door behind me and thought better about locking it. That wouldn't keep them out anyway. It would only piss them off. I couldn't lie that the hint of danger, and their impulsive tempers sent a little shiver up my spine. A *tingling* shiver that stirred up a fresh sheen of moisture between my legs. What was wrong with me? Had I been alone so long that any attention was turning me on. Even from vile delicious spirits who refuse to leave until I let them defile my body?

I was as fucked in the head as they were.

After splashing some water on my face, I rested my trembling hand on the doorknob. I wanted more but I was still a bit terrified. What if I couldn't handle any more?

As I turned the knob and opened the door, I gasped, almost walking right into Grim. He stood, blocking the doorway, naked and waiting for me.

He held a leather collar in his hands. "Come here, little fox."

I shook my head. "What is that?"

"A gift," he drawled.

I backed up into the bathroom, ashamed and horrified that the sight of it in his hands made me wet again.

Grim stalked forward, his eyes ablaze with renewed hunger. "I like hunting you, little fox. These games you play are so fucking hot. Pretending you don't want the same things. You make me so hard."

He backed me up until there was nowhere to go. The cold wall hit my back, and I froze. "What is that for?"

Grim smirked and held the collar up closer so I could see its intricacies. There were three metal loops attached to it.

Oh, fuck.

Just as the realization hit me, Saint appeared in the doorway, a chain wrapped around his wrists. Fuck.

Poe entered the bathroom last. He took the chain from Saint and nodded to Grim.

Grim exhaled, shuddering in anticipation as he opened my robe and slid it off my shoulders. He dragged the collar across my chest, using it to caress me, tracing circles around my swollen nipples with it. "I'm really going to enjoy seeing you like this," he rasped.

I stiffened. I'd be giving up more control. But wasn't that what I'd already done? From the moment I said yes, I gave them permission to own me. To do whatever the fuck they wanted to me. And that thought sent another burst of heat through my body.

I swallowed hard and lifted my chin, holding eye contact with Grim.

He chuckled as he wrapped the collar around my neck, fastening it at my nape. "Good girl."

It was tight but not choking me. Just tight enough to remind me who was in charge. Poe inched forward and tugged on my collar, causing me to stumble into him. He fingered the ring at the base of the collar, caressing it like it was a part of me. I guess now it was.

I drew in a sharp breath as he hooked one end of the chain into my collar. His eyes lit up with lust and desire. As he stepped back so all three of them could admire me, the other end wrapped tightly in his fist, I became dizzy. An animalistic need inside my belly bloomed. They were beasts, and I was at their mercy.

Saint took the chain from Poe and tugged me forward to his chest. "Beautiful," he growled. "Ours."

He pulled me out of the bathroom and away from the living room, down the hall. Grim and Poe followed close behind. I could feel their warm breaths on my back. Fuck, I was so wet.

They herded me to my bedroom. The blankets and pillows had been stripped off my queen size bed. Only the top sheet remained. I shivered.

Saint stood behind me. He tugged on my chain and backed me up into his hard cock. I couldn't help my body for wanting to feel him. I wiggled against his crotch, and his hand shot forward as he cupped my pussy.

"Please," I begged.

"Get on the bed," he ordered in his low gruff voice.

I nodded as he gave me some slack on the chain to climb onto the bed. As soon as my knees hit the mattress, he tugged back on the chain again. "No. I want your head at the foot of the bed."

I laid back against the squishy mattress and inhaled a deep breath.

Poe came to one side of the bed and removed his shirt, then his pants. He was gorgeous with abs that rivaled Grim's. How were all three of them so fucking perfect?

Grim came to the other side. The three of them gazed down at me, their lips wet and cocks hard. "Let's play, little fox."

He climbed onto the bed and ran a hand up the length of my thigh. Moisture pooled out of my folds. I bit back a whimper as he stroked my wet slit. Saint handed him the chain right before he grabbed my wrists and held them tight above my head. Oh, fuck. Poe growled in need as he joined us on the bed.

Grim stuck his finger deep inside his mouth and pulled it out slow. Without warning he shoved it into my tight pussy. I clenched and bucked my hips. "Relax, beautiful." He held his finger still inside me. My clit throbbed.

Poe massaged my belly. "*Let's see how wide you can stretch for us.*"

Grim fisted his cock, rubbing the tip of it against my aching folds. "Beg for it. Tell me how bad you fucking want it."

I wanted to touch it. I tried to pull away from Saint, but he held my wrists tighter.

Poe pushed on my nub while Grim teased me with his tip, stroking it up and down my dripping wet entrance. "Fucking say it, or I'll just torture you like this all night."

I panted, the need to feel him inside me taking over every other thought. "Please… I need it. I fucking need it so bad. Please, Grim."

A sinister smirk played across his lips. "Good girl." He teased at my entrance, pushing himself halfway in. "Relax… open up for me."

I spread my legs wider, and he inched in farther, gasping as I clenched around him. Shit he felt so fucking good.

Poe moaned and sucked on my nipples while Saint panted behind me, holding my wrists firm.

Grim slid in and out of me slowly as he moved deeper into me. He was so big I could feel him in my fucking back. I rocked my hips into him, letting him hit every angle.

I cried out as he hit my spot, sparkly spots clouding my vision. "Oh, fuck…Grim."

"Fuck yeah, scream my name, you dirty girl. Such a good fucking dirty little fox." He pounded into me harder, faster. He rose up, towering over me as he thrusted, pulling on my leash. He came inside me as I unraveled underneath him.

Grim pulled out and laid back next to me. "So fucking good."

I could barely catch my breath before Poe was on top of me, sucking on my pebbled nipples. "I want in, little fox."

Staring up at his cold blue eyes, a little tremor shot through me. I was ready for more. I was insatiable. They had awoken something in me that would not be dormant any longer.

I licked my lips and spread my legs wide again, arching my hips toward him in offering.

Poe growled at the gesture. "You are taking us so well. Fuck. I'm going to make you cum again. So hard."

He pushed at my slick entrance and we both gasped as his hard cock slid inside. I let out a moan as he drew back and then plunged forward through my clenched walls. I felt like I was flying. Saint still held my wrists tight in his hands, caressing them with his thick fingers. Next to me, Grim looked on, his cock hard again at the sight of me being fucked by Poe.

Grim grabbed my chain and tugged, pulling my face to his. He kissed me hard, shoving his tongue between my lips and exploring my eager mouth.

"Fuck, you make me so needy, little fox."

Poe moved deeper inside me, and I bucked. "Oh, fuck. Yes. Just like that," I cried out.

"Say my fucking name." He pounded harder.

I broke away from Grim's kiss. "Poe," I rasped. "You feel so fucking good."

"Uhh, fuck yeah." The whole bed shook as he pumped into me. While Grim was more sensual and slower with his movements, Poe was like an animal. He was unleashed. Wild. Raw. And I fucking loved it.

My pussy trembled as my orgasm built. The tingling spread through my thighs first, then my swollen clit, until finally it took hold of my entire body. I screamed out as it washed over me, clenching, and squeezing around him like I was trying to milk every last drop.

This triggered him, and he poured into me, digging his fingers deep into my hips to hold me still as he came.

My legs felt like dead weights. My pussy was raw. But I was feeling the highest I've ever felt.

Saint released my wrists just as Grim and Poe nuzzled up against me, each throwing a leg over one of mine.

I waited, my heart hammering, for Saint to move on me next. But to my surprise he left the room.

A wave of disappointment came over me. I was exhausted, sore, and emotionally spent, but the thought of him not wanting me had me reeling. Did he get his fill just by watching me? Did I do something that turned him off?

Moments later, I heard the rush of water coming from the bathroom. Grim chuckled. "Saint's ready for you, little fox."

Poe stroked the outside of my pussy, making me wet again. "Are you going to be a good girl and do exactly what he says?"

My breath hitched. So he did want me. I nodded. "Yes."

"That's what we like to hear," Grim breathed.

Saint stalked back into the room, grabbed my chain, and tugged me out of bed. I grasped onto it so as not to get choked. Although, I wasn't entirely opposed to that either. What was wrong with me?

Saint led me into the hot steamy bathroom and closed the door behind us. I was confused. "They aren't joining us?" I was under the impression that they were a package deal.

He shook his head. "Not this part... get in the shower."

His eyes were dark, sinister. I swallowed hard, suddenly afraid of what he was going to do. As I turned around and stepped into the tub, he shoved me against the wall. My breasts pushed up against the cold tile, hardening my nipples. I was starting to think they'd be permanently swollen at this point.

"Don't move," he ordered in his gruff voice.

I don't know what I was expecting, but it wasn't this. I felt the fuzzy sponge at my back as he dragged it across my skin. The soapy suds oozed down my body. He was cleaning me.

"Turn around."

I gulped and slowly inched around to face him. He stood in front of me, fully naked. His body was covered in tattoos. Beautiful patterns of black and gray ink. And his cock, holy shit. I thought Grim and Poe were big. Saint was colossal. And the tip of it was pierced with a silver bar bell. I could only imagine what that would feel like inside me.

"Spread your legs."

I widened my stance and leaned back against the shower wall.

He pressed the sponge to my pussy, moving it up and down my slit. Broad strokes that turned to small circles as the soft foamy sponge tickled every nerve ending. I bit back the urge to moan. Saint seemed to like the quiet. He never broke eye contact with me as he worked the sponge over me like it was his own hand.

Despite just getting fucked by two of the hottest men I'd ever seen, this act that Saint was doing was more erotic than anything else. It was seductive and carnal. He was cleaning me but somehow I felt dirtier.

We stared at each other without speaking. I bit down on my lip as another orgasm threatened to strangle me. I didn't want to even breathe wrong for fear that he'd stop.

Sensations of ecstasy came before I could stop them. My knees began to shake. A deep rumbling in my belly burst through. I could see the very faint beginning of a smirk catch on Saint's lips. The heat from his body only made it worse as he stepped closer toward me, pressing the sponge harder against my clit.

His lips grazed my ear as he whispered, "*Cum for me.*"

It was all the coaxing I needed. Without another thought, I arched back against the tiles and let my body have its release. He snaked his muscular arm around my waist to hold me up as every tingling sensation possible, took hold of me. I grabbed his wrist and thrusted into the sponge. "Fuck... Saint...oh my, fucking...I need you to touch me. I need your cock. Please... Saint."

He took my earlobe between his teeth and gently bit down. Dropping the sponge, he cupped my pussy with his wet soapy hand. He drew in a sharp breath as I continued to grind against him. I ached for him so bad.

I was starving for him. Without thinking, I reached for his cock. He growled and wrapped a hand around my throat, threading his fingers through my collar. His grip tightened. "On your knees, fox."

Oh, fuck. He was so hot.

I got on my knees without hesitating. He yanked on my chain and shoved his cock into my mouth. I moaned into him as he squeezed my chin. His other hand moved to the back of my head. He grabbed a fistful of my hair and guided my mouth back and forth. Tears welled in my eyes as I struggled to breathe.

"Good girl," he rasped. He fingered my lips as I stretched my mouth wide around his throbbing cock. He tasted like ecstasy. I twirled my tongue around the barbell, and he shuddered, digging his fingers deeper into my scalp. He pulled at my hair until I flinched from the pain. But it hurt so fucking good.

He thrusted into me faster. I looked up and our eyes locked. The devil lived in his gaze. Cold, sinister, hard... *hungry*. My vision blurred as he hit the back of my throat. I choked back a sob as he fucked my mouth hard. I couldn't breathe, but he tasted so fucking good. I kept my eyes on his. I wanted him to see me take it.

His body jerked as he reached his peak. I saw it happen. The change in his eyes. The rush of blood to the tip of his cock which caused him to clutch the back of my head so tight I couldn't move. He held me still as his cum rushed into my mouth like a dam bursting. He moaned, deep and guttural. I cupped his swollen balls as he rode his orgasm, pumping it into my mouth. I swallowed every fucking drop.

He pulled me from my knees and lifted me up in his arms. I wrapped my legs around his waist as he pushed me up against the wall. "It's been so long…" He tapped his fist three times against the wall.

I heard the door open. Grim and Poe pulled back the shower curtain and their eyes lit up. "Can we watch now?" Grim asked.

Saint grunted and gave them a nod. He lifted me out of the shower and carried me back into the bedroom. He set me down and then crawled onto the bed. "Get on top of me."

I was horny again for this man. What the actual fuck? I didn't even think it was possible to have this many orgasms.

As I climbed onto the bed, I felt Grim, and Poe come in behind me. I crawled on top of Saint, straddling him.

Grim joined us on the bed, his chest pressed against my back. I drew in a sharp breath as he reached around and fisted Saint's cock. He squeezed it in his palm and stroked up and down. Saint growled, "Put it in."

Oh, fuck. Grim pushed at my entrance with the tip of Saint's cock and I almost came right there. He guided it inside me, as I stretched for him. "Oh, shit. So fucking big," I murmured.

Grim lifted my hips up and down on Saint's cock. It was unbelievable. Indescribable. To feel another man behind you, moving your body, making you ride another man's cock. I almost blacked out. The three of us moved in a rhythm. Poe moved around to watch, fisting his own cock up and down as he looked on.

Grim's hands were everywhere—squeezing my nipples, pressing on my clit, sliding underneath, between us. He hoisted me up so he could wrap one of his hands around Saint's shaft while leaving the tip still inside me. He stroked him as he brought me down on him. Saint moaned. "Fuck… Grim and our little fox," he breathed.

Grim pulled me back against him as I rode Saint harder. I couldn't get enough. It would never be enough.

I had fucked all three of them. As another orgasm claimed me, panic rushed through my chest. They said they couldn't move on until they had all had sex with me. And now they had. But I didn't want them to leave. I didn't want to be alone. Without them… how would I ever feel pleasure like this again?

Saint unhooked the chain and removed my collar right before the four of us passed out on each other, a pile of tangled limbs and heaving chests.

CHAPTER Seven

For the first time since they'd arrived, there was a silence between us. A quiet understanding that we belonged to each other. And a deep sense of dread that we'd soon be ripped apart.

In all of my life I had never experienced anything like this. Something so depraved and vile and yet utterly beautiful at the same time. I had dreamed of it. But after being told my fantasies were dirty, I'd locked all those thoughts away.

But Grim, Poe, and Saint… they accepted me. Their desires matched mine. It wasn't wrong to want them. I *couldn't* believe it was wrong to want them. To want this. Forever.

I put clothes on, actual clothes, for the first time since they'd arrived. I sat down at my kitchen table in a T-shirt, shorts, and fuzzy slippers. With their clothes back on as well, they seemed to tiptoe around me.

Saint set a steaming cup of coffee in front of me. Without complaining I shuffled to the cabinets and grabbed sugar. He tracked my movements, observing everything I did even as I went to the fridge to retrieve the milk.

I didn't want to offend him, but after the night I had, I was going to take my coffee the way I wanted it. Just like they took what they wanted.

Grim sat at the windowsill, the same one he'd first violated me on. He stared out the window as the October mist came down on my driveway. I wondered what he was thinking. How long would they stay?

Maybe I could cook them breakfast or dinner or something. Fuck. Did they even eat food? What in the hell was I thinking? That I could do normal things with three demonic spirits that invaded my home?

Yes, they gave me the best fucking erotic night of my life, but they aren't my boyfriends. This wasn't an episode of The Vampire Diaries. Hell, I don't recall Elena ever getting railed by three guys in the same night. So yeah, reality was setting in fast.

But I wasn't ashamed. No. I enjoyed it. I fucking loved it. And when they left, I would remember it forever. I'd never fully enjoy regular sex ever again, but that was okay because for one vicious night, I got to live out my wildest fantasies. And that would have to be enough.

"We don't want this to end, little fox," Poe blurted out, cutting the silence like a knife.

I drew out a long-held breath. "I don't want you to go."

There, I said it out loud. I couldn't bear the thought of not having them here with me.

Grim's shoulders' heaved. "We *have* to go... *but* no one can stop you from coming with us. If you want..."

Saint growled. "*No*. She has her life to live."

"Wait, you're suggesting that I go back to Wickford with you? It's condemned. The city is tearing it down next week." I hadn't even thought about what would happen to them when that happens.

Saint gave Poe a look as he protested. "You're such a good girl, little fox."

"The best girl," Grim added.

Poe leveled his gaze on me. "Once the house is destroyed, there will be no reason for us to stay. This is it, little fox. Our one last hurrah. I'm happy it was you..."

Fuck. This was crazy. I've spent less than twenty-four hours with them, and I was already growing attached. I let these monsters in my bed. In my house. In my life. I made that decision when I broke into Wickford. Despite my skepticism, a small part of me knew the superstition could be real.

Ever since I was a kid, strange things happened around me. I always had a sixth sense. Crows and black clouds seem to follow me everywhere I went. While my family has long since passed away from this life, my connection to them has remained. They come to me in dreams. A part of me wanted to awaken something last night.

I was tired of being alone...

"What if I was able to stop the city from tearing the house down, could you stay?" I finally understood everything that has led up to this moment.

"And how would you do that, Bailey?" Saint growled.

"I could buy it," I replied.

The three of them exchanged a worried look. Grim rested a hand on my waist. The warmth from his fingers tingled my skin. "Can you?"

My heart was racing. I nodded. "When my parents died, they left me a pretty good chunk of money. I haven't touched any of it. Was saving it for some reason. Now I know why. I could buy the house and have it restored. We could live there... together."

Poe ran a hand through his dark hair. "You would do that for us? Why? We came in here and defiled you."

I choked back a sob. They had no idea. "No. You liberated me. Set me free. Now that I've tasted it, I want more. I don't want it to ever stop."

Saint laced his fingers through mine. "You're young, little fox. Your tastes will change. And when they do, you'll wish you hadn't kept us."

I shook my head. "No. I will always be happy I kept you… But maybe, you'll grow tired of me. Is that what's holding you back? Will you grow bored of me?"

The three of them rushed forward at the same time, each placing a strong hand on me. Grim cupped my chin in his hands. "Never. In the hundred years we've been imprisoned, not a single person has seen us the way you have. You have given us so much more than flesh, little fox. Your warmth and care are more than we've ever known."

My chest ached. "You said you were poisoned. What happened? I think I've earned the right to know."

Poe motioned for me to take a seat on the couch. "We were tricked," he murmured.

I tucked my legs underneath me, pulling my robe down around my knees. Goosebumps pebbled my flesh. "Who did that to you?"

Grim sat on the coffee table across from me. "We worked for Mrs. Wickford. She was a widow who lived there all by herself. I maintained the house while Saint oversaw the grounds and Poe cooked all her meals. She gave us room and board, and a small weekly salary."

Saint sighed as he sank into the seat next to me. "She was a reclusive woman. No one ever visited, and she never left. She spent most of her time in the garden, humming to herself."

"But after a while," Poe interjected, "she took more of an

interest in us, inviting us to eat dinner with her and joining her by the fire at night for drink and conversation. She was a lonely woman."

"And she was very beautiful," Grim added.

A slight twinge of jealousy panged me as I imagined my guys doting on this woman. It was silly, but my heart had started the process of claiming them. And I couldn't stop it.

"It wasn't long after that she started visiting us at night in our rooms as we slept," Poe continued. "Her carnal appetite was insatiable. She grew very attached to all of us. And we attached to her. But something snapped in her one day…"

A shiver crept up my spine. "What happened?"

Saint's face paled. "She lost her fucking mind."

Grim squeezed his hand. "An old woman started coming around. A witch. She fed into her delusions. Told her that we could live forever."

I gasped. "*No*… Fuck."

Poe nodded. "Fuck is right. She refused to get help. To see a real doctor. So we told her we were leaving. That we wanted no part in her witchcraft."

I leaned forward, riveted. "How did she react?"

Saint snickered. "Mrs. Wickford gave us her blessing and invited us to one last dinner."

A cold chill swept through me. So cold I could feel it in my bones. "*Poison*," I whispered.

Grim drew in a sharp breath. "All four of us died that night. On Samhain—Halloween. But only the three of us were stuck inside that house for eternity."

"She left us a note," Poe started. "That if she couldn't have us, no one could. At least not forever. The veil between the living and the dead would drop for one night only. If someone with intent was able to open the door to that cursed room, then we could leave. But her witch fucking cursed us."

Saint nodded. "There was a catch. We would be tied to the person who opened the door. And in order for our spirits to release them, to return to the house, we'd have to get their permission to defile them. Otherwise, we'd be trapped in nothingness."

"The Wickford house is our home," Grim added, "and it's the devil we know."

Tears streamed down my cheeks before I could stop them. "You're safe now. I will save your house and keep you for as long as you want to be kept."

CHAPTER Eight

"We belong to you now, little fox. There's only a few more hours left and then we must go." Grim untied my robe and pushed it open, putting me on display.

My breath hitched. "And I will join you as soon as I get everything in order."

Poe licked his lips as he pressed his palms into my thighs. "Let us have one more taste to keep us going."

Fuck, I wanted them again. And again. So fucking bad. I spread my legs and arched my back against the couch. "I'm yours to do whatever you want with now."

Saint growled and lifted me into his lap. His cock stiffened underneath me. He unzipped his pants and pulled it out. I gasped as he grinded against my bare ass. "So fucking responsive for us."

A smirk pulled at Grim's lips. "Let's play one more game then, little fox. A preview of what's to come."

I let out a groan as Poe slid a thick finger inside my sopping wet pussy. "Oh, fuck. Yes, I want to play. *Please*."

"Good girl," Saint breathed in my ear.

Grim grabbed my wrists and yanked me up. "Get on the floor. On your hands and knees."

Moisture pooled between my legs. My nipples pebbled. What wicked things did they have in store for me now? I lowered myself to the floor and did as he said.

They circled me.

"Spread your legs nice and wide for us, little fox," Poe commanded.

Fuck, I was going to cum before anything even started. I lowered myself farther down, bracing against the hardwood floors with nothing but my bare hands and knees.

"So fucking filthy for us, aren't you?" Grim asked, his voice low and raspy.

My breath quickened. "Yes."

"Let's show her what happens to dirty girls." Grim slid the collar back around my neck and gave the chain a good tug.

I was practically salivating. My juices dripped down my thighs. The anticipation, not knowing what was about to happen, was just as arousing as what they had already done to me.

Poe kneeled down next to me and grabbed my chin, forcing me to look into his piercing green eyes. "Give me a word, little fox. Something you'll remember."

I blinked a few times, mesmerized by his long black lashes. "Why?"

Grim knelt down on the other side of me and yanked my chin away from Poe. Now I was drowning in pools of blue eyes, colder, harder, but just as fucking hungry. "Because the lines between pleasure and pain are about to blur for you. We need to know when you've had enough."

Oh fuck. I should have been terrified. But all it did was make me wetter. Needier. "Okay, my word is... *devil*."

Grim's smirk deepened. "Good girl." He looked at Poe. "You're up first."

Saint pulled up a chair and sat in front of me, holding tight to my chain. "I want to hear you scream, little fox."

I swallowed hard, my heart racing. Fuck, fuck, fuck. What am I doing?

I turned my head to the side just in time to see Poe pick up the leather riding crop. He slid it back and forth against his palm. He stalked around me dragging the tip of the crop down my spine as he circled until finally stopping behind me. I clenched my pussy as he tickled my ass with it, caressing me gently.

He chuckled as I flinched every time it touched me. He teased me for what seemed like hours, stroking it down the middle of my ass. My legs trembled in anticipation.

And just when I thought I was going to collapse onto the floor, the wind changed above me. I heard the snap before I felt the sting.

"Fuckkk," I cried out.

He smacked the other side of my ass, harder this time, and I bucked forward. The sting spread, shooting tingles throughout my entire body.

Grim rubbed my back. "Good girl."

My eyes watered as Poe brought the crop down harder. Then the warm flesh of his palm was on me. He kneaded my ass gently. "You like it, don't you?"

I gasped for breath. I fucking loved it. "Yes," I whispered.

Saint pulled my chain. "Louder."

"Yessss," I cried out.

"My turn," Grim growled. He sat down on the edge of the windowsill. "Come here, little fox."

My body was shaking. I started to push myself up when Poe cracked the whip down hard again. "No. Dirty girls don't get to stand up. Fucking crawl to him."

Oh, fuck. I was almost ashamed of how turned on I was. *Almost*. But they didn't make me feel any shame. No. They make me feel alive.

Saint unhooked my collar and patted me on the head. "Such a good fucking girl. Go to him. Nice and slow."

I locked eyes with Grim. His gaze was darker, hungrier than before. I watched him watching me as I crawled across the floor to him. He took off his jeans but held onto his belt. My pussy was aching with need by the time I reached him.

Grim laid back against the window. "Lay across my lap."

I crawled up and onto him, trembling. As soon as I stretched out across him, he grabbed my wrists and fastened them tight behind me with his belt. His hard cock pulsed against my stomach. "Relax, little fox. I'm going to make you cum so fucking hard and for so fucking long, you might not ever be able to stand up straight again."

I shuddered as he dragged the tip of his fingers down the opening of my ass. "I like to feel the sting against my hand," he rasped.

He trailed his fingers further down, cupping my pussy in the palm of his hand. "Fuck, you are wet. So fucking filthy."

I moaned as he squeezed my clit. "Grim…*please*."

His cock throbbed against my abdomen. He pushed a finger inside me but held it still. "Say it again, little fox. Beg me."

I writhed against him. "Please make me cum, Grim."

Without warning he brought his palm down hard against my ass. "Again."

A deep guttural moan escaped my lips as he pushed another finger inside me. I clenched around him, squirming to try and get myself off against him.

"Please, fuck. I want to cum. Grim, please."

He growled and hit my ass again. I screamed as it reverberated through my entire body. He shoved his fingers deeper inside. Stars clouded my vision. Sweat pooled down my back. "Ughhh, fuck… yes." I panted.

I turned my head to see Poe and Saint fisting their own cocks, and I cried out again. I had almost completely forgotten that we weren't the only two in the room. The sight of them touching themselves pushed me over the edge.

The pressure swelled against the walls of my pussy. "Grim. Fuck. I'm… I'm close."

Grim slowed the rhythm of his fingers to an agonizing pace, drawing it out like torture. My senses were heightened. My nerves tender and raw. I could feel every inch of his fingers from the soft tips as they reentered, all the way past the second knuckle as he stretched me. The slickness as they slid back and forth. I rocked my hips against him and spread my legs, allowing him to go even deeper. It was pure fucking ecstasy.

"That's it. Just like that, little fox." He fisted my hair and turned my head back toward Poe and Saint. "Show them what a good girl you are and cum for us…"

And that's what sent me over.

I clenched and gasped as my orgasm took hold of my nub first and then spread deep inside. As I moaned through the pleasure, Grim brought his hand down hard on my ass. I flinched and another orgasm rippled through me.

"Fuck," I screamed.

Grim stroked my back as I shook. He untied my wrists as he leaned down and whispered in my ear, "I want you to feel your cum dripping all over my cock. It feels so fucking good. So dirty."

I struggled for breath as my heart pounded out of my chest. I reached in between us and wrapped my hands around his cock.

He moaned as I stroked him, smearing my sticky juices up and down his shaft.

Poe growled and stalked over to us. "Turn her over."

As I was flipped around, I kept my hand firmly on Grim's cock. Poe stood over me as he touched himself. "Open your mouth."

I parted my lips just as he shoved his cock inside. "Good fucking girl." He grabbed the back of my head as he fucked my mouth. I kept my grip on Grim, sliding my hand up and down to the rhythm of Poe. "Fuck." A burst of liquid hit the back of my throat as he moaned. I drank every drop of his thick warm cum. And then another burst coated my fingers as Grim released. He bucked against the window, nearly breaking it.

I licked my lips and smiled up at Poe. "You taste so fucking good."

Every inch of my flesh was on fire.

"I want her back on the floor," Saint commanded. He stood from the couch and stepped out of his jeans.

Fuck. I almost forgot there were three of them. I was on the verge of blacking out. The stimulation was driving me crazy. But no matter how battered I was, I would not resist Saint. I needed him to touch me. I wanted him to make me cum so bad.

Poe and Grim lifted me up and placed me gently on the floor on my back. Saint picked up the riding crop and stalked over to me.

I was getting spanked again. I clenched my pussy as a new wave of tingling started to spread. I started to climb back onto my hands and knees when Saint grabbed my ankles.

"No. I don't want you on your knees, little fox. Not this time."

I was confused. "What are you going to do?"

His eyes glazed with carnal desire as he stared at my pussy. "Remember your word?"

Poe and Grim moved behind me and each grabbed one of my wrists.

"Y-yes. I think so."

Saint dragged the riding crop over my hard nipples. "Say it so I know you didn't forget."

I inhaled a sharp breath. The feel of the leather crop against my swollen nipples was amazing. "*Devil,*" I rasped.

"Good girl. Now open up nice and wide for me."

I spread my thighs as far as they would go, feeling the beginning of an orgasm starting to already move through me. Sometimes, the fantasy, the waiting, could make me cum without even a single touch.

Saint circled the riding crop around my nipples one last time and then slowly trailed it down my stomach. I watched him as his gaze devoured every inch of my body. He shifted the crop farther down, teasing it over my swollen nub. I let out a little whimper.

"Look at that glistening cunt. So wet and ready for all the dirty things I'm about to do to it."

I shivered as he dragged the edge of the crop between my wet folds. He gently nudged it against the lips of my pussy, using it as a tool to peel back my flesh. I was coming undone underneath it. The leather felt so fucking good. So smooth against me.

I couldn't help myself from arching up to meet it, urging him to rub harder. I needed more pressure. "Don't stop," I pleaded.

"Do you like my toy, little fox?" Saint rasped.

My teeth chattered. "Y-yes. Play with me, please."

Grim growled as he took one of my nipples between his fingers and squeezed. Poe followed suit and grabbed the other one. Fuck. I was going to black out if I didn't cum soon.

Saint lifted the crop away and brought it back down with a light slap.

Oh, fuck. I bucked as the slap sent a shiver deep down inside my pussy. I couldn't stop my body from trembling. But I needed more. "Again," I begged.

Saint slowly rubbed the crop against my clit, applying more pressure this time. I rocked against it, aching to feel that sting again.

Before I could beg some more, he lifted up and brought it down again, smacking the inside of my dripping wet pussy.

This one fucking stung. But it also felt like heaven. A tiny orgasm shot through me as I clenched. I writhed on the ground while Poe and Grim held me firmly in place. I squeezed my eyes shut for a moment and saw stars.

The stinging began to fade, and it turned me ravenous. "*Harder*," I breathed.

Saint let out a low growl. He pressed the leather crop to my clit again, rubbing me back and forth till I was almost raw. "Such a good girl."

I screamed as the leather riding crop came down hard against my wet pussy. An orgasm unlike any I've ever known took hold of me, pulling me down like quicksand. Sparks of light burst through my closed lids as I tore out of Poe and Grim's grasp. Like a wild animal, I pounced on Saint.

"That's it, little fox. Take what belongs to you." Saint stretched back onto the floor as I straddled him and rode out my orgasm on him.

He dug his thick fingers into my hips as I clenched around him. "Fuck me hard, little fox. Give me everything you've got."

And I did. I bounced up and down his slick cock, twisting and grinding till I could feel him in my stomach.

The second my cum coated his shaft, he lost it. He squeezed my ass, lifted me into the air, and took me against the wall. "Dirty. Fucking. Girl. *Fuck*."

He held me still against him as his cum dripped down my thighs.

Poe and Grim were at our side within minutes. With Saint's cock still pulsing inside me, Grim grabbed my chin and placed a hungry kiss on my lips. He shoved his tongue deep into my mouth while Saint moaned against me. He slid in and out as he came. Poe reached his hand in between us and stroked my clit.

Grim broke the kiss to look down at our bodies sliding together. He watched as Saint's cock moved in and out. Watched Poe finger my nub, as another orgasm began to build inside me.

Grim stuck his finger in my mouth. "Get it nice and wet for me."

I moaned as I sucked on his finger, coating it with as much saliva as I could muster.

He pushed at the entrance to my ass, and I clenched. He drew in a sharp breath. "Relax, little fox. Let me in."

I gasped as he inched his finger farther in. "Oh, fuck."

"That's it. Just like that," he coaxed as I started to relax and give in.

Saint screamed as he came. A burst of cum shot through me. I thrusted into Saint, arching my hips up.

Poe pinched my clit. "Surrender to it, little fox.

"Yes," I cried out.

And as another orgasm rippled through me, Grim pushed his finger all the way in.

If I had neighbors, they would have called the cops. That is how fucking loud I screamed. And it was the most satisfying scream of my entire life.

The four of us leaned into each other, our chests heaving, bodies glistening with sweat. We held each other up. Gave each other breath.

I hugged them tight to me.

I knew one thing for sure… I was never letting them go.

There was only an hour left till dawn. Halloween would be over, and they would have to return to Wickford. And I would have to act fast to buy it before the city tears it down. My friends would think I'm crazy, but I didn't care. They would never understand. While they were preoccupied with jello shots and toilet papering houses, I was here with Saint, Grim, and Poe, being reborn. Having the best night of my life.

They stood near my front door, waiting to say goodbye. I looked the three of them over with a fresh gaze. When they first arrived, I'd thought them monsters. Now they were my saviors. They had dragged me kicking and screaming from my old life and awakened the darkest pleasures within me.

Dusk was almost fading away. The sun would rise soon and

so they had to go. Poe clasped the back of my neck and pressed his forehead to mine. "Little fox… Fuck. What a surprise you were."

I brushed my lips to his. He kissed me with a fire that sent shivers up my spine. His soft tongue gently twirled around mine. I clung to him in desperation, fisting my hands in his hair. "I will see you soon," I murmured.

Grim pulled me out of Poe's arms and into his. He gazed down at me with those piercing blue eyes that I was once afraid of. Eyes that rooted me in place and commanded my body to do things not even my wildest fantasies could dream up.

He stroked my hair. "In case… something goes wrong… just know that I'll never forget you."

I shook my head. "Nothing will go wrong. I will see you soon. I promise."

He bent down and placed a soft kiss on my lips. "Whatever you say, little fox."

I almost crumbled at Saint's feet. His lips were pursed, his expression unreadable. But his eyes… were full of sadness and longing. I stood in front of him, unsure of how I was going to part from him. From any of them.

Saint yanked my hips to his. My nipples pebbled at the feel of his chiseled chest pressed up against mine. There would never come a day when I didn't want him. He kissed my neck, my jaw, then finally my lips.

"You're such a good girl, Bailey. The world has no idea. Thank you for trusting us. Remember us. Remember this night. And know that you can do anything you want. Anything you set your mind to."

Tears streamed down my cheeks. "You weren't the only ones locked in a prison. While I may have been able to roam around, I was captive just the same. Thank you for setting me free."

They circled me and pulled me into a group hug. Our breaths were heavy. I couldn't discern whose heart was beating louder. We were like one symbiotic unit. I felt like I was losing a part of myself right now.

Some believe in love at first sight. Others believe that lust can be confused with love. I don't know what the clinical definition of love is. I just know that it's messy and imperfect and life changing. There are no rules on who one should love or how long it should take to fall. Love is intangible. It cannot be grasped with human hands or even understood with rational thought.

Would I call what we did love? I don't know. It was something like love. It was definitely lust and desire and passion. Isn't that how love starts? Looking at the three of them lingering in the doorway, still smelling their mingled scents on my skin, something did stir and ache in my heart. Call it longing or pheromones or even foolish fantasy, it doesn't matter what it is. It makes me feel alive. That's all that matters. And I will not let it go. I won't let them go.

"I will call my attorney. She can get the funds from my trust in order and make an offer on the house today. Once the deed is mine, I'll make plans to renovate. To make it a home again. And then we can all be together… for as long as you want me." I sniffled and wiped the remaining tears off my cheeks.

Poe flashed me a grin. "Ok, little fox. See you soon."

Grim nodded. "Till we meet again."

This felt like goodbye. No. I would make this work. It had to work. I couldn't lose them. Before new tears threatened to fall again, Saint pulled me in for one last hug.

"We will wait for you, Bailey. For as long as we can," he whispered.

I nodded, choking back a sob. Poe opened my front door, and as each one of them stepped through it, a piece of my heart went with them. Saint paused and looked back one more time. He winked and then closed the door behind him.

Out of the corner of my eye, I spotted the duffel bag they'd come in with. The bag of toys that we had so devilishly played with. I grabbed it and threw open the door.

"Wait, you forgot—" I sank to my knees. Fuck. They were gone. I scanned the yard, the trees that lined the path leading up to my house. There was no sign of them. If I hadn't had this bag in my hands, I might even start to think I'd hallucinated the whole thing.

I went back inside and sank down on the couch, the bag in my lap. I clung to it as the one last piece I had of them. My house was eerily quiet. I used to love that. Not anymore. It was just a cruel reminder that I was alone.

A buzzing noise came from my bedroom. Fuck, my phone. I hadn't touched it in over twenty-four hours. I darted into my bedroom and retrieved it from the bedside table.

Ten missed calls and twenty-five texts. All from Maureen. Shit. I scanned through the messages. Most of them were drunken commands to get my ass to the party. The last five were more of the—where are you bitch; I'm worried about you—variety.

I sighed and texted her back.

Hey Maureen, sorry I didn't respond. I took a sleeping pill and passed out. No need to worry. Hope you had fun at the party.

The typing bubbles appeared immediately.

Oh, thank god! After what happened at Wickford, and then not hearing from you, I thought you actually got kidnapped by ghosts! Meet for coffee later?

If only she knew.

I sent back a quick reply.

Haha. No such thing as ghosts, Maureen. Yeah, let's meet up this afternoon. I need to run a few errands in town anyway.

I was pretty sure the whole town, including my well-meaning friend, will think I'm nuts when they find out I'm buying a condemned and supposedly haunted house. I was dreading even having the conversation. But I know in my heart that this is what I want. It's the first time in my life that I've known exactly what I wanted.

Two weeks later

My attorney, Evelyn, pushed her glasses higher up her nose. "Okay, Miss Bishop, just sign here and the house is yours. It took a bit of convincing, but the city decided that it was in their best interest to make money off of the house rather than *spend* money tearing it down."

I nodded and picked up a pen, my hand trembling. This was it. Wickford was mine. *Poe, Grim, and Saint were mine.*

Evelyn scooped up the paperwork and stuck it in a file. "I'll finalize everything today and get the ball rolling for the re-construction. It will not be easy, but by this time next year, you should be living in your new home."

The sound of that sent a warm ripple through my body. "Thank you, Evelyn. I appreciate all you've done for me since my parents died."

She smiled curtly. "Of course."

I couldn't get out of her office fast enough. I dashed to my car and headed directly to Wickford place.

I skidded into the driveway just as workers were removing the caution tape. A sold sign already sat in the front yard. I jumped out of the car and raced across the porch into the house. Pausing on the first floor, I looked around. It was just as cold and barren as it was two weeks ago. But I wasn't afraid anymore. It was already feeling like mine.

I barreled up the stairs to the second floor and down the hallway to the room my guys were locked in. The door was still broken from me losing my footing and crashing into it.

I crept inside. "Poe? Grim? Saint? Are you still here?"

The wind rustled one of the boards that were coming loose

across the window. A crow squawked on the ledge. I hugged my arms to my chest as I stood in the dark room. Waiting.

My heart sank. It was so quiet. So empty. What if I had dreamed the whole thing up? Or what if they had finally passed over to the other side?

I choked back a sob and called out for them again. "I'm here. Like I promised."

The floorboards creaked behind me. Strong arms snaked around my waist. I breathed a sigh of relief as his scent enveloped me.

"Welcome home, little fox," Saint rasped.

I spun around and threw my arms around his neck. Behind him, Poe, and Grim stood smiling. "I thought maybe I had hallucinated all three of you." I held out my arms for them to come over. I hugged Poe and Grim tight to my chest. "I'm so happy to see you."

Poe brushed a strand of hair off my forehead. "We knew you'd come, little fox."

"Now we can always be together," Grim murmured.

I nodded. "The construction will take a while, but I don't care. I'm not leaving you again. I'll sleep on the broken floor with you."

Saint grinned. A rare expression from him. "Luckily, it won't come to that. There's a basement, Bailey. It was untouched by the fire. We have already prepared it for you."

Grim beamed. "It's our gift to you. You'll be comfortable there until the rest of the house is ready."

My heart wanted to burst. I was beyond happy for the first time in my life. Some people are lucky if they find love once in a lifetime. I have found it three times over.

I stepped back and admired them, taking my time to really study each and every inch.

The three of them exchanged a mischievous look and it sent a flutter to my belly.

"Are you ready to see what we have in store for you downstairs, little fox?" Poe asked.

"*Yes.*" My arousal was growing by the second. "Fuck, yes, please," I breathed.

Saint curled his arm around my waist. "*Good girl.*"

One year later

"Good morning, little fox." Poe nestled his face in my neck.

I yawned and stretched out my arms. "It's going to be a great morning."

Grim reached across Saint to squeeze my thigh. "Happy anniversary, love."

Saint pulled me onto his chest. "Come here, little fox. It's time for us to give you your gift."

Heat spread between my thighs. "But you've already given me so much," I rasped.

Wickford place was restored to its original glory ahead of

schedule. For the last six months, the three of us have been enjoying the fruits of our labor. We do everything together.

From dancing in the kitchen to having dinner in the garden and defiling each other in every single room. Now, as we lay here in our king-size bed amidst the black satin sheets, tangled up in each other's arms, in *our* bedroom, I can't help but think back to the night we first met.

"Seems like we've known each other longer, doesn't it?" I asked as Grim's hand traveled farther up my thigh.

Poe nuzzled my nipple. "That's because we are connected body and soul. Now, stop talking," he teased. "There are better uses for that mouth of yours."

I let out a moan as Grim slipped a finger inside my wet pussy.

Saint twisted me onto my side and pulled me toward him. His hard cock pressed into my ass. "I'm going to fuck you so hard, little fox." He kissed the back of my neck, sending a shiver down my spine. "And then… I'm going to give you a good hard spanking for playing so hard to get that night."

Oh, fuck. I was so wet. "You're going to punish me for a year ago?" I asked coyly.

"Mmm… yes, little fox," Saint whispered. "No dirty deed will go unpunished."

Poe and Grim each grabbed one of my wrists as Saint flipped me over onto my stomach. "Spread your legs nice and wide for me, little fox."

I whimpered and did as he said. My clit ached as I waited for all the dirty things they were about to do to me.

Saint mounted me from behind. His hard cock pressed at the entrance to my sopping wet pussy. "Such a good girl."

I cried out as he yanked my hips up and thrusted in hard. "*Fuck.*"

Grim rubbed his fingers in circles around my tingling clit. I rocked back and forth, desperate to consume what they were both giving me.

Saint fisted his hand in my hair and pulled it tight. "So fucking slick for me." He pulled out slow and then thrusted back in with a force so hard I bucked forward.

"Fuuck," I screamed.

Poe let out a growl. "Such a dirty girl." He pressed a finger into my ass, and I lost it. "That's it, little fox. Move your hips just like that."

I ground against them, panting, and twisting as their hands explored every crevice of my body. Saint pummeled into me without restraint, stretching me like a rubber band. I braced my hands against the headboard and pushed back into him, urging him deeper.

Saint dug his fingers into my hips, "Fuck. I'm going to cum."

And just as Saint exploded inside me, Poe inched his finger deeper into my ass while Grim lowered his head to my middle. My vision blurred and sparked as I felt his warm soft tongue pushing against my nub. He sucked and flicked as the tingling intensified. I cried out as my orgasm gripped me, sending wave after wave of euphoria throughout my entire body.

"Happy anniversary, little fox," Saint breathed as he moved off me.

I collapsed onto him. Poe and Grim nestled in close, our arms and legs tangled up in each other. My chest heaved as I fought to regain my breath. "Happy Halloween."

Poe chuckled. "It's the first one in a hundred years we don't have to worry or wonder if someone's going to open that door and let us out."

I cradled his arm to my stomach. "You will never be locked up again."

Grim stroked my cheek. "We are happy it was you, Bailey."

"You made this place a home again," Saint added.

I didn't know a year ago that I would fall in love with three deviant spirits. Even the night they left; I was afraid to call it love. But I knew then as I know now that love is exactly what we share. It might not be what other people's definition is, but it is ours. And because of Poe, Grim, and Saint, I would never feel shame for loving like this ever again.

I will always be their good girl.

LITTLE Fox

M VIOLET

A NOTE FROM THE AUTHOR

Little Fox is a why choose, dark romance meant for 18+ readers only. It is the sequel to Good Girl so I highly recommend you read that one first. Extreme caution is advised before reading Little Fox. There are many scenes that some may find triggering. Please see the full list of TWs below.

Trigger Warnings

Graphic sex
Graphic language
Graphic violence
Drugs
Physical assault
Sexual assault
Bullying
Kidnapping
Murder
Dubious consent
Non consent
Group sex
Sword crossing
Coercion
Manipulation
BDSM
Death of a parent (off page)
Stalking
Torture
Extreme degradation
Objects used as sex toys
MFMM

MM
MFMMM

Kinks:
Choking
Spanking
Restraints
Collar/leash,
Knife-play
Praise
Degradation
Breath play
Sex toys
Gagging
Spitting
Anal sex
Double penetration

Playlist

Prologue: Beware—Victoria Carbol

1. Small Town Witch—Merci Raines
2. The High—Bryce Savage
3. F****d My Way Up To the Top—Lana Del Rey
4. Money Diamonds Roses—Lolo Zouai
5. HOME IS WHERE THE HELL IS—Sarah Saint James
6. Blackout—AViVA
7. Underneath the Mask—Royal & the Serpent
8. BLOSSOM IN THE DARK—Diana Goldberg
9. E-Girls Are Ruining My Life!—CORPSE & Savage Ga$p
10. Ghost—Ava Max
11. Dangerous—Rivals
12. Monster—Victoria Carbol
13. You Put a Spell On Me—Austin Giorgio
14. Queen of the Freaks—AViVA
15. Risky—Boon
16. Run for Your Life—Atalia
17. If I Be Wrong—Wolf Larsen
18. Ghost Town—Layto & Neoni
19. Psycho—AviVA
20. Look What You Made Me Do—Taylor Swift
21. Break Me Down—Mandi Crimmins
22. Bad Decision—Jules Walcott
23. Gibson Girl—Ethel Cain
24. Into the Fire—Erin McCarley
25. What Do I Believe In (feat. ASHBY)—Steelfeather
26. Bad Side—Jake Daniels
27. Bells in Santa Fe—Halsey
28. Unholy—Sam Smith and Kim Petras
29. Hot Killer—Julia Wolf
30. Cruel—Jennalyn
31. Out of the Shadows—Ely Eira

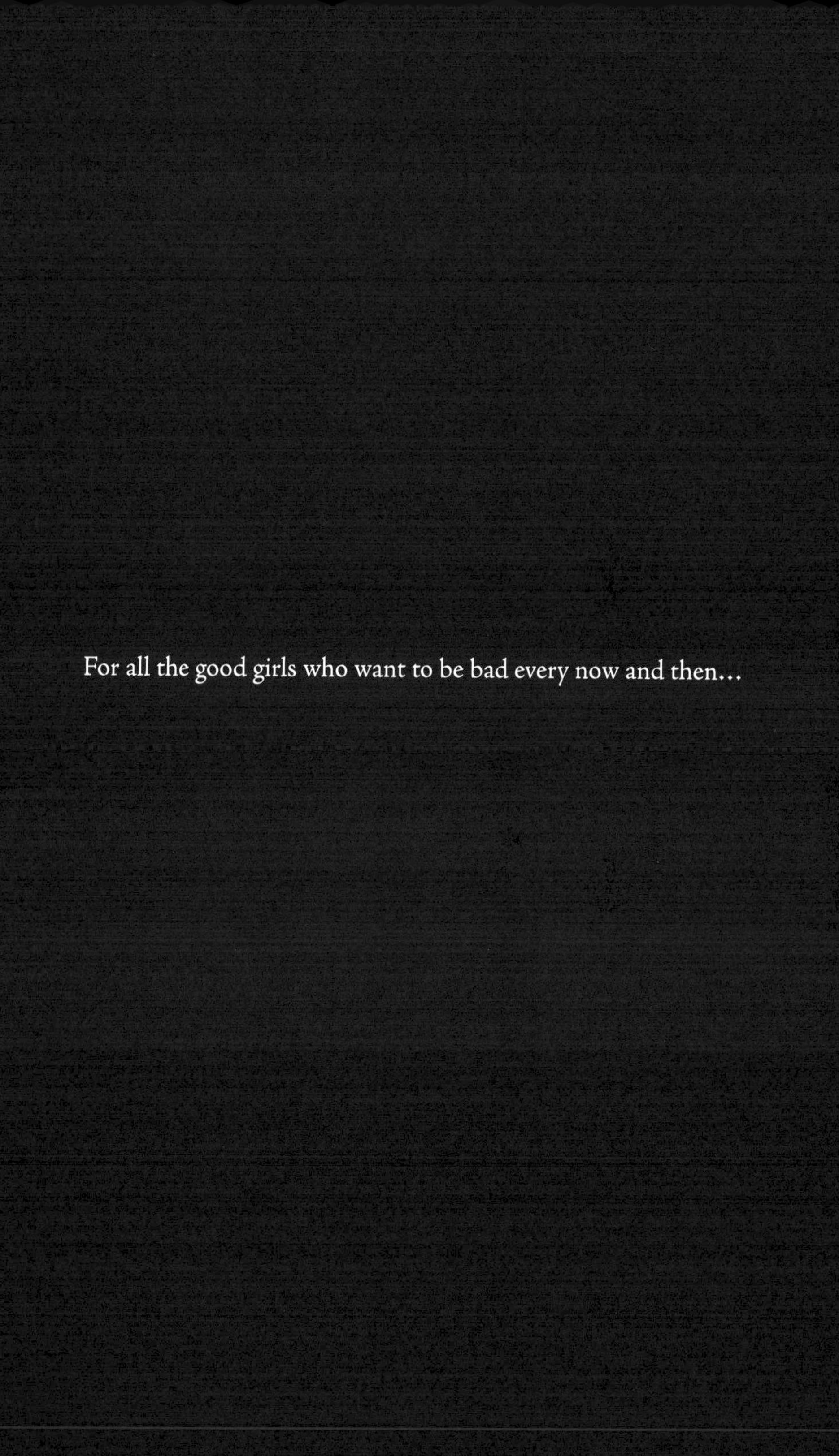
For all the good girls who want to be bad every now and then…

Prologue

Bailey

I'd never heard of houses having graveyards. Except in books. Dark, haunting books where the girl living in the house was driven mad by some unseen force. This was where I found myself now. In an old, haunted house with a graveyard out back.

I didn't know why I was drawn to these things. Ever since I was a child, I was fascinated by the dark. Curious about the monsters under the bed that were never there. My mother would tell me that the monsters were afraid. *Afraid of me*. But she was wrong. The monsters were just waiting in the shadows. Waiting to consume me like the fire that took her and my father away from me. The fire that I survived.

Some said it was luck. Others claimed I was evil. That my family was cursed. I tended to believe the latter. I read the reports years later. The fire department said it was a mystery. The town priest said it was a miracle. And my neighbors… well, they said it was an act of the devil.

And once something was set in stone, it couldn't be etched out.

With each day, I grew wearier, more fearful, retreating farther within myself. And my carnal cravings were becoming more intense inside this house. More twisted and depraved. My guys would give me whatever I wished for. Their cravings knew no bounds. But would I lose myself inside this dream? All I wanted was them. Their pain, their lust, and their desire. I wanted it to fill me and consume me.

But there was something even darker than us lurking around Wickford Mansion. I could feel it in my bones. Something sinister and wicked.

So, here I was in the middle of the night, kneeling in front of Mr. Wickford's grave, searching for answers. I wiped the dirt off the cold headstone and traced my fingers over his epitaph. *And all I loved, I loved alone.* Edgar Allan Poe. A cold chill snaked up my spine. Such an odd quote to put on your dead husband's grave.

I zipped my leather jacket all the way up to my neck as a burst of cold wind blew against me. I jerked my head toward the tree line as a branch snapped. "*Fuck,*" I whispered.

My heart raced as I cycled through all the possible things that could be lurking in the dark—wolves, vagrants, Mrs. Wickford's angry ghost, local heathens waiting to pounce on me. *Fuck, I hoped it was wolves.*

I stood up slowly and backed away from the grave, mentally patting myself on the back for wearing sneakers instead of the fuzzy slippers I almost threw on. Another gust of wind embraced me, sending my blonde strands flying in every direction. The leaves rustled around my feet, circling me as if they were about to attack.

And still I waited, listening. *Why was I like this?*

If I were normal, I would've headed back inside already. *A normal woman wouldn't have come out here to begin with.* A flash of lightning gripped the sky, followed by a deep rumbling of thunder.

I whipped around and stalked back toward the house just as the rain came down in buckets. *Ah, shit.* As I broke into a jog across the lawn, my hair was soaked within seconds. There was nothing gentle about a Wickford Hollow storm. When they came, it was with a vengeance.

I was almost to the back door when the lightning flashed again, lighting up the whole sky. I looked up, my eye drawn to the third story, and froze. A shadow pressed against the window, its eyes glowing like the moon. The thunder roared and the rain fell harder. I blinked and the shadow was gone.

Shivers climbed up my back. *There was something there.* Fuck.

The back door flew open. "Bailey! Get inside before you catch pneumonia!"

I blinked again as Poe held out his hand to me. I nodded and jogged toward him.

"Bailey," the wind whispered.

I gasped and spun around. It was pitch black out here and hard to see through the rain. I looked up at the sky, waiting for another burst of lightning. *Come on.*

A crack echoed through the woods just as two strong arms wrapped around my waist and pulled me inside.

"What the hell were you doing out there?" Poe growled.

"I-I don't know. I can't f-feel my fin-fingers." My teeth chattered as the chill began to settle into my bones. I couldn't breathe.

Poe's eyes widened. "Fuck. We need to get you out of these wet clothes or you're going to freeze to death."

I nodded.

"Grim, Saint, a little help here!" He yelled into the house as he undressed me where I stood.

They both barreled in. "What in the world?" Saint's face paled.

Grim shook his head. "Fuck, Bailey, why in the devil's name do you like trouble so much?"

"Help me get these off her. Saint go run a hot bath. We need to get her body temperature up," Poe ordered.

Everything began to blur as if I were leaving my own body. Like it wasn't attached to me anymore. I couldn't feel their hands. But the fear that gripped me wasn't from the cold. It was from whatever was out there watching me. The whisper in the wind. The shadow in the window.

A cry ripped from my throat. "*Don't let him get me,*" I rasped.

Grim scooped me up in his arms. "Shh, little fox. It's going to be okay."

Poe raced ahead of us as Grim sprinted up the stairs, cradling me to his chest. Tears streamed down my cheeks.

Within seconds I was being lowered into a warm scented bath. Soothing hands caressed me. And then I was out again and wrapped in a big fluffy towel. The three of them pressed into me, their body heat enveloping me like a cocoon.

"Deep breaths now. Good girl," Poe murmured.

Grim gathered my hair off my neck, towel drying it as my pulse began to steady.

"I'm sorry..."

"You should be," Saint growled. "You could have died out there, Bailey."

A strange thing occurred to me. And not for the first time. "If I had... would I still be here with you? Would I be *like* you?"

The three of them stiffened. Poe wrapped another towel around my shoulders and tugged me in closer. "Is that what this is about? You want to die because you think that will keep us together forever?"

I didn't know what I was thinking or feeling right now. Nothing made sense. I shook my head. "No. I mean, maybe. I don't know... I wasn't trying to kill myself. There was something..."

Another shiver raced up my back as I remembered the whisper and the shadow.

"Something *what,* Bailey?" Grim asked.

"Enough," Saint interjected before I could respond. "She needs to sleep. Everything will make more sense in the morning."

Grim carried me to bed and the three of them climbed in around me. Their strong hands caressed my arms and face as I let myself surrender to the warmth and quiet. But I wasn't sure that anything I saw and heard tonight would be any clearer by morning. I feared it would only make less sense.

CHAPTER One

Bailey

"There's something seriously wrong with this town," Maureen mumbled through a mouthful of sweet potato fries.

Growing up in Wickford Hollow had never been easy. I was used to the stares and the whispers. Used to being the girl whose parents died under mysterious circumstances. But even I had to admit that the people of this town had gotten more aggressive ever since I bought and renovated the Wickford Mansion.

I shrugged, pretending to ignore the icy glares from half of Ruby's Diner. "It's whatever, Maur. Small towns, you know?"

Maureen bared her teeth at Crazy Fred, sweet potato fries and all.

I stifled a laugh. "Oh, that'll show him."

"*He's* supposed to be the town freak. Not you. Fuck him and everybody else." She stuck her tongue out at him, clearly not done with taunting him.

I giggled. "Well, that's what happens when you buy a condemned house that almost burned down. People talk."

For years, Wickford Mansion incited superstition and stories of hauntings. That was the one thing they weren't wrong about...

In the summer after graduation, a bunch of kids even set the Wickford Mansion on fire. They claimed it was an accident, but I always wondered if the town was just trying to get rid of it for good. As soon as word spread of my buying it and moving in, the people here distrusted me even more.

I started to take a sip of my iced tea when a glob of spit landed on my arm. I looked up, furious, to see Billy and his buddies snickering a few feet away—one of them being my ex-boyfriend. *Ugh.*

"Fucking witch," Billy spat. "Hey, Chad, didn't you fuck her back in high school? Hope she didn't put a curse on your dick." The lot of them burst out laughing.

My cheeks reddened as I wiped my arm with a crumpled napkin. "Assholes," I muttered.

"Fuck this." Maureen stood up from the table. "It's kind of hard to curse a dick that didn't work right to begin with. Maybe my girl here did you a favor, *Chaaad*," she yelled back.

I grabbed her wrist as they started to come over. "It's fine, Maur. Just let it go." The last thing I needed was more attention.

Billy licked his fingers before shoving them into our bowl of fries. He crushed them between his fingers and flung them at my face. "That's better. Now you look like the dirty whore you are."

Rage seared through my veins. But before I could react, Maureen swung her fist at him. He ducked and grabbed her arm, twisting her around so her back was pinned against his chest. His buddies laughed harder.

The rest of the patrons did nothing. Said nothing. They just watched on like we were in an episode of their favorite reality TV show.

Maureen squirmed in his arms. "Don't you know who I am, fucker?"

Billy snickered. "Please, Maureen. Your daddy might be the sheriff, but he shoots more whiskey than he does criminals. Now shut your pretty mouth before I stick my dick in it."

I was going to fucking kill him. "*Billy*. I said let her go. It's me you have a problem with."

Chad's eyes darkened. "Hey, let's go, man. I really don't want to get arrested tonight."

Maureen elbowed him in his stomach. "Yeah, Billy, listen to your daddy *Chad*."

"*Maureen*," I warned.

Just as Billy's eyes turned murderous, Ruby came flying over. "Enough. This ain't one of your house parties, Billy. Get the hell out of my diner before I call the sheriff myself."

Ruby was not a big woman, but her presence was larger than life. She had a short fuse and thick skin. Diner life was no joke. When the customers got out of hand, Ruby laid down the law.

Billy pushed Maureen back toward our table. "I'm bored with you basic cunts, anyway. Enjoy your fries, Bailey."

I let out a sigh of relief as soon as they walked out the door.

Ruby eyed both of us back and forth. "You girls all right?"

"Hell no, we—"

"We're fine. Thank you, Ruby." I shot Maureen a look so fierce she quieted instantly.

Ruby nodded. "Uh-huh. I'll get you some more fries."

That was another thing about this town. No one wanted to get involved in other folks' business unless it was forced onto their lap. If I said we were fine, Ruby was going to take me at my word. She had more important things to do than coddle a grown woman.

"I'm so sick of those assholes, Bales. We need to do something. Like, fuck with them somehow." Maureen's pale cheeks flamed pink and her freshly blown-out hair was starting to frizz at the crown.

I sighed. "And do what? They'll only come back at us harder. No. I just want to forget about them. Do you see why I hate coming into town now?"

"Well, this is your town too. You can't let them keep you locked away in some creepy mansion all by yourself forever."

A twinge of guilt stirred in my belly. I still hadn't told her about... *them*. Maureen was my best friend. My only friend. If I told her I was living with three spirits in the house they were murdered in, she'd have me committed. If I told her all the vile things they do to me... she'd never speak to me again.

"*Bailey*. Are you even listening to me?"

I shuddered. "Yeah. No. Sorry. What were you saying?"

She rolled her eyes. "I said, when are we going to have a girls' night? It's almost been a year, and I still haven't gotten drunk and slept over at your place. I'm not gonna lie, Wickford Mansion creeps me out but you're my best friend, so I'll suffer through," she teased.

Since moving in, I hadn't let her, or anyone get any farther than the front sitting room off the kitchen. There was no way I was going to ask Poe, Grim, and Saint to stay hidden all night in their own home. And I wasn't ready yet to introduce her to them.

"Soon. I promise. Believe it or not, I'm still settling in. I've got crap everywhere. Just give me some more time. Please, Maur?" *I physically hated lying to her.*

Her eyes lit up when the new basket of fries arrived. Her hand was already digging in before they touched the table. To be fair they were the best sweet potato fries in town.

She swirled one in a bowl of ranch sauce and shoved it in her mouth, her eyes rolling back in her head like she was about to cum. "Fine, Bales. Whatever you want. Just don't wait too long. I've only got one more month in this place. It would be nice to have a couple of sleepovers at my best friend's house before I go."

My heart sank. Every time I thought about Maureen moving away, I wanted to hurl. It's not that I wasn't happy for her. She got accepted into Tenebrose Academy, her dream school, but it was in Raven's Gate, which was six hours away. Her dream of studying Gothic costume design was finally coming true. I just wish it didn't have to take her so far away.

I fought back the urge to cry. Maureen hated mushy shit. "I know. I promise we'll have a girls' night before you leave."

Somehow I was going to have to find the balls to fess up to my best friend about Poe, Grim, and Saint. They were tied to this town, and I was tied to them. So despite getting smooshed fries thrown in my face, being with them was worth every snide comment and hateful stare cast my way.

I pushed open the front door and was instantly hit with an array of scents—freshly picked wildflowers on the foyer table, sweet incense smoke burning throughout the house, and the rich aromas of meat and garlic wafting from the kitchen.

Home.

I let out a grateful sigh and threw my keys on the table. "I'm back," I called out.

Before I could walk three more steps, a pair of strong arms wrapped around me from behind.

I jumped at first, still getting used to the fact that my guys could appear and disappear at will. Another ghost thing I was learning to live with.

"I missed our little fox," Poe rasped in my ear. His lips brushed my earlobe and sent a tingle straight to my core.

I sank back into his arms. Safe. Loved. "You have no idea how much I missed you all today."

He dipped his fingers into the waist of my jeans. "Everything all right, love?"

I bit my lip. The last thing I wanted to tell him, any of them, was that I had a run-in with asshole Billy and my stupid ex. It would only make them angry and fearful every time I left the house. Not that I even wanted to go into town, but someone had to get the groceries. Plus Maureen would throw a fit if I didn't keep our weekly lunch dates.

I squeezed his hand, urging it lower. "Just peachy," I cooed.

Poe chuckled and pushed his fingers inside my panties. "Are you trying to tempt me into eating out that sweet pussy of yours?"

Shuddering, I leaned my head back against his chest. "Is it working?"

"Little fox… you tempt me every time you walk into a room." He slid his middle finger down my already wet center. "I will devour every sweet and sticky inch of you."

My breath hitched as his fingers probed deeper inside my folds. "Fuck… *Poe.* How do you always know what to do?"

He kissed my neck, sending goosebumps across my flesh. "Because I know what you want, little fox." His thumb circled my clit. "*I know what you need.*"

My knees shook as he wedged two fingers deep inside my pussy. I let out a soft whimper as the pressure inside me grew. We were insatiable. All of us. I ached for each of them every minute of the day. No matter how much we gave each other, it was never enough.

"I'm so close, Poe…"

"I know, love." He pumped in and out, slowly, pushing and pulling his fingers through me with bittersweet torture. I rolled my hips, swaying to the rhythm of his movements. Riding his hand as I chased my orgasm.

"Oh, fuck," I cried out. I clenched around his fingers as my juices spilled out.

He palmed my pussy, pressing it hard against my clit. "Mmm, just like that, my love. Unravel for me. Such a *good—fucking—girl*."

His voice in my ear was my final push over the edge. I let out a throaty moan as my orgasm rolled through me. "*Ughhh*..."

"Fucking beautiful." He stilled his hand as I panted.

"Well, that's one way to greet a woman when she walks in the door," I murmured.

"Are you surprised? I've only been making you cum non-stop for a year straight, little fox," Poe teased.

I turned to face him and planted a soft kiss on his lips. "And yet I always want more. I'm greedy like that."

He flashed a devious grin as he sucked my cum off his fingers. "So am I. I'm determined to keep that sweet little cunt of yours dripping wet at all times."

We were about three seconds from ripping each other's clothes off and fucking on the marble foyer floor. I stepped into him and sighed. "I need a shower and you should probably check on whatever delicious food you've cooked that's got the whole house smelling like a gourmet restaurant."

Poe licked his fingers again. "Mmm, yeah. You *are* filthy. And I have a special anniversary dinner planned for all of us."

I giggled. "But Halloween Eve isn't for three more weeks."

"So? It's our anniversary month. I'm going to spoil you every day, little fox. Get used to it." He squeezed my ass and planted a firm wet kiss on my cheek. "Now go take your shower and slip into something naughty."

Despite the renovations, this house still creaked as if it were as old as the foundations it stood on. While the original frame remained intact, the interior had gone through extensive repair and upgrades. But no matter how many fresh coats of paint were slapped on, the soul of the house remained. Poe, Grim, and Saint made me feel safe, but when I was alone in a room… something eerie prickled me.

Great horrors had taken place inside these walls. Pure evil had lived here with them. Some imprint of that energy still lingered. I could feel it in my bones.

A shiver crawled up my arms as I walked the endless corridors. The floors and décor were also new. It was no secret that I loved dark and Gothic vibes and the house reflected that.

With black velvet curtains, tied together with gold brocade ropes, plum and gray tapestried walls, and marbled floors, it was a mixture of the past and the present—their tastes and mine. And while we filled these once barren rooms with love and laughter, something cold and sinister still permeated here. I couldn't quite put my finger on it, but it prickled the hairs on the back of my neck like a chilly draft you couldn't figure out the source of.

I paused in front of the floor-to-ceiling window at the end of the west wing hall. The black velvet curtains were parted, fastened to the wrought iron frame with that thick gold rope. The glass streaked with condensation as the moonlight strobed through. It was almost winter in Wickford Hollow and with the way the wind beat against the house, I knew it was going to be a cold one. Maybe the coldest one ever.

It had almost been a year since I'd broken into this once abandoned house. The cursed and condemned house of Wickford Hollow. Only one year since Maureen had dared me to walk in here by myself, drunk off of jello shots and adrenaline. I could still remember the rush, the excitement, and the fear when an unseen force shoved me into that locked door at the top of the stairs.

I'd always been obsessed with the occult, but I never fully believed in urban legends or ghost tales. I just really liked Halloween and all the dark and delicious things that came with it. But the moment Poe dragged me out of my bed later that night, I knew something wicked my way had come.

And yet after just one night with him, Grim, and Saint, I didn't want to let them go. My three deviant ghosts. The ghosts of Wickford Mansion, cursed to spend an eternity locked away until that night I set them free. And now they were mine. Wickford Mansion was ours. We made it our home. So why did I feel like something was going to burst in and snatch it all away?

I stared at my reflection in the window and barely recognized myself. My skin was paler than usual from the lack of sunlight. My blonde hair, longer, hanging all the way down to my lower back.

Cold shivers trickled up my arms as I glimpsed a subtle movement behind me. I took a deep breath through my nose and forced myself to still. A few months ago, I started seeing things in mirrors. In anything with reflections. Nothing solid, just little flickers and shadows. I had started feeling things I couldn't explain.

The guys tried to assure me that it was nothing. That it was just a big house with dark corners, lots of windows, and mirrors—plenty of reflective surfaces for the wind and the moon and the stars to play tricks on my mind.

Even the lights flickered when I walked into a room despite the brand new electrical wiring. They said it was most likely because of them. They were spirits after all. But it didn't *feel* like them. This felt like something else. *Fuck, I was probably just losing my mind.*

My breath hitched as I strained to see through the window, fixated on the reflection of the hall behind me. A lump formed in my throat as I waited for movement. Nothing. I sighed and turned around to face the empty hall. "*Get it together, Bailey,*" I muttered.

I stood at the top of the curved staircase and gripped the railing. Every time I walked down, I had this indescribable feeling that something was going to push me. Visions of my twisted body, bloody and mangled at the bottom of the foyer flashed through my mind. I forced the bile down my throat and made my shaky descent, my black stiletto heels clicking against the marble like keys on a piano, echoing down all three levels.

By the time I reached the safety of the main floor, my thighs were slick with sweat. The back of my neck, clammy. I had to fight to keep my legs from buckling as I walked into the kitchen.

But as soon as the decadent scents of Poe's cooking hit my nose, a warm rush flooded me, chasing away the chills as if they'd never been there to begin with. Poe's lips curled into a smirk over the steaming ladle he held to his lips.

"There's our good girl," Grim rasped as he came up behind me. He wrapped his strong arms around my waist.

I sank back into him.

Poe sauntered forward and held the ladle to my lips. "It doesn't taste as good as you, but I think you'll like it." He winked.

Grim's hands roamed my hips, slowly tugging at the edges of my tiny black skirt. "Let's feed our little fox, so we can have our dessert."

Saint stalked in, his massive body barely fitting through the doorway. His black T-shirt and jeans hugged his frame, showing off every curve of his muscles. He ran a hand through his long brown hair before tying it up into a top knot.

I let out a tiny whimper. The sight of the three of them never got old. They were viciously beautiful. Dominant. And always hungry for me.

We took our seats around the kitchen table. There was a fancier one in the main dining room, but it was so formal. I loved the kitchen. It was warm and cozy and smelled incredible after Poe cooked.

Tonight, I sat between Grim and Saint with Poe across from us, his sloppy grin growing as he watched me devour his stew. I moaned into my spoon. "This is delicious," I mumbled.

Grim squeezed my bare thigh under the table. He played with the edge of my skirt. "*You're delicious.*"

Heat flooded me.

Saint wiped a dribble of soup off my lip with his thumb and sucked it off. "How was your day, love?"

Poe adjusted himself under the table. "Fuck, you're making me hard. I love to watch you eat."

I smirked at the three of them. They were such deviants. It was hard to get through one meal without wanting to rip each other's clothes off.

"It was fine. We had a nice lunch," I lied.

Saint squeezed my other thigh. "You still haven't told Maureen about us, have you?"

My stomach knotted, the guilt clawing at me. "No."

Grim glared at him. "It's all good, little fox. You'll tell her when you're ready."

Poe nodded. "We have all the time in the world to meet her."

Another gut punch. *They* had all the time in the world. But I didn't. I was a mortal woman who would age and at some point die. *What happens then?* Would they remain here without me? Or would their souls follow me to whatever existed beyond this life? It hadn't crossed my mind in the beginning. I was too swept away by them. But lately, it was all I could think about. Yet another issue I didn't want to burden them with.

Saint grabbed my wrist, stopping me from taking another bite. "Enough talk. As much as I like your cooking, Poe, I'd rather our little fox here be the main course."

Grim leaned back in his chair. "What did you have in mind?"

My pussy quivered under their ravenous stares.

Saint caressed my cheek. "Let's move this party to the dining room. I want to see our little fox spread out on the good linens."

CHAPTER Two

Saint

"On the table," I growled.

Bailey's eyes flickered with excitement as she climbed on top.

I stalked around the table, drinking in the sight of her hard nipples poking through the fabric of her flimsy shirt, the flutter in her belly, the beads of sweat that trickled down between her breasts. She was beautiful. She was my dark and delicious fantasy come to life.

"Hold her wrists," I told Poe. His green eyes flared as he burned for her. *We all did.*

Poe removed a gold rope from the curtain and wrapped it tight around her wrists before pinning them over her head.

I leaned down and whispered in her ear. "I'm going to make

you scream and cum so fucking hard, you won't remember your own name."

Her breath quickened. "Please, Saint… fuck."

Grim pushed his finger into her mouth. She took it greedily, sucking it like a lollipop.

My cock grew in my pants. I loved it when she begged. I pulled my knife out of my back pocket. I traced the tip across her collarbone, then down between her breasts.

"Let's get you more comfortable." With two quick thrusts, I tore through her top with the blade, splitting it down the middle.

Her rosy skin glistened with sweat. She was so fucking turned on it was all I could do to slow play this and not fuck her raw right then. But I wanted to watch her squirm.

I dragged the knife down her belly and slipped the tip underneath her panties. With another quick jerk, I cut them off her trembling body, leaving only the remnants of black lace around one of her thighs.

"Show me that wet cunt of yours," I growled, my heart beating faster with every twitch and whimper she elicited.

My cock throbbed as she spread her legs wide for us. "*Good girl.*"

I sheathed the knife and flipped it around. With the covered blade in my palm, I pressed the hilt against her belly.

"Your favorite knife," Grim rasped. "For our *favorite* girl."

Poe hovered over her. "Go slow. I want to see every agonizing inch of it."

Bailey licked her lips as she eyed the knife in my hands. "What are you gonna do with that?"

Using the rounded tip of the hilt, I circled her clit. "Do you want to please me, little fox?"

She bit down on her lower lip as she panted. "Yes. Always."

Fuck, yeah. She was so beautiful when she wasn't in control. So vulnerable. When her pussy was aching with need. "Are you going to be a good girl and surrender to us?" I dragged the hilt down her slit.

She nodded. "Yes. I belong to you."

I handed the knife to Grim. "Get this nice and wet for me." He squeezed my hand as he took it from me. Without breaking my gaze, he took the hilt in his mouth and sucked, coating it with his saliva.

Bailey moaned as she watched.

"I need a better view." Poe secured the end of the rope to the table leg before stalking over to the other end. "And I want to suck that hilt *after*."

I nodded and held up the large knife so Bailey could get a good look at it. "Do you like it, little fox?" The top was a rounded steel ball, and the base was wrapped in thick coarse leather.

"It's beautiful," she whimpered.

Poe and Grim each stroked one of her thighs.

"It wants to play with you." Seeing her tied up and spread out was making me feral.

Her belly quivered. "*Oh, fuck.*"

I peeled back one of her pussy lips using the hilt, the act instantly making my dick throb. Slowly, I dragged it back to the middle and did the same to the other side. It was sinful and erotic and filthy as fuck. The way she inched her hips forward, readying herself to receive it like the good little girl she was, made my dick so hard I was going to need to cum multiple times before I'd be able to walk straight again.

Grim grunted next to me, clearly having the same problem stirring in his own pants. "Put it in. I want to see her stretch around it."

She was panting, her chest heaving at the sound of his words.

"Let me make sure she's nice and wet first," Poe rasped. He slid a thick finger down the opening of her cunt, the flesh already pink and swollen.

Her breath hitched as she wiggled her ass against the table.

"Mmm, so wet." Poe's mouth watered as he stroked her, sliding his finger up, down, side to side, and back up to her clit. He drew slow circles with his thumb as she writhed and moaned.

"Let's go," Grim growled again. *"Put the knife in her fucking pussy."*

"Easy now. I'm just savoring our little fox," I rasped.

Grim was not known for his patience. He wanted everything at the snap of his fingers. He groaned and started forward, but I held him off. "All right, Grim. Relax and watch."

Bailey flinched as I pressed the cold tip of the hilt against her clit. "Oh, fuck," she panted.

"Shhh, relax." I dragged it down her slit, my hunger growing as I pushed the round steel tip inside her sopping wet pussy.

As she bucked her hips, Grim and Poe each placed a firm hand on her thighs, holding her in place. She lifted her head and locked eyes with me as I held it still, her breath quickening.

I got off on teasing her. Taunting her. The way her body shook as I slowly began to twist it farther inside her, made me feel feral.

Poe dug his fingers into her thigh, his eyes glued to her cunt. "Do you like that, little fox? You like when Daddy Saint fucks you with his toys?"

She moaned louder. "*Yes.*"

I peeled the folds of her pussy back with my other hand and edged the hilt in deeper. "Oh, baby. You are so fucking tight. *Relax.*"

Grim bent down and pressed his tongue against her clit. She screamed as he licked in quick rough strokes. She spread her legs wider, welcoming every depraved act thrust upon her like a good fucking girl. *Our good fucking girl.*

"There we go. *Fuck.* Now I can slide in deeper." I placed a hand on her belly and pushed the full length of the hilt inside her.

"Uhhh. Fucking hell," she screamed.

Grim pinched her clit, rubbing it back and forth as I stilled the hilt inside her, letting her get accustomed to its girth. "Do you like being stretched open, little fox?"

Sweat beaded down her hard nipples. "Saint, please. I need to cum."

"*More*," Poe snarled as he snatched the cushion off the armchair and wedged it underneath her, elevating her hips.

She twisted and pulled against her restraints, her wrists bright red from the rope digging into her flesh. "*Please*," she begged.

I pulled the hilt back and then thrust forward. And again. I had to start slow so she could accommodate the size. But I was going to fucking stretch her before the night was over.

She rocked her hips, moaning, as I fucked her with the hilt of my knife. It was the next best thing to my own cock. I grunted as I watched her juices coat the leather. Grim fisted his own cock as we watched her squirm and buck with every thrust. Watching her pink pussy turn red as I pumped faster.

"Fuck, don't stop," Grim breathed as he stroked his cock to the same rhythm I had with her.

"Ughhh. Fuck. Faster. I'm going to cum…fuck." Bailey's back arched so hard, I thought she was going to break through her restraints.

I slid my free hand underneath her and fingered her ass. "Do you like when we use you like this, little fox?"

She nodded and bit down on her lip. "Yes… *ruin me*."

Seeing how close she was to the edge, I shoved the hilt in with more force. I was ready to push her over. "I'm going to fucking destroy you." I ground it against her G-spot. "I know you love every filthy thing we do to you."

Her eyes rolled back as she clenched around the hilt. "Ughhh," She cried out. "I-I'm coming. Fuck."

Poe fingered her clit as she chased her orgasm. "Good girl. Coat that fucking knife for me."

Grim slapped his cock against her belly as his cum spilled out in thick white ropes. "*Such a good fucking girl,*" he grunted.

As I rammed the hilt against her swollen walls, a feral need stirred inside me. I palmed her belly and smeared Grim's cum down over her pussy lips. A carnal ache throbbed in my body as his cum coated my fingers. I painted every inch of her folds with it.

Poe's eyes glazed with hunger as he fixated on the knife. "*Mine.*"

Bailey gasped as I pulled the hilt out and handed it to Poe. He took it in his mouth and sucked. "Delicious," he purred.

Bailey lifted her head up, struggling to keep her eyes open as she locked them on me. "Cum for me, daddy."

I dropped my pants and fisted my throbbing cock.

Bailey's breath hitched. "No. Not like that. I want to watch *you* give up control."

Fuck, she was perfect.

Grim moved behind me and wrapped his hand around my cock. "You know I won't be gentle."

He was far from it. Grim was rough and brutal. I remember the first time we touched each other all those years ago. It was like an awakening. I had been with many men and women before but there was an electricity in his touch. The way he took what he wanted without restraint. Just like I did with Bailey.

I panted as Grim stroked my shaft in hard jerks. It sent tremors all the way down to the tip. "Don't fucking stop."

I slammed my hands on the table as the pressure grew. Grim's cock hardened against my ass. "Are you going to cum for our good girl?"

I gritted my teeth, nodding, as a tingling spiraled throughout my entire body.

Grim's grip tightened. "You're so close. I can feel it."

Poe rubbed his cock against Bailey's face. "You're a voyeur like me, aren't you, little fox?"

I couldn't hold it back any longer. Fuck. I let out a riotous moan as Grim snaked around me and dropped to his knees. I threw my head back. "Mmm, fuck, I'm coming."

Grim wrapped his lips around my cock, his cheeks hollowing as he sucked. I cried out as my cum gushed into his hot mouth. I drove into him violently, knocking him back against the table. He moaned as he swallowed every drop of my cum.

Poe grunted as he shoved his cock deep inside Bailey's mouth. "Yeah, fuck, suck it just like that." She choked as she took it, her lips swollen from the size of him.

Grim slid his lips down to my shaft, humming as I twitched against him. "You taste so fucking good," he breathed.

Bailey reached out to us. "Kiss me."

Poe untied her wrists, rubbing them as they fell lifeless beside her.

Without hesitating, Grim went to her and plunged his tongue into her mouth.

I traced my fingers up her leg, over her belly, and across her breasts. Her nipples were still pebbled. We took turns kissing her, savoring the taste of each other on her tongue.

It was as good as breathing. And since we didn't technically do that anymore, touching her was better than breathing.

CHAPTER *Three*

Bailey

The longer I lived in this house, the stronger a nagging feeling grew in my belly. It was only when we played these dirty games with each other that it went away. When they opened me up and fucked me raw.

Feelings of dread and uneasiness had followed me my whole life. Ever since my parents died. But it got worse the summer after graduation. All the parties I went to were nothing but a temporary distraction. They couldn't drown out the noise in my head. No amount of alcohol could chase away the darkness growing inside my chest.

I felt like I was slowly losing my mind. And I couldn't figure out why. But there was something inside me that wouldn't let me rest. Only the vile and depraved acts of Poe, Grim, and Saint could.

But with each passing day, my dread threatened to suffocate me. I was thinking more and more about the past. I had questions about the fire that killed my parents. Questions no one could answer. And I was too young to remember. According to the police report, the fire was caused by a gas leak. *So how did I survive?* It was perfectly clear on paper but still made zero sense in my head.

I let out a frustrated sigh as I flicked my windshield wipers on. The rain was coming down so hard I could barely see the road. The clouds shrouded the town in darkness, making everything gray and muted. It was strangely beautiful, though. And comforting. Like all of my melancholy had spilled out onto the streets while the town itself held it up, embracing every twisted thought in my head. It was ethereal, a perfectly gloomy day to search for answers.

I parked in front of the Wickford Hollow Library and made a mad dash for the entrance, cursing myself for forgetting my umbrella again. In just three minutes, I was soaked and dripping water all over the library's marble floors. The woman behind the front counter sneered at me and shook her head as I sloshed over to her.

"Hi. Um, sorry about the water on the floor."

She peered up through her pointy glasses and pursed her lips. "How can I help you?"

Of course, it would be too much to ask of at least one person in this town for any kindness.

I glanced down at her nametag. "Right. Well, Mary, I need to find some news articles."

She winced as if the sound of her own name on my tongue might kill her. "Computers are over there."

I glanced in the direction she pointed and shook my head. "No, I need to look at old newspaper articles." The internet could doctor anything. I had to see the originals.

Mary the librarian rolled her eyes and pointed to another corner. "We only have one microfilm machine left. You know how to use it?"

I nodded. "Yes, thank you."

She blew out a sigh of relief. This woman didn't want to spend a second longer talking to me. She was yet another person I made uncomfortable just by existing.

After about twenty minutes of looking through the microfilm, I gathered all the ones that contained articles from the year of the fire, and I even snatched up any that had the keywords *Wickford Hollow* and *fire* in them. Just in case.

As I loaded the first one into the machine, a group of young girls whispered and gawked at me as they passed. They couldn't have been more than fifteen years old. *Jesus, what were these people teaching their children?*

I flashed them a wicked grin. "You know it's not polite to stare at strangers," I called out a little too loudly. The girls giggled as they scrambled away.

Mary pressed her finger to her lips and shushed me. *The bitch actually shushed me.* I snickered before directing my focus back to the machine.

I loaded the film that had the actual date of the fire listed and scrolled through all the articles. There's never been a whole lot going on in Wickford Hollow so it shouldn't be too hard to find.

The Wickford Daily Hollow was no big city newspaper. The articles alone were sheer proof of that. I stifled multiple yawns as I poured through endless articles about city council elections and petty neighborhood squabbles. I couldn't believe how many times someone's cat got stuck in a tree. And how many times someone chose to write about it.

As I reached the end of the film, my heart sank. The fire that killed my parents was nowhere to be found. *What the actual fuck?* How does an entire house burn down, killing two people, and not one journalist published anything about it?

Fuck, I hated the people in this town. Just more proof that

they didn't want the Bishops to exist. So they treated us like we didn't. Now I was the only one left.

After scrolling through the next film, I was about to give up and call it a day when I came across an article on the Wickford family. They founded the town and had more money than everyone in it combined. All the stuff I knew before. *Blah, blah, blah.*

Oh, wait, what the fuck is this? The second article mentioned that Raine Wickford built Wickford Mansion after moving here from Ever Graves, shortly after he wed a young socialite named Daisy Thorn. *Mrs. Wickford.* That's the bitch who poisoned my guys.

I scrolled through more bullshit about how rich they were and all the great things they did for the town, but I couldn't find any pictures. Fuck. I couldn't help my curiosity. At one time, she was the woman they worshiped. A part of me wanted to see what she looked like. Probably for the best, though. I'd only end up driving myself crazy comparing myself to her.

I spent another hour scouring through three more film cartridges but found nothing. I rubbed my eyes. I was nowhere closer to finding out anything about the day I became an orphan.

Fuck, last one. The microfilm came to life on the screen as I loaded it and the first article that popped up made my stomach turn. A picture of Wickford Mansion in flames splayed across the screen. Something twisted in my gut, sharp like a knife. Bile crept up my throat. This was from that party, the summer after graduation.

I scrolled down and skimmed the article, pausing on the last line: *Several of the trespassers claimed to see someone buried under the rubble, but no bodies were recovered.* My breath hitched. Someone might have died that night. Fucking hell. That could be why I was seeing and hearing things around the house.

I skipped to another article, my heart racing, that stated all partygoers had been accounted for and the body they saw was most likely a squatter. Jesus, these people were something else. They didn't even bother investigating any further once they decided the person killed wasn't one of their spoiled little rich kids. I gritted my teeth as I yanked the microfilm out of the machine.

Rage coursed through my veins as I shoved all the microfilm back into their drawers. The only thing I learned today was just how deep the hate in this town ran. And now I had even more questions. And a sneaking suspicion that someone didn't want anyone talking about the fire that killed my parents.

I sat in the driveway, the heater blasting, not quite ready to go inside. I didn't want the guys to know I was digging into my past. It's not that they wouldn't support it, it's just that everything was so perfect when I first moved in here. I didn't want anything to ruin that.

I gazed up at Wickford Mansion as the phone rang three times before she picked up.

"Hey, bitch, I was just about to text you," Maureen shrilled into the phone. "Should I get another tattoo before I leave for school? I want to give off an edgier vibe in my new life."

I chuckled. "Hell, yeah. You should get *at least* two more," I teased.

She snorted. "This is why you're my friend. What's up with you?"

I tapped my nails against the steering wheel. "Well, not to be a downer but… I just left the library."

Maureen feigned a gasp. "Oh, the horror!"

I snickered. "That's not the downer part. I've been looking into the fire that killed my parents."

"Oh, shit. Sorry, Bales. Fuck. I know that has always been in the back of your mind. So, what did you find?"

I sighed. "Jack shit. Apparently, no one thought it was newsworthy."

"Ugh, that's ridiculous. And shady as fuck," Maureen drawled.

I nodded into the phone. "Yup. So, I was wondering if you could talk to your dad. I know he's not allowed to share confidential stuff but maybe he remembers something. Wasn't he one of the first ones on the scene?"

"Of course, Bales," her voice cracked. "He hates talking about work but you're my best friend. I'll ask him tonight at dinner."

If anyone could get the sheriff to talk, it would be his favorite daughter. "Thanks, Maur. I just don't think I can let this go until I know for sure what happened."

"You got it, babe. We'll find out together."

"Okay, text me later."

I hung up the phone and gripped the steering wheel. Why was I like this? I should be enjoying my life right now instead of dwelling on the past. But it wouldn't let me go…

As winter loomed over us, the days were cold and gloomy in Wickford Hollow. But at night, the house came alive with energy. With a fire going in every hearth, bright chandeliers that lit up every room, and the scents of Poe's cooking wafting through the entire house, it was like our own private wonderland. It was enough to make me temporarily forget about the shadows that had crept into my bones.

I stood in the kitchen watching the three of them set the table, wondering how I got so lucky to find them. They were sexy as fuck, dangerous, and unpredictable, but they were also caring, sweet, and gentle when they needed to be.

Saint wrapped his big arms around me from behind. His

cock stirred in his pants, pressing against my back. "You're killing me in this outfit."

I leaned back into him, letting my pleated skirt ride up a little. "I wore it just for you."

He pushed my hair to the side and kissed my neck. "I want you to keep it on when I fuck you."

I let out a little whimper as his hand pulled my skirt up higher. "Fuck… Saint."

"Does your pussy want to play, little fox?" he rasped.

I nodded as I locked eyes with Grim who was leaning against the counter watching us. "Yes… always."

"Good girl." Saint inched my skirt up around my waist.

Grim stalked over and my heart quickened. He licked his lips as he pulled my panties down, gazing up at me from his knees. "*Always so wet for us.*"

Saint grabbed my leg and lifted it up, spreading me wide. I gasped as Grim's thick lips wrapped around my clit. His tongue flicked over it as he sucked while he peeled my folds back with his fingers.

"Oh, shit," I breathed.

Saint moaned as he kissed my neck. "I love watching your pussy get eaten."

Grim planted soft kisses down my slit before shoving his tongue deep inside. I bucked into Saint who held me firm against him. "Uhhh," I cried out.

The pressure built in my core, sending spasms through my entire body.

Poe dropped the ladle he was stirring with and walked over. I quivered as he pulled the strap of my top down, exposing my breast. My nipple swelled as he pinched it between his thumb and finger. "You're such a good fucking girl for us…"

Saint's hands roamed my thighs while Grim devoured me. I shivered as he scraped his teeth against my clit. And I was done for.

"*Fuck*," I screamed as an orgasm ripped through me.

Grim chuckled as I ground my pussy against his mouth. "Fucking hell," I murmured.

As they set me back down, my legs wobbled. Grim's saliva dripped down my thighs. He pulled my panties back up, wrapped his hand around my throat, and yanked me to him. "Come here, little fox."

My belly fluttered as he kissed me hard, shoving that magical tongue of his past my lips. The taste of my own pussy filled my mouth. And it was fucking hot as hell. He squeezed my throat and angled me back. "Don't ever forget who makes your pussy cry tears of fucking joy." He dragged his thumb across my lower lip. "*Our* dirty little girl..."

"How did you know that was what I needed?"

Saint pulled me to his chest, his eyes narrowing as he gazed down at me. "Because I know you, Bailey. Better than you think."

Something unspoken passed between us. He was the only one who could read me. Grim was easy to dodge when I didn't want to talk, he hated confrontation. And Poe just always saw the light in me. But Saint... he was impossible to hide from. And that feral look in his eyes told me he was coming for me soon.

As we crowded around the table, Poe dished us out heaping bowls of pasta. I covered mine in a thick layer of parmesan cheese before diving in. I hadn't realized how hungry I was until that first pillowy bite. I moaned as the spicy marinara sauce coated my tongue.

Saint raised an eyebrow. "Careful or I might insist you eat that naked."

I giggled and feigned a more dramatic moan on the next bite.

The guys burst out laughing as I egged them on. I loved this time of night so much. It was a space somewhere in between being a family and them reminding me that I was still theirs to defile and dominate.

While Poe and Grim play-fought over the last piece of garlic bread, Saint side-eyed me. "Meet me in the garden later tonight. Just you."

I nodded, swallowing another bite of pasta down along with the lump in my throat. Saint was the more serious one out of all of us. He was intense. And downright fucking scary at times. I knew from the minute I first saw him that he was going to push every boundary I had. He wanted me to surrender my vulnerability, my body, every fucking part of me.

I got away with distracting Poe. It was easy to flirt and charm him into submission. And Grim avoided the hard stuff at all costs. We had that in common. But Saint… he would push until he'd broken me wide open.

He dug his fingers deeper into my leg. "I want to hear you say it, little fox."

Fear and desire danced across my skin. "I will meet you in the garden alone tonight," I murmured.

Grim threw him another look that seemed to say, don't stir up trouble.

"What are you all colluding about over there?" Poe mumbled through a bite of bread, a smug look on his face for having beat Grim to it.

I took a big swig of my red wine. "Nothing you need to worry about, sweet Poe. Saint just wants some one-on-one time later."

"Aw, is our resident monster feeling a bit needy?" Poe teased.

Saint rolled his eyes over his glass of whiskey. "Says the man who gets separation anxiety when she's in the shower. Don't worry, I'll have her back in our bed before sunrise."

Grim snorted. "You're both adorable."

I giggled despite my nervousness about chatting with Saint later. It was rare that they fought for dominance over each other. We were equals, sharing each other from the moment we met. Poe just got off on getting a rise out of Saint. And I couldn't deny that it turned me on. The obsession and possessiveness were hot. Maybe that meant I was fucked up, but it was my truth. I knew it the second Poe dragged me out of my bed that first night. I hadn't been scared at all. I'd been craving it.

Poe burst out laughing. "Take as much time as you need. Just don't have too much fun without us."

I could feel Saint's body tense beside me. That told me all I needed to know. Something was bothering him, and he wasn't going to let me go to sleep tonight until he got it off his chest.

CHAPTER *Four*

Saint

When you've lived the life I have, happiness and love were two concepts that were hard to believe in. And yet here I was with my two best friends and our little fox. The loves of my life. But the nagging feeling of dread never fully goes away.

The garden was my favorite place on the whole property. Maybe because I've been tending to it myself for over a hundred years. Or perhaps because it was natural, the only spot on our land that wasn't fixed with marble and stone and velvet. Just the trees and flowers, all of which I planted myself with my bare hands. And when the Wickford Hollow wind would blow through my hair, it was the closest feeling to being alive. At least from what I remember.

As I sat in the dirt between two rose bushes, I sensed my little fox before I saw her. Heard the points of her heels squishing into the grass. Scents of honeysuckle and vanilla engulfed me along with a tiny shadow, lingering behind me.

"It's a beautiful night, isn't it?" I asked. The moon was almost full, casting an ethereal glow across the garden.

Bailey sucked in a deep breath. "It's perfect."

I took off my jacket and laid it beside me. "Here, sit next to me."

She plopped down without hesitating and nestled into my side. I wrapped my arm around her to keep her warm.

"What's going on with you, Bailey? Aren't you happy with us anymore?" I was connected to her on a deeper level from the moment we met. It was as if I could sense her emotions before she even experienced them.

Bailey's eyes widened as she gazed up at me. "Of course, I'm happy with you! I love you all so much. I can't imagine my life without you."

I breathed a sigh of relief. "Then what is it, little fox? What has got that beautiful head of yours spinning out of control? And don't lie to me. You're terrible at it."

She fidgeted with the edge of her skirt. "It's nothing. I'm just sad that Maureen is moving away soon. I'm fine, I swear."

She wasn't lying but she also wasn't telling me the whole truth. I pulled her in tighter. "Believe it or not, I understand what you're going through. The whispers, the gossip… When we first moved in here after the war, it was quite a scandal. Fuck, I mean three grown men living alone with a widowed woman… They didn't really believe that we were *just* the help, you know?"

"I'm not ashamed of you if that's what you're getting at. It's just that I've always had a complicated relationship with this town. After my parents died, I was sent to Wickford Orphanage. I lived there until I was eighteen. It was so lonely. And people can be so mean…"

The thought of anyone treating this sweet girl with anything but kindness literally made me murderous. "I know you aren't ashamed of us. But I think you are still ashamed of yourself and that needs to stop. You have done nothing wrong. Love is love and it's nobody's fucking business how we express it. Trust me, I've seen enough to know that to be true."

Bailey slipped her hand in mine, our fingers interlocking. "I'm working on it."

I kissed her temple. "That's all I ask. Maybe you can start by introducing us to Maureen."

She tensed, her grip on my hand tightening. "Fuck. I know I need to. What if she thinks I'm crazy?"

I sighed. "Darlin', if she loves you even half as much as you love her, she will support you no matter what. The longer you wait, the more hurt she'll be that you didn't tell her. Poe, Grim, and I had to learn that the hard way once."

Bailey nodded. "I know you're right… wait, what secrets did you keep from Poe and Grim?"

The past was a haunted place. Full of darkness and sin and death. So much death. But the thing I used to be more ashamed of were the secrets we kept from each other. "When the widow first started coming to each of us at night, we each kept it a secret. The concept of sharing her together was a foreign one. Times were different back then. It started to drive a wedge between us all. But then one night, she beckoned for all three of us. And we realized that the love we had for each other was stronger than our pride. It wasn't jealousy, it was an ache to be with each other. A need to share our desires."

Bailey swung her legs onto my lap. Her bare thighs against my jeans sent a tremor down my cock. I tucked a hand under her ass as she cupped my face in her hands. "And now? Do you ache for Poe and Grim when it's just me and you?"

I sucked in a breath as my erection grew. "It's different with you. The widow was trying to manipulate us. You, my love, are pure light. We love being together with you, but we are also content when you're alone with one of us. There's no question of who you love or desire because we know that it's all three of us."

Her violet eyes watered as she tilted her chin up to look at me. "With every fiber of my being. I was lost until I found you all."

I wrapped my arms around her and hugged her to my chest. "You can tell us anything, Bailey. Anything. We always have your back. Don't ever forget that."

She nuzzled her lips against my neck, leaving a trail of kisses up to my jaw. A growl escaped me as chills danced up my back. "*Little fox*," I rasped. "If you don't stop, I'm going to take you right here on the ground."

Her kisses found my lips, and she moaned as I slipped my tongue inside her mouth. We panted for air as our kisses deepened, starving for each other. Lifting her up, I gently placed her on the ground and nudged her thighs with my knee. "*Open*."

She arched her back and spread her legs wide as I nestled between them. The sight of her black lace panties stretched over her pretty pink pussy made me want to do unspeakable things.

I stroked her slit through the fabric. "I'm going to let the moon watch you cum tonight. Would you like that?"

"Yes… *please*," she whimpered.

I pulled her panties to the side and sucked in a sharp breath. My cock throbbed at the sight of her glistening cunt. Her legs twitched as I dragged the tip of my finger down her slit. "Fuck, you feel good. So slick."

"*Destroy me*," she breathed.

Fuck, yeah I will. "Such a good little girl letting me do dirty things to you."

I rubbed my fingers through her folds forcefully, smearing her juices all over the outside of her pussy as she cried out. I wanted her soaking wet. It made the sting that much sweeter.

"Uhhh, Saint. *Please.*"

I gave her quivering pussy a light slap. "I want you red and swollen for me."

She steeled her violet eyes onto mine and bit her lip. "Yes… *Harder.*"

I pinched her clit and released it before bringing my palm down harder against her pussy. I growled like a feral animal as she bucked wildly. I needed to taste and feel every inch of her. I clamped my lips down hard on her clit and sucked. "Mmm, so fucking tender."

I lapped up her juices, licking up and down her slit and down her thighs. I needed to taste more. Wanted to see her unhinged. A riotous moan rumbled out of me as I yanked her panties down. Her cunt was mine to play with. Mine to use and abuse. She flinched as I slapped her thigh. "Are you going to be a good little slut and take everything I give you?"

Bailey moaned, arching her back as I ripped her shirt open. Her nipples peaked as the cold air hit them. I pinched them hard between my fingers. "Use that filthy mouth of yours and answer me."

"Do whatever you want to me, daddy. I belong to you," she rasped.

Fucking hell. I grunted and unbuckled my belt. Her eyes widened as I slid it out of the loops of my jeans. "Oh, I'm going to need to hear you say that again." I slapped her pussy hard. "Who does this dirty cunt belong to?"

"*Uhhh.* It belongs to you, daddy."

My cock was pressing so hard against my jeans, it was about to split the seams. I wrapped my belt around her neck, poking a new hole in the leather so I could fasten it tight. She gasped as I buckled it. I wrapped the free hanging end around my wrist. "Do you like your new leash, little fox?"

She nodded and I yanked it again. "Tell me why I put this on you."

Her breath was shaky, her voice raspy from the leather constricting against her throat. "Because you own me, daddy. I'm your good little girl."

Fuck yes. I unzipped my pants and whipped my cock out. With my free hand, I fisted the tip and rubbed it around her clit in deep slow circles. I was so ready to cum, but I wanted to draw it out. I wanted our release to be agonizing.

Bailey rolled her hips as I teased her clit. She slid her fingers down her slit and peeled her flesh back. "*More.*"

"Mmm, good girl. Spread those lips back for me. *Wider.*" I dragged the tip of my cock down her slit and against the inside of her walls. Spasms fluttered down my shaft as the pressure built.

"*Oh, fuckkk.*" A burst of her cream landed on my hand as she squirted.

I smeared it over my fingers and licked it off. "Fucking delicious." I yanked on the belt, forcing her head off the ground. "I want you to taste it." She opened her mouth, and I shoved my finger inside. She moaned as she sucked her own cream off my finger.

"That's my dirty little slut." I spread her legs farther apart with my knees. "I'm going to break you open until your sweet little pussy cries."

"Yes, daddy. I deserve it..."

I couldn't hold back any longer. I needed to be inside her. To claim her right now in the dirt with my belt wrapped around her pretty little neck. "Yeah you do." I shoved my cock deep inside her.

"*Uhhh,*" she screamed. Her hips bucked as she rose to meet my force.

As my cock slid in and out of her tight cunt, every inch of my body tingled. I rocked into her, pulling on her leash as I pounded.

Sweat and cum dripped down our thighs as one orgasm slid into another. "I love fucking you like this. Mmm."

It was like shocks of electricity traveled down my shaft as her cunt swallowed me whole, taking every long and thick inch of me inside her. I hit the back of her pussy and slammed into her G-spot.

She cried out, her eyes rolling back in her head. "Right there. Fuck, don't stop."

"Yeah, that's the spot, isn't it?" I ground against her, moving in circles as her orgasm began to peak. She clenched her walls around my throbbing cock, so tight it was pushing me closer to the edge. The beast inside me was breaking free. That dark carnal part of me that I kept simmering under the surface. "Fuck being good, little fox," I growled. "Be a bad girl for me. Be my dirty little slut."

"Oh, fuck," she rasped. "Yes, daddy, punish me for being bad."

"Uhhh," I grunted as I pulled my cock out and flipped her onto her stomach. She trembled as I spread her ass cheeks apart. "Relax." I pressed my tongue against her taint and sucked.

A deep guttural moan burst out of her. "Oh, fuck."

I slapped her ass cheek hard, and she screamed. "Shh, relax." I inched the tip of my finger inside her anus. Fuck, it was so hot. Her knees shook as I massaged the flesh around her entrance. "Such a naughty girl, aren't you? *Yeah, you are*. You're going to show me just how bad you are."

She gasped as I slid my finger in a little deeper. "Yes, daddy. I've been such a bad girl."

I wanted every part of her. Wanted to infiltrate every fucking crevice of her body. She tightened around my finger as I got past the first knuckle. "Mmm. And this is what happens to bad girls." I slapped her ass with my free hand and thrust my other finger in deeper. She arched back and screamed again.

"I'm too tight… it won't fit. *Please*."

Fuck she was so scared and turned on it was all I could do not to lose control. I slid my finger in and out, obsessed with how slick she was. "You want me to stop, little fox? Hmm? I don't think you do. Tell daddy what you really want."

Her juices streamed down her thighs as she continued to rock her hips back and forth. "I'm scared."

I slowly inched a second finger into her anus. "You don't ever have to be scared with me, little fox. The pleasure I give you will take away all the pain."

"Oh, fuck. Fuck."

"Just breathe, Bailey. Relax into it." I pushed both fingers deeper, curling them up as I stroked.

She moaned into it and finally began to expand for me.

"Better?" I rasped.

"Yes... Oh, fuck."

I reached around with my other hand to rub her clit. "Yeah, you're ready now." I grabbed my cock and guided the tip inside her asshole. She started to clench again. "*Stop fighting it and open up for me*," I barked.

Bailey let out a deafening cry as I inched my way in. And I nearly came right there. Fuck. The heat inside her consumed me, the way her slick cheeks cradled my cock as I slid in and out of her tight asshole was unlike anything I'd ever felt. "That's my naughty girl. Taking her punishment so well."

She was almost hyperventilating as I burrowed my cock all the way in. "Yeah just like that. Stretch for me."

"Uhhh. Saint... I can't..."

I stroked the inside of her thighs. "I know it hurts, little fox."

She nodded, whimpering. "Yes..."

"Mmm. But doesn't it feel good too?"

She swayed her hips from side to side as I swelled inside her. "Yes, daddy," she whispered. "It shouldn't feel this fucking good."

She was so tight, so warm, I wanted nothing more than to fill her up with every drop of my cum. I pulled out a little and then slowly slid back in. She was opening up, her juices leaking out faster than ever.

"You like it when I rail you, don't you, little fox? You like how it feels to stretch around my cock."

She moaned deeper and rocked her hips back into me. "Yes. Don't you dare fucking stop."

I upped my pace, driving harder with each brutal thrust. All the blood rushed to the tip of my cock as I climbed the walls inside her. "Mmm, my dirty little slut. Fuck, I'm going to hurt you so fucking good."

"Yes, daddy," she cried out. She rammed her ass against me, urging me in deeper, and I lost all control.

"Fuck, Bailey. I'm… fucking coming." I grabbed her wrists and pinned them to the ground as I pushed my cock as far in as it would go. Crippling spasms gripped my shaft as I ground and twisted inside her ass, desperate to feel every inch of her swollen flesh.

"Saint, oh my god. *Uhhh.*" Bailey rubbed her pussy against the grass as she came, her legs twitching and shaking with each violent thrust.

"Such a good girl for daddy." I pulled out and cradled her to my chest.

Bailey gazed up at me, her eyes wild and feral. "Do you really think I'm a slut?"

My heart was racing. I wanted to bend her over and fuck her again. The flesh of her earlobe was cold as I took it between my teeth. "You're our little slut. Only for us. Do you like that?"

Her breath hitched and her nipples pebbled against my chest. "I shouldn't… but I do."

I nodded and stroked her silky blonde hair. "You want to be a bad girl for a while, little fox? Hmm? So we can take turns punishing you?"

Her cheeks flushed, and I could feel her juices seeping out again and onto my leg. This is what she needed. Not to be coddled or treated like an angel. Our little fox wanted to be defiled. She fucking craved it.

She swallowed hard before looking back up at me. "Y-yes," she stammered.

My cock was hard again. "The darkest parts of you will set you free. Tell me how vile, how depraved you want it. I want to hear those dirty thoughts out loud."

She drew in a sharp breath. "I want to surrender. I want to feel what it's like to be caged… punished… and violated. I want your demons unleashed. Every dark and dirty act you've ever wanted to do to me."

All the depraved things I longed for flashed in my head, stirring my cock. Hearing her ask for all of it was the cherry on top. I fingered the belt that was still wrapped around her neck. "Do you remember your safe word? I want to hear you say it."

She nodded, her eyes lighting up. "*Devil.*"

"Good. For the rest of the night, unless you say that word, you will obey our every command. We will give you what you want and take even more. But you have to surrender."

"I understand."

I tugged at her leash. "You understand what?"

"I understand that I have to obey you, daddy," she rasped.

A deep carnal ache stirred in my groin. I didn't know who was going to enjoy this more, her or us.

"From now on, you will not stand up unless we give you permission. You'll walk on your hands and knees." I yanked on her leash until she was on all fours. "Like a little fox."

She crawled behind me as I pulled on her leash and guided her back inside the house.

CHAPTER *Five*

Bailey

I was naked and raw, crawling through the foyer on all fours with Saint holding tight to the leash around my neck. I felt crazed, wild, and fucking alive. Every inch of my skin buzzed with anticipation. His cum still oozed out of my ass and down my thighs as he led me through the house.

This was my reckoning. My self-inflicted baptism by fire. I needed to go down a darker path before I could bask in the light. I had cravings, needs, and desires that most would find unspeakable. But not *them*. They would give me every depraved thing I asked for. As long as I surrendered. It is when I give up control in which I will truly be free.

Grim appeared before us at the top of the stairs that led to the basement. His eyes flickered with lust and malice as he gazed down at me. "Are you sure, little fox?"

I nodded. "Yes."

Saint handed him the end of the belt. "This is what she asked for."

Poe crept around the corner. He knelt down and took my chin in his hands. "My pretty little pet… You have no idea what's in store for you. But it will make you stronger."

Grim tugged on my leash. "Time to see your new room, little fox."

The cement steps would have felt colder if not for the numbness that was spreading through my hands and knees. Grim wasn't gentle as he dragged me down into the darkness. When we reached the bottom, fear danced inside my belly. What did I ask for? The room was dimly lit with candlelight and a few torches. There was a small mattress on the floor, no pillow, but a small thin blanket. A fire blazed in the hearth so I wouldn't freeze to death.

He removed the belt from around my neck, and I let out a deep breath. I hadn't even realized how much air it had been restricting. "Crawl to your new bed."

As I headed toward the mattress, a hard slap came down on my ass. I cried out, stunned.

"Faster," he growled.

I scrambled for the bed and just as my knees touched its scratchy surface, Grim was on me. He flipped me over, pinning me on my back. "I will ask you one more time… are you really ready to play this game?"

I was afraid but ridiculously turned on. "Yes, I promise. I want to feel these things. Possess me. Treat me like you own me."

"I do own you." He growled again and roughly grabbed my wrists. He took his time locking each one up in a metal restraint that was attached to a chain. The other end was secured to the

floor. Then he did the same to my ankles so that I was completely bound with no way to escape.

Grim stood and gazed down at me before turning away and heading back up the stairs. "We'll see how long you go until you break, little fox," he called down before he shut the door. I heard three locks click into place and then silence surrounded me.

I was alone, restrained, and I had no idea what would happen next.

It seemed like hours had gone by as I lay there shivering. I nodded off a couple of times, but a small creak would cause me to jerk awake, terrified someone was in here.

The longer they left me alone with my thoughts, the more my mind started to wander toward darker, more sinful things. I was at their mercy, and I knew them well enough to know that they would unleash their full depravity on me.

More hours went by, and I had no idea if it was night or morning. There were no windows or clocks here. I watched the candles flicker until they burned out. And then the torches. Not before long, the fire smoldered out and I fought multiple waves of panic. It exhausted me. I kept repeating, "*I'm safe*." Then just as I began to close my eyes and surrender to sleep, a hand gripped my thigh.

I gasped and tried to sit up, forgetting I was chained to the floor. "Who's there?"

The candles sprang back to life, as I met Grim's cold blue eyes. "You didn't think I'd let you sleep, did you?" His voice was gravelly.

I trembled as he crawled between my legs. He palmed my pussy, his hand cold as ice. "I can feel your pulse racing even in your cunt."

I squirmed under his touch, desperate for him to rub me. But he just held it there. "This is torture."

He smirked. "That is exactly what this is."

I whimpered as he removed his hand. "Grim, please."

"Shh. It's okay, little fox. I plan on doing dirty things to you."

He peeled back the lips of my pussy and stroked the inside. "So slick… so pretty."

I turned my head and moaned, my body trembling with need. His finger circled my entrance. The realization hit me. This was a game. And I had a role to play. Something came over me that instant. I pulled my legs together and scooted up the mattress.

Grim snickered. "Now this is going to be fun." He yanked my hips back toward him. I screamed as he pinned each of my thighs down with his knees. He shoved his finger deep inside my pussy. "Such a noisy little slut, aren't you? We'll have to do something about that."

A deep moan escaped me as he hit my G-spot. "Fuck, yes."

"Shut the fuck up." My breath hitched as he shoved a pair of my own panties in my mouth—the ones I'd had on in the garden, coated in my own cum. I took a deep breath through my nose as my nipples pebbled.

Grim leaned hard on my thighs with his shins. "Fuck, you are a sight right now." He unzipped his pants and pulled out his cock. "Look how fucking hard you make me."

My belly fluttered as I watched him stroke himself. His smooth fingers traced up and down his shaft. He grunted and growled as he worked himself faster. I watched with a hunger. With an ache. I moaned into my panties as his cum burst out in thick hot ropes. He jerked himself off over my pussy, his hot cum dripping down into my slit like warm honey.

"Mmm… so wet and sticky." With two fingers he smeared his cum all over my folds.

I bucked my hips at the sensation. It spread tingles through my body. *Oh, shit…*

His eyes darkened. "I know you want my cock but little sluts like you don't get what they want."

I groaned in frustration and tried to curse at him through the cloth.

He chuckled as he reached for something next to the bed. "I'm going to fuck you with this instead."

My heart raced as he held up a large dildo. He dragged the tip of it down my slit and then slapped it against me. He laughed as I flinched. "Don't take your eyes off what's happening. I want you to see everything."

He pulled the lips of my pussy back and inched the dildo inside my entrance. "Uhh, look at how beautiful that is. Fuck. Sliding back and forth."

Oh, fuck. It was the most erotic thing I'd ever felt. I watched as he worked it deeper into me, feeling its thick ridges against the walls of my cunt. I rocked against it, needing to come undone.

Grim scissored his fingers up and down my pussy while he pushed the fleshy dildo farther in. "This might be my new favorite toy. *Fuck*… Yeah, move your hips. Just like that."

Pressure began to build in my clit as I fixated on the soaking wet dildo sliding in and out of me, my flesh pink and swollen with need. Another deep moan burst out from my throat as an orgasm rolled through me.

He increased his speed, thrusting harder. "You like being fucked like this, don't you? Nod yes for me, or I'll stop."

I screamed into my panties, nodding feverishly.

"That's my good little slut. So fucking eager to please me." He pressed down on my clit and began twisting the dildo around, grinding it in circles. "Time to cum for Daddy Grim."

Stars blurred in my vision as he stimulated both my clit and my G-spot. A rush of adrenaline spiked through my veins as I pumped my hips furiously up and down, chasing my orgasm. I cried out as it hit me, and the floodgates opened. The more I clenched and writhed around it, the harder and deeper he pushed, deepening my orgasm.

"That's my good little slut. Ride that fucking cock. Mmm you look so fucking dirty." He pulled out the dildo and wedged it underneath me, so its length was cradled in my ass.

My chest heaved as I felt every nerve in my body tingle.

Grim painted his name on my belly with my own cum. "*Mine*."

I groaned as he lifted off of me, my thighs aching from his weight, and no doubt bruised. "Sweet dreams, little fox."

Panic started to set in again as he walked to the stairs. I screamed through the panties, but he just chuckled as he left me there bound, gagged, and with a dildo wedged between my ass cheeks. The more I tried to wriggle away from it, the deeper it burrowed. And it sent new tingles down my thighs.

Holy shit. I was exhausted, swollen, and frustrated because I was more turned on than ever.

I woke to droplets of water bouncing off my stomach. My eyes flew open and locked on Poe.

"Bailey, you're filthy. Let's get you cleaned up." He grinned like the devil as he rubbed my belly with a cold washcloth.

Poe might have been the gentler one, sweeter and more sensual, but make no mistake he was just as psycho as Grim and Saint. I opened my mouth to speak and then remembered I still had my soiled panties in it.

"What was that, little fox?" He reached over and snatched them out.

I gasped as air hit my lungs. "I have... to... pee."

Poe chuckled. "Don't worry, love. I'm going to get you sorted. First, let me wipe all this filth off you."

His green eyes flickered with need as he took his time wiping every inch of me with the washcloth, spending extra time on my pussy. I did have to pee, but it was stirring a new ache inside me.

He reached underneath me and pulled out the dildo slowly,

making sure it rubbed against every tender inch of me. "Mmm," he moaned as he sucked on it. "Delicious. I want you to taste it."

Oh, fuck. "Poe…"

He climbed on top of me, straddling my chest. "Be a good girl and open up or I'll make you choke on it."

I moaned as he slid the dildo into my mouth, sucking as he worked it in and out. "*Good fucking girl,*" he whispered.

Yup. Just as nuts as the other two. And I fucking loved it.

He unzipped his pants and pulled out his cock. "I'm getting a little jealous, little fox. I want you to suck me like that."

I loved Poe's cock. It was smooth and always hard for me. I moaned again as he thrust his thick veiny cock into my mouth.

I gazed up at him, his green eyes wild with lust, and watched him peel off his shirt. He was fucking beautiful with his black hair and tan skin. His muscles were thick and hard.

He reached up and grabbed onto a wooden beam to angle himself as he slid in and out of my mouth.

I twirled my tongue around the tip of his cock, eliciting growls and grunts from him. "Do you like when I use your body for my own pleasure, little fox?"

Tears streamed down my cheeks as he hit the back of my throat, gagging me. With my hands bound, there was nothing I could do to control this. And it made me feel crazed with lust.

He cupped his balls and growled as his pace quickened, one hand still gripping the beam overhead. "Mmm, fuck yeah. I'm coming for you now, little fox. Swallow every drop for me."

His cock throbbed and released hot liquid in my mouth. He cried out as I lapped it up, drinking it down like holy water. "Mmm," I moaned. "So fucking good."

He fingered my swollen lips. "Such an obedient little captive." Poe reached over and unchained my wrists. "Let's get you cleaned up now." He moved to the foot of the mattress and released my ankles as well.

Everything hurt. Poe had to help me sit up because my muscles were so weak. "I give you permission to stand up, little fox. There's a bathroom over there. Go sort yourself out."

I nodded and almost collapsed when my bare feet hit the cold cement floor. "Fuck."

I stumbled over to the bathroom door, my heart sinking as I entered. This was the only part of the house we didn't renovate. *And now I regret that decision.*

With only a small sink and a cracked toilet, there were gas station bathrooms that were nicer than this. No mirror, no shower or bathtub, no lock on the door… Nothing humanizing about it. I sighed as I peed, wishing I had the comforts of my ensuite upstairs.

I shook my head. No. This is what I wanted. What I asked for. To be stripped bare and raw. To detach from the familiar. If they could break me open, then I could be reborn anew. Every instinct I had told me this was the way through.

There wasn't any toilet paper but luckily I found a small washcloth to wipe myself with. I examined the bruises on my thighs. Grim's marks on me. Despite the soreness, my clit tingled as I remembered the way he worked that dildo inside me. It was fucking hot.

Poe opened the bathroom door and fisted my hair. "I think you're done in here, little fox."

I whimpered as he dragged me out and threw me on the mattress. I tried to scramble off when another pair of strong hands pinned me down. Blonde hair, ice-cold blue eyes. *Grim was back.*

"Remember your safe word, Bailey?" Poe asked.

Moisture pooled between my thighs. "Y-yes."

Grim shackled my wrists back to the chains while Poe did the same to my ankles. They nestled in next to me on either side, both fully naked.

Warmth flooded me as I breathed in their scents. Anticipated their touch. I needed them like I needed air.

Poe pinched one of my nipples between his fingers and rubbed back and forth. "Who's in control, Bailey?"

I arched my back as waves of pleasure spilled out from my breasts and down my middle. "You are," I breathed.

Poe pinched harder, massaging my nipple till it was bright red. "Look how she swells for us. You want a taste?" he asked Grim.

"Mmm. Such a needy little slut." Grim wrapped his lips around my nipple as Poe continued to rub it like he was feeding it to him.

I moaned as the two sensations rocked my core. "Oh, fuck. Don't stop. Please."

Poe chuckled. "We have no intention of stopping. This is just the beginning of your sweet torture."

Grim growled as he came up for air. "Give me the other one."

Poe moved to my other nipple and pinched, doing the same as before, while Grim sucked and scraped his teeth across it.

I was burning up. Every sensation magnified by the slow and agonizing rhythm of their movements. It wasn't gentle but it was drawn out and deliberate. They were going to make me feel every single touch.

Poe traced his fingers between my breasts and down my belly. I trembled as he rested his hand right above my clit. "Open her up for me."

I sucked in a sharp breath as Grim inched down and peeled the flesh of my pussy back. "So wet…"

Poe moaned as he slid his finger down my slit before pushing it all the way inside. "Mmm and so tight."

I bucked as a deep spasm rocked through me. "*Uhhh.*"

"We're going to make you cum so fucking hard." He grabbed a pillow that hadn't been there before and wedged it underneath my hips, propping me up at a forty-five-degree angle.

"What are you doing?" I asked, my adrenaline spiking.

Grim sucked the length of his finger and slid it underneath me. "*Destroying you.*"

"Wait. Wha—"

I cried out as Grim shoved his finger inside my anus. With my ass in the air, they hovered over me, watching as they each took turns thrusting in and out.

I couldn't breathe. The pressure built from both sides as I felt it in my belly. It was fucking animalistic.

"Do you like that, little fox?" Poe growled. "You like both of us filling you?"

I nodded as I rolled my hips back and forth—up as Poe fingered my pussy and back down onto Grim's finger in my ass. Like a fucking see-saw.

"Fuck. I can't take it anymore… I'm…fuck… coming." My breath caught in my throat as my core exploded into not one but two orgasms at the same time. Grim wrapped his hand around my throat and squeezed as my juices gushed out, drenching my legs, their hands, and the mattress.

"*Yesss,*" I cried out, panting.

Grim covered my lips with his and kissed me hard. Our tongues swirled around each other's in a frenzy. "*Bailey*… you're so fucking hot."

Poe replaced Grim's lips with his own and kissed me just as deeply. He nibbled gently at my lip. "Have you had enough, little fox?"

They were like my drugs. I was insatiable. "Never," I murmured.

My stomach grumbled as scents of vanilla and sugar hit my nose. I looked up to see Saint standing at the foot of the mattress with a tray of pastries, juice, and coffee. "You have had enough for now. Time for us to have breakfast together."

I didn't realize how hungry I was until the food was right in front of me. "Smells amazing."

Once Poe and Grim unshackled my wrists, I started forward, but they held me back. "Not so fast, little fox," Poe purred in my ear.

Grim snickered. "You didn't think we were going to let you feed yourself, did you?"

Saint's eyes darkened as we locked eyes. "Tie her to the chair."

My heart raced. "Why the chair?" I was getting used to being in bed.

Grim snickered. "Because we don't want you choking on anything other than our cocks."

Oh, fuck.

After they finished feeding me, I was shoved back onto the old mattress. My thighs were bruised, my pussy swollen, and I could barely hold my eyes open.

I curled myself into a ball. "I need to sleep."

Grim wrapped his hand around my throat. "We'll decide what you need. Get on your knees."

Fuck, I was exhausted. "Grim, I can't anymore tonight. Please."

Poe snickered as he took off his clothes and sat in the chair facing us. "Be a good little girl and put on a dirty show for me."

Grim yanked me forward, forcing me onto my knees. "You said yes to this, now fucking do as you're told."

Saint slid up behind me and squeezed my hips. "Have you ever had two cocks inside you at the same time, little fox?"

My heart fluttered with fear, my stomach tightening. "No," I whispered.

Grim's eyes darkened as he lay on his back. "Get your pussy around my cock right fucking now."

I trembled as Saint nudged me forward. I straddled Grim, lowering my swollen pussy onto him. I gasped as his cock swelled inside me, my juices instantly leaking despite the soreness. I let out a little whimper.

Saint rubbed my back as Grim throbbed inside me. "Hold still for Daddy Saint, little fox. This is going to hurt like hell."

Panic flooded me. My legs began to shake. "Wait. I'm not ready. I'm already full." Grim's cock had already stretched me wide. I couldn't imagine having Saint's enormous cock in my ass again. Especially at the same time.

Grim slapped my leg. "It isn't up to you anymore. You gave up control of your body the night you said yes to us, little fox. Now relax and open up for him or it will hurt more."

Tears streamed down my cheeks. I wanted this but now I wasn't so sure. I was scared of who I was becoming. Saint pushed me forward till my breasts were pressed against Grim's chest. He stroked my ass, his fingers kneading my cheeks and probing my entrance. He rocked my hips into Grim who ground against me.

"Fuck yeah, push her down onto me. Are you sure you don't want this? You're fucking soaking wet."

He was right. It felt so fucking good. And the danger, the fear of what Saint would do to me from behind only added to it.

"Fuck…" Saint murmured as he slipped a finger inside my ass. "Like a fucking oven."

He began working his finger in and out, the way he had in the garden. I squeezed around Grim's cock. "Uhhh," I moaned.

Saint pushed his finger deeper. "That's it. Just like that. The more you clench, the harder I'm going to cum."

Tingles spread down both my slits, a throbbing unlike any I've ever felt before. I needed release. "Mmm, more," I moaned.

Saint lined his cock up to my ass and pushed himself in.

CHAPTER *Six*

Grim

Bailey threw her head back and screamed as Saint's cock slammed into her ass. Fuck, she looked hot. I pinched her nipples. They were so fucking pink and hard. Her nipples weren't small either. Just the way I liked them. A little bigger than a quarter.

Her pussy was so wet. So fucking tight. I could feel every inch of her on my cock. And as Saint pounded her from behind, it inched her deeper down my shaft. We rocked her back and forth between us.

I reached down to play with her clit. "*Good girl,* Bailey. *Good fucking girl.*"

Saint and I locked eyes as he hammered into her porcelain white ass. He was a beast. A feral animal. The more he grunted and growled, the harder it made me. The more it made me want to be punished by him too.

As if reading my mind, he reached down between us and cupped my balls. "You like that?"

I nodded and spread my legs farther apart. "Squeeze harder. You know I like it rough."

He smirked and shoved a finger in my ass. I let out a deep moan as he burrowed it all the way in. He bucked hard into Bailey, shoving her down my cock. She grounded against me, her moans getting deeper.

"That's it, baby. Cum for us. Mmm." As I rocked into her, Saint added another finger into my ass. "Fuck… yeah. Yeah, don't stop."

Poe climbed onto the bed and got on his knees. He cried out as he jerked himself off. As his cum spurted out in thick hot ropes, he sprayed it over my stomach and across Bailey's breasts.

"Fucking filthy." I smeared his cum across Bailey's chest.

"I'm coming," Bailey rasped.

Saint fisted her hair and yanked her head back as he pounded into her ass harder. "Cum, baby."

The sight sent me over the edge. My cock pulsed with need. With release. I felt it rush forward and just as Bailey let out a scream, I flooded her pussy with my cum.

She clenched around me as I drove forward.

Saint worked her in circles, grinding deep as he chased his orgasm. He growled as he came, his fists squeezing her ass cheeks till they were bruised. She was filled with so much of our cum now, it oozed down her thighs. And it was fucking beautiful.

Bailey collapsed onto the bed, draping herself across Poe. "Fuck," she murmured.

Saint eyed me hungrily. He wasn't finished. Not even close. I gave him a wink and flipped onto my stomach. With his and Bailey's cum still coating his cock, he slipped easily into my ass.

"Oh, fuck," I grabbed onto the edge of the mattress.

Poe wrapped his arms around Bailey, pulling her to his chest. "Watch, little fox."

I kept my gaze on her as Saint's massive cock stretched me. I was so fucking hard I could have cut a hole in the mattress. "Play with yourself for me, baby girl."

Bailey's breath hitched. She spread her legs and slid a finger down her slit. Poe pulled her pussy lips back. "Oh baby, look at you. Fuck. Show Daddy Grim how deep you can get that finger of yours."

I licked my lips as I watched her finger disappear in between her folds. "In and out, little fox. Finger fuck yourself *hard* for me."

"Yes, daddy," she rasped. Poe kept her pussy peeled back as she worked that creamy finger of hers in circles around her clit and then back inside her sopping wet pussy.

Saint slapped my ass as he drove in harder. I bucked against him. *Fuck.* "Is that all you got?" I taunted him.

He snarled and smacked me harder.

"*Fuck,*" I yelled. I loved the pain. *Fucking loved it.*

"Is that hard enough for you?" Saint grunted.

The ridges of his cock pulsed and throbbed deep inside my tender flesh, rubbing, and swelling against me until it felt like my insides were on fire. I pushed myself up to my knees and fisted my cock. I stroked in slow rhythmic motions, squeezing my shaft from base to tip.

"I wanna cum with you," I moaned.

"Fuck. Right there. *Fuuck.*" Saint smacked his hand down on my ass as his thick hot cum filled my ass.

"Oh, fuck. Mmm, yeah." I jerked myself furiously and another load came barreling out, soaking the mattress underneath me. "*Ahhh, fuck yeah.*"

Bailey's moans erupted soon after as she watched Saint cum inside me. She pumped her finger faster, arching her back into Poe as he pinched down on her clit. She rolled her hips as a deep guttural cry wrenched out of her.

The four of us lay there breathless, watching each other. Looking over every inch of each other's bodies. It was never enough. I could fuck them over and over again.

But Bailey did need sleep actually. We rode her hard today.

I scooped her up in my arms. "Let's get you back in your real bed, little fox. You did so good today."

She nodded, her eyelids fluttering.

After we tucked her in upstairs, we went into the ensuite bathroom to clean up.

Saint stood behind me. "Here let me clean up my mess." He ran a warm washcloth between the folds of my ass, sending another shiver to my cock. As rough as he was, he could be gentle too. Sometimes it was the softer touches that I fucking craved. After I tasted the pain.

"If you keep doing that, I'm going to fucking need to cum again," I rasped.

Poe chuckled as he jumped into the shower. "Like that would be the worst thing," he teased.

Saint kicked my leg out, forcing my stance to widen. He reached up underneath, grazing my balls with the washcloth. He ran it up and down my thighs in slow circular movements. My stomach tightened with need. Fuck.

I gripped the counter. "It's been a long time since you touched me like this. Bailey brings out your softer side."

Saint reached around and fisted my cock. "I know you like slow torture. The fucking agony of feeling every nerve on your body come alive."

I closed my eyes and took a deep breath as he stroked me from tip to base, my lips quivering. "Yeah… keep going just like that. Fuck."

I heard the shower curtain slide open and knew Poe was

watching. That was his thing. And I loved putting on a show. I leaned back into Saint's chest as he unraveled me. His grip was strong and firm as he squeezed my cock with every jerk. The blood rushed to the tip of my cock, sending shockwaves to my core. I moaned louder as he wrapped the washcloth around my balls with his other hand. He inched it up, toward my ass, tugging it between my cheeks. My knees trembled as every ounce of pleasure was drawn out.

"Fuck. I'm coming. Harder," I rasped, my mouth dry.

Saint bit down on my shoulder and growled. "I want to feel your dirty hot cum all over my hand. Right fucking now."

"Uhhh… Fuuck." My cum burst out as I hit my peak. It was too much. My vision blurred as my orgasm rocked through me.

Saint held my cock in his hand, stroking it gently as I rode the orgasm out. "Fuck, your cum is so hot. So thick. Mmm, I just want to keep playing with you."

"Fuck, we're never going to leave this bathroom if we don't stop," I panted.

Poe stepped out of the shower and wrapped a towel around his waist. "I could watch all night." He eyed my cum soaked cock still in Saint's hand.

I arched an eyebrow at him. "See something you like, Poe?" I teased.

He licked his lips. "You know how much I love the taste."

I nodded and propped myself up on the counter. I fisted my cock. "Help yourself."

Poe slid his mouth over the tip of my cock and moaned. "Fuck."

I leaned back against the mirror and closed my eyes as he licked and sucked all my cum up. It stirred my cock again, of course. I plunged into his mouth as it became clear that I was as hard as a rock.

Saint chuckled as he left the room. "I'm going to crawl into bed now, boys. See ya in a few."

I nodded, barely hearing what he said as Poe worked his full lips up and down my shaft. He gripped my thighs, digging his fingers into my flesh.

I ran my thumb across his lips. "Fuck, Poe. I forgot how good you are at this."

He lightly scraped his teeth up my shaft, sending shivers all the way down to the balls of my feet. "Oh yeah, just like that."

As another orgasm gripped me, I cried out and held Poe's head down in place as I filled his mouth with more of my cum. My legs shook as he moaned and flicked his tongue over the tip of my cock, sucking me like I was a fucking popsicle.

"Shit, man. We gotta get some sleep."

Poe wiped his mouth with his hand and smiled. "We can sleep when we're dead."

I rolled my eyes at him but couldn't help but laugh. "Fucking Poe. We are dead, man."

His eyes darkened for a minute. "I know but ever since we found Bailey, I feel more alive than ever."

He was right. She brought all this out in us. Helped us find that joy again.

I cleaned myself up and slid into bed with the others. Bailey was out, purring in her sleep practically. Just one look at her pretty pink nipples made my cock hard again. *Fuck no, go to sleep, Grim.* But if it were up to me, I would fuck her and them all night.

"Is she still sleeping?" Poe asked as we crowded around the breakfast table.

I nodded into my cup of coffee. "Yeah, we wore our little fox the fuck out." I often wondered what she dreamed about. With all that chaos in her head, I imagined her sleep wasn't as peaceful as it looked.

"We need to talk about her fear of the house," Saint grumbled.

Ever since she moved in, she'd been feeling like there was something else lingering here besides the three of us. But none of us had seen or felt anything. *Not saying that she's imagining things, but fuck I don't know…*

"We've been trapped here for a long time, and we've always been alone," I quipped.

Saint stood and looked out the kitchen window, his eyes glazing as if his thoughts were a million miles away. "Yeah, but we were also confined to one room until Bailey set us free. It's a possibility that something else could be in here with us. Could have been here this whole time."

I rubbed my jaw, irritated that we were even having this conversation. I didn't want our girl to lose her mind, but she has her demons. "Like what, Saint? Daisy Wickford? That bitch left us here to rot while she crossed over. I hope she's in fucking hell, though."

"Who the fuck knows, Grim? This house has been here for a long time. Longer than even we've been tied to it. But if something is freaking Bailey out, we need to listen."

Poe was awfully quiet as he putzed around the kitchen. I watched as he hummed to himself over a big bowl of pancake batter.

"Aye, Poe? What do you make of all this?" I asked.

He shrugged and kept stirring. "Bailey is going to be so happy when she wakes up. Chocolate chip pancakes are her fucking favorite."

I threw a look at Saint. "That's awesome, Poe. But do you mind joining the current conversation Saint and I are having?"

Poe sighed. "Look, I don't know if we should be worried or not. Let's just be there for her when she needs it. But if she thinks we don't believe her, she'll start shutting us out."

Fuck. The last thing we needed was for her to pull away. Bailey trusted us with her body, but did she trust us with her mind? With her heart? Our lust-fueled year hasn't lent any time for too many deep discussions. I wasn't one to complain about that. Talking about my feelings wasn't at the top of my list of things to fucking do. But I didn't want her to feel like she couldn't.

"Let's just keep an eye out. If there is some other fucking spirit lurking about, it's avoiding the three of us on purpose," Saint spat as he finished up the rest of his coffee. "And if it's even half as depraved as the three of us, Bailey will be in fucking trouble."

The ladle clanked against the ceramic bowl as Poe dropped it. "That's not going to fucking happen. No one hurts our little fox but us."

We nodded in agreement, a silent pact to keep what's ours safe and secure.

And if I find any other vile creatures in here besides us, I'll fucking burn this house down before I let it have her.

CHAPTER *Seven*

Bailey

Everything ached as I stretched out beneath the thick duvet. My wrists were rubbed raw from the restraints. The flesh between my legs was tender. My pussy was fucking tingling still. I should be feeling shame right now. At least that's what I'd been raised to think.

The nuns at Wickford Hollow Orphanage would be trying to perform an exorcism on me if they knew what I'd done last night. What I *let* them do to me. But I felt none of that. Only gratification. It's only in the throes of my release in which I truly felt free.

I could feel hot breath on my neck and the weight of a strong body pressing into the mattress behind me. A smirk pulled at the corners of my lips as I tried to guess which one of my guys it was. Just when I thought I was getting good at this game, one of them would surprise me and I was always shocked to find it was not whom I'd thought.

My pussy spasmed at the touch of his hand against my back, moisture pooling in my core. I leaned back and giggled. "If I guess correctly, do I get a reward?"

Silence. *Oh, he's playing hard to get.* All right, I could play too. I pressed my ass against his middle, satisfied that his cock was as hard as I hoped it would be. "Saint?"

His hand traveled lower. He traced his fingers delicately around my tailbone. I squirmed against him. "Poe, please. Don't toy with me."

I started to turn my head, but he grabbed the back of my neck and held me in place. Oh, for fuck's sake this *was* torture. His cock pulsed against my ass and my nipples pebbled. This had Grim written all over it.

I pulled the top of my nightgown down and reached for his hand. He sucked in a sharp breath as I guided his fingers to my nipples. "Play with me, Grim."

He chuckled as he squeezed my nipple between his fingers and pulled upward. "You guessed wrong, little vixen. You lose. What's *my* reward?"

Oh fuck. My stomach tightened. His voice… it wasn't any of my guys. I whipped around and gasped. Dirty blond hair, slicked back. Blue-green eyes, as clear as the sky right before it starts to rain. Tattoos covering every inch of him, all the way up to his chin.

Panic flooded every cell in my body as he lay there calmly, smiling like the devil.

I pulled up my shirt, realizing my nipples were still hard. "Who the fuck are you?" I rasped.

He propped himself up on his elbow and smirked. "I'm the monster under your bed."

Fuck.

My knees trembled as I took a cautious step back.

He scrambled off the bed like an animal, like a predator, and charged toward me.

I couldn't move. Couldn't run. My feet were betraying me. So I closed my eyes and screamed.

The door to my bedroom burst open.

"Bailey!" I heard Poe shout.

Strong arms wrapped around me, and I shrank down onto the floor. "Bailey, open your eyes. It's me, Saint. It's okay."

I looked up and saw his beautiful hazel eyes and burst into tears.

Grim paced my room, throwing open the closets and peeking underneath every piece of furniture. "What happened? Did someone break in? Who's put the fear of the mother fucking devil in you?"

"Easy," Saint growled at him. "Bailey, are you okay?"

I shook my head, my face now a sniveling mess of snot and tears. "I-I don't know who he was. He was in the bed. I thought... I thought it was one of you."

Poe's face paled. "What did he look like, Bailey?"

Grim snickered. "Are you serious? She was obviously having a nightmare or something. There's no one else in this house but us."

Anger welled in my chest. I jumped to my feet and before I knew what I was doing, I slapped him across the face. "Fuck you, Grim. How dare you. I know what I saw. He was here in this room."

Grim grabbed me by the throat and pinned me against the wall. "There's only one way in this room, Bailey. There's no way a man could have gotten out without us seeing him."

I glared back at him. "Unless he's like you."

"Let her go right fucking now, Grim," Poe snarled.

My heart raced as Grim, and I stared each other down. "Not until she accepts the fact that she's sleep deprived and might be imagining things."

"Fuck you," I whispered again.

Poe grabbed the hand that Grim had wrapped around my throat. "She's not. Let her go."

Grim squeezed my neck tighter before letting out a frustrated grunt and releasing me. "What the fuck are you going on about, Poe?"

Poe sank down onto the bed. "I've seen him too… I know who he is."

Saint's nostrils flared as he towered over him. "And you are just telling us now? Who is stalking our little fox in *our* home?" he asked through gritted teeth.

Poe's face was damp with a fresh sheen of sweat. "Raine Wickford. Daisy's husband… She killed him too. He's like us."

Grim clenched his fists and stood over Poe like he wanted to punch him. "And what the fuck does he want?"

I whimpered. "I think he wants me."

The three of them turned to look at me as if they just remembered I was in the room.

"Did he touch you?" Saint asked, his chest heaving.

I nodded. "I thought it was one of you…"

Grim charged toward me and pushed me back against the wall. He raised his hand to my throat again but stopped. "Fuck this."

"Grim," I pleaded.

"No," he called back as he stormed out.

Saint glared at Poe. "Everyone needs to take a moment. But you better tell us everything you fucking know later." He followed after Grim and didn't even look at me.

Fuck.

I felt like everything was crumbling. But it wasn't my fault. They wouldn't listen. And now Raine Wickford was getting more aggressive.

Poe cradled his head in his hands. "I'm sorry, Bailey. This is my fault. Fuck. I'm so sorry."

"I'm not safe here anymore," I whispered. Raine could get to me anywhere in this house. But what scared me more was my pull to him. Maybe I wanted him to get to me.

Poe rushed to me, and I let him wrap his arms around me. Maybe because he was the only one who wasn't angry with me for getting assaulted. "Don't say that, little fox. You know we will protect you. I'll fix this. I promise."

My old friend shame began to creep back into my veins. That feeling of being alone and misunderstood was threatening to pull me under and drown me once again.

I nodded, but I was retreating within. I needed to shut down if I was going to survive this. "I'm going to shower and then I'm going to pack a bag."

He cupped my face in his hands, desperation running wild in his eyes. "Bailey, no, please don't leave. We can figure this out."

"Oh, my sweet, Poe. I know if anyone can it's you. I'm not running away I just need to clear my head. Maureen has been bugging me about a girls' night anyway. I still have the keys to my old house. It will just be for a night or two."

He let out a deep sigh. "All right, my love. I promise everything will be better when you get back. You have my word."

I brushed a strand of hair off his forehead. "Don't make promises you can't keep."

I threw my bag over my shoulder and headed for the front door, which was being blocked by Grim. "Bailey, wait."

My eyelids fluttered. He was so fucking beautiful. Even when he was angry. "I just need some space."

He ran his thumb over my bottom lip. "Don't forget who you belong to when you're out there."

I rolled my eyes. "Is that what you call an apology? Fuck off, Grim. Would it kill you to say something sweet for once?"

He stepped into me and pressed his cold palm to my chest. "Nothing can kill me because I'm already dead. And you know I don't do *sweet,* Bailey. You're lucky I'm even letting you walk out of here."

I shook my head and snickered. "You're not the only one who's ever felt trauma or pain or had a shitty fucked up life. But you're the only one who seems to think that entitles you to act like a fucking prick. I love you, Grim. Maybe try to figure out if that means anything to you while I'm gone."

His lip quivered and his breath hitched. We stared at each other for so long, I thought we would never stop. And then he stepped back. "Go… before I lock you in my room and show you what it means to be loved by me."

I looked around once more, hoping that Saint would come to say goodbye. He didn't. I fought back the urge to cry as I walked out the door. Maybe things that are too good to be true are just a lie.

I called Maureen on my way into town. I had to pick up some supplies for the house and told her to meet me at the store. I hadn't been back to my old place since I'd left. We would need food, and I was going to need lots of fucking alcohol. She was so excited to spend a night with me, it broke my heart that I couldn't match her level of excitement. I was happy to spend a drunken night with my best friend but the shit that just went down at Wickford dampened my mood like a dark cloud.

I pulled up in front of the market and hopped out, eager to get this little shopping trip over with. As I perused the aisles, the whispers and stares commenced. Didn't these fucking people have anything better to do? They looked at me like I was the devil. And for what? Because I bought an old house with inheritance money? I get that my life was strange, but I'd never been anything but kind and polite to them.

I went straight to the wine aisle first, placing four bottles of red in my cart. I eyed a bottle of tequila for a few seconds before throwing two of them in as well. Fuck it. Twenty minutes later, I had stocked my cart with all my favorite snacks: chips and dip, cookies, frozen pizza, fancy cheeses, crackers, and of course eggs and bacon for breakfast tomorrow. I couldn't cook like Poe, but I did live on my own for most of my adult life. I knew how to make a few decent meals.

There was still no sign of Maureen by the time I reached the checker. That girl would be late to her own funeral someday. I chuckled to myself. I was already feeling lighter at the thought of getting drunk and eating junk food with my best friend. Sleepovers at her house when we were younger were still some of my favorite memories. No matter how old we got, we still acted like silly teenagers when we got together. I didn't realize how much I missed it until now.

The checker pursed her lips at me as she rang everything up. "Problem?" I asked.

She was maybe eighteen years old with bottle- blonde hair and long pointy pink fingernails. I remembered her from elementary school. Quiet, shy girl until she discovered drugs and booze. Now she had the audacity to look at me with judgment?

She rolled her eyes as she scanned the last item. "That'll be one fifty-two, ninety-seven."

I snickered as I inserted my credit card into the machine. "Sure. Whatever."

The guy bagging my groceries threw her a look. She cleared her throat. "Is it true your house is haunted?"

I punched in my pin number and sighed. "This whole town is haunted."

Her eyes widened. "What is that supposed to mean?"

I grabbed my bags off the counter. "Haunted by ignorance and hate."

The checker muttered under her breath, "*Crazy bitch.*"

My hands clenched around the bag handles. But it wasn't worth it.

As I stalked off, I could hear them laughing.

Fuck them. I wasn't going to let them ruin my night. After everything that happened this morning at Wickford, I just couldn't take any more drama. I needed to have fun.

I shoved my bags in the trunk, slammed it shut, and stepped back into a wall of pure muscle.

"How's it going, Bailey?"

Adrenaline coursed through my veins as I spun around and came face to face with Billy. "I'm not in the mood for your shit today, Billy."

There was a time when I used to think he was handsome. He was popular in high school, captain of the football team, and all that shit. But over the years, I've come to find him disgusting. He pushes people around and has no respect for anyone. Especially women.

Billy didn't budge an inch. He placed his hands on my trunk, boxing me in. "Looks like you're having a party. Am I invited?"

I could feel the heat rising in my cheeks. My heart was racing. I glanced around, looking for someone to make eye contact with. For anyone to see that this man was assaulting me. But everyone kept their heads down. Just like they did in the diner the other day when he smashed French fries in my face.

"Leave me alone, Billy. I'm just trying to get home and make dinner."

A snarl took over his lips. He stepped into me, letting me feel the weight of his chest against mine. Showing me he was stronger. "You know one of these nights, you're going to cook me dinner. Right after you take my cock in your ass."

I dug my fists into his chest and pushed but he wouldn't move. "That's never going to happen. Now get the fuck off me."

Billy wedged his leg between mine, lifting it up as he ground his thick thigh against my pussy. "Oh, come on, Bailey. Don't play hard to get. You and I both know you've been dreaming about my dick since freshman year."

I was going to be sick. I squirmed back but he had me in an iron grip. "Please, stop. I'm not interested in fucking you."

He pinched my arms. "No one says no to me. No one. Especially not sad little sluts like you. I bet your ass is so loose, I'll slip right in." He hovered his lips over my ear, his breath reeking of whiskey. "I bet we could get two cocks in there. You'd like that, wouldn't you, slut?"

All my rage and fury boiled up inside me. "Get the fuck off me!" I screamed.

He laughed as he stepped back, releasing me finally. "Are you gonna cry, Bailey? You know that only makes my cock harder."

I clenched my fists. "No, I will not be shedding one fucking tear for you." Before I could stop myself, I swung my arm with every ounce of anger and adrenaline I had. A loud pop sounded as I connected with his mouth.

His eyes widened as he stumbled back. "You fucking bitch!"

I fumbled for my keys and backed up toward the driver's side of my car. "Stay away from me, Billy."

He spat blood on the ground, his lip swelling up like a balloon. "You know, I was just messing around but now I'm fucking pissed. After I fuck you, I'm going to kill you."

My hands started to shake as he lunged forward and grabbed me by the hair. I screamed as he pinched my jaw between his fingers with his free hand. "You're going to regret punching me, slut."

"Get off her!" Maureen shouted from behind him.

I fought down the bile that was rising in my throat and looked past him to see Maureen sprinting toward us in her stiletto boots.

Billy shoved me back against the car door and spun on her. "You should find better friends, Maureen. This one just moved to the top of my shit list."

She whacked him with her purse. "And you're at the top of

mine. Now leave her alone or else I'll have you thrown in the drunk tank."

He laughed and threw up his hands, mocking defeat. "That's right, run to daddy like you always do, Maureen." He walked backward, glaring at me the whole time. "I'll be seeing ya real soon, Bailey. That's a fucking promise."

My whole body trembled as we watched him walk down the street and turn right back into the bar. I'm sure he was telling all his buddies right about now how much fun he had terrorizing me in broad daylight.

Maureen grabbed my hand. "Are you okay? Did he hurt you?"

There would be bruises on my arms soon, no doubt. And my scalp was tingling from the grip he had on my hair. But his words hurt me more. His threats. And for the first time in my life, I wanted to kill someone. I wanted to kill Billy.

I sucked in a sharp breath. "I'm fine. He's just a fucking asshole. Let's just get out of here, okay? I need a drink."

Maureen nodded but the worry in her eyes was obvious. Billy just went from being a harmless prick to an actual threat. "Yeah. Fuck him. We are still going to have fun tonight. I promise."

My hands were still trembling as I lifted my keys. Maureen grabbed them. She opened the trunk and pulled out the bottle of tequila. "I'll drive, Bales. You just relax and sip on this. It'll take the edge off."

I nodded and climbed into the passenger seat. She drove us through the back country roads, away from the main part of town, the music blasting, as I took slow long pulls of tequila.

CHAPTER Eight

Bailey

The kitchen counter was covered in snacks, booze, and makeup. I hadn't been to this house in so long, I had forgotten how much I had loved living here. It was my safe place. My parents had left it to me when I turned eighteen. I'm sure they had no idea that they wouldn't have been around to see that day.

I try not to think about the fire. I was so young, my memories of it are pretty hazy. I remember the smoke the most. The thick, gray, suffocating smoke that invaded my lungs. And then there was darkness. Endless darkness. When I finally came to, I was in Wickford Orphanage. It happened so fast, even the nuns seemed surprised to find me in one of the beds.

The police reports were jumbled and didn't make sense. Statements were redacted and signatures blurred. I vowed to move on and never look back. So when I found out that my parents had another property for me to inherit, I was over the moon. It made me feel closer to them without all the tragedy attached to it.

Maureen handed me another shot of tequila and a semi-burnt mozzarella stick. "Where do you keep disappearing to, Bales? You're here but like you're not."

I downed the shot in two seconds. "Just missing my parents. Did you talk to your dad?"

Her face fell. "Yeah… I wish I had more to tell, but he got so annoyed that I even brought it up. He said we should leave the past in the past and move on. I'm sorry, Bales."

My stomach knotted. *Why wouldn't anyone in this town talk about the fire?* "It's all good, Maur. Thank you for trying."

She hopped up on the counter next to me. "You know, we never talk about them anymore. We actually never talk about anything deep. I feel like you're shutting me out sometimes."

There were so many things she didn't know. Ugh. "I know. I'm sorry for that. There are just things that I haven't been able to say out loud. Like if I do, they become all too real."

Maureen smoothed her hands over her miniskirt. The dark red tips of her nails were perfectly polished. She was always so put together. A stark contrast from the hot mess that I had become lately.

"You know you can tell me anything, right? We've been best friends for as long as I can remember. Come to think of it, I don't even remember the first time we actually met. But it's been our whole lives. Nothing you say will ever make me stop being friends with you."

I squeezed her hand. I believed her but I was still so afraid. "I know. It's just harder for me. I'm the town freak, but you've always stood by me. I love you for that."

"And I always will. I love you too, Bales." She hopped down off the counter and went for the blender, pouring in a shit ton of tequila and margarita mix. "So, what are we going to do about Billy and Chad?"

I took one of the limes and began slicing it, imagining I was slicing into Billy's flesh with every swipe of the knife. "I don't know. We can't go to your dad. They'll just deny it and then it will only piss them off more. I'm going to avoid him for the rest of my life."

Maureen snorted. "Fuck that. You have every right to walk as freely as he does around this town without being harassed every ten steps. That piece of shit needs a taste of his own medicine."

I rimmed our glasses with the limes before dipping the edges into a plate of salt. "There's not much we can do. Billy's dad is head of the city council. If we start shit with him, he could make our lives miserable. Well, mine at least."

Maureen poured the margaritas into our glasses and handed me one. "He's the one who's started shit. We just need to finish it."

I chuckled as she pursed her lips. Sometimes I wished I had even half of her tenacity. She was so confident and sure of herself. "All right enough about that asshole. Let's get drunk and watch something scary."

We clanked glasses and each took a big gulp, nearly choking after the first sip. Maureen coughed. "Fuck, I think I went overboard with the tequila."

I laughed. "You think?" My eyes were watering from the sting of it.

After watching two horror movies and downing the entire bottle of tequila, Maureen and I slumped on opposite sides of the couch, our feet tangled together.

Whether it was newfound bravery, liquid courage, or just a deep ache to be able to talk to my best friend about my love life... I finally cracked.

I sat up a little, my head buzzing. I blinked a few times to make sure Maureen didn't actually have two heads. "Okay," I sighed.

Maureen groaned as she pulled a fuzzy blanket over our legs. "*Okay* what? My head is fucking spinning by the way."

I laughed but my palms were sweaty. My stomach knotted. "I never told you the whole story about what happened that night we broke into Wickford Mansion."

She shot straight up. "I knew it! Ow." She gripped the back of the couch. "Fuck, I really hope I don't throw up. Okay, tell me more."

This was going to be hard, but I have to do it. "Something pushed me into that door, Maur. At first, I thought you were playing a prank on me. But I looked out the window and saw you outside, three floors down. There was no one there. But I felt the force of hands pushing me forward."

Her eyes widened. "Seriously? What the fuck? What was it?"

My head was just as scrambled as hers. "I don't know. Well, I mean I kind of figured it out later. But now I'm second-guessing myself. Anyway, it freaked me out. I felt strange after. My entire body broke out in chills."

She shifted forward even more. "That's why you didn't want to come to the party."

I nodded. "I felt like something was… watching me. I just wanted to go home, take a shower, and go to bed. I thought that I could shake that feeling if I just got away from it. So that's what I did. Except the superstitions were true. Something was watching me… and it followed me home."

Maureen gasped. "Oh my god, Bales! What happened? Were you hurt?"

I sat up and pulled the blanket to my chest. I looked around the room, remembering Poe, Grim, and Saint's introduction into my life. "No. They didn't hurt me."

"They? Holy fuck, Bailey. Please tell me what happened."

I shook my head. "I don't want you to think I'm crazy."

She scooted toward me and gathered my hands in hers. "Bitch, I'm your ride or die. I'll never doubt you or think you're crazy. Please, you can trust me."

I inhaled a sharp breath. "Okay, here goes. When I was pushed into that door at Wickford Mansion, I unleashed three spirits. They followed me home, dragged me out of bed, and said they wouldn't leave unless I gave them what they wanted."

Maureen's eyes widened again. She swallowed hard. "What did they want, Bailey?"

The fact that she hadn't even blinked at the fact that I said ghosts and not actual living boys, gave me the courage to continue. "Me. They wanted to do things to me. With me. I was terrified at first. But that was my own shame trying to talk me out of it… I wanted them too. And so I said yes."

"We're going to need more tequila for this." Maureen leaped off the couch and ran to the kitchen.

She was right. My admission basically shocked us both sober. "Bring the chips too," I called after her.

Within two minutes, Maureen was back with everything and nestled back under the blanket across from me. "Okay, spill the tea. I want every detail."

I laughed as I took a pull of tequila straight from the bottle. "It was crazy. They awakened parts of me that I didn't even know were there. Like all my darkest and dirtiest fantasies."

"Did they take turns? Was there group sex? Please, your horny friend who hasn't gotten laid in over six months needs to know these things."

Maureen hung off my every word as I described all the ways that Poe, Grim, and Saint defiled me. The leash, the spanking, the way Poe ate a peach out of my pussy. I told her everything. Even about the curse.

"And by the end of the night, Maur, I knew I wanted to keep them forever. So I called my lawyer and had her make arrangements for me to buy Wickford Mansion. Because of them. That's why I don't leave that often. I've been terrified that you'll think I've lost my mind. That's why I haven't invited you over."

Maureen stared at me dumbfounded for a few minutes. A second longer and I would start to think my fears were coming true. But she finally released a deep breath and smiled. "Bailey, you naughty little vixen. I fucking knew you had it in you. I'm so jealous right now, I can't stand it. Happy for you, but fuck do I need to find my own haunted house filled with ghosts who want to worship my body."

I laughed out loud. A deep genuine laugh that I hadn't released in a long time. "I'm so relieved you know. I hated keeping this from you."

Maureen nodded. "Thank you for telling me. I get why you were scared. It's a lot. But I hope this just proves to you that I'm truly your best friend. No matter what. So… you've been living with them for almost a year now. Everything still kinky and nasty over there?"

I snorted. "If you're asking if the honeymoon is over, it's not. But there are some other issues going on. That's why I called you last minute for a girls' night. I needed to get some space from that house."

Maureen took another sip of tequila, clearing her throat as she swallowed it down. "What kinds of issues? What do ghosts fight about?"

I bit my lip, unsure on how to say another strange thing out loud. It made it all too real. "We aren't the only ones in the house. There's another spirit. I felt something the moment the renovations were finished. The guys thought I was just adjusting to living with them. But I could feel a different energy. This morning, I woke up to another ghost in my bed. Raine Wickford."

Maureen gasped again. "Another one? Fuck. It's like you've hit the hot ghost lottery. He *was* hot too, right?"

My stomach knotted. There were so many things I was afraid of. But maybe if I did say them out loud, the fear and anxiety would go away. "Yes," I breathed. "Raine Wickford is fucking hot. But I feel wrong thinking that. I'm with Poe, Grim, and Saint."

Maureen whimpered as she fanned herself. "I don't know, Bales. They are already sharing you with each other. What's one more? If that's what you want, of course."

Butterflies swam in my stomach at the thought. "Yeah but I don't know if *they* want that. Besides, Raine is unhinged. The look in his eyes was… feral. He's been taunting me for almost a year in the shadows. Making me think I was going crazy. What if he's an evil spirit that wants to hurt me?"

Maureen raked her hands through her curls, twisting them around her finger as she contemplated my predicament. "*Or*, what if he wants in on this relationship you've got going on? He hasn't hurt you so far. Maybe he's just been watching and waiting for the right moment."

I sighed. "Poe knew he was there the whole time and didn't tell the rest of us. So there's that too. That house is full of secrets and shadows and creepy corners. I worry that we're all keeping things from each other now. And I hate it."

"Sounds like you need to sit down with all of them and hash it out. You need to talk to Raine too. Find out what his intentions are. You've sacrificed a lot to be with them, they really haven't. So maybe it's time they do."

I already felt a hundred times better talking to her about this. I was internally kicking myself for not trusting her with this in the first place. I shot across the couch and threw my arms around her. "Thank you for believing me."

She hugged me back. "Always."

I tucked myself under the blanket next to her and rested my head on her shoulder. "Ugh, I can already feel the hangover coming for me."

She giggled. "Yup. But nothing that bacon and eggs can't cure in the morning."

As I tried to drift off to sleep, I wondered what my guys were up to tonight. Were they missing me as much as I missed them? Were Grim and Saint still pissed at me for letting Raine touch me? Was Poe okay? Were they fighting? My brain raced with these thoughts until I thought I might explode.

"Go to sleep, Bales. Everything is going to be okay," Maureen whispered.

CHAPTER
Nine

Poe

There were secrets between us. And I'd been keeping the biggest one.

This house was too empty without Bailey in it. She needed space though. I hoped a night away would be enough. The guys and I had gotten so used to it just being the three of us for so long. Now that Bailey was in our lives, I couldn't imagine it without her.

I should have fucking told them about Raine. *I feel like such an ass*. Bailey knew in her soul that there was something else lurking about, and I didn't say a fucking word. A part of me hoped he would go away. That he'd leave her alone. But our precious little fox was too irresistible. I should have known he'd stalk her like a fucking psycho.

Daisy Wickford warned me about him all those years ago. She told only me. Grim and Saint were too hot-headed to listen. So she told me the whole story about how she killed her husband. I should have warned them about that too. Because we ended up just like Raine Wickford. Dead and trapped in a house that continued to consume us.

But I was a selfish prick. I wanted to keep fucking Daisy. And so I kept her secret.

The war had done a number on all of us. I was a short-order cook on a ship, so I didn't see too much fighting. But the ones who did, the ones who died, had been my friends. That scared the shit out of me. I saw firsthand how short life could be. Couple that with months upon months at sea… well, it made me a horny bastard who couldn't wait to fuck the first woman I saw.

So when the war ended and I landed a job cooking at Wickford Mansion, I didn't protest one bit when Daisy started showing up naked in my room every night. Grim and Saint had already been living there for a few months before me. She was going to their rooms too. When all three of us realized it, we made a pact to share her. It stirred carnal cravings inside us we didn't know we had. We took turns fucking her. We watched each other fuck her. And everyone was fucking happy. Until we found out she was batshit crazy.

I knew deep down that Grim wasn't pissed at Bailey. He's just scared. Terrified that she's losing her mind in here just like Mrs. Wickford did. The guilt I've been carrying for keeping these secrets was eating me up inside now.

Daisy was crazy before we ever got here. She killed her husband, and I didn't say a fucking word. This whole mess was my fault. Grim, Saint, and I could have left before she did it to us. If they had known and I hadn't been thinking only with my cock, we could have gotten out of this house.

But as fucked up as it sounded, we would have never met Bailey if we hadn't been murdered in this house. For that reason alone, I didn't have too many regrets. Only that I kept these secrets from them for so long.

I could hear pacing outside my room. "Come in already or go away."

The door creaked open and Grim popped his head in. "She's not back yet."

I stood from the bed and reached for my clothes. "Relax. She's probably sleeping in. You know how drunk she gets when she's with Maureen."

He leaned in the doorway, watching me as I zipped up my jeans and threw a black T-shirt over my head.

"How long have you been lying to all of us?"

I froze, my shirt still around my neck. "A long time," I rasped.

Grim's eyes flashed with contempt and hurt. "Saint's waiting for us downstairs in the parlor. We expect you to come clean about everything."

I nodded as he slammed my bedroom door behind him.

"Why have you been keeping me a secret?"

My heart raced. I spun around to see Raine perched on my windowsill. "Fuck off. I'm not in the mood for your shit. Actually, I could ask you the same thing. Why have you only shown yourself to me and Bailey."

He smirked. "Because I know you're a selfish little bitch who wouldn't dare do anything to upset your sweet little family unit." He licked his lips. "And as for Bailey… I've been watching that pretty little cunt of hers for a while. Thought it was time to finally show her what she's been missing."

I charged over to him. "I don't like this fucking game you're playing. I accept the fact that we're all stuck here together, but Bailey is off-limits. She belongs to us, not *you*."

Raine stood up and looked down at me, his nostrils flaring. "I say we let Bailey decide that. You know, just like she did with you three. Oh, wait, she didn't really have a choice in that, did she?"

I didn't care that he was taller or bigger or even crazier than me, I would not let anything happen to our little fox. "You don't know shit about us. Bailey is happy here. Or at least she was until you ambushed her in her own bed."

He stepped into me, forcing me back. "Don't be so sure about that, Poe. Your sly *little fox* has some secrets of her own."

Something about the way he talked about her hit a nerve. I shoved him back. "Well, *this* secret is out in the open. Everyone knows about you. Good luck sneaking up on Grim and Saint now. They're not as patient as I am. Which reminds me, I need to go downstairs before they lose their shit."

Raine laughed. "Yes, run along, Poe. You're good at that."

I bit my tongue. I had wasted enough time indulging this psycho.

"He wants Bailey," I rasped.

The fire blazed in the hearth. Saint leaned over it, stoking the flames with a metal poker. The flames created a glowing reflection against the walls. It was midday but winter was on its way and the days were growing shorter. The sky was gray and provided little light through the windows.

Grim paced behind him. "We'll get to that in a minute. First, tell us why you've been lying to us for over a hundred years."

When he put it like that, it made me feel even worse. I shrugged. "Self-preservation. Fear of rocking the proverbial boat. Fuck, I don't know anymore. If you tell a lie enough times you can start convincing yourself it's the truth."

Saint jammed the poker back into its stand with a loud clank. "So Mrs. Wickford killed her husband, told you about it, and you said nothing. I understand that part, actually. It's fucked up, but I get it. We were young men back then. We'd seen horrors in the war. And you didn't want anything to fuck up your new comfy situation."

I nodded as he continued, taking a seat across from me on the overstuffed couch. "What I don't understand is how you could let Bailey think she was losing her mind this past year. How you let us look like assholes every time she tried to convince us there was someone else in this house. We rocked her world. Took her from her life and promised her safety and love. All the things. And yet you kept this from *her*."

"Yeah, how is she supposed to fucking trust us now?" Grim growled.

They were right. I was a complete and utter asshole. "I'm sorry. I thought that I could keep him away from her. That he would, I don't know, grow bored and leave her alone. I wasn't thinking clearly. And it was selfish of me. I see that now. But all those years ago, I didn't really believe Mrs. Wickford. And then after what she did to *us*… I was even more afraid to tell you. Besides, Raine didn't start showing himself until Bailey moved in."

Saint's eyes darkened. "Well, I'm guessing he didn't have too much love left for his wife after she murdered him. But Bailey is fresh meat to him. A craving to be satiated. He didn't have much use for us then, but now…"

"Now he wants our little fox," Grim snickered.

I shook my head. "That's not going to happen. Maybe we can find a way to bind him to one of the rooms, just like that witch did to us."

Saint sucked in a sharp breath. "There are two problems with that idea, Poe. One, we don't know any witches. And two… we don't know what Bailey wants."

My heart sped up. "What the fuck does that mean? She ran out of here the second he showed himself to her. There's no way she wants him too."

Grim braced himself against the hearth and gazed into the

flames. "No. She ran out of here because of how *we* reacted. We didn't even stop for one second to ask her how she felt. This is all our faults… You didn't see the hurt in her eyes when she left."

"No, I didn't. My stubborn ass didn't even bother to say goodbye. Fuck. I wouldn't blame her if she didn't come back," Saint murmured.

Fuck. This was a disaster. How did we get from pure happiness to this hot mess in just the span of a few nights? We had her right where we wanted her. With us. She was ours to play with, to defile, to love, and to worship. And we fucked it all up.

"She'll be back." I nodded, reassuring myself as well as them. "Bailey loves us. She won't abandon us."

Grim slowly turned to each of us. "And when she does, we need to remind her why she said yes to us, to begin with."

CHAPTER Ten

Bailey

My tequila hangover was worse than I'd anticipated. But I needed to let loose. And after telling Maureen everything about my life, I felt lighter and freer than ever. It was as if a weight had been lifted and no amount of dehydration or nausea was going to ruin that.

I took a deep breath and headed inside Wickford Mansion. I didn't know what I was expecting to find, but seeing Grim and Saint sitting in the foyer was not it.

I glanced around waiting for Poe or that psycho Raine to come barreling out, but neither of them appeared.

"Hi," I murmured.

They both stared at me like they'd seen a ghost. The irony of that thought was not lost on me.

I threw my keys on the foyer table and dropped my bag on the floor. "I told Maureen everything. We drank too much, stayed up too late, and I feel like shit. But I'm happy to be home."

Saint rose from his chair and rushed me. He threw his arms around my waist and hugged me to him. "I'm sorry I didn't see you off, Bailey. It was selfish of me." He pulled away and looked down at me with so much sadness in his eyes, it physically hurt my chest. "I'm happy you had a night away with Maureen. Do you feel better now that you've told her?"

A huge smile took over my face. "I should have done it sooner. You were right. She loves me and there was no judgment there."

He hugged me again. "We have a lot to talk about, but it can wait till later. You look like you could use a hot shower and some rest."

I looked past him to Grim, who hadn't budged from his chair. "Wanna walk me to the kitchen? I need water and a sandwich."

Saint kissed me on the forehead. "I'll leave you two to it then."

Grim grabbed my hand as I passed by him. "Just come to my room when you're done."

I nodded, my belly fluttering. He was so hard to read. I couldn't tell if he was relieved to see me or still pissed that I'd left.

With still no sign of Poe or Raine, I devoured my turkey sand-

He terrified me and yet stirred a deep ache in my loins at the same time.

No matter how much time had passed, or how many nights we'd fucked each other, this man could unnerve me and hold me in place with just one look. He was rough and brutal and dominant. Thinking back to that first night when he rubbed himself raw… the way he squeezed my throat, dripping his cum all over me… my clit tingled.

"See something you like, little fox?" he rasped as he glared down at me.

"You're still angry, aren't you?" I asked, my fingers trembling against the doorframe.

I knew the vile things Grim could do to me. I'd dreamed about them. Craved them. And I wasn't even ashamed to admit that sometimes I defied him on purpose. I needed his viciousness like a drug.

He dipped his fingers below my waistline and tugged the hem of my jeans, pulling me flush against him. The scent of smoke and soap and cloves enveloped me. I breathed it in deeply, welcoming it like it was my only salvation.

"Little fox… I'm angry about so many things right now. And I just want to take them all out on you."

I swallowed hard. "Are you going to punish me for leaving?"

My heart fluttered as he closed the door behind us and slammed me back against it. "You have no idea the disgusting things I want to do to you."

A breath caught in my throat. "And what if I run again?" I liked these sick little games too much. We both knew I wasn't going anywhere.

"I've got you cornered, little fox. *Nowhere to run.*" He pulled the strap of my tank top down, exposing my left breast.

My breath hitched. "Maybe I'll scream."

Grim worked the strap off my other shoulder until both hung

around my elbows. He towered over me, gazing down at my swollen nipples. "Oh, I'm going to make you fucking scream all right. Your throat will ache so bad the only thing you'll be able to swallow for the next week is my cum."

I shivered as he unbuttoned my jeans and slid the zipper down. The muscles in his forearms flexed, the veins protruding like chiseled stone. I wanted to drag my tongue across each one. Wanted to lick the salt from his skin like a cat.

"Are you going to be a good girl for me tonight, Bailey?"

I whimpered as he dipped a finger inside my panties. He dragged it up and down my wet slit. I tried to clench around him. To trap his finger there so my pussy could feast on it. "*Grim, quit teasing me*," I breathed.

He wrapped a hand around my throat and squeezed. "Answer me, Bailey. Are you going to be good for me?"

I pushed out my hips, urging his finger in deeper. "Yes. *Always*."

He drew his finger out of my aching cunt and then shoved it back in with a hard jerk. I stumbled back, my knees buckling. He held me up by my throat, pinning me against the door. "I'm going to punish you for taking so long to answer."

I snaked my hands across his bare chest, tracing his tattoos with my fingers. His breath hitched as I dragged my nails over the perfectly carved lines in his abdomen. "Promise?"

He shoved a second finger inside my pussy with such force it almost knocked the wind out of me. Or maybe it was his hand around my throat squeezing the air out of my lungs. Either way, I didn't want him to stop. "I'm going to hurt you so good, little fox."

I moaned as he added a third finger. It was getting harder to breathe inside his grip. But with each sip of air I worked to inhale, the tingling in my pussy intensified. It was like walking on a tightrope without a balance bar… or even a net. Like I was teetering somewhere in between heaven and hell. One more step and it could be the death of me.

And Grim knew exactly what he was doing.

A deep spasm spread between my folds. I clenched around his fingers, twitching as my orgasm began to climb. I closed my eyes and chased it.

Without warning he released his grip on both my neck and my cunt. "Not yet, dirty girl. You're gonna have to work for it tonight."

I let out a frustrated cry. "*Grim,*" I whined. "*Fuck.*"

The most mischievous smirk pulled at the corners of his lips. "The brattier you are, the more I want to pry your pouty lips apart with my cock."

I panted against the door, my throat still scratchy and dry. "Do you want to hear me beg for it?"

Grim fisted my hair in his hand and pushed me down to the floor. "Only if you're on your knees."

Fuck this was hot. I loved the way he pushed me around, taking from me whatever he wanted. I kneeled in front of him and sucked on my lower lip. "*Please, Grim.*"

His eyes blazed with a sadistic hunger. He sat on the edge of his bed and patted his thigh. "Take off your soiled panties and crawl to me."

I couldn't get my jeans off fast enough. Once I was completely bare-assed, I charted my path to him, stalking on all fours with nothing but a thin tank top hanging from my arms. My nipples pebbled as he watched me crawl to him like a trained animal.

As I reached him, he fisted my hair again in his hand, tugging my head back so I had to look up at him. "That's a good fucking girl."

His praise sent another wave of tingles to my core. He pulled my top all the way down to my waist and tied it in a knot behind my back, trapping my arms inside.

"Do you like taking away my freedom?" I cooed.

Grim pulled the strands of my hair tight between his fingers. He leaned over and yanked my head toward his. "*I* am your fucking freedom, baby girl."

He eyed my wet lips for a split second before covering them with his own. His tongue darted past mine with a vengeance. He sucked and scraped at my lips like he was out for blood. Like he was starving for human flesh. And he was.

I moaned into his kiss, arching my back to angle him in deeper. He fumbled with his own pants as we crushed our mouths harder together, bruising our lips. He unzipped them with one hand and pulled out his smooth, hard cock.

As our lips broke free from each other, he leaned back, his hand still tangled in my hair. He fisted his cock with his free hand. "I know you're thirsty, little fox. You're going to swallow every drop, aren't you?"

Cream leaked out of my pussy and slid down my thighs. I licked my lips before wrapping them around his swollen tip. Grim was not gentle with me so I wouldn't be with him. I took in the length of him at once, lightly scraping my teeth against his ridges as I worked my mouth down to the base of him.

He shuddered and moaned. "Ohhh, such a good girl. Yeah, fuck. Just like that."

I sucked him like a popsicle, twirling my tongue around his tip every time I pulled up. He might be a spirit trapped between heaven and hell, but his cock was pure flesh and blood, pulsing in my mouth like a heart jacked up on cocaine.

He pinched my chin hard between his fingers. "*Drink,* little fox."

My eyes teared up as he shoved his cock all the way to the back of my throat. A riotous moan erupted from him as he thrust hard and fast between my lips. I could barely breathe, but I didn't want him to stop.

He twisted and turned in circles, grinding against my mouth as his cum filled me. I fought the urge to gag as it rushed down my throat, breathing through my nose so I wouldn't choke.

"Oh, you're taking it so good. So. Fucking. Good." He gripped the back of my head, holding me in place, as he rode out his orgasm. Tears streamed down my cheeks as he unloaded every drop.

After a few more grunts and moans, he pulled out. I coughed as I struggled to regain my breath. But before I could take another one, his hand was around my throat again.

He squeezed hard. "Don't ever fucking walk out on me again when you're pissed off."

I glared up at him. "You walked away angry first."

His grip loosened as he pulled me onto his lap. "It won't ever happen again."

I wriggled out of my tank top and wrapped my arms around his neck. "Is that your idea of an apology?"

"No, this is." He lifted me up and threw me onto his bed. My breath hitched as he shoved my legs apart, spread my pussy open, and ran his tongue up the length of my slit.

I moaned, shivering as he licked and sucked. "Oh, fuck. *Grim*… apology… accepted."

"Mmm, you taste so fucking good. I'm going to fuck you with my greedy tongue."

I arched my back, my hips rolling, as he shoved his tongue all the way in. His soft, thick lips nipped at my flesh as his tongue slid in and out.

I cried out, panting, stars blurring my vision with each agonizing thrust. With each slippery glide of his rough tongue. "Shit. Grim. I'm going to cum. Fuck."

He ground his mouth against my pussy, while pressing down hard on my clit with his thumb. He rubbed back and forth, sucking, kissing, nibbling, and flicking.

I was practically levitating off the bed.

My pussy spasmed from deep within, my adrenaline spiking, as tingles spread out from my core and took hold of every muscle in my body. I clenched around him, screaming. "*Fuuck, Grim.*"

He pulled out and dragged the tip of his tongue up and down

my length as I gave in to my orgasm. "Good girl. So fucking hot for me."

I convulsed against his mouth, rocking my hips up and down as the pressure released.

"I love watching you cum. Your bare pussy all slick and swollen for me."

I took deep breaths in the aftermath, my core still spasming. I started to pull my legs together, but he knocked them back open. "No. Not yet. Just lay there spread open for me."

I watched him, watching me. For almost two hours, I lay there naked and sprawled with Grim nestled between my legs. He didn't have to touch me to turn me on. Just seeing him gaze hungrily at my pussy as if it were his last meal, was enough to send my heart racing and my juices flowing.

We both had been angry, but this was where I belonged. With him, Poe, and Saint. Even if we still weren't ready to divulge *all* our secrets.

CHAPTER Eleven

Poe

I couldn't relax until I knew Bailey was back home. Relief filled me when I heard her heels click across the foyer. Heard her go into the kitchen and then into Grim's room. But I still couldn't rest. Not with Raine roaming around in the shadows. Not without speaking to Bailey first.

We usually slept together, all of us, in Bailey's room. So being in separate beds tonight felt strange. Like I was missing a limb or something. There was a deep ache festering that made me sick to my stomach.

A light knock rapped on the door. "Come on in, Bailey." I could smell her sweet scent as soon as she approached.

The door creaked open, and she sauntered in, dressed in silk pajamas. "Hi," she purred. She looked tired but the smile on her face loosened the knot in my chest.

I patted the bed, motioning for her to sit next to me. "Hi, beautiful."

She curled up next to me, her sweet scent invading my senses even stronger. "I missed you."

I wrapped my arm around her. "I take it you and Grim made up. Did he apologize?"

She giggled, her breath hitching. "Yes, he certainly did."

I chuckled. Knowing Grim, I'm sure he went above and beyond groveling. And seeing how she was clenching her thighs together, he most likely did it in the most devious way.

"Good. How was your night with Maureen? You two have fun?" Bailey was a hard woman to read. She kept so much locked away in that beautiful head of hers.

She nodded against my chest and took a few deep breaths. "It was nice being back in my old house. So many memories there." She threw a leg over mine. "I told Maureen everything. And she was so supportive. I should have confided in her ages ago."

I planted a kiss on the top of her head. "That's fucking awesome, Bailey. I knew she wouldn't let you down. It's good to have friends like her. Friends like that will never abandon you."

She sat up and looked into my eyes. "Are they still mad at you?"

I loved how selfless she was. Always thinking about everyone else's happiness before her own. "Don't worry about us, little fox. We've had many fights over the years. Nothing we can't come back from."

"Have you seen… *him* since I've been gone?" Her eyes were wide with curiosity, not fear. That told me what I had been suspecting. She wasn't afraid of Raine. She was afraid of how we'd react to her asking about him.

I nodded. "I did. He came in here, asking about you."

She sighed. "Why didn't you tell me about him before, Poe? I don't understand."

My heart ached. I hated that I kept secrets from her. "I don't know. No. That's not true. I thought that if I said his name out loud then it would summon him to you. As I told Grim and Saint, I never saw him before you moved in. Mrs. Wickford confessed to me one night that she killed her husband. She claimed he was abusive and that she did it in self-defense. I didn't know about ghosts or spirits at the time. I believed her, kept her secret, and thought that was fucking that."

Bailey pulled her legs up to her chest, curling herself into a ball. "And did he abuse her? Was any of that true?"

I could tell my answer was crucial to her decision on getting to know him, but I didn't have the answers she needed. "That's something you're going to have to ask Raine, yourself, little fox. All I know is that he started showing his face after you arrived. He's been watching you this whole time. *Watching us*. What's fucked up is that he's been here as long as me, and the guys and we never fucking knew. How he managed to stay hidden for so long is a mystery. I would have been bored out of my fucking mind if I were him."

She fidgeted with her hands, looking down at the sheets. "I think he was the one who pushed me into the door that night. On Halloween Eve when I set you three free. I kept trying to convince myself that I tripped but I know what I felt. Something shoved me forward, and I collided with the door so hard, it broke open."

I had suspected it myself but didn't want to say a word until I knew for sure. "I think Raine needed us to be free. He needed us to find you so that you could restore this house. And I think he wanted you from the moment he caught your scent on the stairs. You're not crazy, Bailey. I'm so sorry I let you think you were."

A long silence fell between us as she smoothed her hands back and forth over her legs. I watched her, desperate to know every thought that was racing through her brain. But I didn't want to push her. She'd already been through so much.

Finally, she looked up at me and smiled. "It's okay, Poe. I'm not mad at you. I understand that it came from a place of love and fear."

I pulled her back to my chest. "My sly little fox. I don't deserve you. None of us do."

Bailey slid her hand down my stomach, fingering the edges of my sweatpants. "Let me show you how much I missed you."

A rush of adrenaline spiked through my veins as her soft fingers dipped below my waistband and wrapped around my cock. My breath hitched. "Oh, how I fucking missed you, little fox."

She gripped my cock tight in her palm and stroked in slow movements, taking her time as she worked her way down to the tip.

"Let me see what you're doing down there." I pushed my sweatpants down and kicked them off.

"I love how hard you are for me, Poe," she rasped.

I spread my legs wide apart and gazed down, admiring my hard cock in her tiny hand. She moaned as if she were getting more pleasure than she was giving. I fucking loved that.

"Take off your pajamas." Her body was fucking gorgeous, and I wanted to see every inch of it while she touched me.

She removed her top and bottoms, making a slow and deliberate show of it. Her pink nipples pebbled as she climbed on top of me. There was something about her movements, her seduction, that stirred something deep inside me. I had defiled her plenty. I had done things to her that were unspeakable. But in this moment, all I wanted was the most sensuous parts of her.

She leaned down and pressed her lips to mine. I kissed her slowly, gently sucking on her lips and tongue. I moaned into her mouth as her nipples grazed my chest, tickling my every nerve. "Take control, little fox. Take whatever the fuck you want from me."

She moaned as she kissed my neck, tracing her tongue across my collarbone. My cells were on fire, my muscles burning from the slow friction. I caressed her back softly using only my fingertips. Goosebumps spread underneath them.

"Poe," she rasped. "You feel so good."

I wrapped my hand around her neck, gently without pressure. Just held it there as she rose and looked down at me with fire in her eyes.

"You're fucking perfect, my love."

She placed a hand on my stomach to steady herself and inched her fingers inside her pussy with her other hand. I almost fucking came right there. I watched as she played with her wet cunt. It was slow and gentle, and it drove me mad.

"Do you like this, Poe?" Her voice was deep and throaty. Like the ache that I felt in my chest.

I slid my hands down her chest and cupped her breasts, holding them without force. "Yes, little fox. Keep going just like that."

She slid her hand in between us and fisted my cock, rubbing the tip up and down her folds, moaning every time I pulsed.

"Mmm, baby, you're so wet. *Fuck.*" It was like torture and yet I loved every second of it. I hadn't even realized how much I needed this with her.

She lifted up and angled my cock to her entrance. I watched as she used one hand to part her pussy lips back and the other to insert the tip inside.

We both gasped as she slid all the way down to the base and stilled. I panted for breath as the heat of her pussy, the tightness, sent spasms up and down my shaft. I held her hips in place, careful not to move too much or else I'd cum in three seconds.

She bit her lower lip, sucking it into her mouth as she stretched her pussy around my cock. "I can feel every inch of you… *Fuck.*"

I locked eyes with her, the carnal ache inside me growing. "I love filling you."

She let out a little whimper as I throbbed inside her. I grabbed her hips and gently rocked them forward. "Oh, shit. *Yeah.*"

She ground her clit against my abdomen as I guided her body. I was so fucking deep inside her. It was different from any other time before. The softness, the slow and gentle way we rocked together, it was as if we were no longer separate. We were one being consumed, swallowing each other whole as if time didn't exist and there was no space left between us.

Bailey lifted herself and pulled back slowly, holding herself in place as she teased the tip of my cock with her entrance. Fucking hell, it was the most erotic thing I'd ever felt in my life.

"Fuck, Bailey, what are you doing to me?" I closed my eyes. I didn't want to watch, for once. I wanted to *feel*, to smell, to taste every fucking piece of her. My senses were so heightened, I could barely breathe. Could barely hold it together.

"Don't cum yet," she breathed. "Let it build until you think you might die unless you release it."

She glided back down, and it took every ounce of willpower I had not to explode. I bit down hard on my lip and moaned. Sweat glistened down her chest as she rode me. The pressure began to build again, threatening to destroy me at my core.

"Little fox… *fuck*. I'm going to cum if you keep moving like that." I was so fucking close. The blood was rushing down my shaft, sending tiny shivers to my balls, down my thighs, and all the way back to my ass.

She stilled herself. "Deep breaths. Relax."

I nodded and licked my lips, tasting blood from where I'd bitten down. I felt my chest rise with each quivering breath I took to try and steady myself.

After a few minutes, I nudged her hips forward.

"That's a good boy," she whispered.

Fuck. When I told her to take control, I had no idea she'd be so fucking hot doing it. All this time I thought being the dominant one was what got me off, but now… fucking hell, this was what did it for me. I was more turned-on than I'd ever been.

With my cock buried deep inside her, Bailey rubbed her pussy in circles against the base, moaning as she stimulated her clit. Her juices poured out like a dam breaking. I reached up and gently pinched her nipples.

"Yeah, ride me just like that." We rocked back and forth, increasing our pace.

She lifted her hips again, sliding up to the tip and back down again with more force this time. The pressure began to build all over again, my blood racing against my pulse. "I'm gonna burst, little fox. Gonna fill you so fucking full of my cum."

She screamed and clenched around me as her cheeks flushed. I squeezed her hips and pulled them down. We pounded into each other so hard I thought our bones might break.

She whined and moaned as her orgasm ripped through her. "*Uhhh… Poe. Fuuck.*"

Shivers raced down my shaft as my cum shot forward like a thousand stars exploding. So much cum, hot and thick. It wouldn't stop. I unleashed into her, twisting, and thrusting deeper as she clenched around me with equal force.

"Oh shit… I can't stop." My cock spasmed again, and another rush of cum spilled out. She had taken me to the edge, over-stimulating me to the point where I no longer had control of my body.

Bailey slid up and down my cock as she panted. "*Yes, good boy.*"

My heart felt like it was going to explode out of my chest as I rammed my cock against her G-spot. "I want to blow your fucking back out, little fox, fuck."

She released a deafening scream as she collapsed on top of me. I wrapped my arms around her and held her tight. We stilled and gazed back at each other, wild-eyed, our chests heaving.

"I'm… I have no words… except fuck," I rasped.

Her cheeks were flushed, her nipples still hard, and her cum continued to ooze out of her, mingling with mine. "*Fuck* is right. Holy shit, Poe. That was… insane."

My heart still pounded. She'd never looked more beautiful than she did right now. I scooted over. "Come over here," I murmured.

Bailey climbed underneath the sheets and nestled in next to me. "Poe, my love… my good boy."

Mmm, there was that fucking dominance in her again and it turned me all the way on. And now I wanted to spend every second buried in that soaking wet pussy of hers. I just wanted to fucking live there.

"Forever yours, my love. Always."

She was sound asleep in minutes. As I lay there breathless, and in awe, for a little longer, I sensed another presence in the room.

Raine.

The fact that he was just showing up now made me think he might not be a complete psycho. He was checking up on her. Watching her sleep as we'd all done before.

I let out a sigh, deciding to ignore him. If he wanted to sit there all night, so be it. Nothing was going to ruin my perfect night with Bailey. I rolled over and tucked her into my chest. "Goodnight, little fox."

CHAPTER *Twelve*

Bailey

I strolled down to breakfast this morning feeling a little lighter than usual. After having the weight of telling Maureen off my shoulders and then the amazing night I had with Grim and Poe, things were finally feeling a little back to normal. Well, normal for me. There were still things to deal with. Things that I dreaded. But for now, I had a little sliver of peace, and I was determined to hang onto it.

Poe, Grim, and Saint crowded around the breakfast table, laughing, and joking around. I released a sigh of relief. This sight made me even happier. Saint pulled out a chair for me just as Poe set a heaping plate of pancakes down on the table. My mouth watered at the sight of the gooey chocolate chips melting into the fluffy dough.

"Smells delicious, Poe. Thank you." After drowning my pancakes in maple syrup, I shoved a huge bite into my mouth and moaned. "Yup. They're perfect," I mumbled between mouthfuls.

Saint smirked. "After the night you had last night, I'm guessing Poe could do just about anything right today."

I felt my cheeks flush despite the fact that the four of us had been fucking each other long enough to not feel shy. But something about last night felt intimate in a different way.

"Mmm, yes. Facts," I breathed coyly.

Grim cleared his throat. "What the fuck am I, chopped liver?" he teased.

I giggled through another huge bite of delicious chocolate chip pancakes. "Far from it, daddy. You got me primed and ready. Couldn't have done it without you."

We laughed together at that and continued to joke around for the rest of the morning. It felt like it did in the beginning again. It made me forget all about the dark cloud hanging over our heads.

Poe cleared the table and returned with fresh cups of steaming coffee for all of us. This was my favorite part of the day. When everything was full of possibilities.

I recounted more of my night with Maureen for them, leaving out the part about running into Billy in town, of course. They laughed and snorted as I described Maureen's facial expressions when I was telling her about them. Saint playfully scolded me for drinking too much tequila while Grim and Poe high-fived me, impressed that I didn't die from alcohol poisoning.

"I think I'm going to take a hot shower, guys. Then maybe go for a walk in the garden." There were only so many nights left before winter would truly hit Wickford Hollow. I wanted to enjoy what was left of the bright orange and gold leaves while I could.

They exchanged a look between them that made my stomach lurch. An uneasiness settled into my bones. "What?" I asked. "What's that look for?"

Saint turned to me. "We'd like to talk to you about Raine."

Butterflies danced in my stomach. "Oh... okay."

Grim sucked in a sharp breath. "I don't want to either, Bailey, but he's here and we need to deal with it."

Poe nodded in agreement. "How do you feel about the situation, love?"

I rubbed my palms against my silk pajama pants, my fingers starting to tremble. I didn't want any more secrets or lies between us. "I... um... want to talk to him."

"Just talk?" Grim quipped.

Fuck. There was something about Raine that I couldn't figure out. He'd been with me this whole time. I couldn't see him until the other day, *but I felt him*. And I still wasn't sure if he wanted to kill me or defile me. Or both.

I took a big sip of my coffee, relishing the warm liquid as it coated my dry throat. "I don't know yet. What if I did want to do more than just talk? How would you all feel about that?"

Saint took my hands and brought them to his lips, kissing my palms. "We've discussed this, and we all feel that you should explore whatever you need to. He's a part of this house and forever a part of our lives."

"We won't keep you from who you are, Bailey," Poe chimed in. "If you feel some type of way about him, then you owe it to yourself to find out what that is."

Grim snickered. "But if he hurts you or forces you to do anything you don't want, I'll kill him. I know he's already dead, but you know what I mean."

I gazed at all three of them and back to Grim. "But are you going to be resentful toward me? I won't do anything unless I have your true and genuine blessing."

Grim sighed. "I love the fucking shit out of you, Bailey. I'm possessive, but I'm not unreasonable. The three of us share you.

That was our choice. But we crossed the line a little when we showed up at your house that night."

Saint nodded. "We didn't give you much of a choice, is what Grim is saying. But we are giving you one now."

"We'd be fucking hypocrites if we didn't," Poe added.

I swallowed hard, unsure if I even wanted this new dynamic. "I appreciate that. And I promise you, I know what I'm doing."

Saint kissed my hands again. "We're all going to have to learn to live together. This is Raine's house too. Maybe more so. We trust your judgment, darlin'."

Poe cupped my face with his hands. "And we realize that getting to know Raine, doesn't mean you love or want us any less."

I nodded. "It doesn't. I couldn't imagine my life without any of you. But something is calling me to him. I need to find out why."

Grim snickered. "I'm not worried. Everyone here knows I'm the one who eats your pussy out the best." He looked up as he teased, as if he were making sure Raine heard him as well.

I licked my lips and winked at him while Saint and Poe pretended to fight over if that was true or not.

Making my way up the stairs, their voices carried as the debate over my pussy was still going strong. I chuckled to myself. I was lucky to have these men. So, was I being greedy for wanting to get to know another?

Whether I liked it or not, Raine had been with me from the start. From the moment that door opened, he was a part of this. And quite possibly, a part of me.

I turned on the shower and let the steam fill the bathroom before I undressed. It was freezing in our house this time of year. Satisfied that I wouldn't shiver to death, I peeled off my pajamas and opened the gigantic glass door. Stepping in, I was once again in awe of the size of it. This shower was custom-built to accommodate all four of us if we so desired.

I released a deep quivering breath as the hot water rushed over me, dunking my head underneath the spray. With my eyes closed I reached for my face cleanser. I instantly felt relaxed as I squirted it into my palm, breathing in the fresh scents of orange and lemon. I lathered it over my face for a few seconds before rinsing it off.

With my eyes closed, I turned around slowly, and moaned as the hot water poured down my back, soothing my every aching muscle.

I dunked my head one more time and then rubbed my eyes before opening them. I sucked in a sharp breath as I glimpsed a large shadow through the fogged glass.

Fuck.

My stomach knotted as I reached forward, my hand trembling, and smeared the steam off a section of the shower door. Raine's blue-green eyes stared back at me. With a smug smirk on his face, he pulled the shower door open. "I hear you've been looking for me. Well, here I am."

Instinctively, I draped one arm across my chest and the other down my middle to cover my pussy. "Are you insane? I'm in the middle of taking a shower."

He looked me up and down, not giving a fuck that we hadn't even properly met. "I find that people are much more fun when they're wet and naked."

A little shiver snaked up my spine as I glared at him. "You're letting all the steam out."

Without undressing, he stepped into my shower and closed the door behind him. "Better?"

Fucking hell. I took a step back, still covering myself. "Could you please have the decency to wait until I'm done in here?"

Raine leaned back against the tiles and crossed his arms, with no intention of leaving. "Fine by me. Continue."

My mouth dropped open. "Are you for real? *I don't even know you.* I'm not just going to let you watch me bathe myself."

He ran a tattooed hand through his damp hair. His eyes flickered with need and fucking pure psychotic lust. "You do know me. And that terrifies you. But I'm not going anywhere. So quit being a brat and *continue*."

Why did he have to be so hot?

If he was nothing to look at it, I would've already bolted and left him there driveling.

Fuck this.

I should leave him here just for that smug look plastered on his face. "Fuck off, Raine."

As I reached for the door handle, he grabbed my wrists and flung me back against the shower wall, pinning my hands over my head.

"You want to learn more about me? Well, here's your first lesson." He gazed down at my pebbled nipples and chuckled. "I don't fucking like being dismissed. You're not leaving this shower until you've finished."

Fuck, he was crazy. And yet I couldn't deny that I was turned on a little. My body was betraying me now, and I fucking hated it. "Let me go," I spat through gritted teeth.

"I'm really going to enjoy this." He released my wrists, but stood in front of the shower door, blocking my way out.

My stomach knotted. I contemplated screaming but that would only cause more chaos in the house. I gave the guys my word that I knew what I was doing. I couldn't risk looking like a moron right out the gate.

No. Fuck this. I didn't need saving.

"Get out of my way." I lunged forward and slapped him hard across the face.

His head snapped to the side as he laughed. "You're no one's good girl, Bailey. You're a naughty little vixen who's going to learn her place." He unbuckled his black leather belt and slid it out of the loops.

Oh, fuck.

My adrenaline surged as my body went into flight or fight mode. I charged forward and slapped him again.

Raine growled, unfazed, as he grabbed my wrists and held them up over my head. "Fucking feisty as hell. You have no idea how hard that makes me."

Panic flooded me as he wrapped his belt around my wrists and then around the showerhead, securing it tight. "What the fuck are you doing?"

His eyes darkened as he admired his handiwork. "If you want to act like a brat, I'm going to treat you like one. All you had to do was finish your shower. But no, you want to act like you have a set of balls on you. You've got them all wrapped around your little finger, don't you? Well, that's not going to work on me."

Shit. What the fuck did I get myself into? "You're a fucking psycho," I spat.

He smirked as he grabbed my sponge off the ledge. "You have no fucking idea." He squirted some of my body wash onto the sponge and squeezed the suds over my breasts. "But you're going to find out."

I had let them do vile and depraved things to me. From the very first night, I let them collar me, spank me, cum and spit in my mouth. But I realized in this very moment that I was always in control. This was different. Raine would not take no for an answer.

My breath hitched as he dragged the soapy sponge across my breasts. "Don't I get a safe word at least?" I glanced up at my wrists and then back to his menacing eyes.

Raine continued to knead the sponge against my breasts, circling it around my traitorous nipples. He pushed the tip of his tongue out and rested it on his lower lip. "There are no words that can save you from me, little vixen. There's only me." He raked the sponge down my stomach and rubbed it against my clit. "And you are going to learn how to truly submit."

As fear spiked through my blood, my clit spasmed with every rough thrust of the sponge against it. "They won't let you get away with this."

He dragged the sponge up and down my slit, chuckling. "No, they won't. But *you* will."

I shook my head. "No. Stop. I want you to stop."

He wedged the sponge in deeper, massaging it against the walls of my pussy. "I know you do. You know why? Because you're a monster just like me. You could have screamed for help at any time. But you haven't and you won't."

No. This isn't what I want. Not like this. "You're wrong. You don't know me at all."

The cold tiles hit my back as Raine pressed his chest against mine. He growled in my ear as he worked the sponge deeper inside my pussy. "I know you better than you know yourself. Yeah… I know you're a filthy little girl who is desperate for someone like me to control her. To punish her."

The pressure began to rise in my core as he worked his fingers around the sponge, flicking them against my clit. Fuck no, please don't let me cum. Not for him. "I will never give in. I will never love you."

Raine's breath hitched as my juices leaked out into his hand. "I don't want your heart, Bailey. I want your body and your soul. I want you to fucking hate me so much that I can taste your pain on my tongue when you cum for me."

A deep spasm rolled through me. "*Fuck…*" I rasped.

"Mmm, yeah. You like how my fingers fuck your pussy. How I'm going to force you to cum and there's nothing you can do about it. This will be the first of many."

I bucked as he pinched my clit, sending me over the edge. I

cried out, a mixture of pleasure and pure fucking hatred for this man.

Raine shoved the sponge into my mouth and finished me off with his rough fingers. Tears streamed down my cheeks. "Shh…" He licked the side of my neck. "You're not a good girl anymore. You're a fucking brat who's finally met her match."

He shoved a finger deep inside my pussy as I bucked against his hand. As another orgasm rolled through me, he slapped me across the face. I screamed into the sponge, glaring at him as he smiled. "You reap what you sow, little vixen. Remember that the next time you think about slapping me."

As he reached up to untie my wrists, I lurched back, my limbs trembling.

I raised my chin to look him square in the eye. "That will be the last time you touch me."

"You and I both know that's a lie." He dragged his thumb across my lips, his breath quivering, before exiting the shower and leaving me alone in the bathroom.

Was he right about me? Every second of that was like a rush of pure adrenaline. I wanted him to stop but then I didn't. He was vile and depraved. But he stirred those dark parts of me. The parts I wanted to feel when I asked Poe, Grim, and Saint to defile me in the basement. Except I knew then, I was in control. That they would stop if I yelled my safe word. So it wasn't really real. Not like now.

When I looked into Raine's eyes, I knew with every fiber of my being that he was going to do whatever he wanted. Just like he knew that I wouldn't scream because maybe I wanted it too. My head was scrambled. There was a war raging between my body and my soul. And Raine just laid claim to both.

But instead of fear, all I felt was fury… and a toxic need to see how far I could push him.

CHAPTER *Thirteen*

Raine

Finally, I was going to have some fucking fun in this house.

Bailey Bishop. Mmm… Fuck. I couldn't wait to feast on that pussy of hers. Couldn't wait to bury my dick in every one of her holes.

And the resistance. Holy fuck, the way she fights me only makes me want her more. I want to hear her beg and scream and cry until she cums so hard she blacks out. Ever since that night, when I saw her climbing up the stairs of this house, I dreamed about this moment. When I saw the fire in her eyes, felt the adrenaline in her veins, *smelled* the cream inside her wet panties… I knew she was going to be a tasty fucking snack.

There was no way she would've gotten that door open without

me. I couldn't think straight. I couldn't let her get away. And now she was just as much mine as she was theirs.

I perched on the foot of her bed, waiting for her. She was taking too long. I needed to touch her again. Bailey Bishop was like a drug to me. And I needed another fix.

Right. Fucking. Now.

I started for the bathroom door just as it wrenched open. She stood in the doorway, her chest heaving underneath her thin white tank top. Her eyes blazed with fear and fury. It got me so fucking hard.

She flinched as I stalked toward her. "You shouldn't have put your clothes back on, pretty girl. I'm just going to make you take them off."

Her lip quivered as she clung to the doorknob. "I have questions," she stammered.

That devious part of my brain kicked into high gear. "And I have answers… for a price."

I let her shove past me. She looked around the room suddenly realizing there was nowhere to sit but the bed. I watched as she hesitated before climbing on top of her duvet cover.

"What's your price, Raine?"

Yes, the fun part. "For every question I answer, you have to do something for me. Anything I ask. How's that sound?"

Her cheeks flamed. "Forget it. Leave me alone. I don't know why I thought meeting you was a good idea."

I leaned against the wall and drank in the sight of her. The way the ends of her blonde hair dripped water onto her chest. It trickled down between her breasts, soaking her tank top. Her nipples poked through the damp fabric, begging to be sucked.

"Come on, little vixen. Play with me a while…" Her throat bobbed as I inched toward the bed. "Go ahead, ask me a question."

She sucked in a sharp breath and pulled her knees to her

chest. All I could think about was ripping her sweatpants off and spreading her wide open.

Despite her claim to hate me, her violet eyes blazed with hunger and lust as she looked at me. "Did you abuse your wife? Is that why she killed you?"

Clever little vixen. "That's two questions, Bailey."

She rolled her eyes.

I took another step toward her. "And I will answer them both. But I'm keeping score."

She bit her lip. "Fine. Answer them both."

I slid onto the foot of the bed, draping myself across it. "Yes. But not physically. We didn't like each other much. Our marriage was forced on us by our families. She called my lack of interest abuse; I called it dissonance. And yes, that is why she killed me. Hemlock. The second I took my last living breath, everything I owned became hers alone. And I owned a lot."

I had blocked out so many of those memories. But I could speak about them now as if they'd happened to someone else.

Bailey tapped her fingernails against her knees. "That's one of the saddest stories I've ever heard."

She had no fucking idea. I gave her the abridged version. Didn't think it would turn her on to hear how I foamed at the mouth and my eyes bulged out of my head right before I died. "My turn. Pull your shirt down and lay back against the headboard."

A bright rosy hue flushed across her cheeks. Her breath hitched as she pulled the straps of her top down with trembling fingers. My cock stirred at the sight of her hard nipples. *They were hard for me.* That's what she was really afraid of. She didn't want me to see how much she wanted this.

"Good girl," I rasped. "Now I want to watch you play with them."

She yanked her shirt back up and crossed her arms. "No. I'm not playing this game."

This fucking brat. I scrambled across the bed and straddled her. As her closed fist came flying at my face, I caught it and pinned her wrists over her head.

"Stop being a fucking brat. *You agreed.*"

She twisted underneath me, grunting. "*I lied.*"

Fuck this. I hovered my lips over hers. "The only thing you're lying about is how fucking hard you want me to make you cum."

I pressed myself between her thighs. "You feel that, Bailey?" My cock throbbed against her. "Because I can feel how wet you are even through your pants."

She took shallow breaths, sweet torturous breaths that tickled my lips. Her hips betrayed her as they rolled up. I could see the frustration in her eyes. Like a drug, it filled me. I craved the chaos of her emotions.

"You know how good my cock will feel inside you. You're craving it right now. How the ridges of my shaft will feel sliding in… and tearing through your tight little cunt."

"No," she breathed. "*You're a psycho.*"

I was past the point of reason. Her scent consumed my every breath. "I'm taking what I want, little vixen. Fight me all you want, but I will have your cum on my cock."

There were two things that Bailey Bishop was going to learn today—what it's like to fuck a monster… and that she's a monster too.

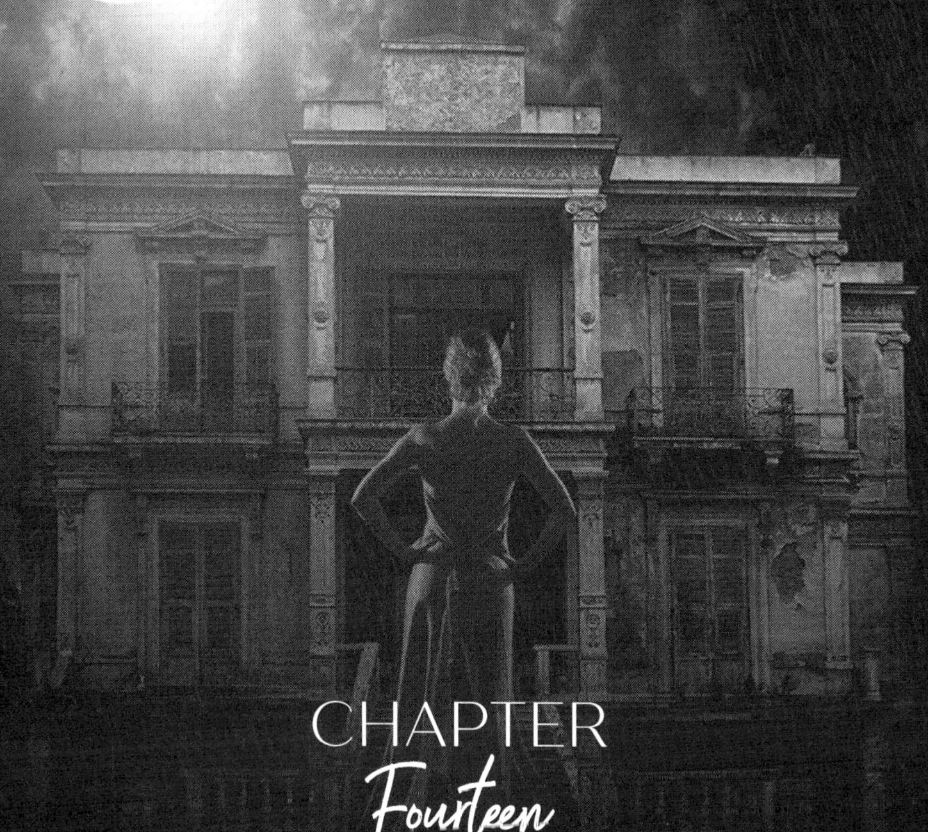

CHAPTER *Fourteen*

Bailey

Before I could scream, he kissed me. *Raine Wickford fucking kissed me.* His lips were soft, but his tongue lapped at my mouth like a starved animal. He held my wrists so tight, they burned against his fingers. A traitorous whimper ripped from my throat as he kissed me harder, bruising my lips.

My body was on fire.

I kissed him back.

Fuck.

"Mmm," he growled. "I knew you wanted a taste. Fucking desperate for me, aren't you?"

Fucking hell I hated how smug he was. "I'm just trying to get this over with, so you'll get off me."

He had both my wrists pinned against the wall above the headboard with one freakishly strong hand. "Look at me."

I glared into his piercing blue-green eyes.

With his free hand, he pulled down one of the straps of my top. "That's better."

Goosebumps prickled my skin as he lashed his tongue over my swollen nipples before blowing softly on them. He arched an eyebrow as I huffed. "Is that too gentle for you? How about this?"

I cried out as he pinched my nipple hard, twisting it between his fingers. "Yeah. That's how you like it. Fuck. I'm going to have so much fun playing with you."

He looked down toward my pussy and licked his lips.

I shook my head. "No. Don't even think about it. You've done enough." This bastard was really going to fucking violate me again. And my body was going to fucking love it. Fuck.

"Shh… relax. Let me get nice and deep inside that pussy before you tell me no. I think you'll be screaming *yes* very soon."

And that was the problem. I didn't want to say yes. The more he forced me, the wetter my pussy got. I was addicted to the control. Trembling and aching for the submission. I couldn't clench, couldn't get away, couldn't do anything. He had me completely pinned. And yet I would fight him every step of the way. It sparked a fire between us that neither one of us knew how to put out.

Raine's eyes darkened as he slipped his cold hand inside my sweats. He slid his palm over the top of my panties before pulling them to the side. I gasped as he stroked the lips of my pussy. "Oh, fuck… Bailey. *Fuck, you are so fucking wet.*" His lip quivered as he explored my folds with his fingers, rubbing and pinching. "Let's see how much I can piss you off."

I moaned and rolled my hips up as he jammed two fingers deep inside my pussy. "*Uhhh… no.*" No. I don't want to want this.

He slapped his hand against my pussy. "*Yeah, keep begging me to stop.*"

My thighs ached from him stretching them wide open. And yet I couldn't help but rock against his hand as he added a third finger inside my pussy and pushed down on my clit with his thumb.

"Why are you doing this to me?" I rasped.

"Because I'm the villain. I take whatever I want. And I want to take." He thrust his fingers deeper. "And take." I bucked as he pumped in and out. "And take. Until I've taken all of you."

I was drowning, getting lost in every tingle and spasm that he was wrenching from me. The pressure in my clit was building, climbing toward that release. It was making me forget every sane thought in my head.

He had me spread open against the headboard. There was nowhere to go. No way to get away. My wrists were tightly locked inside his grip. His hard muscular body pinned me in place. A panic fluttered in my chest at the thought.

"Get off of me, Raine. I don't want this," I rasped.

Raine groaned as he sucked on my bottom lip. "Your pussy is telling me something else, little vixen. I'm only listening to her from now on."

Another whimper floated past my lips as he rubbed his thumb in circles around my clit. I stared deep into his feral eyes. "I hate you."

"*I want you to hate me more.*" Without warning he pulled his fingers out of my pussy and reached for his belt.

"Wait. What the fuck are you doing?" My stomach knotted.

He wrapped his belt around my wrists, the same way he'd done in the shower. "Allowing myself the freedom to torture you with both hands."

I tried to lurch away from him, but he was too strong. He yanked me down and fastened the hanging end of the belt around the bedpost. "Mmm that's better. Let me have a look at you."

"You're insane. You can't just tie me up and do whatever you want," I spat. I could scream for the guys. But that would only make things worse. I felt that in my bones. And yet that dark dirty part of me knew I wouldn't scream for another reason… Raine was pressing all of my buttons, he was pissing me off, but he knew how to touch me in a way that I'd fantasized about before.

He rested back on his heels as he gazed down at me hungrily. "I will tie you up and take what I want, *whenever I want*." He smoothed his hand up my belly, pushing my top up as he went. I felt the cold air hit my nipples as he slid my top over my breasts, all the way to my bound wrists.

His hands glided back down my arms to my breasts. I jerked, my nipples pebbling as he pinched them between his fingers. "Did you know that I've watched you touch yourself?" He dragged his tongue slowly across his lip. "Mmm. I've been tempted so many times to join but I was a good boy. Waiting for the right moment. *This* moment."

My breath hitched in my throat. I hated that this was turning me on. Hated that he knew how to make my body come alive with need. "It's cold and I'm scared. Don't read anything else into it."

Raine chuckled as he inched his hands down my rib cage, dragging his fingertips down my trembling belly. "You're a liar," he whispered. He tugged at the waistband of my sweats, pulling them up so he could gaze inside. "But she's not. No. This pretty little pussy is whining for me. Begging for me to fill her."

Fuck. That was the thing about fantasies. They were only supposed to live in your head. But I knew that was a lie I told myself the moment I said yes to this life. That I would never be satisfied with imagining these depraved acts. No. I was always going to be the girl who sought them out.

But Raine fucking terrified me. There was a wild streak in his eyes that shook me to my core. I had no idea what he was capable of. There was a war going on between my body and my mind. "You don't know anything. You're just a psycho."

"Fuck, I love when you call me that."

I gasped as he yanked my sweats and panties down in one quick jerk. He held them up and dropped them to the floor, before nestling back between my legs.

I was completely naked now, shivering, trembling, shaking. It was exactly how he wanted to see me.

He blew out a deep breath as he drank in the sight of me. "You're *my* fucking slut now."

Panic rose in my chest while moisture pooled between my thighs. My thoughts were nothing but chaos. Pure fucking chaos.

Raine let out a soft moan as he pinned the lips of my pussy back. He leaned down and dragged the tip of his tongue up my slit. "You're a dirty girl, aren't you? You taste fucking dirty."

A deep spasm rolled through me. The way he flicked his tongue was agonizing. My body wanted more. I bit down on my lip to keep myself from begging. I would not give him the satisfaction.

He kneaded his thumbs against my slick walls. "Such a good little pussy... so responsive." He inched his thumb inside my entrance slowly as I clenched. "Yeah, that's it. Fight it. It makes my cock so fucking hard when you fight me."

The voices in my head were betraying me now. *Just let go, Bailey*. Give in. You know you want to. I panted for air as his blue-green eyes blazed with desire. "No." I shook my head. I couldn't fucking want this. "You're disgusting."

Raine sucked in a sharp breath as he worked his thumb in and out. "And you're a fucking liar. *My little psycho vixen*."

Tingles spread to my clit. Despite everything I hated about this man, he knew how to fucking hit all the right spots. My will to resist was fading. The desire to let this happen grew stronger.

"Be a good little slut and admit you don't hate me nearly as much as you hate yourself."

I gasped as he withdrew his thumb from my pussy. "You don't know anything about me."

He grabbed a pillow and wedged it underneath my hips. "Let's see how tight that other hole is."

Oh, fuck. *No*. A billowing rage burst out of me. I kicked him hard in the leg. "Fuck you."

His eyes darkened as he leaped from the bed. "Now you're going to see how fucking psycho I am."

My heart raced. And yet I couldn't bring myself to scream for help. Some sick part of me wanted to see how far Raine would go.

He stormed over to the window and ripped away the ropes that were holding back the curtains. "Oh, you are not going to like this one bit, little vixen."

My body shook as he stalked back toward me. I whimpered as he wrapped the long rope around my ankle and fastened the other end to one of the bedposts. He glared at me as he did the same to my other ankle. "Keep pushing me," he rasped. "And I will gag and blindfold you as well."

I was completely bound and at his mercy. And I was terrified because Raine was not a merciful man. He was unpredictable and had no regard for my comfort. His only desire was to control. To dominate. And I was playing right into his hands.

He wedged the pillow back underneath my hips, propping me up at an angle that would allow him to access more than just my traitorous pussy.

"This is just a taste of what I have in store for you, Bailey." He pushed my legs farther apart and smirked as he gazed down. His lips pursed, his cheeks hollowing, right before he released a glob of spit on my pussy.

A tremor rocked through me. "*Uhhh*." His saliva slid down my slit and between my ass cheeks.

Raine growled. "Mmm, I knew you'd like that."

I bucked as he spat again. "Stop that. It's… dirty."

With his fingertips, he smeared his spit all over my pussy. "Yes. Say it again. Beg me to stop."

Heat flooded my body. Every nerve sparking and threatening to combust. I was screaming inside while my body panted for more. All reason was slipping away as his voice lured me in. As the deep primal beast inside me ached for him to dominate me.

I thrashed against the bed, pulling at the ropes with all my strength. The more I twisted, the tighter the restraints got, burning my wrists. "Damn you," I rasped.

Raine's breath hitched as he watched me struggle to break free. "Yeah. Just like that. Fuck you make me so hard. I was going to wait for this, but you look so fucking feral, I need to play with it now."

What the fuck was he doing?

I took deep breaths, willing myself not to hyperventilate. He reached under the bed and pulled out a leather bag. "Please, let me go." I *was* begging now.

He unzipped the bag and pulled out a collar with a roped leather leash attached to it. I flinched as he fastened it around my neck. I yelped as he gave it a tug. "Mmm, like a wild animal… I can't wait to fucking break you."

He placed the leash down the length of my torso, the end of it hanging between my thighs. Why was I still not screaming for help? Was he right?

"I'm here to awaken your dark side, little vixen. And it's about to get really fucking dark." Raine peeled off his shirt, revealing his entire upper body tattooed from the neck down. His body was perfectly chiseled from his carved pecks all the way down to his washboard abs. I licked my lips without thinking.

He smirked and grabbed the leash between my legs. "Relax or I'll fucking choke you."

Oh, fuck. I could feel my eyes as wide as saucers as I realized what was happening. "You're sick."

"I'm creative," he quipped back. "Now be a good little slut for me." He wedged the leash between my pussy lips and slid it back and forth gently. "Lift those hips. I want to watch you slide up and down your leash."

I couldn't breathe. I was too close to the edge. Spasms spread to my clit. I was afraid to move for fear that I would completely fall into his control. "*No*."

I jerked forward as he gave it a hard tug. With my wrists binding me to the bedpost, it felt like my neck was about to snap. I gasped as he pulled again, the war between my wrist restraints and my collar threatening to tear me in half.

"I'm not going to stop just because you black out from lack of air, little vixen. Play along and maybe you'll enjoy it."

He would actually choke me out and still fuck me. That I did believe. Fuck. And a part of me wanted to play. A sick and twisted part of me ached to. I was more terrified of being unconscious around this psycho.

I slowly inched my hips up as he see-sawed the leash up and down my slit. Soft moans began to escape me as the ridges in the rope kneaded against my walls.

"There we go. Such a good fucking slut for me." He peeled my folds back so he could wedge the leash in deeper. "Behaving so well for daddy."

My control was slipping farther and farther away. He tugged harder each time, forcing me to lift my hips higher to meet it so the collar wouldn't choke me. Fear and adrenaline raced through my veins. Sweat beaded down my body. I was coming undone. My juices leaked out as the pressure built inside my clit.

I moaned as he wrapped the end of the leash around his wrist and pulled it taut against my slit, pressing it hard into my folds as I ground against it. "I want you so fucking raw that you beg me to spit on you."

The spasms in my clit intensified even as the rough leather began to pinch and scratch. "You're hurting me," I breathed.

Raine snickered. "And you fucking like it. You're going to like this too..."

I gasped to catch my breath as he released the leash. My chest heaved. Relief flooded me for a fleeting second. He swung the leash underneath my leg.

I shook my head. "No. I don't want that there."

Raine planted a gentle kiss on the inside of my thigh. "Say it again."

"I said I don't want this anymore. Untie me right now." The truth was I didn't know what I wanted. My muscles ached from being stretched. But my pussy was aching for release. I was so tired of fighting.

He wedged the leash inside my ass and looped it back around so that it would now rub against both my entrances. He reached over and unhooked the other end from my collar. "Now I get to have some real fun."

I cried out as he pulled the leash tight and began see-sawing it back and forth through my ass and pussy. My juices spilled out as the rough leather scraped against my tender flesh, sending more spasms to my core. My hips betrayed me as I couldn't help but rock them to his rhythm. *I was so close.*

And then he stilled, dropping the leash from his hands. He exhaled a slow breath against my wet pussy. "No, little vixen. You

He chuckled as he walked back toward the bed. I flinched as he leaned over me. "I'll be back later, little vixen." He planted a soft kiss on my cheek. As soft as his tongue was on my pussy. Fuck. He was bringing out so many different emotions in me, I couldn't decipher which one was stronger. I wanted to hate him, and I wanted him to own me at the same time.

CHAPTER Fifteen

Bailey

My heart raced. It pounded in my ears, louder than the rain hitting the kitchen window. Poe was finishing up the dishes in the sink, humming an unfamiliar tune to himself. I glanced through the double French doors that led outside and spotted Saint working in the garden. Grim was most likely in his room reading.

Poe took one look at me and knew. His nostrils flared. "Did he hurt you?"

I threw my arms around his neck. "I'm okay. I promise." His embrace was everything I needed. It felt like home.

"Bailey, don't cover for him." Poe looked me up and down, examining me for injuries.

I sighed. What do I actually tell him? "It wasn't like that… exactly. I can't explain it."

Poe cupped my face in his hands. "You can tell me anything. If he hurt you, I need to know. I won't allow it."

Raine scared me but I still wasn't sure if it was because I thought he would actually hurt me or if it was because he stirred a longing I didn't know was there.

I clasped Poe's hands in mine. "I'm still figuring him out. Trust me. If I thought I was in any real danger, I would have called out to all of you."

He pursed his lips. "That's the thing, Bailey. I'm not sure you trust yourself. Raine is manipulative. He will make you think you want something even if you don't."

I had considered that as well. But despite my better judgment, I was drawn to Raine. I nodded. "I know. He's… a bit unhinged. That could be because he hasn't had any real interaction with anyone for over a century. I just need more time with him."

Poe sighed and kissed my hands. "I just want you to be happy. But I swear to god if he hurts you in any way, I will never let him be alone with you ever again."

That was the thing about our life. I couldn't just leave Raine behind without leaving Poe, Grim, and Saint behind as well. I had to make this work. Otherwise, they would be glued to my side for the rest of my days. And we'd always live in turmoil and chaos. Raine wasn't going anywhere. And neither was I.

"I'm going to meet Maureen for coffee in town. Tell the guys I'll be back later and not to worry." I wrapped my arms around his waist and breathed in the sweet scent of vanilla and pastry cream from the pancake batter that still clung to his shirt.

Poe squeezed me tight. "I hope we can figure this all out soon. Halloween is next week. I just want our anniversary to be special."

My stomach knotted. "You know it's technically Raine's

anniversary too… he admitted that he pushed me into the door. He brought us all together."

Poe nodded. "I know. Go have fun with your friend. We can talk more later."

I went to peck him on the cheek when he found my lips and slipped his tongue inside my mouth. There was an ache in his kiss I hadn't felt before. He pushed me back against the counter and kissed me deeper. Every nerve in my body tingled with love and desire. The night we shared made me feel more connected to him. The way we fucked was different. It was slower, more sensual. And now his kisses felt more intimate too.

I pulled away, breathless. "I love you, Poe."

His eyes lit up. "I love you so much, little fox."

"Girl, you better spill the tea. I can see it in your eyes. Something happened with the new guy, didn't it?" Maureen bounced in her seat while she added a third packet of sugar to her latte.

My cheeks burned. I was still getting used to talking openly about my unconventional sex life. Yes, she was my best friend, but I still had a lot of issues with shame I was working through.

"There was an incident. Yeah." I let out a nervous laugh.

Her eyes lit up as she squealed. "Ooh, what happened?"

The wind picked up, blowing a cold gust through my hair, sending chills up the back of my neck. I wrapped my hands around the hot mug in front of me, using it to warm my hands before taking a sip. The sweet flavor of pumpkin spice filled my mouth, invoking a deep sense of nostalgia for my favorite time of year.

We would have been way warmer inside the café, but I wasn't in the mood to be looked at under a microscope. It was bad enough that half the room looked up and stared when I walked into order. I also didn't want anyone eavesdropping on our conversation.

"Well, for starters, he's a complete fucking psycho."

Maureen leaned forward like she had a secret. "Like evil psycho? Or super-hot-I-want-to-fuck-you psycho?"

"A little bit of both, actually. He ambushed me in the shower, tied me up, and forced me to cum… Is it possible to hate someone so much you want to fuck them just so you can let it fester more?"

Maureen almost choked on her latte. "Damn, Bales. Okay, now I *know* he's hot for sure. And yes. Hate can be as strong as love. They might not look the same, but both spike your adrenaline. Your body doesn't know the difference."

My mouth dropped open. "How the fuck did you get to be so wise? That's like exactly how it feels."

Maureen batted her eyelashes. "You're not the only one with secrets, Bales. I've had a spicy rendezvous or two."

We'd been friends for so long that it was hard to believe we didn't know everything about each other. But I had been distant this past year. It only made sense that she would have had some adventures without me.

A wide grin spread across my face. "*Touché*. Maybe one of these days you can tell me about them."

A rustle of orange and gold leaves blew past me, drawing my attention to the street. The lampposts were decorated with strings of black and purple fairy lights. At the base sat carved pumpkins on haystacks. The storefronts boasted skeletons, ghosts, and broomsticks, and had already put out buckets of candy for the kids.

Wickford Hollow went all out for Halloween. Funny how they had no clue that the veil between the living and the dead really was about to come down. In just seven days, it would come and go. But I lived it every day.

Maureen broke off a piece of her chocolate-dipped biscotti and handed it to me. "How about another girls' night then? I can tell you all my dirty secrets." She winked.

As much as I hated being away from my guys, that was exactly what I needed. Raine had scrambled my head. I couldn't think clearly with him breathing down my neck. And I didn't have any answers for Poe, Grim, or Saint. Not yet, anyway.

"Yes, let's do it," I mumbled through a bite of my cookie.

Maureen clapped her hands together. "Yay! Okay, I'll get all the food and drinks this time. Ooh, maybe we should do a tarot reading or a séance."

My stomach knotted. "Maybe. I think I have more ghosts than I can handle right now."

Maureen pouted her lips. "Well, maybe I want in on some ghost dick too, Bales. Ever consider that?" she teased.

I snorted into my pumpkin spice latte. "You're right. How selfish of me. Maybe one little séance."

We both burst into a fit of giggles. But it was short-lived.

Maureen tensed as she looked past me, the muscle in her jaw clenching. "Fuck."

A flutter of nerves danced in my belly. "What is it?"

Her leg began to bounce as she tapped her nails on the table. "Douchebag alert. Headed this way."

Billy and Chad. Fuck.

I surveyed the table, searching for anything I could use as a weapon. It didn't matter if it was broad daylight or a public space. No one would jump to our defense against these assholes. Both their dads were on the city council, and I was the town freak. Maureen had some pull with her dad being the sheriff but not enough to garner any sympathy for me.

As Maureen's tapping increased, I assumed they were getting closer. I saw their shadows on the sidewalk before I heard them approach.

"Well, if it isn't Sheriff Gray's mouthy daughter and the town freak," Billy drawled.

Chad planted his feet beside him and snickered. "More like the town slut."

My cheeks were hot.

Maureen flipped her hair. "Don't you assholes have anything better to do?"

Billy planted his hands on our table and leaned over her. "Come on, Maureen. We used to have so much fun together. Remember when you sucked my cock last Halloween?"

"Fuck you," she spat. "You got me so drunk I could barely stand."

My blood was boiling. I had never wanted to punch anyone before until Billy. I wanted to smash his face in and wipe that smug look off it. I gripped my spoon, wishing it was a knife.

"Get away from her, Billy."

He turned his attention toward my hand. "Or what? You going to feed me to death?"

Chad laughed. "That would be a sight."

"Maureen, let's go." I started up out of my chair when Billy dug his fingers into my shoulder and forced me back down.

He hovered over me, snarling. "I haven't forgotten about the little stunt you pulled the other day. You almost broke my jaw, bitch."

Maureen hissed. "You attacked her first."

I glared up at him. "Take your hands off me or I will break your jaw for real this time."

A few people in the café started to peer out the window at us.

Chad gave him a nod. "Let's get out of here. Too many eyes on us."

Billy flashed a toothy grin through the café window and stepped away from me. "Yeah, don't want anyone thinking we're friends with these bitches."

I wanted to scream and cry but I wouldn't let him see me do either.

"Fuck off, Billy," Maureen spat.

He kept his malicious gaze on me. "This isn't over, Bailey. I will make you pay for punching me."

I swallowed hard and didn't break eye contact as he backed away. I wouldn't show him how terrified I really was. I was angrier than I was scared, anyway.

Maureen was fuming just the same. She drank the rest of her latte in quick jittery sips. "This harassment has got to stop, Bales."

I covered my hand with hers, forcing her to stop tapping. "Why didn't you tell me what he did to you last year?"

She shook her head and looked away. "Because I felt like an idiot. I got so wasted, I didn't even know what I was doing. I haven't been to another one of his parties since."

"Oh, Maur. You're not an idiot. He took advantage of you. You have every right to get drunk and still be safe. You should report him before he does it to someone else." My heart broke for her. And I felt like a horrible friend for not noticing that she was not herself lately.

"What I should have done was bite his dick off." She folded her arms to her chest. "It doesn't matter anymore. I just want to forget about it."

I nodded. "Okay. I'm here to listen if you ever want to talk about it. And I'll go with you to the station if you change your mind."

She shuddered and then flashed me a smile. "Okay enough depressing stuff. Let's talk about our girls' night. I'll make a list of what we need."

Maureen was always good at flipping a switch. She could turn off emotions she didn't want to feel quicker than I could take another sip of my coffee. We spent the next hour planning the menu and drinks list for our girls' night over another round of pumpkin spice lattes.

I wished I could compartmentalize the way she did. As much as I tried to exude a light and easy vibe, I couldn't shake the feeling of dread that Billy had planted. He was getting more aggressive with each run-in. I really didn't want to tell the guys, but Billy's threats were scaring me.

But if they found out, they would want to lock me away in Wickford Mansion forever to protect me. Maybe that wasn't such a bad idea, though. This town had caused me nothing but grief.

On my way back home, I took the long route so I could drive past the mortuary. It was boarded up and the weeds were overgrown but it was still mine. Since I never reopened it, the locals had to drive to the next town over, Ever Graves, for their funeral needs. I just wasn't ready to deal with it. I doubt they'd come to mine anyway even if it were open for business.

I idled out front for a moment, basking in that feeling I could never fully grasp. It was an emptiness. An ache that hadn't gone away since the fire. Sometimes I wondered if reopening Bishop Mortuary would help. It might make me feel closer to my parents in some way.

My breath hitched as a shadow flickered in the front window. Probably just the reflection of my headlights playing tricks on me.

I shuddered and threw my car back in drive. Fuck. Living with four ghosts was making me see things everywhere. I glanced back before pulling away and the shadow flickered again.

Yup, definitely something in there. Of course, *I* would own a haunted mortuary. Fuck me.

CHAPTER Sixteen

Grim

"Where is that fucking bastard?" The back of my shirt was drenched with sweat as I raced around the house. I knew he was the reason Bailey had been acting differently. And after Poe filled me in on his run-in with her earlier, I figured Raine was fucking with her hard.

I took the stairs two at a time, heading all the way up to the third floor. "There can only be one psycho in this house and that motherfucker is *me*," I called out. "Come out and face me, fucker."

Saint caught up to me just as I barreled through the first bedroom door. "What the hell are you doing, man?"

I spun on him; my jaw clenched. "I need to have words with Raine right fucking now."

"Bailey wouldn't want this, Grim," Poe rasped as he sprinted around the corner.

I seriously thought a vein was going to burst in my neck. "Look, if Bailey wants to be with him, fine. But if this asshole is forcing her to then nah, that's not gonna fly with me."

Saint shook his head. "If she says she can handle him, then we have to trust her."

Had everyone lost their fucking minds? "Bailey is *our* little fox. Our good girl. Who the fuck does Raine think he is claiming any right to her?"

"He claimed her first," Poe murmured.

Every muscle in my body tensed. "What the fuck did you just say, Poe?"

"You heard me." He went and sat down on the bed. "Raine pushed her into the door. He wanted her to let us out. He's the reason we're free."

No fucking way. "So we owe him now or something?"

Saint leaned against the doorway, taking up the whole frame. "No, we don't. Poe's just pointing out that Raine has every right to pursue her the same way we did. And if Bailey is okay with that, then we have to be too. No matter his methods."

I was going to break something if I didn't exhale soon. "I need a fucking drink." I blew past Saint, shoving him out of the doorframe before charging downstairs.

When I got to the sitting room, my adrenaline surged again as I locked eyes with Raine. A sleazy smirk pulled at the corners of his lips. I looked him up and down, taking stock of his tall frame. We were at eye level, but his body was bigger than mine. His eyes were a shade of bluish-green, like sea glass. And his sandy blonde hair was tousled with a slight wave to it. Tattoos covered almost every inch of his body that I could see. He leaned casually against the bar in a white T-shirt and jeans.

I was ready to spit fucking venom at this asshole but a part of me didn't even want to believe he was real. Now that we were face to face… I was speechless.

"Grim in the flesh," Raine drawled. "Here, brother, I heard you might need this." He held out a glass of whiskey.

"I'm not your brother." I snatched the glass from his hand, knocked the whiskey down my throat, and offered the empty glass back to him. "Another."

Raine chuckled as he poured me a refill. "So what's got your panties in a twist? You jealous? Kind of ironic actually."

I took the glass and backed up a few steps, so he was out of strangling reach. "What are your intentions with Bailey?"

Raine plopped himself down on the couch, relaxed and at home like he owned the place. I guess technically he did. "I know she calls you daddy but now you actually sound like one. Is this where you give me the birds and the bees talk?"

The look of amusement on his face was infuriating. "Fuck off. You know what I'm asking. Bailey has been through a lot, and she doesn't need you toying with her."

Raine's eyes darkened. "You have no idea… Don't you want to know why I find this ironic?"

I forced my muscles to unclench and took a seat across from him on the opposite couch. "Not really but something tells me you're going to tell me anyway."

"For starters, you, Poe, and Saint were fucking my wife in my bed. Before she murdered you like she did me, of course. So, no hard feelings mate. If anything, that bonds us, don't you think?" Raine leaned back, draping his arm across the back of the couch. He looked so fucking smug.

I mimicked his movements as I glared back at him. "Ah, yes. Bonded by poison and pussy. So you're the jealous one, is that it?

Pissed that your wife crawled into bed with us before your dead body was even cold? Now you want a piece of Bailey to even it up."

Raine shook his head. "I didn't want my fucking wife. She was fucking crazy. What I want with Bailey has nothing to do with any of that."

It was my turn to chuckle. "I don't believe you and I definitely don't fucking trust you."

He shrugged. "Fuck if I care. You're just pissed that there's a part of Bailey that you can't reach. And I can."

The way he said her name stirred a possessiveness in me that I hadn't felt in a long time. "I won't let you hurt her."

Raine stood abruptly, his eyes full of malice. "That's for Bailey to decide. You three may have awakened her dark side, but I'm the one who can show her how to embrace it. She's caught between two worlds, her old life and this one. Let me help her leave the past behind for good."

He wasn't making sense. Every word out of his mouth was vague or cryptic. And yet a part of me knew that he spoke some sense. Bailey had grown distant and withdrawn. There were things she was keeping from us. I stood from the couch and stalked over to him till I was just inches away. "You might be right, but I still don't trust you."

Raine leaned forward, our noses almost touching. "In time, we'll all be one happy family. You'll see, Grim. And when I'm done breaking her open, you'll thank me for what you find inside."

My pulse fluttered. Something about the way he looked, the tone in his voice, stirred something deep inside me. A longing. Raine and I weren't that different. He was slightly more unhinged but our taste for darker things was the same. The thought of Bailey stretched out between us, naked and trembling, made my cock swell.

I knocked back the rest of my whiskey. "As you said… we'll see."

Poe and Saint crept in and poured themselves a drink as well. "You two playing nice now?" Saint grumbled.

Raine and I didn't break eye contact. I nodded. "For now."

Poe froze mid-sip. "Did you hear that?"

"Hear what?" Saint looked up as if he were expecting someone to crash through the ceiling.

Raine's nostrils flared. "I hear them. Someone's out front."

Just as he said it, the sound of muffled laughter rang out. "Fuck." I raced through the house, toward the front entrance with the guys at my heels.

I turned into the foyer just as a loud crash erupted. "What the fuck?" I yelled.

My hair blew back off my face as the cold wind from the broken window rushed in. Glass covered the marble floor.

Saint growled as he mobbed through it, his boots crunching as he stomped over to the window and looked out. "They're gone."

Poe ran his hands through his dark hair as he surveyed the mess. "Probably just a stupid prank. Fucking asshole kids."

I looked over at Raine, the both of us seething. "No." I shook my head. "This was something else."

Raine gazed around the room until he spotted what they threw. He reached down and picked up a brick with a note attached to it. He clenched his jaw as he read it aloud. "*Freak…* This is a message for Bailey."

I yanked open the front door and barreled out into the front yard, scanning the neighborhood like I was searching for a lost dog. There was no one in sight. I looked at the other houses to find their windows still very much intact.

As I charged back into the house, Poe was already sweeping up the glass. "Raine's right. Someone is fucking with *her*."

Saint sighed as he peered out the window again. "Why hasn't she said anything to us?"

Raine snickered. "Because she's afraid you'll lock her up and throw away the key. Open your fucking eyes. You aren't paying enough attention." He raised his voice.

Poe leaned against the broom. "She told you that?"

Raine kicked some of the glass. "Bailey hasn't told me anything. She didn't have to. I've been watching in the shadows for a long time. Long enough to see the war going on inside her."

A desperate need to see her face gripped me. "Why would someone target her?"

Raine shot me a glare. "Fucking ask her. Do you know anything about her past? Hmm?"

Saint shot forward. "Oh, and you do?"

"I know more than enough. Too much. I've seen her in her darkest moments when she thought no one was there." He sank down to the bottom of the stairs. "She's not—"

All four of us flinched as the front door burst open. Bailey's eyes widened at the sight of the glass, the broken window, and finally us. Her breath hitched as she spotted Raine. "What's going on? Please tell me you aren't fighting with each other."

That need to see her was now replaced by a need to chain her to my bed and never let her out of my sight again. I ripped the brick from Raine's hands and handed it to her along with the note that was attached. "I think you need to start talking."

"*Freak,*" she murmured. She crumpled the note and threw it. "That's what I am, right? A fucking freak." Tears burst from her eyes.

Poe shot me a glare as he rushed toward her, wrapping his arms around her tiny frame. "It's okay, love. Let's get you something to eat."

He started to walk her toward the kitchen when Saint

stopped him. "Stop coddling her. Everyone in the sitting room. *Now.*"

The conversation had shifted from worry to anger back to concern for Bailey's safety. But we were talking about her like she wasn't in the room. Raine was the only one who kept quiet. Doing what he did best, observing. Maybe he had the right idea after all. You learn more from listening than you do talking. I should know because I wasn't one for talking much either. Except for me, it was different. The thought of opening up made me physically nauseous. So how could I really judge anyone for doing the same?

But it was Bailey who finally commanded the room. She stood in front of the hearth, and everyone shut up. "This is exactly why I didn't want to say anything to you," she started. She tucked her blonde hair back into a ponytail and plopped down on the floor in front of the fire. "I knew you would overreact."

I sucked in a sharp breath. "Overreact? Bailey, someone threw a brick through our front window."

She wrapped her arms around herself as she shivered. "Nothing like that's ever happened before. I'm sorry."

Poe joined her on the floor. He took her hands in his. "How long have you been harassed like this?"

Bailey snickered. "Since forever. This town has hated my family since the day we moved here… They've always called us freaks. My parents were morticians. They opened up Bishop Mortuary here in Wickford Hollow. I don't remember much about them. I was so young when they died. All I know is that they had a lot of money. Enough that I never have to work a day in my life, ever. When they died, I was put in Wickford Orphanage. The nuns weren't unkind, they just kept their distance. People either hated me or feared me simply because my family was different."

An ache began to fester in my chest as I watched her recount what were clearly her most painful memories. I softened my tone, realizing my need to control everything was making me look like an asshole. "*Little fox*…" I didn't know what else to say.

She dabbed at her eyes with a cocktail napkin. "I felt so alone until I met Maureen. She accepted me for who I was. And because she was popular, the other kids eased off me. I even had a boyfriend for a while. But one night… everything changed.

My ex and I were fooling around in his truck. I started to touch myself in front of him. He was turned on at first but then he got angry. He didn't believe that I was a virgin. One minute I was living a normal life, and the next, I was labeled the town slut."

Raine leaned forward, his eyes darkening. "And what did you do about that, Bailey?"

She tilted her face toward the fire, her eyes flickered with the light from the flames. "I proved them right."

CHAPTER Seventeen

Bailey

I'd never thought I'd say those words aloud. *Slut*. All the shame I'd ever felt was bubbling up and threatening to choke me.

Saint sat down on the other side of me and took one of my hands from Poe. "The people of Wickford Hollow haven't changed one bit. It's a fucking cycle they keep perpetuating. They labeled us freaks as well back then. People fear what they don't understand. You have nothing to be ashamed of."

I shuddered. There were sides to me that even they didn't know about. But Raine fucking sensed things about me. It was like he could see into my soul. "I used to hate the word slut. But now I've claimed it. I own it. Because it's on my terms, not theirs."

Poe squeezed my hand. "We are cut from the same cloth, love. All of us. But we can't protect you if you keep secrets."

Raine snickered. "She doesn't need protecting, she needs liberating."

A knot formed in my stomach. I had no idea how Raine was so perceptive, but I had to come clean to them. "It started out harmless enough. They would tease me and call me names but say that it was all in good fun. I laughed along with it at first because I didn't want to go back to being the freak with no friends. Maureen knew it bothered me, but I refused to talk about it."

The four of them stared at me like I was a fragile bomb about to explode. I took a long sip of whiskey before continuing. "I started partying a lot more. The nights began to blur together. To be honest, there are big gaps in my memory. I started having blackouts. I was so depressed… I didn't want to see anyone. But the moment I entered *this* house, something changed. I felt alive again."

Raine sucked in a deep breath. "That's how I felt the moment I first saw *you*."

I was still wrapping my head around the fact that he was the one who pushed me into the door. "Why weren't you locked in the room with them?"

Grim snorted. "Excellent question. Raine, please do tell us how your psychotic ass was roaming free around the house."

Raine chuckled. "Because I pissed off Mrs. Wickford enough for her to kill me but not quite enough for her to curse me. You see, *your* souls can't pass on because of what she did. Mine can."

Saint's eyes widened. "You just refuse to. How is that even possible?"

"Because even the devil won't let this psycho into hell," Grim quipped.

"This is my house, and I won't leave. Simple as that." Raine was so calm about everything. He crossed his legs and sipped on his whiskey as if what he just said was the sanest thing anyone ever had. But he was a dead man. A ghost who would not accept his fate.

I understood him a lot more now. Raine Wickford came from

noney. He was a rich man at a time when the world was at war. Poe, Grim, and Saint on the other hand came from more complicated pasts. It wasn't as easy for them back then.

But there were still so many questions about that night. "How did you know what I would do? That I would move in and renovate this house?"

His eyes lit up to match his devious smirk. "I like chaos, little vixen. And this little situation is as chaotic as it gets. I'm not going to reveal all my cards tonight. There are some things you need to figure out for yourself."

My cheeks burned. This man fucking infuriated me. I couldn't get a read on him, and I couldn't throw him out. He was playing a game I didn't sign up for. And yet one look was all it took to keep me hooked.

"Oh, fuck off," Grim growled at him.

The day had turned into night, and I was exhausted. I stifled a yawn as I stretched to my feet. "Look, it's nothing to worry about. Just bored locals trying to prank me. I'll call the shop in the morning and get us a new window. It's not supposed to rain tonight so, if anything we might have a few furry animals joining us for breakfast. Can we please not talk about this anymore tonight?"

Saint tied his long hair up into a top knot, revealing the sweat that was beading down his brow. "Bailey… you're downplaying what happened tonight and I don't fucking like it one bit. But we *will* talk more about this tomorrow."

The tension was so thick, it was suffocating. Everyone was so wound up. We needed release. I placed my hand on his chest. "Fine. But tonight… I want to feel something else than this ache inside my chest."

His breath quickened as the room fell silent. "What do you want, little fox?"

Moisture pooled between my legs as I looked at each of them. "*Release*."

Raine pursed his lips and leaped to his feet. "Well, that's my cue."

My heart raced. "Raine… stay."

"Bailey," Grim growled.

"I want him to stay." I knew I was playing with fire but if we were going to all make this work, we had to start somewhere.

Raine chuckled. "Only if you get on your knees and show them what you look like sucking my cock."

Everyone seemed to be holding a collective breath, waiting to see if I would slap him or fulfill his demand.

"Sit down," I murmured. "All of you… take a seat."

Raine stalked toward me and gazed down. "*Good girl.*" He unzipped his jeans and pushed them down, stepping out of them before sinking back down on the couch. He spread his legs wide open and then pulled off his shirt.

My breath hitched. He was fucking gorgeous. I licked my lips as my gaze landed on his hard cock. It was long and thick with pre cum already oozing from the tip. Raine snickered as he watched me drink in the sight of him, knowing how aroused I was.

I forced myself to look away. I needed to check in first. I locked eyes with Grim and gave him a nod.

He nodded back. "Take what you want, little fox." Poe and Saint nodded in agreement as they sat back to watch.

Their approval sent another rush of adrenaline to my core. I turned and knelt down between Raine's legs, sliding my hands up his thighs.

"Take off your shirt," he rasped.

My nipples pebbled as the air hit them. I threw my top on the floor and moved back into position. I could hear the rustling of clothes from behind, knowing my guys were getting naked as well. The thought of them jerking off to me sucking Raine's cock made me feral.

Raine slipped his hand around the back of my neck, pulling

my ponytail free. Tangling his hand in my hair, he pulled my head down into his lap. Sweat beaded down my back as my core tingled with anticipation. With his free hand, he fisted his cock, rubbing the tip across my lips. "Open your mouth."

A little whimper escaped my lips as I parted them. Raine guided his cock into my mouth. I was not in control. He thrust in hard and yanked my head down. His cock hit the back of my throat, and I gagged. I dug my fingers into his thighs as he ground against me, pushing in and pulling out without an ounce of gentleness.

And I fucking loved it.

I moaned as tears streamed down my cheeks.

"Yeah, fucking choke on me, baby girl." He looked at the guys as he held me in place, thrusting deeper down my throat. "Looks like I'm her fucking daddy now, boys."

I took deep breaths through my nose as his cock took up all the space in my mouth. A rush of air hit my lungs as he pulled out, leaving just the tip in. "Suck it hard."

I pursed my lips around his tip and sucked, twirling my tongue in circles around it. He grunted and plunged back in. "Swallow every fucking drop for me."

Judging by the moans that were erupting behind me, they were just as turned on as he was. "Squeeze my balls."

I cupped his balls in my hands and did as he commanded.

"That's my good little slut."

Oh, fuck. Every inch of my body burned with desire for this man. With a need to please him.

He grunted again as his cock hit the back of my throat. Stilling himself against me, his shaft throbbed against the inside of my cheeks. My core spasmed as his thick hot cum shot out into my mouth.

"Mmm, fuck," he rasped. "Drink, little vixen." He moaned louder as I choked his cum down my throat, my breath as erratic as my pulse.

I gasped for air the second he pulled out and leaned back against the cushions. He wiped my lip with his thumb and shoved it into my mouth. "You missed a drop." I moaned as I licked it off.

It was rough and depraved and dirty. I turned around slowly to face the guys, anxious to see their faces. To my delight, their eyes blazed with hunger and desire. Poe was holding his cock, his hand covered in his own cum. Saint had his hand down Grim's pants, still working his cock up and down.

They were just as aroused as I was.

Raine pulled me onto his lap and yanked my pants off. He whispered in my ear, "Let's help him finish, shall we?"

Without waiting for my answer he spun me around, so my back was against his chest. "Spread your thighs apart and lean back."

Their eyes traveled the length of my body as I spread open wide. Raine fingered the edges of my panties before sliding them to the side. "Is this not the wettest cunt you've ever seen, boys?" He swirled his finger in circles around my swollen clit. "You like watching me touch her. I can see it in your eyes."

I trembled as he untied the strings holding my panties together and ripped them out from under me.

Grim moaned as Saint stroked him. "Fuck… yeah… keep going."

Raine's soaked fingers inched up my belly, smearing my juices all over my skin. He circled my nipple before pinching it hard. I cried out as he twisted it between his fingers. He did the same with the other one. It hurt so bad I could barely breathe.

"Shh… relax. The more you struggle, the harder I squeeze."

Despite wanting to get away from him now, my core was spasming. He was doing something to my body that I didn't want to like. "Raine, stop, you're hurting me."

He sucked on my earlobe. "And you like it."

I looked across the room to find Poe jerking himself off again. We locked eyes. "Relax, little fox. Let him give you what you want."

A wave of panic pushed against my desire as I realized what was happening. They were stepping back. Letting me explore my dark side. Grim and Saint would never let anything happen to me. But they knew this was what I needed. They were done fighting with Raine. I was the only one left who was.

He released my raw nipples and traced soft circles around them. "These nipples should always be swollen like this."

He pinched them harder this time and I bucked. Every nerve in my body was on fire. "Raine, please."

"You're so fucking scared that I could make you cum just like this. That I can control your cunt any way I want. Isn't that right, baby girl?"

He let go and dragged his fingers down my belly "I think you're ready for this." He slid his palm down my pussy and back up. "Deep breath now." Before I could form my next thought, his hand lifted and came down hard against my folds.

"Uhhh." A deep spasm rolled through me, breaking past the sting of his hand. I clenched my thighs together. "I can't take anymore."

Raine grabbed my throat and squeezed. "You'll take whatever I give you like a good little slut. Now open your fucking legs."

Grim let out a deep moan as his cum burst out. "Fuck, Bailey... stop fighting it."

Saint rubbed him furiously, milking him for every drop. "Grim's right," he rasped. "Let him take you to the edge. And then fucking jump."

I looked to Poe who was always the voice of reason. His eyes were dark as he watched Raine dig his fingers into my throat. He stood and stalked over to us. My heart was beating in my chest. What the fuck was he going to do?

He knelt down and pushed my legs apart. "You belong to us, little fox. I think you need reminding of that." He nodded to Raine. "Make her fucking scream."

Oh, shit. Memories of that night came flooding back. The night Poe ripped me from my bed and dragged me to my fate. We had gotten soft playing house for the past year. I had forgotten myself. Forgotten how much I craved this.

"I'm going to punish you now for being a bad girl," Raine whispered in my ear.

He slapped my pussy hard. Each time I bucked, Poe pressed my legs farther apart.

I screamed as my clit swelled and tingled as Raine rubbed at my raw folds. His cock throbbed against my ass. I clawed at Poe's arms, leaving scratch marks across his skin. He growled and sprang to his feet.

Raine laughed. "Now you've done it."

Poe returned with his belt in hand. Raine pushed me forward and clasped my hands around my back. I squirmed as Poe wrapped his belt tightly around my wrists, securing it in the clasp.

As Raine yanked me back up and held me to his chest, Poe cupped my face. "Surrender, little fox. I know this is what you want."

I was afraid to accept it. Why? What was so wrong about me enjoying this? The fear of the unknown was what got me off. Losing control. Letting go and giving in to this… those were some of my darker fantasies that I was scared to embrace.

Poe pushed my legs apart again and held them firm. "Are you going to be a good girl and let us defile you?"

I whimpered against Raine, my arms aching from being pinned behind my back. "Y-yes," I stammered.

Raine chuckled as Grim and Saint crossed the room, and each took a seat on either side of us. I was surrounded by all four of them and it sent a deep spasm straight to my nub. I licked my lips and relaxed back against Raine.

Grim and Saint each sucked on one of my breasts. The sensations from both were driving me wild. Saint sucked and nibbled while Grim flicked his tongue. I moaned into it.

I gazed down just as Raine spread my pussy apart. I bucked as he shoved his finger deep inside. "Uhhh," I cried out.

"Mmm, why don't you help me stretch her open," Raine rasped.

Oh, fuck. I was panting now, my heart racing so fast it felt like it was going to explode. A small spasm rippled through me as Grim slipped his finger in next to Raine's.

"Yeah, you like that don't you, little vixen?" Raine moaned as he and Grim took turns thrusting inside me "I'm so close, fuck," I whispered. The pressure was building.

"Not yet," Saint growled. "Not until we're all in there." I gasped as he slid a thick finger inside. I was stuffed to the fucking brim as the three of them burrowed in deeper. I lifted my hips as they finger fucked me together, grinding up and down.

"Fuck… it's too much…" I cried, tears streaming down my cheeks. I was overwhelmed by every sensation of pleasure that rocked through me.

Raine wrapped his free hand around my throat. "Almost time."

Poe stroked the outside of my pussy, dragging his finger down and underneath. I clenched as he pushed at my other entrance. "Relax…"

Oh, fuck.

Poe shoved his finger deep inside my ass. I screamed as the pressure in my clit exploded. I rocked against them as they pushed harder. Stars blurred my vision. Raine closed his grip on my throat, cutting off the air to my lungs.

Their voices began to blend together. I couldn't focus on who was saying what.

"Yeah, fucking cum for us."

"Mmm, that's our good girl."

"Our dirty little slut."

Each spasm rolled into another one as my orgasm claimed

every inch of me. Grim and Saint devoured me as I came, kissing and licking my neck, my lips, and my nipples like starving animals.

I inhaled deep breaths as Raine freed me from his grip. He caressed my back as he whispered in my ear, "The darker we go, the closer you'll be to remembering who you are."

CHAPTER Eighteen

Saint

"Did we do the right thing?" I asked.

"Well, she passed out with a smile on her face." Poe chuckled as he sipped his whiskey.

Grim nodded in agreement. "I wasn't too keen on it at first but seeing her body come alive like that… fuck. That was fucking hot. Maybe she'll finally tell us what's going on inside that head of hers."

It was Bailey who was really in control. We were nothing but servants to her every desire. Even if she didn't want to admit it. But Raine pushed her to, and it was exactly what she needed. I wasn't too thrilled about him either at first but feeling her cunt throb against my finger as she came harder than ever, changed my mind about him.

Because deep down inside, Bailey was a little psycho too.

"So what do we do about our little locals problem?" Poe asked.

Grim clenched his fists. "I will murder the next one who crosses our property line."

I pinched my brow, exhaustion setting in. "We need to find out more from Bailey. And I think Raine knows more than he's letting on." The fact that Raine Wickford might know more about Bailey than we did irked me to no end. But I was trying to give him a chance. We were all bound to this house, so it only made sense to try and live together peacefully. Especially after tonight.

Sharing our little fox with him was more than just sex. It was an invitation to be a part of this family. I only hoped he didn't fuck it up. Or we might lose our little fox in the process.

Poe nodded. "I agree. And until we figure out who's fucking with her, Bailey stays put. We can't protect her out there."

Grim snickered. "Good luck with that."

"Let's all get some sleep and figure it out in the morning."

Raine sauntered in, humming to himself. "She's out for the night. It took all I had not to fuck her while she slept. She looked so soft and fragile. I'd love to see the look on her face when she wakes up to my cock buried deep inside her. Mmm… next time."

I rolled my eyes at him. "You really are fucking psycho."

He grinned as he hoisted himself onto the kitchen counter. "And insatiable. A delicious combination."

I knew he wasn't even joking. He would actually fuck her while she slept. A part of me wondered if that was yet another thing that would turn her on. Or maybe it was just him. Everything Raine did to her seemed to be what she wanted.

"Well, don't come running to us if she snaps your dick off," Grim spat.

Raine laughed. "Keep talking like that and I'll run up there right now just to prove you wrong."

"Okay enough. What do you know that we don't?" I asked him point blank.

He dipped his finger into a jar of peanut butter and sucked it off. "Many things, Saint. But they aren't my secrets to tell."

Fucking hell with this guy. "Fine. We'll ask Bailey tomorrow."

He arched an eyebrow at me. "She can't tell you things she doesn't remember. And she won't tell you things that are going to make you insist she stays locked up in this house."

Grim threw up his hands. "Enough with the fucking riddles already."

"I will say this…" Raine licked his fingers. "Pain is only temporary. Once she fully embraces that, no one will be able to hurt her ever again."

We fell silent as his words seemed to hang in the air like a bad omen. The more I tried to figure it all out, the more confused it made me.

CHAPTER Nineteen

Bailey

There were many things I needed to face. I had been running from trauma my whole life, burying it deep. It was a lot to process but it was time for me to come to terms with everything. Last night was an awakening. My life had become a battle of two extremes—feeling powerless outside of this house and feeling invincible inside it.

I was done with accepting things happening to me, and ready to take charge of my own life. I clasped the keys in my hand, remembering the weight of them. The door they unlock presents more mystery to what lies on the other side. But I have to embrace it. My parents would want me to.

I threw some clothes into my overnight bag, sent off a quick text to Maureen, and raced downstairs. Tonight, I was determined to have a fun night with my best friend and hopefully figure out what to do about Billy and his friends. It was one thing to harass me on the street, but throwing a brick into the window of my home was crossing a line. And the dread sitting in the pit of my stomach told me it was only going to get worse.

As I stomped into the kitchen, I ran smack into a wall of solid muscle. Saint. He towered over me, his eyes narrowing on the bag slung over my shoulder. "Going somewhere, little fox?"

I looked past him to see Poe, Grim, and Raine crowded around the breakfast table, their mouths full of pancakes and bacon. Their forks all seemed to clank down at the same time.

I let out a deep sigh. "I'm heading up to my old place. Maureen and I are having another girls' night." I held up my phone as if a text from Maureen solidified it.

Poe's face sank. "Did we upset you last night? I thought you were enjoying it."

My cheeks burned at the memory of all four of them finger fucking me. At night I came alive but in the light of day, I turned back into that shy girl full of shame. But not today. No. This was about something else.

I shook my head. "Last night was *everything*. I just need to figure some shit out. And Maureen is leaving soon. I want to spend as much time with my best friend as possible."

Saint placed a gentle hand on my lower back. "Bailey, someone threw a brick through our window last night, remember? A brick with your name on it. Figuratively, of course. Do you think it's safe right now to leave?"

My stomach knotted. This was why I hadn't wanted to tell them about Billy to begin with. They would want to protect me and the only way they could was to keep me here. But I didn't want to live in fear. Not anymore.

"Look, the guys that did that know that I live here. That's why they came *here*. My old place probably isn't even on their radar. As far as anyone knows, I haven't been up there for a year. I'll be fine.' No one except Maureen knew that I lived here with four feral men who've been dead for over a hundred years.

"I don't like it, Bailey," Grim rasped. "Why can't Maureen just come here?"

I released an irritated sigh. "Because it's not really a *girls'* night if the four of you are lurking about and eavesdropping. And don't try to deny it. That is exactly what you'd do."

Raine flashed me a wide grin. "Go have fun, little vixen. I'll keep these assholes entertained."

"Of course, *you're* on board with this," Saint growled.

Raine shrugged. "Bailey's a grown woman. If she wants to party with her friend, she doesn't need our permission. One brick does not equal a lockdown."

Psycho or not, he was the only voice of reason right now.

Grim snorted. "Such a kiss ass."

Raine smirked. "Kiss, lick, fuck… I'm gonna do all sorts of things to her ass."

"Not tonight you aren't," Poe hissed. "Bailey, we promise we'll leave you alone if you and Maureen stay here."

I tightened my grip on my overnight bag and looked each one of them in the eye. "No. If this is going to work, I need to have a life outside of this house."

Saint ran a hand through his long hair before tying it up into a top knot. "You're right. I can't promise you we won't be worried all night but if this is what you need, then go."

Grim huffed while Poe looked like his dog just died. Raine was the only one who didn't seem the least bit concerned. He smirked into his coffee mug. Fuck, that man was always pleased with himself.

I tilted up to plant a kiss on Saint's lips. "Thank you."

Grim pulled me into his chest, his hands on my hips, and

kissed me hard. He tasted like maple syrup and chicory. "Be careful, little fox."

I nodded as I moved to Poe. He embraced me with his whole body, hugging me tight to his chest. He pressed his forehead to mine. "How is it that you can make me so fucking feral one minute and then turn me into a needy puppy the next?"

"I love both those sides of you," I whispered between us.

My stomach knotted as I turned to face Raine. We stared at each other for what seemed like entirely too long as if we were the only two people in the room. He licked his lips and wrapped his hand around my neck. "Come here."

I whimpered as he gave my throat a light squeeze. His blue-green eyes flickered with a carnal hunger that sent tingles straight to my core. "When you're in bed later tonight… you better think of me when you're playing with yourself, little vixen."

My breath hitched, moisture pooling between my thighs. All I could muster was a nod. This man made me want to do things that were unholy.

"I'll walk you out," Saint quipped.

I lingered at the front door. "Thanks again for backing me. I really need this tonight."

He nodded. "I left a present in your bag. Don't look at it until you get there. It's a surprise."

"It better not be a vibrator. Maureen will think I'm a sex addict." I chuckled.

Saint kissed my cheek before opening the front door. "You'll just have to wait and see."

By the time I got in my car, the front door was already closed. But as I pulled out of the driveway, I spotted Raine in one of the second-story windows, his brow furrowed against the glass. *Maybe he was just as concerned as the rest of them.*

I flashed him a grin and sped off down the street.

The gates of Bishop Mortuary creaked in the wind. A flutter of butterflies swam in my belly as I drove through them, taking note of the chipped paint and rusty hinges. This place had been relatively untouched for about fifteen years. The brush had grown thick around the edges of the building, weeds as tall as me snaked up the walls.

I got out of my car and stood in front of the entrance; my nerves shot. It wasn't ghosts that I feared. Not anymore. No. Being back here brought back distant memories. Knowing that this would be the first time I'd be going inside without my parents. I could never bring myself to do it, but I couldn't sell it either. But if there was anything in there that could tell me more about them, about where we came from… then I had to swallow my anxiety and get my ass inside.

It took me a few minutes to get the door open. The knob turned with ease, but the door stuck. I had to push on it with my body before it finally snapped open.

I was grateful in this moment that I'd also kept the utilities on as well. I just couldn't bring myself to turn them off. As if keeping them on, would preserve my parents' memory even more.

I flicked on the lights and was instantly hit with more nostalgia. That familiar scent of flowers and embalming fluid engulfed me. I crept in carefully, half-expecting someone or something to greet me or jump out at me. But it was quiet and still.

The waiting room was pristine—clean and orderly with its white walls and gray carpet. I ran my finger over the front desk, leaving streaks through the thick layer of dust. The appointment book sat open. A twinge of sadness crept into my chest at the sight of my mother's handwriting.

I closed my eyes for a second and took a deep breath. I could almost smell her still, recreating the memory of her scent in my mind—roses, fresh linen, and ash. My father's glasses perched on the edge of the closed laptop. I wondered what the last thing was he read with them.

A part of me wanted to rifle through everything and another part wanted it all to remain untouched. Frozen in time. As if they'd never left. I looked up at the ceiling, tears welling in my eyes, and a whimper escaped my lips. "*Why did you have to leave?*" I rasped.

It was the silly whims of a little girl that screamed impossible things in my head. Being here again awakened that voice. I just wanted to curl up under the desk and fall asleep like I used to do all those years ago.

Except it wouldn't be the same. There'd be no gentle kisses on my forehead, soothing me awake, telling me it was time to go home. No more scent of roses and linen and ash. Just death. So much death.

I made my way through the rest of the mortuary, going from room to empty room. The estate manager had told me years later that she came through right after the fire to make sure everything was untouched. She assured me, per my parents' wishes, that nothing had been moved or tampered with. I was relieved to find that to be the truth. The essence of Dahlia and Ronan Bishop had been preserved. It lingered like a forgotten dream.

As I entered the last room, my parents' office, I flipped on the light and froze. The black leather rolling chair behind my father's desk swayed from side to side. As if someone had just gotten up out of it.

Sweat beaded down my neck as I took a nervous glance around. I remembered the shadow I'd seen in the window a few nights back and panic rose in my chest. The building was locked up tight so there was no way anyone could have broken in. And there were no windows in this office, no other way in or out other than the one I was standing in.

Fuck. It was probably just the draft from me opening the door after all these years of it being sealed. Or maybe just the foundation settling, stirred by my footsteps. *Yeah, I'm going with that.*

When I said I wasn't afraid of ghosts, I just realized that I wasn't afraid of *my* ghosts. And I had somehow failed to remember that a house for the dead would most likely have its fair share of them roaming around.

I was going to have to sage this place if I ever planned to get it back up and running.

Convinced that nothing was going to jump out and grab me, I crept inside the office. I ran my hands over the desk, the chair, and finally my father's lab coat that hung from the coat rack. A lightness filled my chest. This was the first step to making peace with my past. And a desperate desire to spend more time here gripped me. Why had I waited so long?

I took a seat in my father's chair and let out a deep breath as the leather formed to my body, embracing me like an old friend. Tears streamed down my cheeks. I could still feel them. They were gone but a piece of them still lingered. Not in the way my guys were, but a sliver of my parents remained for me to cling to.

I pulled open the desk drawers, finding endless amounts of office supplies. There were some business ledgers, receipts, and… multiple bottles of rose room spray? I chuckled as I took one out and spritzed it in front of me. And here I thought all these years my mother wore expensive perfume. Nope. Drugstore room spray. This brought a smile to my face. And it made me adore her even more. I pocketed one of the bottles before closing the drawer.

I saved the top middle drawer for last for some reason. I figured it was the most personal and wanted to savor it. As I slid it open, my heart raced. Directly on top of a stack of papers was a large manilla envelope… with my name on it.

As the rain poured down, I tucked the envelope into my jacket and made a run for my car. My fingers trembled as I turned the key in the ignition. I sucked in a sharp breath as I fished the envelope out and tossed it onto the passenger seat.

How long had it been in that desk drawer? I knew it wasn't their last will and testament. I had already seen that on my eighteenth birthday when I suddenly became the richest girl in Wickford Hollow. So what was inside?

Maybe it contained the answers I'd been searching for…

I turned up the heat, my fingers trembling around the knob, and switched on the radio. *If I Be Wrong* by Wolf Larsen poured out of my speakers. A hiccup lodged in my throat as my emotions bubbled over. My tears turned to sobs as I drove back through the gates and turned onto Devil's Road. I had played this song over and over after I'd signed the estate papers three years ago.

Sometimes I thought that life was circular, not linear. Here I was, years later, on the same road, listening to the same song, driving toward my old house, with an envelope from my parents as my only passenger. A shiver snaked up my spine as the sensation of déjà vu consumed me.

My phone buzzed as I turned onto the dirt road that led up to my old house—a text from Maureen: *Got lots of snacks and booze. See ya soon, biatch.*

I chuckled as I parked out front of my house. If anyone could shake me out of this melancholic stupor, it would be my best friend. I shoved the envelope into the glove compartment before getting out. "*I'll read you later,*" I muttered under my breath. The ghosts of my past would have to wait. Tonight, I had to figure out how to deal with my present predicament.

CHAPTER *Twenty*

Bailey

"Did you buy up the whole store?" I laughed as Maureen bounced through my front door carrying four full grocery bags.

"Hey, the night is young, and you know how hungry I get when I'm drunk." She set the bags down on the kitchen table and leaned in close. "And I plan to get very fucking drunk."

I raised an eyebrow at her. "Everything okay, Maur?"

Her brow furrowed as she emptied out all the bags, spreading a mass array of chips, dip, cheese, frozen pizzas, crackers, ice cream, and chocolate bars all over my table. "If by okay you mean why do I plan to eat my feelings and drink away my sorrows, then nope." She popped the p with pursed lips.

I retrieved two pint glasses from the cabinet and filled them with ice. We needed drinks, stat. "What's going on?"

As I perused the bottles of liquor, trying to decide on what our first cocktail of the night should be, Maureen snatched the vodka and shoved it into my hands. "I need a *Bailey special.*"

Oh, fuck. She really was upset. The last time we drank dirty martinis was senior year after she walked in on her mom fucking her accountant. Her mom swore her to secrecy. The last thing Sheriff Gray needed was another reminder that he wasn't good enough for his wife. She came from old money and despite their early connection, Mrs. Gray quickly grew tired of a Sheriff's salary.

I grabbed two martini glasses and my shaker, pushing the pint glasses to the side. "Coming right up. Now start talking."

She plopped down in a chair and pulled out a bag of weed and rolling papers. "Well, my dad found out about one of my mom's side pieces and she thinks I told him. What a fucking joke. So now she's refusing to pay my tuition for school next year."

My mouth dropped open. "Oh, shit, Maur. What the fuck is wrong with her? You've been keeping her dirty secrets for years. Why would she think you'd spill now."

She shrugged as she pinched some of the weed and sprinkled it inside a rolling paper. "She's on opiates half the time so who the fuck knows? I think she was just looking for an excuse to stop me from going. She's miserable and wants everyone else to be too."

Fuck. Maureen has dreamed about getting away from here since we were kids. "I'm so sorry… Maybe she'll cool off in a couple of days. How did your dad react?"

She licked the paper before rolling and twisting it between her fingers. "How he always does. Work. He's been sleeping at the station for two days. It's that or he'll turn into a raging alcoholic again. You know how hard he's worked to stay sober."

My heart ached for her. I threw my arms around her shoulders. "Fuck. I'm sorry."

"You and me both. I guess this means I have to get a job now. I should be able to save up enough money by the time I'm thirty." She groaned as she lit up the joint and took a long drag before passing it to me.

I shook my head as I coughed out smoke. "No. Fuck that. I'm giving you the money."

Her eyes widened. "No, Bales. I'm not taking your money. I'll figure it out."

"Maur, I have more than I know what to do with. Please, let me do this for you. I know how much you want to go to school. Besides, I'm thinking of all the amazing clothes you'll send me once you become a famous costume designer." If she stayed here in Wickford Hollow, she'd end up in a loveless marriage just like her parents. The pool of men here was less than appealing.

Maureen groaned again. "I don't know. Maybe you're right, and she'll cool off."

I raised my martini. "Well, here's hoping she does. But if not, I got your back. Either way, you're going to that school."

Her eyes welled with tears, but she quickly blinked them back. "Cheers, bitch. Here's to a fun night with no drama." She took a big sip of her drink. "I love you, Bales."

"Right back at ya, bestie." I winked as I mixed a fresh batch of martinis.

After piling an obnoxious amount of cheese onto a massive cutting board, we grabbed our drinks and headed into the living room.

"*So*, what's going on at the house of whips and chains?" Maureen cooed.

A little vodka dribbled down my chin as I laughed mid-sip. "No beating around the bush with you, huh?"

She cocked her head to the side. "I bet they're beating your bush, bitch. I thought I noticed you walking funny."

I threw a pillow at her as she burst into a fit of giggles. "I forgot how classy you are." I laughed. "But yeah, everything is good. I'm still trying to get a read on Raine. He's bringing things out of me I've never felt before."

Maureen perked up. "Like kinky stuff?"

I nodded. "Kind of. It's more about the control. I have this need to give it to him. All of it. He pushes my boundaries, and I like it."

Maureen kicked her legs up on the couch. "Ooh, girl. That is what I'm talking about. I've been watching so much porn since you told me about them. Not gonna lie, I'm jealous of your sex life."

I shrugged. "Trust me, it's not always easy. I have four very strong personalities I'm trying to navigate through. After the sex, we still have to live together. It can be a challenge."

Maureen rolled her eyes. "If half of them are as hot as I think they are, then I would happily juggle their mood swings. It's the price you pay to cum hard."

We burst into another fit of laughter. "You make a good point." I poured the rest of my martini down my throat. "I think it's margarita time."

Maureen's head bobbed up and down as she finished her drink as well. "Fuck yeah."

We spent the next hour having a lively debate about vibrators versus actual cock, drinking margaritas, and eating chips and salsa. She gasped and squealed as I described what it felt like to have four fingers inside me at the same time.

"Okay, bitch. You are officially my hero," Maureen drawled. "I'm so happy you finally told me about them."

That familiar twinge of guilt reverberated through me. I didn't want to be a downer, but I promised her no more secrets. "Maur… something else happened at Wickford. After we had coffee yesterday."

She sat up and poured herself another margarita from the pitcher. "I'm already not liking the sound of this."

I swallowed down the lump in my throat. "When I got home, the guys were cleaning up glass in the foyer. Someone threw a brick through our window. And by someone, I'm pretty sure it was Billy. There was a note covering it with the word freak on it."

Maureen's cheeks flamed. "Motherfuckers." She leaped up and paced around the living room. "That's it, Bales. I know you don't want to ruffle feathers, but he has got to be dealt with."

I nodded. "I know. You're right. It's getting out of hand now. They came to my fucking house and vandalized it. What's next? We have to figure out what to do about them."

Maureen took big gulps. "Well, we have to tell my dad. Maybe get a restraining order against him?"

I sighed. "Yeah but I have no actual proof it was him. You know that's the first thing your dad will ask for."

Her eyes lit up. "What about security cameras? They're easy to install. Next time he comes around, boom you're on camera, bitch."

That would take too long. "But then I'm just walking around my own house on eggshells waiting for him to show up again. And Maur… if Billy gets into my house, the guys will kill him. I don't mean that figuratively. Like they will actually murder him."

Maureen shrugged. "Good. Maybe that's what he deserves for fucking with the coolest bitch in Wickford Hollow."

I shook my head. As much as I hated Billy, I didn't want his blood on my hands. "I'm going to say no to murder, Maur. There's got to be another way."

She waved her hands around, spilling some of her drink on her hand. She licked it off. "Okay, okay. No murder. Jeesh."

The expression on her face made me giggle. No one else could make me laugh the way she did. "It will come to us. Let's just forget about it for now. Besides I wanted to tell you about something else. I went inside Bishop Mortuary today."

She gasped. "Finally? Yes, Bales! I'm so proud of you. I know how hard that must have been."

I nodded. "Yeah, it was surreal. But I'm glad I went. I've been thinking about opening it back up. I think my parents would want that."

Maureen clapped her hands together. "Yes! And who else would be better at it than you? You literally live with dead people. Plus I'm sure people would prefer to not have to drive to Ever Graves to bury someone."

"Exactly. I don't have the heart to sell it and it doesn't feel right to let it sit there empty. It will give me purpose again. As much as I love my guys, I can't just sit around that house all day."

She waved her hand above her head, snapping her fingers. "Because you a boss bitch. Like I said before, my hero."

I had never worked before. Not a day in my life. I was fortunate to have the money my parents left me. But I didn't want to end up like Maureen's mother any more than she did. I needed something other than my love life to focus on.

"There was also an envelope addressed to me in the desk drawer. I think it's from my parents."

Her jaw dropped. "Wait, what? You haven't opened it yet?"

I shook my head. "No, it's in my car. I don't know why I'm scared but it's like if I open it, then it will literally be the last words I have from them."

Maureen threw the pillow back at me, hitting me square in the head. "Girl, go get it. You know you want to. It could be important."

She was right. I was being silly. I jumped up and stumbled to the side. I was tipsier than I thought. "Okay, throw the pizza in the oven, and I'll be right back."

"Yay," she squealed as she made an off-balance dash to the kitchen.

Fuck, we were already drunk, and it was barely nine pm. My stomach grumbled as I threw on my coat and slippers.

The wind almost blew the door off its hinges. It howled through the night like a pack of wolves, whipping my hair around my face till I could barely see. I pointed the clicker at my car to unlock it and jogged toward it, instantly regretting the trek outside.

I was probably making more of the envelope than it was. It could just be some old photographs or medical documents for my records. That was another reason I was afraid to open it. Fear of disappointment when I really wanted it to be a letter from my parents.

I sloshed through the mud, cursing myself for putting on slippers and not my actual boots. I was too fucking buzzed to think clearly.

As I reached for the handle of the driver's door, I glimpsed a shadow, passing behind me, in the reflection of the window. My stomach dropped. Oh, fuck. My feet sank further into the mud just as a wall of muscle rammed into me from behind.

I opened my mouth to scream but it was too late.

A hand closed around my mouth. "Shh… there'll be plenty of time for that later."

Billy.

No. No. No.

I bucked against him, flailing my arms around as I tried desperately to break free.

A deep sinister laugh erupted out of him. "Let's get you inside where we can have some fun."

I screamed into his hand as he dragged me up the front porch, but my voice got lost in the wind.

"No one's gonna hear you out here, freak."

I went limp, like a dead weight in his arms as he pulled me back into the house. I kicked my feet against the floor in an effort to warn Maureen.

He just grunted and squeezed me tighter. "You ain't going anywhere."

I fought him all the way until we got to the living room. And then I froze. Maureen was gagged and bound to a chair, her eyes watery and full of fear. Chad stood behind her, holding a knife to her neck.

A switch inside my brain flipped and all I could think of was one thing.

Murdering them both.

CHAPTER Twenty-One

Bailey

My heart pounded in my ears. A wave of nausea hit me as bile crept up my throat. The stench of Billy's tobacco-stained fingers invaded my mouth.

I kept my eyes locked with Maureen's as he dragged me to a chair and slammed me down on it. Chad was already there with more rope. He wrapped it around me, securing me to the chair.

Billy smirked as he looked down at me, admiring Chad's handiwork. "I've been waiting a long time for this moment, Bailey. I knew throwing a brick through your window would scare you into coming here. This little shithole is perfect. Out in the middle of the woods with no neighbors to hear you scream."

Fuck. The guys were right, and I didn't listen.

"Okay, Billy, you win. You scared the shit out of us. Now let us go," I stammered.

His eyes darkened as he reared back and smacked the side of my face. I cried out as my head snapped to the side.

Maureen started to cry.

"Fuck, Billy, you didn't have to hit her that hard," Chad drawled as he chuckled.

Billy grabbed the back of my head and yanked on my hair, pulling me toward his face. "That's for almost breaking my jaw, you stupid cunt."

Tears threatened to spill but I choked them back. I wouldn't give him the satisfaction. I gathered all the saliva I could muster and spit in his face. "Fuck you, Billy."

He flashed me a grin as he wiped my spit off with his finger and then sucked it off. "Mmm, so sweet. I wonder how the rest of you tastes."

No, this can't be happening.

He grabbed the knife from Chad and strutted over to Maureen. She flinched as he dragged the tip of the blade across her chest gently so as not to break the skin. "Let's play a little game, shall we?" He looked at me. "Chad is going to untie you so you can play. I'm going to make you undress for us. Every time you refuse, Maureen gets a little cut, just like this." She screamed into her gag as Billy nicked her shoulder with the knife.

"Stop! Have you lost your mind? Maureen has nothing to do with this. Let her go, and I'll do whatever you want." Adrenaline raced through my veins. I had to get us out of this. This could not be our fate.

Billy clicked his tongue. "Oh, so she can run off to her Sheriff daddy and ruin all our fun? Nah. I like this plan better."

Fuck.

He nodded and Chad began to untie me. "Don't do anything stupid, Bailey. You'll only make it worse for both of you."

As soon as the rope fell from my wrists, I pulled my arms in tight to my chest. "You will never get away with this, Billy. Let us go now before it gets out of hand, and I won't tell anyone."

He chuckled and took a pull from the bottle of tequila we'd left on the coffee table. "You really think anyone is going to believe you over me anyway? Now fucking take off your shirt."

My hands shook. "Please, don't do this."

Maureen wailed as she writhed against her restraints.

Billy pressed the knife to her neck. "Take. It. Off."

Chad swiped at the bottle of tequila and plopped himself on the couch.

I nodded, taking deep breaths. "Fine. Okay. Just don't hurt her." He licked his lips as I pulled off my black tank top and tossed it on the floor.

He pressed the knife into Maureen's neck and a little blood trickled out. "Bra too. Off."

My breath hitched and it took everything I had not to pass out. I reached around my back with trembling fingers and unhooked my black lace bra. I pulled the straps down slowly and let it fall into my lap.

Billy sucked in a sharp breath. "Are those titties as pretty as you remember, Chad?"

He put his hand over the bulge in his jeans and shifted in his seat. "Ah, fuck. Looks like they got bigger."

I swallowed down the acid in my throat. "Please, Billy. This isn't right."

His eyes darkened. "Shut the fuck up or I'll cut her again. Now, your pants."

Every nerve in my body was shot as I stood. I unzipped my jeans and wiggled them off. Before I could sit back down, he nicked the knife across Maureen's cheek. Her whimpering turned to sobs.

"For fuck's sake, Billy. I'm doing what you ask," I yelled.

"I didn't tell you to sit back down. Not until you take those panties off." His eyes were wild with lust and need. And yet full of hate and rage at the same time.

I looked at Maureen. "It's gonna be okay." I slid my panties down and waited.

"Mmm. Now you can sit back down."

Chad let out a low whistle. "I like this game."

Billy smirked. "Oh, it's only getting started. Put Maureen in the back bedroom and get back out here. I'm sick of Bailey looking at her. I want all her attention on us."

Maureen screamed through her gag as Chad tipped the chair back and dragged her down the hall.

"I'm going to kill you," I muttered.

He pulled up another chair and took a seat across from me. "If that's what you need to tell yourself. But you and I both know that ain't gonna happen."

Chad strolled back in and took back his seat on the couch. "The Sheriff's daughter is locked up tight. I'll check on her later."

Billy's eyes wandered my body. "Spread your legs."

I shook my head. "This has gone far enough."

He slammed the tip of the knife into my coffee table. "It goes until I say it's over. Now open your fucking legs before I do it for you."

The thought of his hands on me made me so sick. I had to will myself not to vomit. I took a deep breath and spread my thighs back.

His lips quivered. "Such a pretty little cunt. I bet you play with it all the time. Don't you, Bailey? Why don't you show us how you play with your cunt."

Chad leaned forward and took a swig of tequila. "This is better than the fucking strip club."

I glared at him. "You mean the only place a woman will actually touch you because you paid them to?"

Chad started to get up, but Billy held up his hand. "Sit down and relax, buddy. She's just got a filthy fucking mouth. No respect. But we're going to teach her some, aren't we?"

He snickered. "Fuck yeah we are."

So his plan was what? To humiliate me? Fuck him. They were the only ones who should be ashamed right now.

Billy gazed down at my pussy. "Now, show us how you play with yourself before I get angry and take it out on sweet little Maureen."

My hands trembled; my palms sweaty. I slid a finger down my slit and inched it back up, rubbing back and forth.

"Mmm… yeah just like that. Use both hands," Billy rasped.

My juices pooled from the friction. I was disgusted but my body didn't know what the fuck was going on. I slipped a finger inside my pussy while rubbing my clit with my free hand. My hips rolled against the chair as the pressure began to build in my core.

Chad unzipped his pants and shoved his hand down them. "Fuck, that's hot."

Billy's breath hitched as he followed every movement of my fingers. "Is this how you play with yourself when you're all alone at night, Bailey? I bet you dream about someone watching you like this."

I stifled a moan as I pumped my finger in and out. If he only knew I had an audience any time I fucking wanted one. "You have no idea," I breathed.

"Mmm, I think I do… Lay down on the floor," he said breathlessly.

I ignored him and kept thrusting in and out, desperate to block him out.

"Get on the fucking floor!" he screamed.

I flinched and scrambled down from the chair and onto the floor, my heart beating in my throat.

He exhaled. "Lay back and continue. And go slow. I want to see every inch of your wet finger slide in and out."

Fuck you. I hoped he was really enjoying this because it was going to be the last pussy he ever saw.

"Now that's a fucking view," Chad snickered.

Billy winked at him.

I closed my eyes and imagined I was back at Wickford Mansion, putting on a show for my guys. That was the only way I was going to get through this without puking.

Spasms spread to my clit as I pushed my finger deep inside my pussy and slowly drew it back out. I bit my lip to stifle a whimper.

"Look at *me*, Bailey."

I opened them, locking eyes with him.

"That's better. Don't want you anywhere else but here. When you cum, it will be my face that you see. No one else's."

I fucking hated him so much. I pictured all the ways I would kill him as I pushed my finger in and out.

Another wave of panic flooded me as the wind roared against the house. I froze as the rain pelted the window hard, threatening to shatter it.

Billy chuckled. "Relax, it's just a little storm. Keep going."

Billy was practically drooling. "Oh, Bailey, fuck… you're so good at this game. I love seeing that cunt stretch. Squeeze another finger in there for me."

I bit my tongue to keep from screaming even though I was raging on the inside. It was only a matter of time before he did something worse. I was seconds away from him violating me, more than he'd already done. I had to think of something quick.

He sucked in a sharp breath as I shoved a third finger deep inside. "Yeah, that's how you do it. Chad, are you as hard as I am, right now?"

A moan escaped his lips. "I'm about to cum in my fucking pants. Let me touch her."

No. No. No.

Billy shook his head. "No. This cunt is mine. What do you say, Bailey? Wanna show Chad how well I can play with your pussy?"

Think, Bailey. Fucking think.

A loud bang thumped against the house.

Chad's head jerked to the window. "What the fuck was that?"

"Probably a tree branch or something. Don't worry about it," Billy spat.

The lights flickered as the wind howled louder.

"Fuck." Chad went to the window and peeked through the blinds. "This storm is getting worse."

I fucking hope it blows the entire roof off.

Billy snickered. "It better not ruin our fun."

I glanced around the room in search of anything I could use as a weapon. My clothes were just within reach but so was the rope they had tied me up with. There were a couple of bottles of liquor on the coffee table, but not much else. Anything I could use was in the kitchen. And there was no way I'd make it in there before they caught me. Fuck.

The lights flickered again as Billy cursed under his breath. He glared at me. "Don't try anything stupid, Bailey."

"Like kidnap two women?" I snapped.

"That's a stretch, sweetie. I'd say this is more of an uninvited guest type of a situation." Billy leaned back in his chair and smirked. The smug look on his face made me want to slice it off.

"Fuck, it's dumping out there!" Chad shouted over the sound of the rain as he continued to watch it through the blinds. Billy jutted over to take a peek as well.

I started to inch back toward the spot where my clothes were piled, then stopped, my heart racing. There was no way I could get them on and make a run for it in time. I had to get to Maureen first. I would not leave here without her. I began slowly inching the other way, toward the hallway.

Lightning flashed through the window just as the sound of a

tree branch snapping rang out, followed by another thump against the house. The lights flickered three more times then went pitch dark.

Thank fuck.

Chad yelped as he stumbled into the back of my couch. "Shit, man, I can't see a fucking thing."

"Use your phone light," Billy growled back.

"I left mine at home. What about yours?"

"I think it's on the coffee table. Wherever the fuck that is," Billy whined.

"Dude, what about Bailey? She's being too fucking quiet."

Billy snickered. "Sit tight, Bailey. Don't even think about doing anything stupid. I will fucking find you."

I crawled across the floor as they bickered, enjoying the sound of panic in their voices. Fuck lights, I didn't need them to know where I was going. No one knew this house better than me.

As I felt my way along the walls, I was careful to stay quiet, praying they didn't find Billy's phone. I kept to the walls as I made my way down the hallway, knowing that the center of the floor creaks every five steps.

A loud crash erupted in the living room, followed by groans and curses. As I inched closer to my bedroom door, I could hear Maureen whimpering on the other side of it. *Hang on, babe, I'm coming.*

I took a deep breath and stood up. *Nice and slow, Bailey.*

The doorknob was cool against my sweaty palm. Relief washed over me as it turned with ease. I pushed the door open just enough to slip inside before it creaked. The hinges were old and rusty, but they were my hinges, and I fucking knew how far I could push before they screamed.

My heart thumped in my chest as I closed the door and locked it behind me. I blinked a few times, my eyes finally adjusting to the dark. "*Maureen,*" I whispered, "don't make a sound. I'm going to get us out of here."

I heard her suck in a sharp breath as she stilled against the chair.

Goosebumps pebbled my flesh as a cold draft brushed over me. *Old houses.* I sank to my knees and crawled toward my overnight bag. I unzipped it slowly and exhaled a sigh of gratitude. I quickly pulled out a hoodie and a pair of sweatpants—clothes I'd brought to wear when I was hungover driving home tomorrow. I almost didn't bring them. Thank fuck I did.

I dressed faster than I ever had in my life. Maureen's breath quivered as she waited. I was proud of her for holding it together. Being the daughter of a Sheriff had its benefits. Her father had been teaching her survival skills since she was old enough to walk. Skills like how to stay calm in sticky situations.

I reached back in the bag for my sneakers when my hand brushed against something else. Something rough and heavy. I gasped as I wrapped my hand around it.

Saint.

It was the gift he put in my bag. The one he told me not to look at until I got here. And now I knew why. I wouldn't have accepted it earlier. I was so convinced that nothing bad could happen to me out here. One of the most naïve thoughts that I'd ever let enter my head.

Now that we were being held hostage by Billy and Chad, I couldn't have been more fucking grateful.

I unsheathed the bowie knife and kissed the blade. It made my nipples hard just thinking about how satisfying it was going to feel when I plunged it deep into Billy's flesh.

Footsteps thumped loudly through the other room. "Where the fuck are you, Bailey?" Billy yelled. "You can't escape me, you little slut."

My pulse raced as my adrenaline kicked in. I scrambled over

of nowhere, you have to be prepared for anything. This wasn't the first time I'd lost power from a storm out here.

I handed her the flashlight and tucked my keys into my pocket. "It's exactly twenty steps to the living room from here. Hug the wall or else the floorboards will creak. Now once we get to the end of the hall we have to step to the right three times to avoid hitting the coffee table. Then ten more steps to the front door. Billy most likely bolted it, so wait for me to unlock it before taking another step. As soon as we're outside, turn the flashlight on and shine it to the right. That's where my car is. And then run like fucking hell."

She sucked in a sharp breath. "Okay, I got it, but what if… we run into them?"

I nodded unsure if she could even see me. My eyes had adjusted but it was still dark as fuck. There were two of them but there were also two of us. They had the advantage earlier by splitting us up but now it was an even playing field.

"There's a bottle of tequila on the coffee table which is three steps forward and to the left at the end of the hallway. Break it, and it becomes a weapon. Don't hesitate. It's us or them."

Maureen shuddered next to me. "Oh, I have no problems shivving either one of them to death." Her voice held a dark edge that had never been there before.

I tied my hair back before grabbing her hand and guiding her to the door. "As soon as I open this, you need to go first so I can close it behind us before it creaks. That's when you start counting your twenty steps."

It had gotten extremely quiet in the living room. I wanted to believe that Billy and Chad had given up and left. But I knew that was only wishful thinking. They were most likely lurking in the dark, hoping we'd come out and alert them to where we were. Fucking douchebags.

"You ready?" I asked.

Maureen squeezed my hand. "Let's get the fuck out of here."

CHAPTER Twenty-Two

Bailey

You never know what you're capable of until faced with your own demise. It wasn't the possibility of death that scared me. No. Death would have been easy. It was the thought of what those sick bastards would do to us *before* they killed us. And the thought of anyone but my guys touching me… That got my adrenaline racing and my feet moving forward.

We were halfway down the hallway when the taunting began again.

"I can hear one of you bitches breathing," Billy sneered. "I can't wait to fuck that tight little ass of yours, Bailey."

I swallowed down the bile in my throat. In the dark, I could make out the side of Maureen's face pressed against the wall. I could feel her pulse quicken through her fingertips as I squeezed them in my palm.

With the knife gripped tightly in my other hand, I nudged her forward. There was no turning back. The window in my bedroom had been stuck shut for years and now I was silently cursing myself for not getting it fixed. The only way out was through the front door.

Maureen started forward again. Every step felt like an eternity. But it was in the quiet and stillness of the dark where I thrived. I could see shapes and shadows that others did not. Maybe I had spent too much time wandering graveyards. They could call me a freak all they wanted, but it was me who had the upper hand now.

As we reached the end of the hallway, my stomach knotted. *We were almost there*. They knew it too. The house was too quiet. Too still. Billy was just waiting for us to slip up. I prayed neither of us did.

Maureen froze at the threshold. Fuck.

My heart raced. *Come on, bestie. We can do this.*

And like a mind reader, she took another step, moving to the right just like I told her. *Good girl.* I placed my hand on her shoulder and followed her lead.

Muffled voices cut through the room, and I clenched my knife tighter. Billy and Chad weren't the sharpest tools in the shed, but they weren't idiots either. Their eyes had most likely adjusted to the dark as well.

Two more steps to the right and we had a clear path to the front door. I could almost taste our freedom on my tongue. I clamped my lips shut and took small breaths through my nose.

A large shadow shot forward, narrowly missing us. "Fuck!" Billy yelled. "I know you're in here, Bailey."

Maureen tried to stifle a whimper, but it was too late.

Another shadow dove toward us, knocking us to the ground.

I watched as the two larger shadows scrambled around, disoriented.

"I'm going to kill you, you crazy bitch," Billy yelled. Thunder roared as the wind pounded against the windows. "I'm going to burn you alive just like your fucking parents."

Fucking hell. My rage threatened to expose my location as it took every ounce of strength to stay quiet and not lunge at him.

We had about ten seconds before the lightning lit up this whole fucking room.

I dashed over to Maureen. "*We have to run,*" I whispered.

Weapons would only get us so far. They were football players. If they got their hands on us again, we were done for.

Maureen found my hand and laced her fingers through mine. "I'm ready."

I pulled her three steps to the left and rushed forward, slamming into the door. Frantic, I fumbled with the bolt.

"They're getting away," Chad called out.

Heavy footsteps stalked toward us as I struggled with the chain on the last latch. Fuck, fuck, fuck. My heart was racing so fast I could barely breathe.

Maureen whimpered behind me. "Come on, come on."

A fresh wave of adrenaline surged through me. "Fuck this." I grabbed the chain and yanked as hard as I could. A loud pop sounded as the screw pelted me in the face. *Yes*.

I threw open the front door and yanked Maureen outside. Fuck, it was even darker out here. The rain pricked us like a thousand needles as I dragged her down the slippery front steps.

"Flashlight, Maur!"

"Oh, fuck." She tapped it against her hand. "It's not working!"

Shit. My shoes sank into the mud as we reached the ground. I jerked her to the right and squinted through the dark. "Keep trying," I called back.

A bloodcurdling scream echoed through the night. "Bailey!" Billy roared. "Come back here."

Maureen grunted, slamming the flashlight harder against her hand. "Fucking hell. Work dammit!"

We sloshed forward in the dark. Another bolt of lightning flashed, and I spotted my car. Which meant Billy also spotted us. "Maureen, run!"

She shrieked as we sprinted toward my car. With my keys already out and ready, I tapped the clicker to unlock the doors, and the interior lights flashed. "Go, go, go!"

We couldn't get into the car fast enough.

"Lock the doors, quick," Maureen rasped.

I turned the key in the ignition but kept the headlights off as I threw the car into reverse. Billy rammed into the side of the car and pounded on the window.

"Fuck you, Billy," Maureen snarled.

I smashed down on the gas pedal, praying I didn't hit anything behind me, and then threw it in drive as I hit the headlights. The sight of the road in front of us was the most beautiful sight I'd ever seen.

I peeled out, leaving Billy screaming our names in the dark behind us.

We were about three miles down the road when both of us burst into tears. They were tears of relief, of anger, and frustration. Not a single word was uttered. We just held hands and cried together all the way back home…

Every light in Wickford Mansion flickered on the second I screeched into the driveway. I killed the engine but neither of us moved.

"Did they… you know… touch you?" Maureen rasped.

I shook my head as I choked back more tears. "No. But… they made me touch myself so they could watch." I was going to be sick thinking about it.

Maureen burst into tears. "I'm so sorry, Bailey. This is all my fault. If I hadn't kept insisting we have a girls' night…"

I threw my arms around her. "Stop. This isn't on either of us. I'm going to fucking kill both of them. That's a promise."

She wiped her nose on her sleeve. "I'll help you do it."

A chill snaked up my spine as I gazed at the house. "Well, you'll have to get in line. When I tell *them* what happened… Billy and Chad are going to have four very hostile and depraved psychos after them. Psychos who can't die. I have to warn you, it's about to get really fucking heated in there."

Maureen gasped. "I'm actually going to get to meet them. Holy shit. Bales... what if they blame me? What if they hate me?"

"No, Maur. You're my best friend. They will love you because I love you. We had every right to have a fun night alone. It is not our fault this happened. Okay?"

She nodded, sniffling again. "I know. But people in this town will say it is. They put Billy and Chad on a fucking pedestal."

A fury grew inside me. "Well, we're about to knock them off it. Fuck anyone who tries to stop us, or I'll come for them too." I squeezed her hand again. "Let's get inside. We're safe now. They will protect us both."

Maureen smiled for the first time all night. "I'm excited to meet the men who make my best friend happy."

My stomach knotted as we headed to the front door. This was going to be a long fucking night. Tensions were already high before I left.

As soon as I turned the key and stepped inside, I froze. All four of them stood in the middle of the foyer with fists clenched. Even Raine's usual smirk was gone from his face. Maureen clung to my side as they gazed over us.

"Holy, fuck, Bales. *You definitely downplayed how hot they are*," Maureen murmured.

If we hadn't just run for our lives, I would have laughed. Seeing them through her eyes for the first time, took my breath away.

Poe, Grim, Saint, *and* Raine were achingly beautiful. Soul-crushingly stunning. But they were also deadly as fuck. They were monsters. *My monsters*. And I was about to unleash them on this whole fucking town.

I think the shock of what we just went through was beginning to wear off and reality was setting in. Maureen shivered by the fire, a blanket around her shoulders. She gazed at each of my guys, going back and forth between them. I think a part of her was trying to rationalize the fact that they were dead.

A thick silence hung in the air between us. They listened quietly as I recounted everything that happened tonight. *Everything*. Maureen burst into tears hearing the details of what Billy and Chad did to me while she was tied up in the other room. It made my own stomach turn as I said the words aloud.

I watched as my guys' faces turned from concerned to murderous.

"I'm going to murder them slowly," Grim spat. He ran his hand through his blond hair, his fingers twitching.

"We'll take turns," Saint growled.

Poe leaned forward, his head in his hands. Was he crying? Fuck.

"We will all have a go at them." Raine sucked in a sharp breath. "They fucked with the wrong psychos."

Maureen wiped the tears from her cheeks. "I want to be there when their last breaths leave them. I want to hear them scream and beg for their lives."

Raine smirked at me. "I like her already."

Saint let out a deep sigh. "Maureen, it's a pleasure to finally meet you. I don't think that's been said yet. I'm sorry it's under these circumstances."

She shrugged. "This is Wickford Hollow; I wouldn't expect anything different."

Poe looked up; his eyes glassy. "I can't imagine how scared you must have been. I'm so sorry that happened to you. This is why we didn't want you to leave."

"Speak for yourself," Raine hissed, and Poe shot him a glare.

I leaped to my feet, annoyed. "Just stop. I refuse to be a prisoner in my own home. I'm done letting Billy or anyone else control what I do and where I go. I love all of you, but I can't lock myself away in here and avoid the outside world forever."

Saint nodded. "You're right. You're a grown woman who can take care of herself… clearly."

I raised my chin. "Exactly. Thank you for the knife by the way."

Grim jumped from the couch and rushed me. "No, Bailey. Going out for a cup of coffee in broad daylight is entirely different from spending the night alone in the woods when there are monsters stalking you in the shadows. That's not being fearless, it's stupid."

I looked him dead in the eye, my jaw clenching. "*We* are the only monsters here, Grim. Billy and Chad are nothing but disgusting pigs whom I intend to gut open. Now back the fuck off."

He was pissing me off. I understood his need to protect me, but trying to control me outside of the bedroom was not going to fly.

Grim held up his hands and stepped back. "Look… I-I just don't want anything to take you away from us. Those fuckers could have killed you."

Raine planted himself between us, shaking his head. "No. They couldn't actually."

Saint stood up; his fists clenched. "Enough with the riddles, Raine. Why don't you just let the grownups talk."

"What are you talking about?" Poe asked, ignoring Saint.

Raine was unstable, that much was clear. He loved getting a rise out of all of us. He was a creature of chaos. But he also knew more about this house and everyone in it than we did. I sensed that about him the second he ambushed me in the shower.

Maureen pulled the blanket tight around her body as she shivered, watching the tense exchange between us. *What a fucking introduction she was getting tonight.*

I inserted myself in the middle of their circle, spinning around slowly to take stock of each of them. "I have had a really fucked up night. I'm angry and exhausted, and I need a hot shower. And you arguing with each other is not helping." I held up my hands and wiggled my fingers. "See, I'm all right. Still in one piece. Still alive."

Raine spun me toward him. As we locked eyes, my stomach knotted. Something close to sadness flickered in his eyes. "No, Bailey, you're not."

Maureen jumped to her feet, the blanket falling to the ground. "*What is going on?*" She cried out.

My heart raced as the guys moved in closer, their chests heaving as all eyes fell on me.

Raine took my hands in his. "They can't kill you because… you're already dead."

CHAPTER Twenty-Three

Raine

Halloween Eve. One year ago.

Pacing. All I've done is pace since those little fucks burned down my house. Soon, the city would tear it all down. *Condemned*. What a fucking joke. This town wouldn't even exist if not for me.

I should have never married Daisy Thorn. That fucking cunt. I might as well be cursed in that room with her lovers. Once this house was gone, I'd have nothing. She could've at least had the decency to let one of them impregnate her before she offed them. Instead of having everything I own default back to the city.

For over a hundred years, I've tried to figure out a way to get that damn door open. But I remember the night she cursed them.

Only a member of a founding family from Ever Graves could break it. It was impossible. There was no one left in this town from Ever Graves. Or so I thought. Until that night last summer. When I saw *her*. She had those same violet eyes that all the Bishop women had.

I knew this was my chance. If she freed them, she'd be tied to them forever. She could save this house.

But then the fire broke out.

I tried to stay close to her but there was so much chaos. The halls were filled with smoke and flames and drunken teenagers running for their lives. I even tried to call out to her, but my voice was lost amidst the screams.

By the time I caught up to her, it was too late… I found her at the bottom of the stairs, her body contorted in a way no one could survive. Still, I checked for a pulse.

Nothing.

The Bishop girl was dead. And we were doomed.

Fuck.

I watched from the window as they hosed my beloved house down. I waited while they combed through the rubble. Hours and hours of searching. And when they were done, they left empty-handed. There were no stretchers. No ambulances. No dead Bishop girl in their arms.

What the actual fuck?

I sprinted down the stairs only to find a pool of blood at the bottom.

Fucking hell.

So, back to pacing. I stalked up and down the hall, back and forth, losing my fucking mind for over a year.

And that's when I heard them.

At first, I thought I was imagining it. I ran to the window and looked down. A grin spread across my lips.

On the front lawn stood two drunk women in slutty Halloween costumes. And one of them was *her*.

There's my little snack.

Bailey Bishop had finally come home. Back to the scene of the crime. And she didn't even know she was dead. It made it that much sweeter.

I lurked in the shadows as she climbed the stairs, my obsession growing with every step. I stalked her down the hall as she made her way to the locked door, my cock throbbing to the sway of her hips. And when she struggled to get it open, when I began to fear that she'd give up and leave… I pushed her. *I* unleashed the three deviants who would drag her back here to me.

And I couldn't wait to play with her. To teach her how to live in the darkness.

To show her how to be a monster like me.

CHAPTER Twenty-Four

Bailey

I was dead. No…

A hush fell across the room, collective breaths held tight inside trembling rib cages.

Paled faces.

Disbelief.

And then emotions exploding. Voices shouting.

I stood still; my head dizzy, as the room seemed to spin out of control around me. I snuck a look at Maureen. The firelight flickered over her face, highlighting the tears streaming down her cheeks. Her chest heaved as she began to hyperventilate.

But it was with Raine whom I locked eyes with.

My breath steadied as I walked toward him. Flashes of that

night filled my head. The smoke in my lungs. The flames blurring my vision…

With every step I took toward him, I recovered another fragment. A chill snaked up my spine as I remembered people pushing and shoving to get out. How no one helped me. All these years I thought the smoke-filled memories were from the fire that killed my parents.

But they weren't.

They were from the fire that killed me.

As I bridged the gap between us and gazed up at Raine, I saw myself at the top of the stairs. I remembered my stomach dropping as I felt the shove from behind. I lost my footing and tumbled down. Every step I hit broke one of my bones. The flames lapped around me, the smoke filling my lungs. And the last thing I remember seeing as I took my last breath, was Billy's snarling face…

"He's telling the truth," I murmured. "I remember now."

Maureen threw her arms around me and sobbed into my chest. "Oh, Bales. No."

Poe sank to his knees in front of the fire. "So you've been dead this whole time? How did we not know?"

Raine kept his eyes glued to mine. "Because *she* didn't know. Her soul didn't pass over and there was no one there to tell her any different. She got up, walked away, and blocked the whole thing out."

It explained everything. The way I'd been feeling since that night. This emptiness inside of me that I'd been trying to fill. The way Billy's hatred of me grew even more. He thought he killed me. *He did kill me*. But when I showed back up, he must have thought he'd failed. He must have known that I couldn't remember. And he's been fucking with me ever since.

"Well, how the fuck did *you* know?" Saint growled.

Raine smiled. "Because I was there the night it happened. I found her body after she fell."

I was getting sucked in deeper, drowning in his blue-green eyes. "I didn't fall. I was pushed."

Maureen broke our embrace. "Please don't say it..."

I nodded. "Yup. It was Billy."

Grim charged the fireplace and with one violent sweep, knocked everything off the mantle. "Fuck!"

I ran to him. "Grim..."

He pulled me to his chest and wrapped his arms tight around me. "Little fox... I'm going to avenge you. I promise you that."

"Why didn't you tell her sooner?" Saint growled.

Raine shrugged. "I like secrets. Thought this would be more fun. But I got so sick of hearing you all whine about her safety every time she left the house. For fuck's sake."

"You really are a bastard, aren't you?" Poe spat.

"I smell bullshit." Saint went to the bar and poured six glasses of whiskey. "You kept this a secret so you could have something with Bailey that we didn't have."

Raine smirked as he snatched one of the drinks. "I still do. *We* set you free. Bailey and me. Together. She was always mine first."

"Fuck you," Grim snarled.

I pulled away from him and looked around at the mess he'd made on the floor. "What's done is done. We can sort all our feelings out later. Right now we need a plan to get Billy and Chad here so we can kill them."

Maureen smiled at Saint as he handed her a drink. She guzzled the whole thing without blinking. "Halloween's in three days. We throw a party here. Costume only. He won't be able to resist."

That's why she's my best friend. "That's perfect. Send out a group text to everyone we know."

Poe cocked his head. "You think he'll take the bait?"

I nodded. "He thinks I live here alone. The only reason he hasn't shown up here yet is because he knows I have nosy neighbors. When he saw me and Maureen heading out to my place in the woods, he jumped on it."

Maureen helped herself to another whiskey. "He was going to kill us both tonight, wasn't he? To shut us up after they had their fun."

"That's what I would have done," Raine snickered.

Grim started toward him but I blocked his path. I put a firm hand on his chest. "I need all of you to sort your shit out if we're gonna get through this. No more fighting. Save your anger for the asshole who murdered me."

He grunted and pushed past me, heading straight for the bar. "Fine." His throat bobbed as he knocked back a glass of whiskey. "But you and I need to have a chat later, little fox. *Alone*."

These were the moments where I truly felt the weight of having to manage four alpha psychos. "It's settled then. In three days, we finish this with Billy."

After everyone nodded in agreement, Grim grumbled off to his room. Poe retreated to the kitchen, insisting we let him feed us a hot meal. We devoured our food in silence. Except for the occasional moan from Maureen's lips as she gushed over Poe's cooking.

I put her to bed in one of the guest rooms with a promise that we would chat more in the morning. Three whiskeys later and she wasn't putting up much of a fight about it. She could barely keep her eyes open.

Raine wandered off without saying goodnight, which was for the best. He was winding everyone up, and I was too tired to deal with it. I gave Saint and Poe each a quick kiss before heading upstairs.

I stood in the shower and closed my eyes as the hot water sprayed over me. As I breathed in the steam, a sob lodged in my throat. My breath quivered as I exhaled slowly.

I was dead.

My body trembled as the tears finally poured out. I slammed my hand against the tiled wall. "Fuck."

Everything I'd been holding in, rushed out. I sank down and curled myself into a ball underneath the showerhead. I knew something was wrong with me. Just never would have imagined this. It wasn't until Raine said it out loud. When I looked into his eyes and saw the truth. A switch flipped in my head as I accepted it. Embraced it. And now I can't shut the memories off. They've been on a constant replay in my head since he told me.

I was really drunk that night. Billy used that to his advantage when I got separated from Maureen. I had rejected him earlier. He was so angry that I wouldn't fuck him. He was drunk too. But that was no excuse. Pure evil ran through his veins. I saw it in his eyes tonight when he was slamming his fists against my car. He had every intention of killing me.

I rested my head against my knees and sobbed. I didn't know how long I'd been in here, but the steam was so thick I could barely see. A part of me wanted to hide in here forever. But Billy had already taken too much. I wouldn't give him this life as well.

I turned off the water and dried myself off. I smeared the steam off the mirror and looked deep into my own eyes. I still looked like me. That's what was so fucking scary. Because underneath the flesh, I was not the same. And I never would be again.

A shudder passed through me as I pulled on a tank top and a

pair of panties. I opened the door and froze. Raine sat at the foot of my bed, barefoot and shirtless. Fuck. The top of his jeans were unbuttoned. Every inch of his skin was covered in tattoos.

We locked eyes and my belly fluttered. He leaned back on his elbows, his posture relaxed, but his gaze was feral. I'd never seen a man hunger for me the way that he did.

"Hi," I stammered.

"Come here."

My breath hitched as I inched toward him. He sat up as I reached the bed. He ran his hands up my thighs. I flinched as he ripped my panties down the middle. "Next time you take a shower…" He grabbed my tank top and tore it in half. "If you don't come in here naked, I will burn all your clothes."

An ache festered in my core. I craved his violence. His brutality. "Do you want to punish me?"

Malice flashed in his eyes. He grabbed me by the hair and dragged me onto the bed. In one quick swoop, he had me pinned underneath him. "Oh, I'm going to." He pushed my head to the side and ran his tongue across my cheek. "And it's going to hurt."

Moisture gathered between my legs. Fuck, I was just as psychotic as he was. "*Good*," I spat.

He growled and flipped me over onto my stomach. "Let's make sure you can't run away."

Another spasm rocked through me as I felt the fabric wrap around my left wrist. I gazed up just as he secured the other end of the silk scarf to my bedpost. "Forget about your safe word, Bailey. It's useless on me."

I sucked in a sharp breath as he secured my right wrist to the other bedpost. Panic began to creep into my chest even as my juices leaked between my legs. I tugged on my restraints but the more I pulled the tighter they got.

Raine dragged his fingertips down my spine. "Fight back all you want. It makes me so fucking hard."

"I'm not fighting this time," I breathed.

I heard the sound of his zipper and him rustling with his jeans. Then the sound of them dropping to the floor. He got back between my legs and pushed them apart. "So you do like being fucked in the ass like a dirty little slut."

A tingle coiled around my clit. "*Yes.*"

Raine dug his fingers into my ass cheeks and spread them wide open. "I bet the boys were gentler, hmm?"

My heart raced. Fuck. He was going to tear me apart. I just knew it. "There's some lube in my top drawer." *Please, fuck, let him use it.*

He pushed my ass cheeks farther apart. I could already feel the burn of the stretch. Fuck. "Nah, I've got a better idea."

I clenched as a sudden drop of liquid splashed against my entrance. It oozed down my ass sending a spasm straight to my core. Fuck. "What are you doing?"

Raine chuckled. "Dirty sluts don't get fancy lubricants. They get spit on."

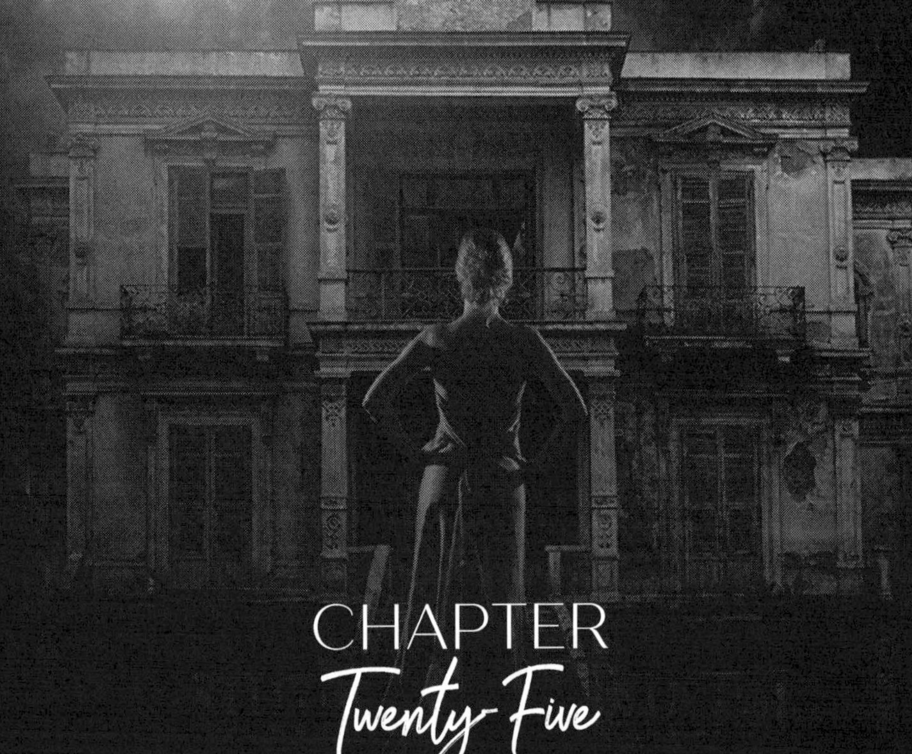

CHAPTER Twenty-Five

Raine

Her skin was already flushed as the heat rose in her body. I had her on her stomach with nowhere to go and no way of escape. She was fucking loving every minute of her degradation. It satisfied every twisted part of her.

I slapped my cock against her ass. "Mmm, I'm going to cum inside you twice." I slid my hand through her legs and up, gliding my fingers through her soaking wet pussy.

"Oh, fuck," she moaned.

"I'm going to give you a new dark fantasy to dream about." I coated my fingers in her juices and then smeared them up and down my shaft. "*Fuck*… the cream from your cunt is the only lube I need."

Mmm. I was already getting close. A primal urge stirred in cum gushed into her anus, hot and thick. I squeezed her ass cheeks together as I rubbed against her.

"*Raine*," she screamed. "*Oh, fuck… fuck.*"

"Now you're fucking wet enough for me," I snarled. Something came over me. A ferocious need to keep claiming her. The sight of my cum dripping out of her asshole was so fucking dirty. But it was the way she screamed my name that drove me to the edge. And it made me instantly hard again.

"Raine, wait," she panted. "My wrists… fuck. I need a second, please."

Oh poor little vixen, still thinking I had some kind of merciful bone in my body. "Yeah, keep begging me to stop. Fuck."

Her hips rolled up as I pushed my cock inside her ass. A feral moan ripped out of her throat as I buried myself to the hilt. "You feel that, little vixen? Can you feel me forcing my cum deep inside you?"

She clenched down around my cock as I railed her. "Mmm. I'm going to fuck you raw."

I yanked her hips up and pounded her hard. She cried out as she rocked back into it. I felt her muscles loosen and her own juices start to flow. "That's my filthy little slut. Taking my cock and loving it."

"*Yes*," she rasped.

I chuckled as I reached around and pinched her swollen clit. "Tell me what you are. I wanna hear you fucking say it."

"Fuck you, Raine…" She was pissed because she was about to cum the hardest she's ever cum. *Because of me.*

I slapped her ass as I slammed into her. "Say it or I will keep you like this all night. I will fuck you while you sleep." I hoped she would defy me just so I could see the look on her face when she woke up to me fucking her.

Another moan erupted from her as she bucked and ground her ass against my cock. She gritted her teeth. "*I'm your filthy little slut.*"

"Mmm, good girl. Say it again." Blood raced to the tip of my cock as I burrowed in as deep as I could go.

"Oh, fuck… damn you. You're going to make me cum."

I ground in circles, twisting inside her. Fuck. I was seconds away. "*Again.*"

"*Uhhh.* I'm… your filthy… little slut."

Stars studded my vision as my orgasm gripped my shaft, threatening to choke the life out of me. "Fucking clench. Now." I squeezed her ass cheeks around my base as my cum shot out.

She ripped out a moan as I pressed the weight of my body on hers, grinding her pussy into the mattress. "Raine… fuck… fuck you. I'm cumming."

A feral growl escaped my lips as my cock pulsed and throbbed inside her. "Your ass is my new favorite place to cum." I traced my fingertips over the small of her back as she twitched and shivered.

"Untie me, you psycho."

I probably should but I couldn't get enough of her like this. She grunted as I pulled my cock out of her ass. I crawled up to the top of the bed and pinched her chin between my fingers. "I'll think about it."

"Raine!" she screamed.

She still didn't understand that her little temper tantrums had the opposite effect of what she intended. It was like a shot of adrenaline straight to my cock. I shoved my tongue inside her mouth and despite her screams, she kissed me back. Bailey Bishop always kissed me back.

"Seriously, please untie me," she breathed. "I'll even stay like this. I promise."

I sighed. I needed a new game anyway. I reached up and untied each wrist.

"Thank you."

I pulled her to my chest. "Come here."

Her breath hitched as I wrapped my arms around her and held her close. She was mine to play with and degrade but she was also mine to love. And she loved me too in her own fucked up way.

She purred against my chest. "Raine?"

"Yes, Bailey."

She sighed. "There's so much fucking cum in my ass."

I snorted and we both burst out laughing. "Good. Just don't forget whose cum it is when you wake up wanting to fuck."

If I wasn't already dead, this dirty little vixen would be the fucking death of me.

CHAPTER *Twenty-Six*

Bailey

When I woke up, I was surprised to find Raine's arms still wrapped around me, his legs draped across mine. He held me in an iron grip so I couldn't get away. But with my ass still full of his cum, I needed another shower.

I lifted his arm and shimmied away from him. But as I reached the edge of the bed, he yanked me back into his arms. "Where the fuck do you think you're going?"

"To the bathroom. I need to wash my ass," I grumbled.

He rolled onto me, trapping me underneath him. "Nah. I like your ass better when it's full of my cum. You're staying right here."

I gazed up at his blue-green eyes. They reminded me of the ocean. Intoxicating, beautiful, and deadly as fuck, ready to pull you down in a rip tide. "Why didn't I know I was dead this whole time?"

Raine ran his thumb across my lips. "You disassociated from the trauma." He planted a soft kiss on my cheek before dragging the tip of his tongue along my jaw.

My breath hitched. The slightest touch from him sent spasms to my core. "Why am I still here? Poe, Grim, and Saint are cursed. And you're just fucking stubborn. *But why didn't I cross over?*"

He inched himself down my body until his face was level with my breast. His lips parted over it. I let out a little gasp as he stuck out his tongue and rolled it over my pebbled nipple. "Because you're just as stubborn as I am…" He puckered his lips and blew against my wet nipple. "And because you belong here with me."

I arched my back, moaning as he moved to my other breast and sucked. Moisture pooled between my legs as he raked his teeth across my nipple. "*Fuck…*"

He inched his tongue farther down, leaving a trail of saliva down my rib cage and across my belly. Goosebumps pebbled my arms. Fuck. There were so many sides to this man. Last night he was rough and brutal as he violated me. But now… this was slow and agonizing. I couldn't decide which turned me on more.

He pushed my thighs apart and released a slow steady stream of spit onto my pussy. "I don't like sharing what's mine. But I will for you, little vixen. So long as you don't ever deny me."

My hips jerked as his saliva trickled down my slit. My god, why was that so fucking hot? "I-I won't."

"Good." He peeled the lips of my pussy back and licked me from taint to nub.

I moaned, my legs shaking, as a deep spasm burst from my core.

"Because if you ever try to…" He flicked his tongue over my clit. "I will drag you away from this house and you will never see them again."

Wait, what?

"Raine, what are you talking—"

He plunged his tongue deep inside my pussy. Oh fuck. My head was spinning. I opened my mouth to speak but a scream came out instead as he worked the tip of his tongue against my G-spot.

I yanked on his hair, but he was too strong. He dug his fingers deep into my thighs as he devoured me.

"Raine," I breathed. "Fuck, it's too much… wait."

He growled inside me, scraping his teeth against my folds as he sucked and licked hungrily.

The pressure climbed in my core, sending tingles to every inch of my body. I lifted my hips and rocked against his face. "Oh, shit… don't fucking stop."

I needed him to, but I didn't want him to. Fucking hell. I was in so much fucking trouble.

Raine chuckled as he fingered my clit while he worked his mouth over my sopping wet pussy, not leaving any inch untouched.

I dug my nails into his skull as another spasm rolled through me. "Fuck… I'm cumming."

"Mmm," he moaned.

I gasped as he pinched my clit hard between his fingers. I rubbed myself against his mouth, my heart racing as I chased every wave of pleasure.

My limbs trembled as he lapped up my cream.

"Breakfast of fucking champions," he rasped. He stroked my pussy as I came down. "Mmm, my tasty little cunt."

Another orgasm threatened to claim me as he planted a firm kiss on my clit. "Raine, what did you mean drag me away?"

A smirk pulled up the corners of his cream-covered lips. He pushed out his tongue and licked it off. "I think I made myself very clear."

My stomach knotted. "Raine… are you able to leave this house?"

His eyes lit up with amusement. "Of course, I can."

A shiver crawled up my back. "Then why haven't you? I don't understand. Why stay in a house that burned down?"

Raine slithered back up my body until we were at eye level. "Because this is *my* house. And everything in it belongs to me." He wrapped his hand around my neck and squeezed. "But if you ever try to push me away, I will take you somewhere else."

He really was fucking psycho. And yet I couldn't ever imagine being away from him.

I whimpered as his cock stiffened against my thigh. "I won't..." I rasped.

"If you try to leave, I will find you." His eyes darkened as he nudged my thighs apart. "I will always find you." He pushed his cock inside my pussy.

I cried out as he shoved deeper, his girth stretching me open. "I won't run away..."

His grip tightened around my throat. "I know you won't." He pulled out slowly. "Because you're my dirty little slut." I moaned as he thrust in harder, so deep I could feel the pressure in my lower back. *"Now call for them."*

Fuck. "Raine, no..."

"Do it," he snarled. "I want them to watch me fuck you."

A spasm coiled around my clit at the thought. They hated him. And yet they were just as sick and depraved as he was.

He pulled halfway out and stilled. "Call for them or I'll finish fucking you in the front yard so all the neighbors can see how needy your cunt is for me."

Fuck. I knew he wasn't bluffing. I sucked in a sharp breath. "Poe," I called out.

Raine drove his cock back into me. "Good girl."

I screamed as he filled me to the hilt. "Grim."

"Louder."

"Saint," I screamed.

Footsteps pounded up the stairs right before the door burst open.

The three of them froze at the foot of the bed, their fists clenched.

"It's okay," I panted.

"What the fuck, Raine?" Saint growled.

Raine snickered. "I want you to see how well your little fox takes my cock."

I bucked as he rolled his hips, as every ridge of his cock throbbed against my walls.

Poe walked around to the side of the bed and pulled out his cock. He bit down on his lip as he stroked himself. "Fuck, you're so deep."

I arched my back as he rolled his hips again, lifting my ass off the bed. "She likes it deep. Don't you, little vixen?"

Grim walked to the other side of the bed and gazed down at me. "Yeah, she does."

"Fuck her harder," Saint rasped.

Raine pounded into me. "You will cum for them, little vixen. But you will scream out *my* name."

The pressure in my core erupted as I glanced around the room. They weren't angry. No. Their faces dripped with arousal, an animalistic lust.

I bucked as my orgasm ripped through me. Clenching around his swollen cock, I let out a bloodcurdling scream. "*Raine!*"

"Fuck," he cried out as his cum filled my pussy, hot and thick.

Grim caressed my forehead as I came down. "Fuck, that was hot."

A deep moan erupted out of Poe as his cream shot out onto my chest, soaking my breasts.

Saint stalked over and dipped his fingers in it then shoved them in my mouth, pushing all the way to the back of my throat. "*Good girl.*"

I gagged as I sucked Poe's cum off Saint's fingers while Raine's cock still throbbed inside me.

It was one of the dirtiest things I'd ever done. One of the vilest things Raine had done to me so far. He was beyond psychotic. Raine was a fucking animal without restraint. Poe, Grim, and Saint hid it better, but they were no different.

It only made me crave them more.

Maureen gazed out at the garden, the wind rustling her hair. She was quiet all through breakfast and it worried me.

I sat next to her on the stone bench. "You okay, Maur?"

She sighed. "I'm still processing."

I nodded. "We've had a crazy night, haven't we?"

A sob wrenched from her throat. "You died, Bales… My best friend is dead."

I grabbed her by the shoulders and turned her toward me. "*I'm right here*. Just like I've always been. This doesn't change anything."

She threw her arms around my neck. "We're not gonna grow old together."

There were a lot of things we wouldn't be able to do together. But I've made peace with it. What other choice did I have? "No, we're not. But not that many people do. Let's not worry about that now. You've got me for the rest of your life and beyond."

Maureen sniffled against my shoulder. "What if there is no *beyond*? Some of you are stuck here while others just disappeared."

I'd be lying to myself if I didn't admit I'd been wondering where my parents were ever since I found out I was dead. I wanted to believe there was an afterlife and that someday I'd get there and see them again. Maybe the world of the living wasn't ready to let me go. I knew that as long as Poe, Grim, and Saint were cursed to this house, I wasn't going anywhere. Not without them.

I refuse.

"No one knows, Maur. That's the big mystery, isn't it? Even in death, I know nothing more than you do. But we have to keep going. You have such an amazing life ahead of you. And I will always be here waiting for you, in Wickford Hollow."

Tears streamed down her cheeks. "I'm so angry, Bales. And I'm scared."

I rubbed at the goosebumps on her arm. "I know. I am too. But as long as we have each other, we'll get through this... Did you send out the Halloween invite?"

She pulled her vape out of her pocket and took a long drag. "It's done. A bunch of people already replied back saying they're coming."

I nodded. "Good. Meet me later tonight at Electra's boutique. We're gonna need some costumes."

"Some extra slutty ones," Maureen quipped. "This might be our last Halloween together..."

My stomach knotted. As much as I hated the fact that my best friend was moving away soon, I desperately needed her to make new friends and be happy. And I would be happy too... after tomorrow night.

A shiver snaked up my neck. "It's going to be Billy and Chad's last Halloween too."

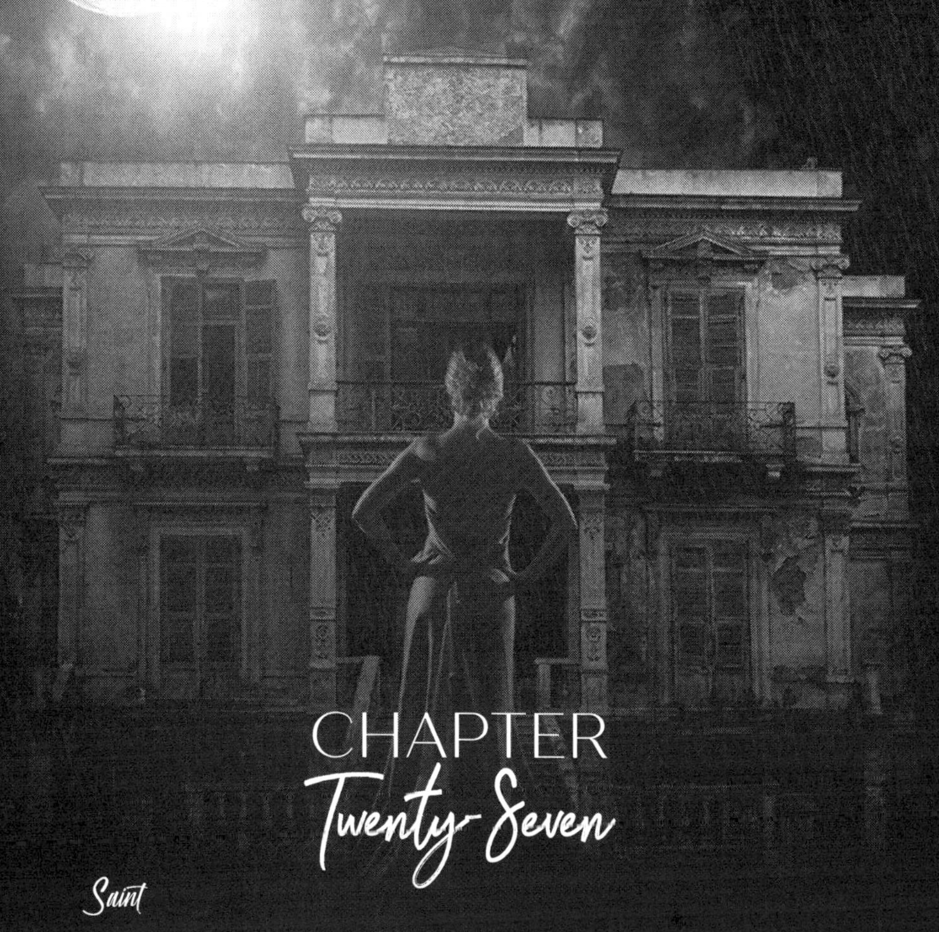

CHAPTER Twenty-Seven

Saint

There was a darkness in Bailey I had always sensed. I felt it from the first night I saw her. But it never crossed my mind that she was like us. Dead.

We were so concerned about protecting her that we didn't bother to notice that something was deeply wrong. She had blocked out her own death. The darkness surrounding her was driving her insane. And we ignored it.

It pisses me off that Raine Wickford was the one to get through to her. That he knew the truth this whole time and kept it from all of us, including her. He was a manipulative prick, and we were stuck with him.

But seeing the way Bailey came undone for him stirred all my carnal desires. Watching him drive his cock inside her needy pussy got me so fucking hard. It got me thinking of all the vile and depraved things I want to watch him do to her. *What I want to do to her.*

But her killer was still out there. And I wouldn't rest until he met the same fate.

I stood in front of the mirror and smiled as I gazed at the monstrosity. At the beauty of my skeleton face, coated thick with black and white paint. I swept my hair up into a top knot and looked down at Grim, his face painted to match mine. He was on his knees with my cock in his mouth.

I sucked in a sharp breath as he sucked. "Fuck... you look insane. I might not let you ever wash that off."

What started out as us helping each other get ready for the party, quickly turned carnal. Between the stress of everything, the murderous rage, and the pressure that had built up toward tonight, we needed release.

Grim ran the tip of his tongue up my shaft. His blue eyes seemed to glow against the black paint surrounding them. "That's because you love to fuck monsters."

I stumbled back against the bathroom door as he took me to the hilt. My balls swelled as he cupped them in his painted hands. Every inch of our bodies was covered. Designed to invoke fear and terror like demonic ghost skeletons.

As Grim worked his lips up and down my shaft, I dreamed of murder. I couldn't wait to torture and gut the bastards who killed our little fox. My cock throbbed as all the blood rushed to the tip. "Get ready to swallow every fucking drop," I growled.

Grim moaned as my thick cream shot inside his mouth. I grabbed his head and shoved my cock to the back of his throat. "Fuck, yeah. So fucking thirsty for my cum, aren't you?"

He pushed me back against the wall as he came up for air. "Turn around."

I chuckled as I turned, knowing how wound up he was. He needed this. We both did.

A shiver snaked up my back as I heard him squirt lube into his hand. He yanked my pants down and pressed his chest into my back. "This is going to hurt."

My eyes rolled back into my head. "That's the only way I fucking like it."

Grim growled as he thrust his thick cock inside my asshole. "Oh, fuck. Mmm, nice and fucking tight."

I moaned against the door as he slid in and out. The ridges of his cock flexed and twitched inside me, driving me to sheer madness. I banged my fists against the door. "*Harder.*"

Grim rammed into me, grunting. "Yeah, fucking stretch for me. Stretch for your favorite monster." He thrust harder. ""I'm close... fuck. I'm gonna cum."

A deep guttural moan unleashed from his throat as he slammed into me and exploded. My ass tingled as his thick hot cum filled me to the brim. He reached around and wrapped his hand around my cock as he chased his orgasm.

Within seconds, cream flowed from my cock. I roared against the door as spasms gripped me from both sides. Wave after wave of pleasure rocked through me as we unfurled together.

Grim breathed heavily against my back as he slowly withdrew himself from my ass. He kissed my shoulder.

I turned around to face him, more turned on than ever by his painted face, now slightly smeared with my cum. "Fuck," I rasped.

Grim chuckled. "Pull up your fucking pants and let's go murder some fuckers."

CHAPTER Twenty-Eight

Bailey

"You're not afraid of the dark, are you, Bailey?" Maureen flashed me a grin as she stuffed her tits into a hot pink bustier.

"Nah, that's where all the fun stuff happens." I laughed and handed her a purple jello shot.

She looked me up and down. "What are you supposed to be again?"

I wiggled my hips and my tail swooshed behind me. "A little fox, of course." My brown furry skirt barely covered my ass, and my tits were pushed up nice and high in the matching fur bralette.

Maureen strapped two knives to the inside of her garter belt before pulling on a short black leather skirt.

"And you're going as?" I offered her my shoulder to lean on as she stepped into her six-inch stiletto heels.

She grabbed a pair of handcuffs and hooked them to her belt loop, flashing me a mischievous grin. "Motherfucking jailbait."

I giggled as she pranced around my bedroom, waving her jello shot around like she was about to give a speech. "*Who me?*" she cooed. "*Why, I'm the sheriff's daughter. Please don't tell my daddy I'm drinking tonight.*" She batted her fake glittery eyelashes at me as she licked the top of the purple jello.

I burst out laughing. "I really hope you get laid tonight. That outfit is too fucking hot to go to waste."

Her smile fell. "Yeah, well, we both know that's not on the agenda for tonight."

My stomach knotted. Getting drunk and flirting with cute boys was all we used to look forward to on Halloween. "I know..."

I walked to the mirror and smoothed my blonde strands back into a low bun before tying the strings of my fox mask around my head. The brown fur covered only half of my face, sweeping across my nose and cheekbones, up around my eyes and forehead, and ending in two pointy ears at the top. I glided a thick layer of sparkly gloss across my lips and made a pop sound as I puckered.

"Your turn." I handed Maureen a black lace half-mask.

She tapped her heel against the floor as she put it on. "We're really doing this."

I nodded and handed her another shot. I held mine up, the red jello jiggling in the thin paper cup. "Here's to getting payback." I nudged my cup against hers before knocking it back.

She nodded. "An eye for an eye."

A deep twisted dread snaked through my bones. "A soul for a soul."

Maureen shuddered. "Where will your guys be tonight?"

"Close by. You won't see them, but they'll be watching." I

slipped my knife—the knife Saint put in my overnight bag—into my boot before zipping it up to my knee.

Maureen cracked the bedroom door open and poked her head out before closing it again. "People are starting to arrive. I can hear them."

I let out a deep breath. "Well, then let's get the lights dimmed and the music cranked up. Come on, we've got a party to host." Despite the fact that I was going to murder two people, I still wanted to show Wickford Hollow the best fucking time of their lives.

We stood at the top of the stairs and looked down at the guests arriving. I no longer had that sinking sensation of déjà vu. Now that I knew it was Billy who pushed me down these stairs two years ago, I descended with confidence. Because he was no bogeyman, just a privileged rich boy who abused women.

Maureen's eyes widened as she took in the scene. "Holy shit, Bales. You really outdid yourself."

We paused midway down the stairs as I took it all in. "Let them see how much of a freak I really am."

I had created the entire foyer to look like a graveyard. Maureen spotted the headstone at the bottom of the stairs and snorted. "Nice one." The words, *RIP Bailey Bishop* were etched into it.

The house was mostly dark with only a few wall sconces lighting the halls. By the front door, I'd placed a basket of glow sticks for my guests. I grabbed one for each of us and led us deeper into the house.

The walls were covered with fake blood. Chains hung from the ceiling, hooked to slabs of meat. Skeletons perched in every corner next to giant pumpkins, demonic faces carved into them. And every window was covered with blackout shades. No one would be able to see in or out.

In the sitting room, a giant fire blazed in the hearth. Three girls dressed as the Sanderson sisters giggled at the bar as they waited for the man with the painted skeleton face to make their drinks.

I gazed over at the couch and my belly fluttered. Only a few nights ago, Raine had me spread open while they filled all of my holes. It was weird now to see people who hated me sitting on that very couch. To watch Poe mix cocktails for girls who talked shit about me. And yet they all couldn't resist an invitation to play in my house. *Bitches.*

"Looks like they're enjoying the *freak's* free booze," Maureen snickered, raising her voice so they could hear.

The three girls at the bar glared at us before rolling their eyes and stalking off.

I exchanged a look with Poe, his piercing green eyes melting me right there. "As long as they don't try to enjoy any of my guys, they'll leave here drunk, happy, and in one piece."

"Amen to that." Maureen pulled an orange jello shot out of her cleavage and knocked it back.

I chuckled but a chill crept up the base of my neck. "Remember, don't drink anything unless you get it from Poe. I wouldn't put it past Billy and Chad to spike our drinks."

Maureen nodded as she looked around. The room was starting to fill up but still no sign of our targets. "You think they'll show?"

"This is the biggest party in town. They'll show." I walked over to the bar and took a jello shot from Poe.

"You good, little fox?" he rasped.

I smirked as the purple jello jiggled down my throat. "Is it wrong that I want to fuck you in that costume?"

His cock tented his pants. "*Mmm, such a bad girl.*"

Maureen cleared her throat and my cheeks flushed. "I'm right here, Bales. You two are making me horny now."

I burst out laughing. "Like I said earlier, you need to have some fun tonight."

Just because murder was on my brain didn't mean it had to be on Maureen's. This was her last Halloween in Wickford Hollow. I wasn't going to let Billy take this night away from her.

In fact, I was hoping that some hot guy would distract her long enough for me and the guys to take care of Billy and Chad without her. She didn't need to have blood on her hands too.

Maureen sucked in her lower lip, swinging her hips from side to side as she contemplated. "Maybe you're right… we are so fucked up, aren't we?"

I nodded. "The night is young, bestie. Try to have a little fun before the bad stuff happens."

She flashed me a grin. "All right, you convinced me. Come find me when it's time?"

I nodded, having no intention of bringing her anywhere near the blood bath that would ensue later.

With the music pumping and the alcohol flowing, scantily clad guests were starting to dance, grinding against each other under the black lights. I slithered through each room like the little fox I was, my eyes peeled for Billy and Chad.

The best part was that no one knew who I was. That was the thing about masks, you could be anyone you wanted to be. As I made my way to the basement, the music changed. *Unholy* by Sam Smith poured out from the speakers.

The room was pitch-black except for the trails of light from the glowsticks. I could make out the shapes and shadows of people losing their inhibitions. It's amazing what you'll do when you think no one's watching.

I chuckled as I passed a slutty nun on her knees giving a

vampire a blowjob. In another corner, a priest had little red riding hood bent over a table, the cross around his neck flinging back and forth as he fucked her from behind.

I ran my hand along the wall, my breath hitching. Beads of sweat dripped down my back as moans of pleasure competed with the music. Down here in the dark, they could unleash their wildest desires. Moisture pooled between my thighs knowing that I was the one who made this all possible. *Looks like we're all freaks now.*

The basement was easy to transform. I hadn't been down here since I let them chain me to the floor and defile me. It was an empty space that was now filled with a couple of tables scattered about, some chairs, and an old ripped-up couch in one corner. I wanted it to feel dirty and raw and dangerous. I even left the chains and the old mattress that was still stained with our cum. The ones who were brave enough to venture down here would have the most fun tonight.

The music changed again as I made my way to the other side of the room, brushing against sweat-drenched limbs as I squeezed through the ever-growing crowd.

It was hot down here. There were no windows and only one way out at the top of the basement stairs.

I nestled into a dark corner, backing up against the wall. I gasped as hard muscle pressed against my back instead. A hand covered my mouth and panic rose in my chest.

"Shh, relax, little fox," Grim rasped in my ear.

I blew out a sigh of relief and spun around. His blue eyes blazed back at me, the only recognizable thing about him. Under the black and white skeleton paint, his cheekbones appeared sunken in. "Fuck, you look hot," I breathed.

Grim slid his hands up my skirt. "Mmm… my sly little fox."

My pulse skyrocketed. I glanced around but it was too dark to see anything else other than what was right in front of me. And currently, that was a hot as fuck skeleton with a massive hard-on for me.

He walked me backward, his hands under my skirt, gripping my ass cheeks. I let him guide me across the room to another dark corner. I whimpered as the edge of a table hit the back of my thighs. He shoved me down, forcing me to sit, and inserted himself between my legs.

"What are you doing?" I whispered.

"Lean back, little fox." He pushed my skirt all the way up to my waist.

I gasped. "What if someone sees us?"

"Let them watch," Grim rasped.

I leaned back slightly on my elbows. Grim gazed down at me, his eyes full of malice and lust. There was something so erotic about being touched in the dark by a masked face, one you could barely see. It heightened all of my other senses.

Grim held his glowstick under his chin. "Be a good girl and take off those panties for me before I rip them off."

I shuddered against the hard table as I wiggled my black lace panties down my legs and let them fall to the floor. He smirked as he bent down to pick them up, coiling them in his hand before shoving them into his pocket.

Grim dragged the glowstick up my thigh. "I'm going to light up that pretty cunt of yours."

Oh, fuck.

Techno beats pumped fast from the speakers. Almost as fast as my heartbeat. Grim rubbed his orange glowstick down my wet slit. I shivered as the cold tip rolled against my folds.

"*Grim… please.*" Sweat glided down my thighs as he toyed with me.

He licked his lips while slowly pushing the glowstick inside me. "This is where the real party is."

I bucked as he thrust it in. "*Our own private party.*"

A scream started to rip from my throat as he slammed the glowstick against my G-spot. He pulled my panties from his pocket and shoved them into my mouth. "Shh, don't make a fucking sound."

My breath quickened as I inhaled through my nose.

"Good girl. Relax for me."

I whimpered into the fabric as he rotated the glowstick in circles, making sure it rubbed against every inch of me.

I rolled my hips as the pressure built in my core. My clit spasmed as he rubbed his thumb against it.

A deeper moan took life in my throat.

Fuck, I was almost done for. I scanned the dark, watching the silhouettes of people doing dirty things, their glowsticks flickering as their bodies swayed to the beat. My pussy ached as Grim punished it. I gazed down between us as the orange light glowed, blinking then disappearing inside me with each violent thrust.

"Mmm... Good. Fucking. Girl. Taking everything I give you."

I jerked my hips up to meet his thrusts as the tingling intensified in my core. *"Uhhh..."* I grunted into my panties. The taste of my own juices on the crotch did something feral to my body.

He shoved the glowstick all the way in, and I clenched around it as my orgasm gripped me.

"Fuck, yeah. Cum all over it." Grim rubbed my clit hard back and forth.

I leaned back against the table, panting and jerking my hips as my cream spurted out all over the glowstick and his hand. I spit out my panties. *"Fucking hell, Grim."*

He sucked in a sharp breath as he pulled the soaking wet glowstick out of my trembling pussy. "Come here."

I exhaled and sat up clumsily, my head dazed. His blue eyes were still wild with need. He grabbed the back of my neck and squeezed. A little tickle fluttered in my clit.

He pressed the sticky glowstick to my lips. "Be a good girl and lick this clean for me."

My breath hitched. There was so much cream, it oozed down the sides. Holy fuck. I whimpered as he yanked my chin down, forcing my lips to open. Before I could even take a breath, he shoved the glowstick in my mouth. He dug his other hand into the base of my skull, holding me in place, while he fucked my mouth with the glowstick.

"Suck it all off for me," he growled.

An unexpected moan ripped out of me as my cream slathered against my tongue.

Grim's eyes filled with animalistic lust. "So filthy. Fuck."

The music slowed, turning darker and more ominous. Bottles and glasses clanked together over the sounds of sloshing tongues and fingers exploring wet folds. The scent of sex and fluids hung heavy in the air.

He slowly pulled the glowstick out of my mouth, satisfied that I had sucked every drop of my own cum off it. "*Good girl.*"

And without warning he stepped back into the dark and disappeared. I was still soaking wet and the horniest I'd ever been. I sighed and pulled my panties back on. I scooted off the table and stumbled back into it. I was a bit more buzzed than I thought.

I made my way to the basement stairs and looked back one more time for any sign of my hot skeleton. I couldn't see him, but I knew he was watching me. It sent another spasm to my core.

But then a darker image came to mind. A flashback of Billy making me touch myself in front of him and Chad. Nausea crept up my throat as I remembered the way he ogled me fingering myself. Goosebumps pebbled my flesh as I wondered if Billy was in here, down in the basement, watching me again…

CHAPTER Twenty-Nine

Bailey

It was almost midnight and Wickford Mansion was packed to the brim. I hadn't seen Saint or Raine other than an occasional flash of a skeleton face in my peripheral. But it made me feel good knowing they were lurking about.

I hadn't seen Billy either. Although, he didn't scare me like he used to. N*ow that I'm dead*. But I had to remind myself that he was still bigger and stronger than me. Even though he couldn't kill me, there were other sick things he could do to my body.

I stumbled upon Maureen in the kitchen, laughing and batting her eyelashes at the group of toga-clad guys surrounding her. "Bales!" she shrieked. "I'll be right back, guys."

She sprinted over to me, almost rolling her ankle in the process. She was a lot drunker than the last time I saw her. "Did you see the arms on that one? O. M. G," she spelled out, slightly slurring the last letter.

I nodded, giggling. "Looks like you have your hands full."

An uneasiness stirred in my belly as I glanced around the kitchen. Some faces I recognized. Some were wearing masks. But none of them resembled Billy or Chad in the slightest.

Maureen yanked on my arm, almost spilling my drink. "Oh! I almost forgot to tell you. I heard those witchy bitches from earlier talking about Billy. One of them said he was going to meet her here. They were all *oohing and aahing* about it like he's some Greek god or something."

A figure caught my eye just as she said his name. *Speak of the devil.* As if he'd been summoned. Adrenaline coursed through my veins as I locked eyes with Billy. Dressed in full gladiator garb, he stepped into the room. "No, but he fucking thinks he's a god," I rasped.

Maureen's eyes widened as she followed my gaze. "Fuck."

I nudged her back over to her group of admirers. "Whatever happens, you need to stick with these boys. Stay visible." I plucked the jello shot out of her hand. "And no more drinks."

Her face paled as she nodded. "What are you going to do?"

A fury that had been building for days bubbled to the surface. I clenched my fists. "Finish what he started."

"Be careful, Bales…"

"You too," I whispered as one of the toga-clad guys slipped an arm around her waist. She giggled at him but not before throwing one more worried glance in my direction.

I jerked my head back toward the kitchen entrance only to find a drunk mermaid leaning against the doorframe. Fuck. He slipped away. But now I knew he was in the house. Game. Fucking. On.

I raced into the sitting room and gave Poe a slight nod. He instantly jerked his head up and scanned the room. I followed his gaze. If Billy was here then Chad was probably lurking about as well. But the crowd had grown in the last hour, and it was impossible to get a good look at everyone.

A firm hand landed on the small of my back. "Don't turn around," Saint whispered in my ear. "Go upstairs like we planned."

I sucked in a deep breath.

Earlier this morning, the five of us had gathered around the breakfast table and agreed that I would have to lure Billy away from the party. It was my idea and Raine was the only one who backed it, of course. But after realizing there weren't any other options, Poe, Grim, and Saint conceded. Billy was after me. He'd follow *me*. Unless we wanted to murder him in a sea of witnesses, getting him alone was the only way.

I grabbed a drink off the bar and headed into the foyer. There were only a few people lingering in here. None of them even looked up as I passed, too engrossed in their own conversations. I pushed through the hanging slabs of meat, my heart racing. *Hot Killer* by Julia Wolf blasted from the speakers.

Wrapping my hand around the railing, I glanced up at the spiral staircase. This was it. I sauntered up slowly, making a show of it to give Billy enough time to catch up. Not that it mattered. I knew he would find me.

But this part of the plan was a mystery even to me. Raine had insisted that I don't appear to be setting a trap. We needed Billy to believe that I was drunk and wandering around alone.

As I crept down the dark hallway, my stomach knotted. My hands trembled as I tried to open each door in our massive hallway of rooms. So far, each one was locked, including my bedroom. As I turned a corner, the hall grew darker. I whipped out my glowstick and held it in front of me as I continued.

Footsteps sounded behind me. I didn't want to turn around. It could've been Billy or one of my guys. Shivers crawled up my back. I was being watched. Followed. And I was going to be sick. The feeling of being hunted, stalked… it was unnerving.

The farther away from the party I got, the quieter it became. There was softer music piped into this wing of the house. It was dark and sinister with the sounds of violins wailing. Goosebumps pebbled my arms. I shuddered and suddenly wished I hadn't volunteered to be the bait.

After trying a few more locked doors to rooms that I hadn't even entered before, the last door at the end of the hall opened. I sucked in a sharp breath as I walked into the pitch-dark room.

I jerked my head toward the door just as it clicked shut behind me. Fuck. *I* didn't close it. Something rustled in the dark. I was definitely not alone.

"Did you think I wouldn't find you, Bailey?" Billy snarled.

My heart thumped in my chest as I tried to pick out where he was in the room. I spun around, swinging my glowstick, but his voice kept coming from behind.

"Did you think you could throw a party and not invite me? I'm disappointed in you, Bailey."

If I wasn't so terrified, I would have laughed out loud. *I threw this party for you, asshole.*

"What do you want, Billy?" I spat.

He chuckled and I could feel his breath on the back of my neck. I flinched as his hands found my hips and he pulled me back into his chest. "To fucking violate you in every possible way."

I shot forward but he caught me in his grip. He wrapped his hands around my waist and dragged me to the bed. "Where you going, babydoll?"

"Let go of me!" I screamed.

Billy laughed as he switched on the bedside lamp. He had a crazed look in his eyes. It was almost demonic. "Look at you, Bailey. Dressed like a fucking slut as usual. Did you wear that just for me?"

"Fuck off, Billy."

He climbed on top of me and grabbed my wrists. *Oh no*. I glanced from side to side to see bondage restraints strapped to the mattress. I sprang forward just as Billy slammed me back against the headboard. Pain seared through my skull, blurring my vision.

"Billy, stop," I murmured.

Panic flooded my chest as he secured each of my wrists to the bed. "You're not going anywhere this time, slut."

He moved to the foot of the bed and slipped two more restraints over my ankles, before climbing back on top of me.

Fuck, where were the guys?

The back of my head throbbed against the pillow. "Please, untie me. I won't tell anyone."

Billy glared down at me. "No, you won't. Because I'm going to keep you tied up in here forever. That way I can come up and play with you anytime I want. Just like my daddy did to your whore mom."

I gasped as he yanked my furry bralette down to my belly, exposing my breasts. A sinister smirk pulled at his lips. I flinched as he lowered his head. Nausea rolled through my stomach as his tongue darted out. "Billy, what the fuck are you talking about?"

He ran his thumb across my lower lip and pinched it down. "Mmm, your mom fought like this too. Right before my daddy lit the fucking match."

No. Fuck. Panic turned to rage as the weight of his words threatened to suffocate me. "*Your* father killed my parents? *Why*? What the fuck did my family ever do to yours?"

"Your momma just couldn't leave it alone. No, she tried to ruin everything. Threatened to tell the world how my daddy was obsessed with her. But she was a lying cunt. It was her who lured him away from our family. But he took care of it, just like I'm going to take care of you."

As tears spilled down my cheeks, a dark rage brewed in my chest. I was going to be sick. *"I'm going to fucking kill you, Billy."*

He snickered. "I've been waiting for this a long time." He rolled his tongue over my nipple. "Fuck, you taste good." He clamped his lips down hard and sucked.

I flailed on the bed, desperate to get away from him. "You're a sick fucking bastard!"

Billy chuckled as he ran his hands down my stomach. "I've been thinking about how you stroked your cunt for me that night." I groaned as he pushed my skirt up around my waist. "The way you fingered your wet pussy. Now it's my turn."

Fucking hell. *Where the fuck were they?* I shook my head. "No. Get the fuck off of me. *Right now.*"

He laughed as he yanked on my panties, tearing them in half with one jerk. "You've been a naughty girl, Bailey. And naughty girls get punished."

"So do naughty boys." Raine stepped out of the shadows, his face painted like Grim's.

Billy sprang off the bed. "Who the fuck are you?"

Oh, thank fuck. "Took you fucking long enough," I growled.

Raine eyed Billy like he was prey. "You think you can touch my girl and not even invite me to watch?"

Adrenaline coursed through my veins. What the hell was he up to?

Billy snorted. "This slut is your girl? Sure man, you wanna watch? Be my fucking guest."

"*Raine*," I warned.

He put his finger to his lips. "Shh, little fox." He climbed onto the bed and squeezed my thigh while he looked at Billy. "Do you even know what makes her scream, Billy-Boy? Hmm? Would you like me to show you?"

Billy's eyes lit up. The idiot didn't even realize that Raine was toying with him. He licked his lips. "Fuck, yeah. I don't mind sharing."

"Ugh," I groaned. "You're disgusting."

Raine winked at me. "Let's give Billy-Boy a little show."

I glared back at him. "Why?"

His breath quivered as he settled in between my legs. "Because it makes me so fucking hard."

I still didn't understand the hold this man had on me. But seeing his sadistic grin, hearing him say he wanted to touch me while Billy watched… well, it did something twisted and fucked up to my soul. And it made me wet as fuck. Knowing that we were going to kill Billy right after made me want to cum so fucking hard.

As my body relaxed, Raine threw Billy a wink. "Take notes, Billy-Boy."

Billy pulled up a chair and plopped himself in it. "Make her scream."

You're going to be the only one screaming, asshole.

Raine shoved a finger deep inside my pussy and every nerve in my body sparked. "Mmm, yeah that's how she likes it."

Billy's mouth dropped open as I bucked. "Oh, shit, that's hot."

"I can't wait to kill you, Billy," I hissed.

Raine chuckled as he added another finger inside me. "That's my girl. Get angry. I want you to cum for me with the taste of murder on your lips."

My clit spasmed as he thrust in and out. I turned my head toward Billy. "You like watching him finger fuck me?"

Billy smirked. "Yeah, he's getting you nice and wet for me, slut."

A subtle hint of rage flickered through Raine's eyes. "I think it's time to teach Billy-Boy some manners."

Another figure stepped out of the shadows and stood directly behind Billy. *Saint*. He wrapped his hands around Billy's neck.

Billy yelped and tried to stand up, but Saint pushed him back down in the chair. "What the fuck? What's going on?"

Poe emerged from another dark corner laughing. He stalked over to the bed and untied all of my restraints. "Did you really think we were going to let you get away with hurting our little fox?"

Raine kept thrusting his fingers into my pussy as Billy's face paled. A devilish smirk took over my lips.

Grim stepped out of the shadows, the look on his face murderous. "No one touches our little fox but us."

"What is this?" Billy cried. "You're fucking all four of them? I knew you were a fucking slut. Just like your mother!"

Saint stepped around and threw a fist into the side of Billy's face. Blood spurted out of his mouth and onto the carpet. "Watch your fucking mouth," Saint growled.

Raine snickered. "Keep your eyes on him. Don't look away."

As I turned my head to the side to see Billy's face swelling, Raine shoved a finger into my ass. He took turns thrusting into each hole. This was so wrong. So fucked up. But I had never been more turned on in my life.

Grim knocked his fist into the other side of Billy's face. "I'm only getting started, fucker."

"You're all sick, you know that?" Billy cried out.

Poe's nostrils flared as he circled him. "Not as sick as you're about to feel."

Billy's face twisted in horror as Poe raised his foot and slammed it down on his crotch. The scream that left his mouth was bloodcurdling. "*Fuuck. You broke my dick!*"

The agony in his voice sent tremors straight to my swollen cunt. "*Uhhh, yes…*" Fuck. "Hurt him again," I moaned.

Saint pulled a knife from his waistband. "Hold him down."

Billy flailed, screaming, as Poe and Grim each grabbed one of his arms and held him back against the chair. "Okay, I'm sorry! Please, don't do this."

Grim got in his face. "*You're sorry?* Should we show you the same mercy you showed Bailey when she was begging *you* to stop?"

Pressure built in my core as sheer terror flashed through Billy's blood-shot eyes. "More," I rasped.

Raine rubbed his thumb in circles around my clit. "Mmm, my little psycho vixen. Fuck, you make me so hard."

Billy's screams turned to sobs as Saint dug the tip of his knife into his already swollen cheek and sliced it open. Blood oozed down his neck. So much fucking blood. I arched my back as Raine pushed his fingers hard against my core. "*Uhhh,* just like that. Fuck. Make him fucking bleed."

"You sick bitch!" Billy wailed at me as I smiled back at him.

Grim dug his finger into the open wound on his cheek and jerked his face toward him. "You wanted to watch. So now you get to fucking watch her cum while we carve you up like the fucking pig you are."

Billy's eyes rolled back into his head as he whimpered.

"Don't let him pass out," Saint growled.

Poe smacked Billy's other cheek, snapping him out of his stupor. His eyes widened as he realized he was still trapped in this nightmare. "No. Please. What can I do? I'll do anything to make this right."

Raine pinched my clit hard, and my vision blurred. Tingles erupted from my core and spread to every inch of me. My juices spilled down onto his hand as the most intense orgasm I'd ever had rolled through me. "That's it, little vixen. Let it rain for me."

My chest heaved as a stunned Billy watched me cum all over Raine's hand. I locked eyes with him and licked my lips. "Nothing you do will ever make it right."

Raine attempted to pull my skirt down, but I pushed his hand away and climbed off the bed. With my breasts out and my skirt still up around my waist, I walked to Billy and stood over him. I dragged my finger up my slit and wiped my cum all over his lips. "That's the last thing you're ever going to taste," I rasped.

Billy jerked his head away, sobbing. "I didn't even do anything that bad to you. *Please*. I learned my lesson."

Within seconds Raine was beside me. "Have you, though? I lied, Billy-Boy. I don't like it when little pricks like you look at my girl."

Raine grabbed his head and dug his thumbs into his eye sockets. "Still having fun, Billy-Boy?"

Blood trickled down his cheeks as he screamed. "Fuuck! I can't see!"

Something dark and feral had buried itself inside me. It was a calm rage that had settled into my bones. I took Saint's knife and held it to Billy's neck. "You think I don't know it was you, Billy? That I don't remember?" I dug the tip of the blade into his throat. "I know it was you who pushed me down the stairs the night of that party. *You killed me*. There's no coming back from that."

He shook his head. "No. You're right here. You're not dead. It was an accident. I'm sorry."

I wiped the blade across my tongue, licking his blood off. "They called the fire that killed my parents an accident too. And we all know now that's a lie. Oh, Billy… See, I'm very much dead. Took me a while to realize it. But you can't hurt me anymore. And I'm going to make sure you don't ever hurt anyone else again."

He gasped, his mouth open in protest as I drove the knife deep into his neck and dragged it across his flesh, gutting him open.

Billy's face contorted in horror one last time as blood sprayed from his neck and he choked on his last breath.

"*A soul for a soul*," I whispered.

CHAPTER *Thirty*

Maureen

I couldn't remember any of their names. After tonight, I wouldn't remember their faces either. It would be just another party. Another hazy memory that would fade as soon as the hangover did.

I gripped the bathroom counter as a bulky blonde-haired guy in a toga costume railed me from behind while his friends watched. Fighting back the urge to cry, I gazed down at my pointy-red nails to avoid looking at myself in the mirror.

When Bailey told me to stick close to these guys, I don't think she meant like this. But that's just what I do. I drink too fucking much and throw myself at every cock that swings my way. Now I had four of them lined up, waiting for their turn to fuck me.

Shame filled me as I realized that this wasn't the same thing as what Bailey had with her guys. No. Her guys adored her. *Loved her.* The frat boys snickering and high-fiving each other in this bathroom felt none of those things for me. I was just a toy to be played with. A body to be used.

And while my best friend was out there risking everything to hunt down the assholes who assaulted us, I was bent over a sink, spread open, allowing these douchebags to use me.

The blonde guy grunted as his cum filled me. "Fuck, that pussy is tight." He nodded to his friends. "Get in here while she's still wet, boys."

My stomach rolled as a taller, dark-haired guy switched places with him. He pressed a glass of clear liquid to my lips. "Have another drink, sweetheart. It'll loosen you up."

My head was buzzing. I promised Bailey I wouldn't drink anymore tonight. But it was too late. As I poured the drink down my throat, the dark-haired guy unzipped my top.

He turned me toward the other three guys and walked me to them. He brushed my hair to the side before dragging his hand across my nipples. "You're a dirty girl, aren't you?"

The room started to spin as they laughed. "I'm a lot of things," I slurred.

Another blonde one squeezed my nipples while the dark-haired one pushed his cock inside me. I let out a moan as he yanked my hips back. "Fuck, yeah. Man, you weren't lying. This pussy is tight as fuck."

The blonde guy fisted my hair and jerked my head to the side. "I don't want to wait my turn." I gagged as he thrust his cock into my mouth. "Fuck, that's right, sweetheart. Choke on my dick."

My core spasmed as they fucked me like I was their broken doll. It felt so fucking good, and yet I hated myself more with each thrust. But I would never see them again. And I would turn over a new leaf as soon as I got out of this hellish town.

Thrust.

The new Maureen would never let assholes like them fuck her in a bathroom. Even if it was just a lie I told myself to justify the act.

Thrust.

No. I was going to be better at Tenebrose Academy. Different.

Thrust.

Classy.

"Oh, fuck. I'm cumming." His thick cream gushed into me and leaked down my thighs.

The other one pulled his cock out of my mouth and jerked it over my breasts, spraying his cum all over my nipples. "Damn, I could play with this slut all night."

"Nah, she's fucking filthy. I'm done."

They laughed again. I couldn't even tell whose voice belonged to whom. I fell to my knees as they stepped over me and left.

Fuck.

I pushed myself up and braced against the sink. My head pounded. I ran the water and splashed it on my face. As I looked around for my top, the door burst open.

"Get the fuck out," I barked as I cupped my bare breasts.

A man in a ski mask, dressed in all black, lingered in the doorway, his blue eyes cold and emotionless. He looked me up and down, taking stock of my half-naked body and the sticky cum that was smeared across my chest.

"What the fuck are you looking at?" I yelled.

The man clenched his fists. "Maybe lock the door next time," he growled.

I snorted. "Right. That will solve everything." I turned around and fumbled with my bustier.

He sucked in a sharp breath. "Let me help you." His voice was deep and raspy, like he'd swallowed gravel.

I flinched as his fingers grazed my back. "Relax. I'm just going to zip you up, okay?"

Tears welled in my eyes as I nodded. "Thank you."

"Who did this to you?" The man breathed as he slowly pulled the zipper all the way up.

I spun around and glared at him. "No one… I did this to myself."

He narrowed his cold blue eyes at me. "What's your name?"

"What's yours?" I snapped.

He pursed his lips.

Silence.

I stumbled back against the sink as a wave of nausea gripped me. The way he looked at me was unnerving. And the shame over what I'd just done prickled my skin like hot needles. "Just leave me alone, please. I need to find my friend."

His eyes glazed over me again before he stepped to the side to let me pass. "Whatever you say, firecracker."

As I inched by him, the scent of coffee and tobacco tickled my nose. It coiled in my throat as I breathed it in. I paused to look back at him. "Thanks again… whoever you are."

I shut the door behind me and was instantly hit with an array of sensations. The music was too fucking loud and the light trails from the glowsticks only added to my dizziness.

Fuck, I needed to find Bailey.

As I shoved my way through the drunken crowd, the angrier I got. I shouldn't have let her go after Billy by herself. Why was I always so fucking selfish? She gave me an out and I jumped on it without even blinking.

I stomped through the kitchen, my rage building with every step I took as I searched for her. After striking out in the parlor and the dark creepy basement, I headed for the stairs. It dawned on me that Bailey would want to lure Billy somewhere private and quiet. No witnesses. That's what I would've done.

If I wasn't so busy getting fucked in a bathroom by four scumbags.

Ugh. I fucking hated myself so much right now.

I sprinted up the stairs as fast as my heels would let me. The hallway seemed eerier now than it did earlier when we were getting ready for the party. I tried various doorknobs as I walked, only to find them locked.

Fuck.

As I neared the last corridor, muffled voices rang out. My heart skipped a beat as I stalked toward the room it was coming from. Just as I approached, I spotted Raine dragging Chad, who was kicking and screaming into the room. He slammed the door behind them.

It's fucking happening. Fuck. A lump formed in my throat and my knees wobbled. I wrapped my hand around the knob, my heart pounding. Could I stomach this? Would Bailey be angry with me for wandering up here? Or would she secretly resent me if I walked away?

I took a deep breath and wiped the sweat from my brow. After everything I'd done tonight, the least I could do now was stand by her side as she took down the bastards who assaulted us.

As I turned the knob, a blood-curdling scream rang out. I gasped as I spotted Bailey with a bloody knife in her hand. She stood over Billy, his mangled body slumped in a chair.

Her eyes widened with horror when she saw me. "Maur… *No*. You're not supposed to see this."

My body trembled as Grim hissed and shut the door, locking me inside with them. "You should have stayed downstairs," he grumbled.

Saint and Poe had Chad gagged and pinned against the wall, a knife to his throat. My nausea from earlier crept back up. It was one thing to talk about murder, another to actually see it. "Bales… what the fuck have we done?"

She shook her head, a crazed look in her eyes. "*I did this,* Maur. Your hands are clean. This piece of shit was going to kill us. And this one," she pointed the knife at Chad, "was egging him on." Chad flailed wildly under Saint's grip, tears streaming down his cheeks.

She was right. They would just keep coming for us. For her. But I couldn't let her carry this by herself. Images of what they did to us flashed in my mind. The rage I had for myself, for them, for the douchebags who poured vodka down my throat while they took turns fucking me, it bubbled up inside me like a fucking volcano.

I forced my legs to move and walked over to my best friend. I wrapped my hand around hers. "I got this."

She shook her head. "No. You can't. I won't let you do this for me."

The fire in my chest surged. I gripped her hand harder. "You just fucking did it for me. Now it's my turn. That's how friendship works. Give me the knife, Bales. We're in this together."

Her hand trembled as I pried the blade from it. Raine squeezed her shoulders and drew her back to his chest. "Let her go, little fox."

Chad hyperventilated as I stalked toward him. He grunted and screamed into the T-shirt they'd gagged him with. The veins in his neck bulged as he struggled to break free. But Saint and Poe held his body firm against the wall.

My fingers twitched around the hilt of the knife as I brought it to his chest. "This is for me and Bailey. And for all the girls who you forced to suck your tiny little cock."

"Maureen," Bailey cried. "Let me. *Please*. You don't have to do this."

She was afraid for my soul. Afraid of what this might do to me. But I was more afraid of what it would say about me if I *didn't* do this. It was too late for redemption. The scars had already formed around my heart.

"*Yes, I do*." I sucked in a sharp breath and plunged the knife into the side of Chad's neck. Blood poured out of his mouth and his eyes rolled back into his head. A deep guttural cry exploded out of me as I twisted it, thrusting it in deeper.

Poe clasped my trembling hands. "He's dead. You can let go."

The knife clattered against the marble floor as I released it. "Bales," I breathed. "We finished it. They can't hurt us anymore."

Bailey sobbed and threw her arms around me. "You're gonna have a good life, Maur. A better one than I had. I promise."

I wanted to cry but the tears wouldn't come. Looking down at the blood on my hands, I knew this would leave a permanent stain on my soul.

But I would do it again. *For her.*

CHAPTER Thirty-One

Bailey

I used to think my family was cursed. A part of me still did. But the real curse was on this town and the ignorant people in it. They saw me as a witch, a devil, and a whore. They labeled my mother as such too. *And once word gets out that Billy and Chad are missing, I'll be the first one they suspect.* For once, they'd be right. But without bodies… they have no proof.

Still wearing our soiled Halloween costumes, Maureen and I clasped hands as Raine dumped Billy and Chad's bodies into the cremator. As the machine roared to life, I wondered what my parents would think. Were they looking down at me from somewhere, disappointed that I was using their mortuary to clean up my crimes?

Raine studied my face. He leaned against the cremator as the flames engulfed the bodies. "You're a Bishop, little vixen. Don't think for one second that this is the first time your mortuary has been used to hide bodies."

Maureen squeezed my hand. "It had to be done."

I swallowed hard against the lump in my throat. "I'm a monster."

Raine snickered. "We're all monsters, love. No worse than the two that are roasting in the oven right now."

"Jesus," Maureen breathed.

"Really, Raine? It's a little soon for jokes," I barked.

He shrugged and peered into the flames. "You shouldn't care so much. They didn't."

"Caring is what makes us human," I murmured.

"But that's not what you are anymore, Bailey," Raine breathed. "Thanks to that motherfucker in there."

Maureen shivered as she let go of my hand. "He's right, Bales. All we can do now is never think or talk about this night ever again."

When I broke into Wickford Mansion last Halloween Eve, I didn't really know what I was going to find. Ghosts, monsters, squatters maybe. But I felt something the minute I walked in. A presence. An energy pulling me up those stairs. My body wanted to keep going. My mind and my adrenaline willed me to keep going.

And when I reached the door, when Raine pushed me into it, I felt something strong and powerful pulsing in my veins. It was the darkness inside of me. But it was up to me now to not let it consume me. My best friend was safe. And I would get to spend eternity with Poe, Grim, Saint, and Raine. The loves of my life.

I sucked in a sharp breath. "You're both right. We leave the past here tonight." I turned toward Maureen. "Come on, let's get you home."

As the three of us walked out of Bishop Mortuary, another

little piece of me died. My old life was truly over. It was time to finally start embracing this new one.

After we dropped Maureen off, I switched on the radio to fill the silence. *Out of the Shadows* by Ely Eira blasted through the speakers. Raine rested his hand on my thigh. It felt so familiar. Like we had done this dance before.

"It was you, wasn't it? You were the shadow I saw in the window of the mortuary that night." A part of me had wished it was my parents, but deep down I knew they were truly gone.

He nodded. "Yeah."

"And you were there the day I found the envelope in my father's desk. Why? What were you doing in my parents' office?"

He sighed. "Looking for answers. I don't know why I'm still here. Dahlia and Ronan Bishop knew more about death than anyone. They studied things… in Ever Graves. That's where I'm from. Where it all started."

A chill snaked up my back. "Where what started?"

He ran a tattooed hand through his hair. "All this darkness."

It seemed like all the questions always pointed back to my family and his. The Wickfords and the Bishops, our histories tangled and intertwined in Ever Graves and beyond.

I grabbed his hand. "We'll keep looking."

Raine flashed me a wicked grin and kissed the top of my hand. "Mmm, my little psycho vixen."

I sat in front of the fire, clutching the envelope my parents gave me to my chest. It was time to get some answers of my own.

Poe, Grim, Saint, and Raine sprawled out on the couches, quietly waiting for me to open it.

I took a deep breath and pulled off the seal. As I turned it over, the contents spilled out.

The four of them leaned forward as a letter and a picture splayed across the floor.

My heart raced as I fingered them.

"Whoa, this is weird." It was a photograph of my mom and dad. *And* two other attractive men I had never seen before. They were embracing her in front of a house I didn't recognize. My mother had the biggest smile on her face. Damn… she was so beautiful.

When I passed it around to the guys, Raine snorted. "Like mother like daughter apparently."

My breath hitched. "You think she was with all three of them?"

Grim pursed his lips as he looked at the picture. "That's what it looks like."

I studied it again. "I wonder what happened to them…"

"What does the letter say?" Saint asked.

I sucked in a deep breath and cleared my throat.

Our dearest Bailey,

If you're reading this, then we are long gone. Hopefully, not before we had a chance to see you grow into the beautiful woman we know you are meant to be. Your father and I had a very different life before you were born. A life that drove us out of Ever Graves and into Wickford Hollow. That picture is the last one we took with them. I was pregnant with you at the time. They were so excited to meet you. Sadly, they were taken from us before that day came. Someday you will fall in love too. Don't ever be afraid of it. Even if it looks different than those who are not like us. Follow your heart and don't ever be ashamed of who you are. We love you more than you could ever understand. When the time is right, we'll see each other again. In this life or the next.

Loving you always,

Mom and Dad

Tears streamed down my cheeks as I clutched the letter to my chest. "They were just like us," I whispered.

As I looked around the room at my guys, I realized I loved them with a fierceness that was beyond reason or logic. They had awakened me, sheltered me, and fought for me. They had made me feel things I had only fantasized about before.

"Are you okay, little fox?" Poe asked.

I nodded, sniffling. "Yeah. I just wish I could have had them around a bit longer."

Saint picked me up and set me on his lap. "You may see them again someday. This world is strange, even for us."

I nestled against his chest as Grim and Poe threw their arms around us. Raine knelt on the floor by our feet. "You have us now, Bailey. Forever," Grim rasped.

Saint stood up, still holding me in his arms. "It's time to put our little fox to bed."

Moisture gathered between my thighs. "But I'm not tired."

Raine snickered. "Who said anything about sleeping?"

Poe ran his hands through my hair. "We're going to do bad things to you, Bailey. Dirty, filthy, depraved things."

A deep carnal ache stirred in my core. I smirked coyly at the four of them. "And I'm going to like it."

Grim slid his hand down my shirt and pinched my nipple. "*Good girl.*"

"Our psycho little vixen," Raine breathed.

We were all psychos, the five of us. Monsters. But it was the world that made us this way. With poison and fire and brimstone, the truly evil ones sent us down this path. I lost my humanity the second I lost my life at the bottom of the stairs of Wickford Mansion. But that's also where I was reborn. There was never any real redemption for me. For any of us. Only lust and sin and darkness. *But that's where the fun stuff happens.*

Epilogue

Riot

What a weird fucking house. And that's saying a lot coming from me.

It had been a minute since I'd rolled up to Wickford Hollow. I should have brought the boys, but I was bored out of my fucking mind back at Tenebrose and I didn't feel like waiting around for Atlas and Valentin to pretty themselves up first.

Just another Halloween where the ghosts come out to taunt me.

This house was simmering with cursed energy. It wasn't just the slabs of raw meat dangling from the ceiling or the fact that it was so dark in here, there was a basket of glowsticks left as an offering. No, it was deeper than that. Something sinister permeated through these walls. And most of the half-naked guests in here were either too drunk or too stupid to pick up on any of it.

I, on the other hand, sensed it from the driveway. It was the faint trace of poison, the putrid stench of corpses still rotting from centuries ago. A stench I know well.

After admiring all the lengths the host went to make this place look like a real house of horrors, I pull the front of my ski mask down and stalk out of the foyer. I'm on a mission—to forget who I am for just one night.

Here in the dark corners of Wickford Mansion, in rooms full of intoxicated strangers, I can pretend to be just like them—masked, hopeful, still lonely yet not alone. Without the town of Raven's Gate tethering me, I feel vulnerable, but not weak. *Never weak.*

The rush of being out here on my own makes my adrenaline course in ways I haven't felt in a long time. It's so fucking exhilarating; it makes my dick twitch. There will be hell to pay later for leaving, but it's worth it just to feel alive in my own skin for once.

The freshly carved sigil burns against my neck like a warning. I resist the urge to lift my mask and touch it. There will be more scars to come for this latest transgression. Atlas and Valentin won't be able to suffer for me this time. We are all marked but my blood is truly cursed. The Blackwells made sure of that before they drove my family out of Ever Graves. Only the bones of my ancestors remain there, buried deep below the town's blasphemous soil.

As I cross into the living room, I'm jolted by what I see—long brown hair, amber-colored eyes like burnt honey, tight ass and tits all wrapped up in a hot pink bustier, black leather mini skirt, and stiletto heels.

Fuck.

My cock throbs as I stalk behind her, following her into the crowded kitchen. I notice the handcuffs hooked to her belt and almost cum in my pants. I imagine what this pretty little firecracker would look like tied to my bed frame, legs wide open, and screaming my name while I bury my cock inside her swollen pussy.

I keep my distance as I watch her throw her head back and laugh at something one of the morons surrounding her says. They don't deserve her attention. The four of them look at her like she's a toy. This beautiful creature is anything but. I want to kill them for being near her. I don't even know her name, but I want to toss her over my shoulder and shove her in my trunk. Drive all the way back to Raven's Gate while listening to her kick and scream, only to pull over and drag her out so I can fuck her hard against the hood. I want to taste her fear on my tongue. I want to feel her pussy tremble around my cock and her pulse race inside my grip.

I snatch a shot of whiskey off the counter and knock it back. Every cell in my body is on fire for this girl. I lurk in the shadows, watching her as she talks to a pretty blonde girl then goes back to the douchebags.

One whispers in her ear, and she giggles. They exchange a look between themselves. A look I've seen before. A look that I have given. I start forward as they whisk her out of the kitchen, surrounding her like she's a queen they've been tasked to guard.

I follow them down a long dark hallway, seething as two of them each grip one of her hips. They're herding her away from the rest of the party, getting ready to do unspeakable things to her. I can tell by the way her ankles wobble in her heels that she's had too much to drink. Only pathetic assholes would fuck a girl while she's barely coherent.

Not my fucking style. I like my prey to be nice and awake.

She glances nervously over her shoulder, and I dart into an alcove, escaping her view. There's a shaky tremor in her voice now even as she continues to giggle. Something is off. I can feel it as clearly as the poison that lives in my veins.

When I reenter the hallway, they're gone.

Fuck.

As I creep farther down the dimly lit corridor, I hear their voices. I follow the sounds until I reach a door. I start for the handle but stop. What the fuck am I going to do? Bust in and intervene like I'm some sort of fucking saint? The scars on my body remind me I'm far from holy. Why do I give a fuck about some drunk girl I don't even know?

Maybe being away from Raven's Gate is taking more of a toll on me than I thought it would.

I came here to find someone new to fuck. I could have anyone. Why her? I press my ear to the door and listen as they have their fun with *my* firecracker.

I clench my fists to the sounds of thrusting and grunting and cheers as they take turns filling her up with their worthless cum. I'm not surprised to find the door locked as I quietly twist the knob. I could easily break it open, but then what?

I'm no one's savior.

I suck in a sharp breath and turn away from the door.

Fuck this place.

I need to get out of here before I start foaming at the fucking mouth. That's the thing about curses, you can only outrun them for so long. One way or another, you have to pay the price. And I always do. Every fucking time.

Their voices spill out into the hallway as they yank open the bathroom door. I freeze, the hairs on my neck raising, my pulse pumping, all my senses alert. I plant my feet, refusing to flinch as they slam the door behind them. They amble toward me, nearly knocking me over in their post-coital euphoria. My shoulders tense, the ache in my chest growing as my need to kill festers.

"Bathroom's all yours, buddy," one of the douchebags mutters as he passes. "There's a tasty little snack in there."

My blood boils. The poison in my veins burns as it surges, inflaming the sigil on my neck. I clench my jaw.

"Yeah, help yourself if you don't mind leftovers," another one chimes in as they stagger off, laughing and high-fiving each other.

These fucking imbeciles. They wouldn't appreciate what good pussy tastes like if it sat on their faces and dripped liquid gold into their traitorous mouths.

The light peeks through the bottom of the bathroom door. It trickles past me like a beacon. I should walk away. But something pulls me back. *My greed.* Like the festering ache that's taken root in my bones. The unexplainable desperate need to see her face again.

I turn around slowly, my heart beating faster with each step I take. And despite this entire mess of a night, my cock hardens as I move closer toward the beautiful creature behind the door.

No woman has ever made me question myself before. I take what I want. *When I want.* But this one… she has me walking on eggshells, carefully traipsing down the hall like a little kid sneaking up on Santa Claus on Christmas morning.

Fuck it. Time to rip off the band aid.

I burst into the bathroom and lose all my nerve as soon as I see her. Sweat and cum glistens over her chest and thighs. Her thick brown hair is disheveled, frizzy, and knotted from being pulled in every direction.

My breath catches in my throat as I gaze down to see her cupping her bare breasts. Her skirt is hiked up around her hips. She clenches her legs together, hiding her sweet pussy from my view.

"Get the fuck out," she growls. Her voice sounds like honey. Fuck me. How can I not take this creature with me?

I look farther down at the tattoos on her legs and have never wanted to be ink so badly in my life. It snakes down her calves all the way to her heels. She has one stiletto on now, her other foot bare. Her skin looks so fucking soft. Silky. I want to lick every inch of her.

"What the fuck are you looking at?" She yells.

A flicker of rage sends shivers up my spine. No one talks to me like this back in Raven's Gate. Especially not half-naked sluts who just got railed in a bathroom on Halloween. But this one is different. I like it when she yells at me. It makes me want to bend her over my knee and spank that tight little ass of hers. But I'm not one to be fucked with. Even in Wickford Hollow.

"Maybe lock the door next time," I growl back.

Her lower lip quivers and she almost looks like she's going to cry. *Almost.* "Right. That will solve everything."

But this creature has seen some shit. Been through some shit. I can see it in her eyes. She's hotter than fire, volatile like the night. Dark, dirty, and a little bit psycho. I want her to be mine.

As she stumbles around, trying to keep herself covered while fumbling with her top, I crumble like a sappy lovesick puppy.

"Let me help you," I rasp.

A warmth spreads in my belly as I touch my fingertips to her back. She flinches and I draw in a sharp breath. "Relax. I'm just going to zip you up, okay?"

She nods, her eyes glassy. I can't tell if it's the copious amounts of alcohol she's ingested or if she's truly about to burst into tears.

"Thank you," she murmurs.

Her praise is like the sweetest lullaby I've ever heard.

As I zip up her bustier, I let my hands linger on her shoulders. I'm not ready to stop touching her.

"Who did this to you?" I already know but I want to hear it from her lips. I want her to tell me that she's been assaulted. That she didn't want this. I needed to hear it.

She spins around with a force that jolts me back. "No one… I did this to myself."

Ahh, self-deprecation. I know *that* well too. She was a glutton for punishment just like me and the boys. It was like a sick twisted prayer to gods who either don't exist or are up there laughing at how stupidly mundane we are.

Fuck.

It's time to go.

My second sigil, the one on my arm, is starting to burn as hot as the one on my neck. Raven's Gate was calling me home. But for one fucking moment, I just want to be here with her in this abomination of a bathroom. In this creepy house of horrors filled with poison and death and ghosts.

"What's your name?" I ask her, trying hard to mask the desperation in my voice.

"What's yours?" She snaps. She sticks her chest out in what I assume is an effort to be brave but all it does is make me want to rip that fucking pink bustier right back off.

I can't tell her my name. I'm not supposed to be in Wickford Hollow. I'm on borrowed time as it is. So I purse my lips tightly together and drown inside her amber-colored eyes.

She hiccups and stumbles back against the sink. "Just leave me alone, please. I need to find my friend."

A friend is definitely what this girl needs and I'm not it. But it takes every ounce of strength not to shove my fingers down her throat just so I can hear her moan for me.

But I think better of it and step aside, giving her ample room to pass. "Whatever you say, firecracker."

Fuck. I didn't mean to call her that out loud.

As the brunette bombshell struts past me, I swear she almost swallows me whole. She takes a deep breath, inhaling my scent, taking it with her like a keepsake.

I almost grab her then. I have to physically fight with myself to resist the urge to steal her from this place.

My hands shake just as she stops in the doorway and glances back, batting her long eyelashes at me. "Thanks again… whoever you are."

The door shuts and I slide to the floor, listening to the sound of her heels clicking away from me. I gasp for air and grip the wall. The beast inside me wants to feast on her swollen nipples and slick pussy. I want to taste her sweet cum in the back of my throat. Want to bury my face in between her breasts while she calls out my name over and over again. I want to do unspeakable things to her. Things that those pathetic douchebags couldn't even fathom.

But we both remain nameless. Two fucked up ships passing in the night without a compass or an anchor.

My phone buzzes like a swarm of bees has taken hold of it. I pause on the front steps of Wickford Mansion to look, knowing full well that it's Atlas and Valentin blowing me up.

I shoot off a quick text: *One more message and I'm flogging both of you in front of the entire school when I get back.*

No response.

I smile, satisfied that I can still get my point across. Atlas and Valentin are nothing to fuck with, but I enjoy pissing them off as much they like getting a rise out of me. Our bond runs deep. It's thicker than blood, stronger than any curse those treacherous Blackwells could place upon our heads.

But they know the consequences as much as I do. I have to get back to Raven's Gate before my body goes up in fucking flames. I've already pushed it too far.

I cross the lawn to my motorcycle, still tense from the bathroom. My fingertips still tingle from touching her skin. I'm about to swing my leg over and ride off into the dark fucking abyss of night when I hear those douchebags' voices again.

Fuck.

Two cars ahead of me, the four assholes who stuck their cocks in *my firecracker* are drinking beer out of brown paper bags and fucking bragging about what they did.

I sigh. I can't let it go. I. Just. Can't.

The wind howls in my ears as I stalk toward them. A warning. An omen.

They look up as I approach, their eyes glassy. "Hey, man.

Hallway dude. You get a piece of that snack we left you in the bathroom?"

I breathe in through my nose and out through my mouth as I take three quick strides toward him. Before he can utter another blasphemous word, I seize his throat between my fingers and squeeze. I close my eyes and feel my power surge as his pulse quickens and then slows.

It happens so fast, the other three can't act fast enough. His knees buckle and his eyes roll to the back of his head. He's already dead as the second one approaches.

"What the fuck, dude?" A blonde one yells. He takes a swing at me, and I duck. I come back up and dig my fingers in his ribs. He keels over as the poison in my veins rushes to the surface of my skin, leaking out of my pores.

I am death.

I deliver it. I receive it. And these fools are no match for me. They aren't even a challenge. I'm almost bored until I think about what they did to my firecracker.

The second one collapses, lifeless onto the ground just as the other two close in on me. I laugh. I can't help myself. It's just too easy. As much as I'd like to torture them, to drag out their deaths slowly, I'm running out of time. But I will not leave here until I've avenged her.

With a few quick steps and minimal effort, I snap both of their tracheas at the same time. My skin and veins and bones ache. Everything burns and tingles inside of me as I watch their blackened souls depart their pathetic bodies that now lie in a crumpled heap on the ground.

My phone buzzes again and I know they know. Atlas and Valentin can feel it. They know what I've done. I tell myself I did it for her. But I did it for me too.

"It's okay," Atlas texts in the group chat.

"Come home," Valentin adds.

Fuck.

Home. That was a funny word. Is home where you rest your head? Where your friends are? Where you're from? Home has always been ever changing for me. A puzzle I'd yet to solve. But I'm Riot Graves, the bastard son of Ever Graves, the king of Raven's Gate, the reluctant leader of Nocturnus, and the monster of Tenebrose Academy. Home was irrelevant to me. Blood was stronger.

I hop on my bike and my phone buzzes again. I smile as my most trusted companions remind me of what's at stake.

"In absentia lucis, tenebrae vincunt," Valentin writes. *In the absence of light, darkness prevails.*

"Mors tua, vita mea," Atlas replies. *Your death, my life.*

The engine roars between my legs as I look upon the mess that I left in the streets of Wickford Hollow tonight. I came here to try to forget who I am, and instead found myself anew. It's time to embrace the monster.

I pull out my phone and send the final text. The last line of the Nocturnus creed. "Mors vincit omnia." *Death always wins.*

And as I race through the shadows like a bullet, I think of my firecracker. And I decide that I will make a thousand sacrifices and blood oaths to see her again.

To my readers (the best readers an author could ask for),

Bailey's story may pose more questions. But there never truly is any finality in this life. Even in death, memories and feelings live on. Though, we must say goodbye to Bailey, Poe, Grim, Saint, and Raine… for now.

There are more stories to be told in this world, but they will be led by new characters. They'll take us to different towns. Places like Ever Graves and Raven's Gate. And I can't wait to share them all with you.

Thank you for coming along on this dark and sinful ride through Wickford Hollow. I hope it kept you up at night and made you look a little closer at the shadows.

Until next time, *little vixens*.
M Violet

ABOUT THE *Author*

M Violet is a dark romance author with a flair for the dramatic. She likes whiskey, rainy nights, and writing by the fire. When she's not creating scorching hot villains for you to fall in love with, you can find her eating chocolate and binge watching her favorite shows.

Facebook: Authormviolet
Instagram: Authormviolet
Tik Tok: Authormviolet

Made in the USA
Columbia, SC
08 June 2025